About the Author

Michael Jenkins MBE served for twenty-eight years in the British Army, rising through the ranks to complete his service as a major. He served across the globe on numerous military operations as an intelligence officer within Defence Intelligence, and as an explosive ordnance disposal officer and military surveyor in the Corps of Royal Engineers.

His experiences in the services involved extensive travel and adventure whilst on operations, and many major mountaineering and exploration expeditions that he either led or was involved in. He was awarded the Geographic Medal by the Royal Geographical Society for mountain exploration and served on the screening committee of the Mount Everest Foundation charity. He was awarded the MBE on leaving the armed forces in 2007 for his services to counterterrorism.

The Moscow Whisper is Michael's third novel. His debut novel, *The Failsafe Query* was published in July 2018 and his second novel *The Kompromat Kill,* was published in June 2019.

THE MOSCOW WHISPER

THE MOSCOW WHISPER

MICHAEL JENKINS

Failsafe ·Thrillers

This edition first published in 2020

All rights reserved

© Michael Jenkins, 2020

This book is a work of fiction and, except in the case of historical fact, any resemblance to actual persons, living or dead, is purely coincidental.

ASIN (eBook): B083MWQZH9

ISBN (Paperback): 9798643505518

To my mother, whose Welsh passion inspired me.

And in dedication to the men and women involved in counter terrorism who serve to protect us.

'The fog of war swirls within the darkness of hybrid conflict where proxy soldiers, unmarked special forces, cyber espionage and propaganda confuse as ghosts to obscure its true purpose....'

MJ, Barcelona 2020

WHISPER

Speak very softly using one's breath rather than one's throat, especially for the sake of secrecy.

Prologue

The Balearics

A few years ago

Sir Rhys Eldridge stood at the window and watched the helicopter pilot manoeuvre his Sikorsky S-76 before it hovered for a short while, then landed with a double bump on the front lawn. This was a moment of some delight for the British Minister of State who knew that the Canadian man disembarking from the aircraft was about to make him an offer he could never refuse. This wasn't a negotiation. There was no deal to be done. But there were some loose ends to tie down after the offer was made. An offer that few men in the world would ever be privy to.

Sir Rhys grinned and made his way to the 1950s bar bureau to pour a quick sharpener. A small whisky delicately poured from a copper still shaped decanter. A gift from a Scottish oil tycoon, the Glengoyne decanter once had a lacquer finish on the copper which had now come away from years of polishing. A gift from an elderly man who had set him on a pathway from his youth to a destiny of wealth and power.

Sir Rhys was a former oil trader and multi-millionaire who had flirted heavily over the years as an investment magnate making an even bigger fortune. He was also mired in controversy. Mainly through his dubious association with shady oil deals that included companies that had been fined heavily for providing kickbacks for oil deals in the Balkans. The gossip of his links to dubious businessmen never went away. But despite it all, he had still forged out a highly successful political career in the Conservative party, rising quickly through the ranks to become a Foreign Office Minister by the age of fifty-five.

Casa de Pere Caria was one of several homes owned by Sir Rhys. A white marble mansion overlooking the resort town of Palma de Mallorca where the fresh sea breeze and the brightness of the sun flowed easily through the floor-to-ceiling windows into the living areas of the two-storey mansion. Surrounded by lush grounds and patrolled by two Belgian Malinois dogs and their burly handlers, it had two swimming pools and several large terraces providing stunning views across the Balearic sea.

One of Sir Rhys's business associates ushered the Canadian gentleman past the ornate marble staircase and into his office. Sir Rhys stood at the entrance to greet the man as the yowl of the helicopter engines waned during shut down. He had agreed to join a highly secretive cabal, and this meeting was the formal invitation to join which would be followed by the much-rumoured induction of its membership. He was piqued with curiosity.

'Welcome to my home Christian,' Sir Rhys said, holding a long arm to guide his guest into the office. 'I think we can safely say that I look forward to your messages this afternoon. Drink?'

The Canadian was a handsome man in his early fifties, with a bold nose, hooded eyes and neatly trimmed grey hair. Sir Rhys, dressed in a tailored blue suit with a Carlton club tie, was not expecting too much chit-chat from the man stood in front of him. By all accounts, he was an inveterate worrier who rarely smiled, and was chosen as the perfect gatekeeper to the covert society he represented.

'Tell me about your trip Christian. A long way to come for an induction my friend.'

'Well, we need to talk at length, and very much in private. There are many aspects I am duty bound to inform you of in our tight business.'

Little did he know, his comment was more apt than he realised. His statement, and every word that would be uttered that afternoon was being recorded.

'I am grateful for the invitation to join your organisation,' Sir Rhys said, nodding gently. 'It's most certainly a privilege to be asked to join after all these years, and if I'm truthful, it did seem to come out of the blue.'

He and Christian's associates were interested not just in making money from machine guns and rocket-propelled grenade launchers, but also in developing insider intelligence on global businesses that they could hold to ransom in their quest to become even more powerful and wealthier than most of the membership already were. Christian assured Sir Rhys that joining this most secretive cabal was safe, and people like himself were well hidden from the nefarious deals and negotiations that happened in a far darker world. But what came with membership was a solemn oath to secrecy, and a loyalty to the executive branch who never met the dealers on the ground. They were the investors, the leaders, the elite.

'The only concern we have,' Christian continued, before providing a polite cough, 'Are your links to a former Serbian warlord.'

The comment caught Sir Rhys completely cold. How did they know? He had been accused of many transgressions in his past: oil deals fuelling conflicts in the Balkans and Nigeria, setting up illicit investment groups capitalising on Libyan fuel supplies drying up, and even an affair with a notable actress. But his links to Goran Dozich had never ever been aired. At all. How did they get this information?

A lengthy pause. A twinge of anxiety. Sir Rhys glanced at his Patek Philippe chronometer before answering. 'I'm not quite sure what you mean Christian?'

The dance. The jockeying for position. The uncertain nature of what might come next for Sir Rhys. He was a master at negotiation, at concealing his hand, but this was different. The offer was too good to lose for a thirty-year relationship with a Serbian warlord which until this point, he had kept most secret.

'We simply need full disclosure. Today Sir Rhys. Once you verify what we know, the offer to you becomes firm, your position in our organisation sealed, and we can begin a new set of operations with your contacts. Think of it as a vetting meeting. You know, like the one you lied in to get your developed vetting certificate when you became a Minister.'

Sir Rhys grimaced. He noticed his ageing white cat stretch like a panther, before she pottered across the room to take up a ringside seat on the leather sofa. A purr and a long pause later, Sir Rhys began to tell the complex story of how he and Dozich had met, and how he'd retained a level of business association with him for just shy of three decades.

'In for a penny in for a pound,' Sir Rhys mused as he began the story which lasted just over twenty-five minutes to tell in its full glory. Always well groomed, and ostentatiously well-mannered, Sir Rhys had an air of roguish elitism about him, and he now relished the opportunity to tell not just of his connection to Dozich, but of his global network of politicians who he'd bring to the table to support the cabal's cause.

'Arms dealers are an indispensable, if unsavoury, instrument of geopolitics,' he suggested to Christian, 'And in my current job, I should know that, better than any man.'

Devoted to the legacy he wanted to leave, and surrounded by political friends and former business associates, Sir Rhys was a jovial and gregarious man, well known for his hospitality and lavish parties. He once appeared in Tatler magazine where they ran a double spread describing him as sharp-toothed and bright-eyed, with a keen prosecuting intellect and a strong right-wing ideology. The piece went on to explain how a Tory party Chairman had once said to a serving Prime Minister that Sir Rhys had the teeth of a killer.... 'This man must have meat or die.' Such was his hunger for power and wealth.

Sir Rhys poured himself another whisky and passed a glass of Perrier water to Christian who was now in full swing explaining how the operations worked. 'Most often, when we set up our core transactions, we have a number of European third-party brokers. From their homes across France and Spain, they can negotiate between a supplier in a second country and a buyer in a third. The weapons can then be shipped directly from the second country to the third, while their commission is wired to a bank in a fourth. Neither you, I, nor our brokers ever set foot in the countries where we ship from or sell to. And most often in Spain, no one can ever be accused of committing any crime. It's tight. It's safe.'

'Much as I thought, and much as I have seen and heard before Christian. As you know, the Americans have been doing this for years now with brokers supplying arms to jihadists and rebel irregulars that support their causes in the Middle East. Very complex supply chains to mask the reality from the public.'

'And that's the model we plan to replicate Sir Rhys. Very much with your influence and political power.'

In an historic part of central London, from an office decked out in fifties style retro furniture, a man called Jack H was listening in to the entire conversation. He glanced over at the A4 briefing note in front of him. It was marked top and bottom with TOP SECRET. UK EYES ONLY.

He read a small passage from the three-page document again. It referred to a transcript taken some days ago from a British gentleman known as Gerard Fox who had been placed under surveillance and was known to Jack's team by the cryptonym SCARAB:

Intelligence Collection from business associates of Codename SCARAB:

'... everything in the business is ninety-nine-per-cent straight, up until the moment of delivery. We will use an end-user export certificate from one country to smuggle arms into another as a diversion tactic.' Indistinguishable words followed by: *'... Intend to pay for the arms with drug money...* (too quiet, indistinguishable) *... and I can get the export certificates at a much better price.*

Jack flipped the page of the stapled document to reveal a map with a few coloured arrows on it. It showed a route that one of the arms shipments would take: from Europe to Ghana, then overland to the Sahel region of Africa. SCARAB and his team were planning to obtain the arms from manufacturers in Bulgaria and Romania, and so long as he presented them with the export certificate from the Ghanaian government as the end users, all the parties to the deal would have plausible deniability.

Jack turned to his American friend who was also listening into the conversation taking place in Palma de Mallorca. 'This isn't going to be for the weak of heart,' the American woman warned.

'This is for the long haul and it's going to cost both of us lots of money and resources to take these people down.'

Chapter 1

Tuscany

Gerard Fox was feeling pleased with himself as he glanced out of the Cessna Latitude aircraft, admiring the sun-drenched coastline of the Tyrrhenean sea as the pilot lined up on his final trajectory for landing in northern Italy. As the only passenger on the seven-seat business jet, Gerard was carrying intelligence vital to the needs of his old friends. He had no idea he was approaching the final hours of his life.

Gerard heard the faint scrunch of the jet's undercarriage begin to deploy its wheels and took a final hit of the gin & tonic that had been neatly placed on a doily in front of him with a white napkin beside it. He smelt the perfume of the young female steward as she leant in front of him. She took the glass, and smiled keenly at him, intimating for him to buckle up. He returned the smile enjoying the attention. It was nice at long last to have hit the big time, to travel in style and have all his wants catered for.

Gerard was a senior British spy, recently retired from MI6, but with a decade of cleverly disguised plans under his belt to make his fortune. No one in Vauxhall Cross had ever carried suspicions of Gerard for he was one of the Secret Intelligence Service's gentlemen. A quiet operator, a loyal servant for well over thirty-five years. Or so they all thought. He had, however, been nurturing his contacts in the dirty world of the illegal weapons trade with deep secrecy, through a cabal that met across the globe formally once per year, but covertly in smaller groups many times more.

Gerard stepped off the private jet at Pisa airport, placed his Armani sunglasses across his eyes, and made the short walk to the VIP terminal without a care in the world. Short, but stocky, he'd kept himself fit through a rigorous exercise regime as he approached his sixtieth birthday. A clean deal today, with his other business partners, would see him become a multi-millionaire by his sixty-first.

It pleased him immensely that he had retired early as the Deputy Director of MI6 only a few years earlier, eager to put into place his plans to have some fun, make money and finally be shot of the prison-like bureaucracy that had ruled his life since he was a young man. The shackles were off, and his newfound desire for wealth drove him incessantly to make the most of his latter life - with expensive cars, a yacht in the Mediterranean, classy company and some fun women. And gold. Lots of it.

But someone had noticed a change in his lifestyle over the last year or so. Enough to warrant a closer look. Most would think a seasoned spy would be able to keep his secrets secret, to keep a low profile, to be discreet and to reap the fruits of his labour for Queen and country. He had planned to retire with a decent sized pension having suffered for decades with a public service salary that was an insult to those who served, he had thought. The shockingly low wages were anathema to many intelligence officers, but a sacrifice they were prepared to make as they set out on their careers to serve their nation. Until, later on in life, the attractions of wealth, private sector salaries and even corruption might just tempt them out, and make them greedy. The power of Gerard's role was one thing, but now he had tasted the good life, he wanted more.

Gerard walked confidently towards the black Mercedes that awaited him outside the terminal. Dressed smartly in a light blue short sleeved shirt with a high collar that was neatly pressed, and khaki brown shorts with blue deck shoes, he looked to all around him as a man with power, wealth and class. His baggage, two small art deco suitcases, were placed into the boot by a terminal porter, and Gerard passed him a crisp twenty Euro note before settling into the plush leather seat in the rear of the vehicle. He didn't notice the small Fiat 500 estate pull out from the fuel station and follow them onto the SS1 towards Siena. There were two agents aboard.

The medieval town of Montepulciano stands fiercely on the ridge of Monte Poliziano in the province of Siena in Tuscany. Below this renaissance city, the magnificent countryside of the Val di Chiana rolls neatly into the distance, interspersed with small villages, farms and grand mansions scattered across the gentle hills. Montepulciano dominates the terrain from above the valley and captures the very heart of every view, every journey and every piece of life in the huge landscape below it.

It was early summer, and three men sat looking at the rolling farmland beyond the neatly manicured lawns of their thirteenth century Tuscan mansion, perched on an isolated hilltop, three kilometres from the great city. Each took tea in bone china cups, taking turns to comment on their plans for the days ahead. Each man was in his early sixties, ordinary looking, with faces easily dismissed in crowds, but on closer inspection, they were all men who once wielded power, now only shown by their expensive clothes and extravagant tastes.

The ancient farmstead was immersed in one of the most beautiful areas of Tuscany with an isolated panoramic position, surrounded by woods, vineyards and olive groves. To their left was a large terrace, most often used for evening dining and cocktails, and to their right below them, two tennis courts and a newly developed twenty-five metre swimming pool. All of this was shrouded by lavender plants and a ring of tall cypress trees: a symbol of immortality that signified the sacred space these men would occupy for the days ahead, and a detachment from their everyday mortal world.

An early afternoon breeze swept across the patio, and the men took in the expanse of the nearby fields, with the distant sound of a lone tractor chugging up a steep hill, leaving behind it a perfect line of deep brown furrows. The deeply scorched clay was turned over with immaculate precision by an elderly farmer.

Two of the men stood up and took a walk around the terrace, whilst the other, a man with long greying sideburns, beckoned their sole helper and minder. There was no security, no men with pumped up muscles, no weapons and no close protection. Just the gated perimeter of their mansion, their tightly honed sense of secrecy, and their discretion. The minder took an instruction from the side-burned man sitting at the wrought iron table and walked back into the kitchen where a chef and a waiter were preparing the evening dinner.

'Are you sure Gerard isn't a risk to us? Maybe conning us?' the taller of the three men posed to the man sat at the table.

'That's what we'll each have to agree on after he's arrived, and after we've had a good chance to probe him,' side-burn man replied. He was a former CIA officer whose authority on their plans for the day's business was accepted by each.

'In truth, he gave us some very good intelligence on the matters at hand,' the tall man said, scraping his chair to sit closer and placing his hands behind his head. 'It's just, well, I've never quite figured Gerard out, and I wonder if there's more to this than we're hearing?'

'Look. It's quite obvious that we have a very serious competitor who could quite easily screw this next deal for us. All of our deals. That's my focus right now, to quell that danger, and to make sure we get the deal we want with the Serbian. He holds the key to our future wealth, and he's delivered the goods for us time and time again. The fact that someone else is now touching him up is very grave for us all.'

'Agreed. But I hope Gerard has a plan for taking this competitor down. Damn, we have never in years had such a quarrel with anyone, let alone a splinter branch of our very own people.'

'Indeed. Times are changing and we need to be quite robust in keeping our cabal very tight and stopping this nonsense as soon as we can.'

The tall man stood again. Himself a former intelligence officer in the Canadian Army. The third man, a stout ageless figure had now joined them at the table. He spoke quietly and mildly in a posh English accent. 'Gerard is good. He'll have some evidence I'm sure, and he'll help us take the man down. His job for years, was to provide collateral to Her Majesty's government to cut the legs from under those who were a threat to the administration or the nation. By foul means or fair.'

'Treacherous ways you mean,' the Canadian proffered.

A sly laugh from each of them.

'My job as a senior civil servant in Whitehall may not have been the most glamorous gentlemen, but I can assure you we never lost the art of treachery when it came to wrecking a man's political career. That is exactly what we will do to take him down, and out him at the same time.'

'With Gerard's intelligence you mean?'

'Precisely. Now, I think we ought to look at some other ways of wargaming what lies ahead gentlemen. We have one member of the British Parliament who has gone rogue amongst his own people, and now he seems to think he can go rogue against us. Let's play it out, in detail.'

The minder returned with a small brown briefcase, handed it to the CIA man, and placed a carafe of local red wine on the table. Famed for its eponymous variety of red grape and testified by the valley's endless vineyards, Montepulciano was a renowned centre for fine wine producers who satisfy a prolific global demand. The three men poured themselves a glass and contemplated their surroundings while watching a dog steer a flock of sheep up a steep hill towards a dilapidated building on the opposite hillside. The sounds of a distant sheep bell and the murmurs of appreciation for the 2007 Emidio Pepe were all that could be heard.

The CIA man reached inside his briefcase and placed an agenda on the table. 'So, the man is a Member of the British Parliament, a maverick by all accounts, and a bit of an arrogant fool I hear.'

'He's no fool,' the civil servant replied. 'During my time in Whitehall, he was always known as being devious, ambitious and very wealthy. He's now overreaching his greed by the looks of it.'

'How did he make his money then?' the Canadian chipped in nonchalantly, sloping back in his chair.

'He was an oil trader before becoming an MP. Made his money and wealth before stepping into politics. An old Oxbridge piece of advice, have a career first, make your wealth, then step into the power of politics. Today, in his late fifties, he's a Minister of State, has a tight hold on a range of corrupt business activities outside of politics, and somehow became part of us.'

'Until now,' CIA man said bullishly. 'He sat quietly on the inside of our organisation, he watched, learnt our tricks, and is now seeking to churn off our deals, our profits and our legend. He's setting up his own secret organisation from the methods we taught him. He must be stopped and dealt a lesson.'

The stout civil servant took out his reading glasses and paused for effect. He read some notes he had made for this moment. 'The problem with Sir Rhys Eldridge gentlemen, is not his predilection for money, but his way of bullying using other hands. He is very good at hiding himself through organised criminals and remains outside the reach of the law. He has now gone beyond the realms of our justice and must be taken down. Permanently.'

Warren Blackburn, known to his SAS friends as Swartz, looked at the computer screen that had been skilfully fitted onto the dashboard of the Fiat 500 estate. The tracking antenna had been hidden in the enclosed roof box above him. He tapped a couple of buttons and listened to the radio traffic coming across his earpiece. The screen showed a high-resolution video feed from an unmanned aerial vehicle flying some six hundred metres above Gerard's car. It was crystal clear imagery, allowing Swartz to follow Gerard from a couple of kilometres behind him.

Swartz watched the Black Mercedes turn off the motorway and slowly navigate the wide arcing bend to come back on itself, before turning right onto a single carriage road heading towards Montepulciano.

'Speed up a little bit Samantha,' he instructed, putting his pen into his mouth and thumbing the map. 'I want to be close to him in case the aerial coverage goes down. It looks like he's close to his destination now.'

'What are the orders when we find where he's going then?' Samantha asked, keeping her eyes on the tricky junction ahead.

'There are none. That's the beauty of this job, lots of money for the longer it goes on, simply pretending to be on holiday. We just follow SCARAB to see what he does, and who he meets. Easy job for a change and just what I need right now.'

'Let's see, eh? When you're involved, things generally don't go to plan.'

'Pipe down, and keep your eyes on the road. This one will be fine.'

Chapter 2

Tuscany

Swartz handed Samantha the binoculars. It was just before six o'clock and the Tuscan light had a vivid majesty about it providing a brightness that sharpened the distant landscape. Perfect for close target imagery, Swartz thought.

'Here, keep an eye out, I'll get some brews on for us,' Swartz said, stretching his arms and exhaling a hefty sigh.

'Take your time, and bring the doughnuts,' Samantha replied. She had settled into her surveillance position that provided her with a discreet view across the valley to their targets. 'This will be a long evening of multiple courses I suspect, and some very fine and expensive wine.'

Swartz and Samantha were ensconced in a dilapidated farm building opposite the mansion where Gerard had sat on the terrace awaiting his first course. Swartz had set up two high powered sets of binoculars, a small stove for making brews, and had improvised some comfort by building a makeshift spy shack inside the derelict building, complete with cushioned stools to sit on. He had assembled two digital cameras on tripods and had taken photographs of each person sat on the terrace where SCARAB had been greeted by his fellow emissaries. The images were relayed by a secure satellite link, using end to end encryption, to a team of MI5 operators situated in a cold war bunker at RAF Bentwaters in Suffolk.

Unseen, and high above the farmstead, an unmanned aerial vehicle was being operated remotely by Jugsy, the imagery intelligence operator and good friend of Swartz. He was sitting in the rear of a Mercedes sprinter van some five kilometres away, providing persistent surveillance on the target buildings using two

C-Astral airframes that had a loiter time of six hours over the target. The fixed-wing drones would provide aerial surveillance of any other vehicles or people approaching the farmstead and provide Swartz with security cover for his own location.

Swartz returned with two cups of coffee and four jam doughnuts laid out on a sheet of cardboard and placed them on an old wine box between the two stools. He checked his phone for secure texts from the UK HQ, then took a sip of his coffee.

'Aperitifs before fine dining perhaps,' Samantha quipped as she leant forward to peer through the binoculars. 'Who do you reckon these guys are?'

'I'd say all three of them are the business associates of Gerard - or SCARAB as he's known in the reports. They've obviously come together for some careful planning.'

'Planning what though?'

'That's why we're here Madam.'

'Mademoiselle if you please.'

'SCARAB made a name for himself as the Deputy Director of MI6, by building up alliances in the political world of the *five-eyes* community before he retired. It seems he might be carrying on with some other, more illegal stuff now. Perhaps with the very same people.'

'Within AUSCANUKUS and New Zealand you mean?'

'Yup. All five-eyes community people. Unhealthy political alliances according to the intelligence report. It seems they want us to find out what he's up to, and why he's travelled all this way for dinner and a chat.'

Swartz picked up the second set of binoculars and trained them on the terrace. Four men in the latter stages of their lives enjoying dinner in the brilliant Tuscan sun. There was no obvious security. Just a group of friends having a short holiday away from home, laughing, joking, telling stories, drinking fine wine and toasting something. Maybe it's all innocent he thought, maybe nothing in it at all. Then he remembered how his new boss, Jack H, operated. He was rarely wrong on activity that might be nefarious and needed a good look at.

Swartz thought back to the day he had read about SCARAB. A simple intelligence report provided by Jack, who ran MI5's covert overseas operations. Jack had been assigned some years ago to leading MI5's most secret internal unit who ran deniable operations. It was a highly capable paramilitary organisation known as 'The Court'. A secret unit that had been born out of a need to retain secrecy well beyond the probing powers of political institutions. Its aim was to collect top-secret intelligence that would never see the light of day outside of the immediacy of The Court HQ, and only acted upon by deniable assets if it warranted intervention. Swartz thought back to the day Jack had shown him a note about SCARAB in a law chambers just off the Strand, a front for The Court's London office.

TOP SECRET STRAP 3 UK EYES ONLY

For C/Ops Desk Circulation only

Surveillance Requirement: Codename SCARAB

Urgent intelligence collection requirement using surveillance measures on Codename SCARAB: This requirement is a priority for C/Ops to conduct immediate and persistent surveillance on SCARAB utilising intrusive and covert capabilities in order to better understand the risk SCARAB poses to UK national security. Current intelligence suggests SCARAB is transferring high-grade intelligence to foreign nations.

Surveillance on SCARAB may provide further intelligence to give us an insight into the aims, objectives and tactics, techniques, and procedures of a threat group we are monitoring via SIGINT and other means. This office requires information on his pattern of life, associates he meets, digital documents, online activity, and close target surveillance on a 24/7 basis until further notice.

Swartz glanced across to the small screen that enabled him to monitor the live video feed from Jugsy's military grade drone circling four hundred metres above the villa, observing and recording every move of the secret quorum who had settled in for dinner. He tapped the touchscreen and pressed the magnification button. The drone's electro-optical lens spurred into action and the telemetry zoomed onto the terrace focusing on the sharp features of SCARAB who was now animated in discussion. Behind him, a small stage was being set.

'Have a look, what do you think is going on here?'

Samantha peered over Swartz's shoulder. 'Looks like they're setting up a microphone to me.'

She pointed at the screen. 'Look, two speakers on the ground, all ready to go. Evening entertainment I'd guess.'

'I wonder who the performer is?'

'We'll find out soon I'm sure. I'll adjust the sound.'

Samantha walked around Swartz to stand over a grey piece of hardened plastic technology known as a phased array antenna. The three square feet microphone array was designed for audio surveillance using acoustic radar. She lifted it high into a small alcove, fixed it into position with a couple of brick ends, and nudged its direction to allow the long-range antenna to pick up audible conversation from the four men through the gap in the wall.

'Do you know how to set up the IMSI grabber or do you need a hand?' she asked Swartz.

Swartz didn't answer but cut her a look. He knew exactly how to set up the phone tapping software. Or so he thought.

'Well it's a long time since you conducted surveillance you know. The tech has changed since those days.'

'Very funny. I'll call a friend if I need to.'

'Sean Richardson is not available as you know. He's tucked up in a psychiatry session, probably fucking with the therapist's mind.'

Swartz momentarily wondered how Sean was getting on with the psychoanalysis interrogation that Jack had ordered before he was allowed back onto Court operations. Swartz had been called in at the last moment to conduct the surveillance, mainly because Sean had gone off on a bender again in Nice and failed to call Jack, who wasn't best pleased.

Swartz and Sean were great friends. They had been lucky to stay alive on their most recent Court operation and had a penchant for bailing each other out when one or the other was in trouble.

Swartz manoeuvred the mouse to launch the software for the IMSI grabber. The ruggedized laptop took a few minutes to whir into action for the software to obtain the lock and hold from the UAV high above the target mobile phones. Swartz tapped his fingers waiting for the data to download and leant forward to view the landscape. The views were stunning. The mid-evening light dazzling. The air was still, and he could hear the bells on the sheep in the far distance, an oddity he felt might be unique to the Tuscan hills.

The software was now up and running. He scrolled down the screen to check which mobile phones had been penetrated by the IMSI grabber that was housed in the nose cone of the UAV circling the sky above. He heard Samantha shuffle behind him. She was laying out the cords from the antenna before plugging them into a small amplifier. Swartz watched her connect a socket to a separate laptop which would record the conversations and beam the audio thousands of kilometres away into The Court HQ in Suffolk.

'Have you got a lock on the phones yet?'

'Three, so far. It's still searching for the last.'

Swartz clicked on the small box next to SCARAB's phone which was now showing its IMSI number. The International Mobile Subscriber Identity, a number unique to the SIM card, that the 'grabber' had intercepted on SCARAB's phone to gain vital intelligence of the calls and texts he had made.

A faint breeze swelled through the open frame that Swartz had camouflaged to conceal their spy location. He now had the full suite of technical capabilities in place to conduct what looked like being a lengthy surveillance operation.

Samantha was right. It had been almost five years since he had last conducted surveillance like this, and he wasn't really sure now how he'd agreed to work with Jack and Sean if this was as lively as it got. It was bloody boring most of the time. Christ, he'd been tricked by Sean over a few lively beers to join The Court but wondered if managing his father's Herefordshire dairy farm might have been the better choice. Jack had nailed the deal and the salary, and the enticement of working on a few more of Jack's infamous operations was too much to hold him back. In the end, Swartz felt compelled to join up as a veteran, just to keep an eye out for Sean who was forever embroiled in dodgy situations that demanded a brotherly eye. Strewth, Sean needed it, he thought. Twice he had broken Sean out of jail, and on too many occasions he had saved him from his own broken soul. Swartz had a lot of empathy for him. After an utterly brilliant intelligence officer career, Sean Richardson had plummeted a decade ago when his wife had suddenly died, which set off a rollercoaster ride of trouble. Swartz knew he had struggled with his shame as a disgraced agent who had been kicked out of the service, and he knew Sean was lucky that Jack had saved his livelihood by bringing him into The Court as a fully paid-up mercenary. 'Mercenary,' he thought. That's all we are now. Paid-up veterans that could be thrown to the wolves at any time.

A tap on the shoulder. Samantha told him to get his headphones on, suggesting that there was an interesting conversation amongst their quarry after all the previous banal chat. Swartz leant over the makeshift bench, grabbed his headset, and placed the cups over his ears. He immediately noticed that the tone from SCARAB had changed to one of frustration and anger.

'Listen to me. All of you. Sir Rhys Eldridge is a danger to us. He's gone completely rogue and my sources tell me that he's set up an exact replica of who we are here. He has his hands in exactly the same pie as ours.'

'How can you be sure? You said you'd bring evidence,' the elderly Canadian responded.

'Sir Rhys Eldridge has dedicated all of his efforts in the Houses of Parliament to being promoted into the right ministerial roles at exactly the right time to further his corrupt activities in the arms trade. My sources are solid. Ex-intelligence officers who have penetrated his Anglo-French cabal, they've collected first-hand intelligence on financial transactions that show he's now poaching our clients.'

'Bastard,' The former CIA officer exclaimed.

'Indeed.' SCARAB stated, ready to explain his story further before being interjected by the Canadian.

'Evidence please, Gerard. You talk of intelligence and evidence, but we need to see it. In full.'

'I have it here in my briefcase gentlemen, in all its detail. Bugged conversation records, financial transactions and insider information showing how he stole our contacts in the Balkans and how he has undercut us. He's taking money from our pockets, our wealth, our very existence. Stealing our arms routes, and probably all of our political contacts too. He's easily able to influence export licensing to a number of nations given his ministerial position, and he's penetrated the market with the singular aim of putting us out of business. This is as bad as it can get for us and we must act hard and fast against him.'

'What do you propose we do then Gerard?'

'That is why what we need to decide. Right here, right now.'

Swartz listened intently. Four elderly men, each of them very successful in their former careers, now running corrupt arms deals by the sound of it, and with a competitor that needed dealing with. He looked through his binoculars to see the Englishman stand and walk around the table whilst addressing the group.

'We decided earlier Gerard, that if your evidence is verifiable, then we will take Sir Rhys Eldridge out of the game permanently.' The former senior civil servant leant on the table looking each man in the eye. 'Now, who do we bring in to cull this threat?'

An hour later, Samantha placed a steaming mug of coffee in front of Swartz. The light was now fading, creating a mesmerising sunset that fused into the clouds, crystallising the brightness into a vignette of orange and red hues. It cast a curious illumination onto the stage that Swartz was watching from afar. A drama full of intrigue, and a cast of players that would draw the eye of many a screen director.

Swartz watched the stage intently as a young female strolled from the villa to the microphone that had been set up for her performance. It gave him a bit of a jolt. She was stunning. The woman stood at the microphone placing both hands around its stand, swaying slightly with a beaming smile. She uttered a few words of welcome, and gracefully threw her hair over her shoulder before starting her performance. Swartz adjusted his long-range spyglass to take a much closer look. He liked what he was seeing.

The singer was tall and slender, her symmetrical face provided an allure that was fresh as well as strong. She wore blue jeans and a tight, sleeveless crop top showing off her midriff, and her long dark brown hair flowed neatly across her right shoulder. Swartz's eyes were drawn to the large circular earrings she wore and the intense purple lipstick that strengthened her aura. But what was most astonishing was her voice. Within seconds of the first song Swartz recognised its magnificence. A contralto. A rare thing of beauty. He began to fire off a series of close-up photos of her. A barrage of shutter exposures that might provide a lead to who this woman was. He didn't know it at that time of pressing the button, but Yelena Hardy was one of the most sought-after singers on the west London circuit, an imperious icon of Camden clubs, with a deep, dark voice that oozed sheer class.

Swartz was thrilled listening to her voice and her songs. Incredibly strong vocals that were infused with the influence of soul, blues and jazz greats, as well as contemporary neo-soul songs. Stunning he thought, intent on finding out more about her.

'All this waiting around is making me restless,' Samantha barked, trying to get Swartz's attention after an age of him admiring the woman.

'Spying is a waiting game, you know that,' Swartz replied, refusing to move from his camera. 'Get on the radio to Jugsy. See if he saw how this woman arrived. Her car, her route in. Who dropped her off, what time she arrived and what she was carrying.'

'Why?'

'Just a hunch.' He repeated it in his mind. 'Get him to track her exit route too. She'll be leaving soon.'

Swartz sighted his binoculars on the woman. She was receiving applause from the cohort and had received a gift of some sorts from the Canadian. A small pink box with a bow on it.

'She's on the move. Get Jugsy on it quickly.' A sense of urgency lingered in his gravelly voice. Something didn't seem right to him. It was a sixth sense from years of experience. He watched her move quickly towards a chauffeur driven car at the end of the long gravel track where the driver held the door open.

Swartz put the binoculars down and frowned. It's going to be a long night he thought, still fascinated by the female vocalist. He switched his gaze to the video monitors that showed the live pictures from the UAV above him locking onto the Mercedes that was now exiting the villa grounds making its way down a stony track towards the main route to Siena. He watched the car drive slowly down the final gradient before it turned onto the tarmac road that led to the dual carriageway.

What happened next was incomprehensible.

A thundering explosion took place on the patio where the men were dining. The first Swartz knew of it was the loud eruption before the blast wave shot across the valley ripping into the derelict ruins, causing Samantha to drop to the ground as if protecting herself from rocket strikes.

Were they under attack? No. Swartz gripped himself, then lurched from his hunched position to check what the hell had happened. He peered across the valley in the half-light to see the devastation of the dining area that was now the scene of an earth-shattering explosion. A huge bomb. He grabbed his binoculars and glanced over to watch the overhead imagery on the monitors. It showed four bodies strewn across the patio and a small fire at the seat of the explosion, which must have been under the dining table.

He trained his lens onto the carnage to inspect the bomb scene. Within seconds there was a second explosion. A searing ripple of explosions emanating from the kitchen, causing a large ball of flames to shoot through the lower ground windows and a blast wave that Swartz felt seconds later across the valley.

'What the fuck happened,' Samantha shouted grappling to get to her feet.

'A mass assassination,' was the only answer Swartz could muster.

Chapter 3

Cagnes sur Mer

Sean Richardson dropped his bag at the base of the bar stool and nodded to the barman who was already pouring his favoured Maltsmiths pale ale from the tap. He placed his jacket on the brass hook under the bar and loosened his tie. It had been a long and tiring journey from London back to his home turf of Cagnes Sur Mer on the Cote d'Azur. But a journey well worth taking as he struggled to find his soul and his being. The traumas were many and varied.

Beer will help, he told himself. Quite a few actually. Specially imported pale ale. He was in no rush to return to his small villa a short distance away and felt blessed that he'd found a small local bar that served proper beer. A local place of refuge where he could occasionally meet with English speaking tourists and colourful French locals. A place he had frequented far too often of late. Three nights a week, and a run out on Saturday nights into Nice was taking its toll on his liver, and much as it pained him to know it was damaging, he could never find a better way to deal with his angst - other than taking long runs in the hills surrounding Vence.

Maybe this was his destiny? Payback for being a disgraced spook kicked out of Her Majesty's service, and only occasionally brought back for deniable operations where his loss would be of no great concern to MI5 or The Court. His role in foiling an Iranian terror plot just a year ago was never released to the wider world. He was simply placed back into suspended animation in the south of France, and made to wait, yet again, for whatever Jack H might need his skills for. Sean Richardson would never get another medal, nor any further citations, and to the small group of people who knew of his existence, he was still the shamed agent who had been jailed in Kabul after the fraudulent charges of being an illegal weapons dealer had stuck. A man not to be trusted on team operations, and a man with a short fuse whose maverick nature resulted in four Armenian weapons dealers getting killed on his last operation. Those were the rumours floating around the corridors of The Court, but the reality was far from being widely known, and would likely never ever be heard in full. His highly sharp judgement on that day had seen the lives of thousands of innocent people saved from a weapon of mass destruction.

'Merci Alain,' Sean said, placing a crisp fifty Euro note on the bar. 'Keep it in the pipes and have a couple of reds on me.'

Alain, who wore a French rugby jersey, planted his elbows on the bar and scratched his immaculately trimmed beard. Sean had always warmed to him, and chuckled knowing he was of French Iranian heritage with a glowing smile and a heart of gold. He wondered what Alain would have thought after he'd killed one of Iran's most notorious secret agents in a standoff in the Asturias to avert a catastrophe at the G8 conference in Biarritz the previous year. Or the fact that he'd now found out he had a son of Iranian descent. Sean smirked and shook Alain's hand with a tight grip.

'You're a good man Alain, gifted with your discreet nature. Maybe you're a spy?'

Alain laughed out loud and thumped the bar. 'And maybe you're an undercover police officer,' he responded with an animated gesture. Sean admired his jovial oration, tinged with a melodic French accent. Never a grouch, always the gentleman.

'If I am a spy, you would never know Monsieur Gavin.' Alain had referred to Sean's legend before continuing. 'What have you got in your bag this time then? Handcuffs, or guns, or both?'

Sean glanced at his bag momentarily. A bag that held all the items he needed to maintain his legend and deep cover in France and overseas. 'Nothing so exciting, just a stash of banking software and a hefty list of potential clients across the south coast. All overpriced and all heavily overrated, but it makes me a clean living.'

'Have you been anywhere nice, I haven't seen you for a while.'

Alain was called to the far end of the bar, so Sean didn't get a chance to answer. Instead, he cast his mind back to London and the bizarre appointment that was still ringing in his ears.

'Tell me about your drinking habits these days,' the psychiatrist had asked Sean pointedly.

'Only a few, nothing too serious,' Sean had answered abruptly, now wishing he'd refused to take part in this session that Jack had insisted he attend. *Maybe he might take me back on a full-time basis* Sean had thought, before agreeing. *Maybe he had a plan to bring him back on a more formal basis within MI5? No. Don't be so stupid. He was now just a blunt tool of the Security Service who could be discarded at will or thrown into the maelstrom of one of Jack's high-risk political stings. Or maybe Jack does actually care? Who knows?*

Working for The Court on a part time basis, the psychiatrist was a scruffy bloke in his early forties. Unkempt, trousers that didn't fit, odd socks, and breath that made Sean wince when he first shook hands with him. Sean had little time for psychiatrists anyway. They were all disordered in some way, giving them a path to take up such a profession as a means to understand and fix their own issues. Sean could play them like his own guitar after all the years of being assessed for post-traumatic stress disorder. Never once did he ever reveal the true nature of the PTSD he had initially suffered, now ten years on. An incident of such gruesome detail, that it still pierced through the other layers of trauma that he struggled with. The aggregated pain finally saw him plummet.

'It's OK to be honest about the drink you know Sean?'

'I know. And I am being honest.'

'What about drugs? Do they help soothe you?'

Sean sighed. *This bloke was clueless and a half wit.* 'Haven't taken any for a long time. I used to deal them in Afghanistan though.'

'I see. What about the loss of your girlfriend who lived with you in France? How have you dealt with that?'

The question pained Sean. He took a moment and looked around the room. It was too dark and moody. Depressing even. Sean had started the day in fine form, and plumped for a pampering with a wash, cut and blow dry at his favourite hairdressers in Marylebone. He'd dressed in a light blue suit, white shirt, matched with a polka dot tie and was looking forward to having lunch with Jack after the brain assessment. He enjoyed having a few wines with Jack, who had promised him a full lunch at Benares in Mayfair after the therapy session. But for now, Sean needed to get the grilling tucked away. A bit like the virtual chest of drawers where Sean stored all his bad memories before nailing them shut. Only this time, he was being asked to prise them open. He had no intention of taking them further out than was absolutely necessary - that was for sure.

'It really didn't work out. It's a shame she left, but hey ho. It was great while it lasted.'

'But why did she leave?' the shabby looking doctor probed. A bit too much Sean thought.

'Listen. She had probably had enough of me and my baggage. There's lots of it you know.'

'As well as your drinking?'

'The baggage included me having a son I didn't know about. That probably didn't help. He's only ten years of age now, and I need to find a way of spending more time with him.'

'Go on.'

'Well, that plus the stuff I was dealing with from losing my wife some years ago, probably shot me away. It got too much for her with my latest episodes.'

'Drinking episodes? Is that how you cope?'

'Of course. You bloody well know that. As well as how I place all my bad stuff in drawers so that I can slam them shut. It's a great way of visualising them being put away and neutered. Out of mind, and out of sight.'

The doctor reached for his reading glasses and made a note. 'Jack needs to know what levels of depression you've been having and how we can help manage that. He has your interests at heart you know, and he wants to make sure you get some therapy to keep you operationally in good order.'

'That's all fine and dandy mate. I cope. I cope well and can pretty much deal with anything thrown at me if I need to.' Sean knew he was skewing things now, right on the edge of truth, but he carried on anyway. 'The fact that I have a son has kept me sharp. It's given me an edge, and I get to visit him every time I come to the UK. I'm in a good place Doc. Well, in the sense that I see a good future now. My quiet time is awkward, but painting helps me deal with lots of the bad memories when they come flooding back. The easel is my heart, and the paint is my lungs. The results help me breathe well.'

'Good to hear Sean. These sessions are really important for you if Jack is going to use you again.'

Important for you Sean thought. He played along anyway, hopeful that Jack might see he was now of decent mind and relatively sane. Well sort of. Sean knew that this was a game to be played. The doctor knew everything about him, but he was checking his stability, his triggers and his reactions to awkward and well-designed questions.

'Don't you think you made too many mistakes on the last operation in Istanbul? You went off-piste and could have jeopardised the entire show.'

'No.' A trigger right there, Sean thought.

'There were a few surprises for everyone. You can't just go off on a drinking session halfway through a job you know.'

'Listen. I achieved all the aims and more. I recruited the Iranian spy, turned her, and Jack got to handcuff a long list of sleeper agents embedded in Britain, as well as taking down a terrorist extortion plot. Anyone else would have got a bloody medal or two for Christ's sake.'

'It wasn't without its collateral damage though was it. How do you feel about that?'

'I regret the deaths of the weapons dealers. The Kapitan and the New York man. We really could have used them again and again for other operations with their connections. But sometimes things go pear-shaped. They go wrong. That's the way it is. Neither Jack nor I knew that the Iranians planned on killing them all. That was tragic but I ended up in a bloody cell again because of that cock-up.'

'And do you still suffer flashbacks from those incarcerations?'

'I have flashbacks from lots of things. I live now for a good cup of tea and a good night's sleep. The memories of those rotten jails never leave you, the globules of snot, the stench of dying men and the sounds of torture. They are haunting.'

'You've been a lucky man to live through those experiences,' the doctor said, taking his jacket off before looking again at his notes. 'I understand your best friend rescued you on both occasions. Swartz, I think he's called. Is he someone you can share your experiences with? To talk, drink tea, and talk some more?'

'He's the only one I can do that with. It's still tough to open the drawers in my mind and talk about everything. It's my way of shutting out the past and looking forward to the future with my son. But Swartz always finds a way of helping those drawers open, and the thoughts just flow then. He's a great friend.'

'Now. Your other close friend. Samantha. Tell me about her.'

Sean laughed. 'She's great. Vibrant, sassy, a top operator. What about her?'

'Well, Jack tells me you're really close?'

'Kind of. On and off you might say.'

Sean relaxed into the high-back chair and started fiddling with the tassels on the end of the arms. He recounted his long on and off relationship with Samantha who was The Court's signals intelligence expert. He didn't mind talking to this shrink about himself, or anyone. But he knew it was pointless. It was just another drill he had to endure. But every time the doctor hit a nerve, Sean would crunch his jaw and tense up. An old foible that he rarely knew he was doing, until he felt his jaw ache. He knew what was coming next and tensed up in readiness.

'And your wife was a great source of release for you too, I think? Did you tell her everything? Share everything?'

A pause and a grimace. Sean tried to focus on something in the room to avoid the shrink's eyes. He found himself focussing on an odd shaped pineapple on the round table next to the psychiatrist. He might as well have put a fruitcake there Sean thought. He composed himself. 'She was my rock. The only woman I could easily share everything with. She was a wonderful person.'

'I know. I'm sorry that she passed away so suddenly Sean.'

Sean felt himself falling into a trance. A flood of memories of Kate came at him, all in one go. He scrunched his face. Then that innate sense of survival came right back at him. It was she that drove him on. To find his way in life. His dreams of a wife and family had been taken from him in one fell swoop when she suddenly died of a haemorrhage when he was overseas. He knew she'd want him to be successful in life after spiralling into his dark hole, baring his soul on many an occasion.

'Maybe we can go all the way back to that first major incident in Iraq Sean. The one that started all this off. Let's walk through all the layers to see where we can go with this.'

'What, now? Right now?' Sean said, irritated. He tapped his Belmont watch, a present from Swartz for his forty fifth birthday. 'I'm due at lunch with Jack.'

'Jack has a new job for you soon. He wants me to really drill into this. Just ten minutes or so Sean.'

Sean winced as he remembered that last part of the session. The drawer that he hated opening up - to spill the beans. He adjusted himself on the bar stool and settled in for a good session with Alain and anyone else who fancied a chat in his local French bar.

'Alain, let's have some of that fine wine of yours please. I feel like a celebration.'

'You're always celebrating Gavin, that's why we like you. Always smiling, having fun, trying your worst at speaking French, and making the locals smile.'

'Well, no point dwelling on things too much eh? Carpe Diem and all that.' Despite everything that had been thrown at him, Sean was not a man for self-pity, but he was restless. He didn't want to spend the rest of his life in bars drinking and partying, nor reflecting on how his life had imploded numerous times, or hoping that one day his service would bring him back into the fold and give him a life of structure again.

Sean leant over to grab an English newspaper. A benefit of the bar being an attraction to tourists. He noticed a small leader at the bottom of the Times. *Exclusive: new Islamic State Caliphate planned for Mali and the Greater Sahara.* Exactly as Jack had briefed him at lunch. A curious development he thought. It was as if Jack had been teasing him into a new job if he brought Mali into the conversation with all the horror that had been happening over there.

Just as he turned the page, a large glass of San Emilion arrived, and his phone rattled on the bar. It was Jack. Sean lunged into his pocket for his cigarettes and made his way onto the street.

'Jack, what's up?'

The lack of immediacy from Jack worried Sean. Maybe he was about to sack him? Maybe he'd been on a bender too far? Then came a voice of despair. A haunting voice that Sean knew could only mean very bad news.

'I'm sorry to phone you like this Sean, and not tell you in person…' Sean lit a cigarette, his hands now shaking.

'It's not my son is it?'

'No, he's fine.'

'His mother…?'

'No.'

'Jack, speak up man, what?'

'It's Swartz. He's been killed.'

The words came at Sean like thunder. Like a knockout blow in the ring you just don't see coming. His hand shook and he gagged as his breathing shallowed. He tried to make sense of it all. His best mate. He was too good an operator to be killed. Surely not?

'How?' was all Sean could muster.

'I'm not entirely sure. But he was compromised on a mission in Tuscany. A surveillance operation that went wrong and he was shot.'

Chapter 4

London

Jack H stood at his office window overlooking Devereux Court just off the Strand. He looked up at the sky, noticed the dark clouds, and decided he would take his brolly after all. The weather forecast looked about right, a seventy percent chance of rain on a drab Wednesday afternoon that was as dark as Jack's soul.

He took personal responsibility for Swartz's death, and wondered if the tight knit operation had been compromised. Had he been so lax as to fail to see there might be a mole in his organisation? He immediately thought of his Russian agent, Sergei Krupin. If there was a leak, was it him? Had his judgement been so badly clouded that he missed something obvious when he took personal responsibility to become Sergei's case officer? 'I'll find out soon enough,' he muttered, intent on testing Sergei's loyalty. A barium meal test, he thought. A long used technique by MI5 to smoke out moles.

Jack flicked through a couple of pages of reports related to SCARAB. It would have to be a sting operation he told himself. A tight plan to weed out who was behind the bombing in Tuscany and the murder of Swartz.

Jack was formally MI5's Director of G Branch, but he was also the commander of the agency's most secret weapon: the covert internal unit used for deniable operations known as The Court. In the words of 'D', his former boss, too many intelligence leaks over the years had severely damaged Britain's ability to protect itself and he had wanted a covert team to operate beyond political intrusion. Jack cussed the sad and untimely death of the man who had created the clandestine unit that worked closely with the CIA's Special Activities Division. The late Director of MI5 had tragically died of a heart attack only a year ago and had been Jack's closest confidante and mentor. He had left a legacy in The Court that Jack felt was his own personal responsibility to improve and expand its hidden capabilities.

Jack leant back into his fifties retro chair to scan a note that had been translated from Italian. It provided the initial assessment of the forensic explosive analysis at the bomb scene in Tuscany. It had been discreetly conducted by the Italian *Agenzia Informazioni e Sicurezza Interna*. He made a mental note to contact his opposite number in AISI, a flamboyant character by the name of Fabrizio Gabrelli, the deputy head of the Counter Terrorism Division. He needed his help to keep the issue quiet, and to allow Sean and his team to view the forensic intelligence that might provide them with a crucial lead.

Jack found himself mulling a few options in his mind to trap the murderers, then he sensed a whiff of treachery feeling certain it would lead to a perfidious individual in the dark corridors of Whitehall. His gut feeling was rarely wrong. After decades of operating in the shadows, Jack had an instinctive sense for modern-day spy-craft, that also included a skill for weeding out corrupt officials who were on the wrong side of the law. It was an ingrained part of his DNA: to uncover the evil and the corrupt, especially in Westminster. His craft dealt not with weapons, gadgets or high-tech equipment, but with political tactics to achieve an aim. This spy was a master of espionage operations, where deception, guile, coercion and meticulous planning were the hidden tools of his trade. The deceased D had always referred to him as a genius tactician.

Jack fiddled with his tie, contemplating a few ideas that were beginning to get traction in his mind. He adjusted the red paisley tie to line up with the buttons so that it was sitting perfectly in the centre of his shirt. A quirk from countless years of masking his anxiety, and a habit he'd honed from sitting in edgy intelligence meetings wearing his trademark navy blue suits and Charles Tyrwhitt ties.

Jack sighed, kicked the desk, and stomped across the small office to an antique black safe in the corner of the room. He needed more intelligence quickly if he was to identify a mole in his organisation. He turned the black dial three spins anticlockwise, adjusted it to sit on the zero mark, then dialled the five-pin code. He heard the comforting click of the four bolt locks disengaging and opened the small door. He retrieved a file and looked briefly at a black and white photograph on the inside of the red cover. Taken some time ago in the eighties, it showed two Russian GRU intelligence officers shaking hands and smiling at each other. He tutted, then turned the first page to search for the information he required. He copied the data onto a small white card, placed it into his inside jacket pocket, and slammed the door shut.

Simmering now, Jack shouldered his coat, grabbed his black umbrella and made his way down the stairs, stepping into Devereux court. Three barristers were hastily making their way to the cover of their nearby chambers. He watched the middle woman place a briefcase over her head before she broke into a gentle trot to avoid the intense downpour. He looked at the smouldering sky, shrugged his shoulders, and pressed the gold button on his brolly propelling the black fabric into its arc. His mind was deep in thought about the death of SCARAB, and the intelligence he had uncovered on a few former members of the intelligence services linked to his cabal. Then there was the Member of the British Parliament, linked to SCARAB, who he placed firmly in his crosshairs. He couldn't quite join all the dots and the linkages, but one thing was for sure, the secretive nature of an organisation called Le Cercle kept appearing in the reports.

Jack steered a course around the puddles in the narrow passageway that led to the Strand. He had received a signal of some urgency from his Russian agent who had indicated that Jack needed to make his way to a secret Mayfair location as soon as possible. He'd been running Sergei for over two years, and the vetting on his character and background had been intense. The Russian was providing high-grade intelligence in return for an eventual life in the West where The Court would one day provide him with a new life. But first he had to earn it.

Though they rarely met, Jack had formed a good bond with Sergei who, to date, had provided impeccable intelligence on Russian GRU activity in London and the West. Sergei had a son in Moscow who had been providing access to secret intelligence, knowing that if he kept the tap open, he would one day be repatriated with his father somewhere in the north-east of England. Surely they wouldn't jeopardise that, Jack thought, or had he been duped? Sergei's son was working as an engineer on one of Moscow's most secretive weapons projects, a high energy laser weapons system known as *Peresvet*.

As he made his way to the drop, Jack reminded himself of the high-grade intelligence Sergei had provided him after he had walked into a Sussex police station in early 2018. As his handler, Jack had conducted a series of intensive interrogations to satisfy himself that Sergei was clean and his motives genuine. He'd always felt they were, but Swartz's murder was like an itch that wouldn't go away. His mind kept returning to the fact that Swartz had most probably been compromised, but he couldn't be fully sure. Yet.

The era of cyber espionage, digital forensics and hacking had meant that Jack and Sergei had turned to reversionary methods of tradecraft which included dead letter drops and disguises. Sergei's role as an unregistered senior GRU officer in London meant that he could be under scrupulous attention from Russia's advanced surveillance teams based in their embassy. There were three dead letter drops that Jack had established. One was in Regents park located in the void of some brickwork at the rear of the open-air theatre. The second was located under a bench in St Marylebone Parish Church, cleverly concealed in a small wooden pocket purposely designed for a drop. And the third was located in a toilet cubicle at the Connaught Hotel in Mayfair. Jack would use this opportunity of collecting the drop at the hotel by having lunch with the CIA station chief at the sommelier's table in the exquisite Hélène Darroze restaurant.

It wasn't long before Jack had stepped out of the black cab when the well-dressed doorman nodded politely to him and clicked the pressel on his radio. The immaculately polished door opened, and Jack stepped into the lobby. He straightened his tie and cruised slowly to the restroom where he entered the furthest cubicle.

Lowering himself to one knee, Jack reached around the base of the toilet casing to feel for a single bolt that secured a small wooden panel. He twisted the screw one short turn to the left and felt the spring unload to give him access. Now on both knees, he opened the panel and reached inside with his fingers to feel a small plastic envelope that had been taped to the inside of the casing. He retrieved the envelope, closed the lid and sat on the toilet to study the contents. He pulled out an aide memoire from his jacket pocket to reveal a series of numbers and letters in two long columns. The cypher key to decode the text that Sergei had dropped off.

Jack used a hefty Monte Blanc ballpoint pen, a gift from D, and began transposing the Vigenère cypher. Within less than three minutes, a new set of words appeared on Jack's piece of paper.

We must talk in the next 24 hours. I have urgent weapons intelligence involving 387 and 233 to give you. Extensive.

Chapter 5

London

The décor screamed of grandeur and tradition at the Connaught hotel in Mayfair. A timeless gem of opulence loved by the Americans, graced by A-listers of the film industry, and revered by wealthy Londoners looking for the cult of celebrity. Stunning paintings, grand portraits, captivating grandfather clocks, glistening chandeliers, and a magnificent antique staircase all added to the charm of the luxury hotel.

Jack wasn't one for such luxurious surroundings, preferring his simple life of the odd beer in his local Marlow pub, or an occasional night out with his wife in one of the town's many quaint restaurants. But D had always insisted on going big if he was entertaining members of the CIA on his turf. 'They like history, they admire style,' he could hear him say. D was a charmer, and Jack felt it was appropriate to bring a little class to his meeting with Laura. He'd booked the sommelier table in the hotel's Hélène Darroze restaurant. An atmospheric and discreet private dining experience in the limestone wine cellar within the hotel foundations, and a basement containing around 15,000 bottles of wine.

'Hey Jack,' the middle-aged woman said in her striking Californian accent. 'Another great place for lunch. Are you romancing me today?'

'If only,' Jack said, standing to greet her. 'Lovely to see you again Laura. You look really well.'

'Well thank you Jack, I like that you always notice,' she said kissing him on the cheek. 'Another venue you have on your payroll then?'

Her cheerful manner relaxed Jack, as did the huge smile she threw, looking him in the eye for what seemed an age.

'D often used this venue for discreet meetings with many of his sources,' Jack said taking a seat. 'It's no secret that he coached me well, and yes, we still use this place for the occasional piece of work.'

'Vetted staff?'

'One or two trusted eyes, yes.'

'You Brits always do things with style,' Laura mused, checking her lipstick in a small mirror. 'That's why we love you, and probably why we make a great team Jack. You set the scenes, and I punch through.'

'We do. Lots more to play for as well.'

'There is, especially as you turned down the Director job. I knew you would, and I understand your reasons Jack. How is your daughter?'

Jack's eyes dropped momentarily as he reached for his napkin. 'You know, she's a tough one. Multiple Sclerosis at such a young age needs a resilient head and she seems to have that tenacity about her. She's full of adrenaline and a fighter. Thanks for asking. My family circumstances weren't the only reason I turned the role down though.'

'Darn it, Jack. You don't need to explain anything to me, even though you were offered the job on a plate.'

'Of a sort. But you know better than anyone that it's just not me. I want to stay in operations, driving The Court forward with you, not acting as a diplomat. It's bad enough as it is with the politicians trying their damnedest to hamstring the security of this nation without me having to play a diplomatic role within it. I'm not cut out for that.'

'You are, Jack. But I get it. And besides, it means we get to play ball together a lot longer.'

A gentle nod. Jack took a moment to reflect on how far they had both come since their heady days working together in Moscow some fifteen years ago. He was always pleased to share his inner angsts with Laura, despite the fact she had dropped him in a whole heap of trouble in Moscow that shook his career progression for a good few years. He'd never really shaken off the memories, but the events of a single day in Moscow had created a lifelong bond of trust between him and Laura.

Laura Creswell was known as a gritty operator, a superb leader and a hugely talented spy after many years working the Middle East circuits. She had worked a highly acclaimed career with only one blip, when she was asked to leave Berlin as station chief in 2014 after her teams had placed surveillance bugs on the German Chancellor's phone. London had always been her dream posting, but it came at the cost of a shot at the top role as Director of the CIA. For Jack though, her posting to London was an added bonus for his world of deception. He admired her tenacity and 'say it as you see it' attitude. They had become close friends for over twenty years and Jack trusted her like no other American intelligence officer.

'Anyway Jack, after our last mission, and the success that came with taking the Iranians down, Washington is nicely placed to give me more funding for our covert ventures you'll be pleased to know. I'll keep my hand right on that tiller.'

Jack smiled, knowing exactly how the relationship between The Court and the CIA had now reached new heights. The motto of the CIA Special Activities Division is *Tertia Optio*, which means 'The Third Option'. In the UK, MI5 had an option of legal amnesty for agents needing to commit crimes for the greater good, known as 'The Third Direction'. Together, Jack and Laura had brought together all options through what they called 'The Third Avenue': an amalgamation of The Court's activity and the sheer might of the SAD to form the most potent covert partnership in the world.

'Do you remember Sean Richardson?'

'Oh, I do Jack. Proper hunk. Would have been top of my list in my day you know.'

'I know.'

'I'm looking forward to meeting him again one day Jack. I might need to steal him from you. Well, for a short while anyway.'

Jack chuckled. 'Well, he always cites that astonishing speech you gave before we took the Iranians down.'

'Which bit? I was thumping hard that day.'

'The bit about the monster. It's a monster riding through a blue moon on Halley's fucking Comet. I think that's what you said and the whole room loved it.'

'Well, it was a bomb destined to screw up the whole G8 conference Jack. It needed something special.'

'The whole room quaked in their boots.'

'A power play, it was an awesome job.'

'Agreed. I need your help soon though, on another one.'

'Another what?'

'A whisper from Moscow on something big going down.'

'How is it Jack, that you always speak with a forked tongue. Spit it out man. Tell me what's happening?'

Jack tucked into his meal, enjoying the sharp, honest exchange. They laughed and joshed lots, an unlikely couple reminiscing about their previous forays across the globe. They dined on bluefin tuna tartare, laced with *oscietra* royal imperial caviar, finished off with a tandoori, carrot and coriander sauce.

Jack paused and placed his knife and fork at the edge of the plate before touching his mouth with his napkin. 'I need your help to set up a sting Laura.'

Laura's eyebrows rose. 'A sting you say. You've been plotting again. Tell me about it.'

'Well, you know how you've been arming the Syrian rebels by stealth? With a wider aim. I want to try something similar.'

'Where?'

'Mali.'

'Jesus, that's just a small blob for us Jack. It's something of nothing for us, in fact hardly on the radar. Especially when you compare it to the Chinese, Iranian and Syrian issues we face. This better be good.'

'It is. It's taken me a while to put the jigsaw together and I think the coded message that I received an hour ago will probably bond it together. You see, the Russians are arming the Islamic State in the Greater Sahara.'

Jack passed Laura the deciphered message, looking for a reaction. She was right of course. Africa was not the US Administration's core priority right now, but Jack could see what was coming over the horizon.

'This better be bloody good Jack. I can't shovel money at your whimsical plots if there is no return for the US. Christ, you'll have me sacked again.'

'It's not whimsical and you won't get the sack. They want you as Director one day and you know that. Just enjoy the ride a bit.'

'Oh, You know I do. Whatever this is Jack, you'd better be right if I'm going to back you.'

'They're supplying weapons through a number of proxies who are using quite sophisticated supply chains. The funding is coming from some very dubious sources in Europe too. It's the very next Caliphate that's being formed in Mali, and Al-Qaeda and ISIS are merging to launch attacks way beyond its borders.'

'If you're implying that we've taken our eye off the ball Jack, you're badly wrong. The US has plenty of intel gathering in the Sahel and we're watching the place as much as you are. We're just not shovelling money after bad money.'

'I think you have taken your eye off the ball.'

'For fuck sake Jack. I'm going to need a lot more than just your thoughts. Show me the evidence.'

'Well, it's just like when you armed the Syrian rebels. But this time the Russians are copying you. Same playbook. The weapons and ammunition that the Pentagon supplied to Syria were dispatched illicitly through a sprawling logistical network, including an army of arms dealers, shipping companies, cargo airlines, German military bases and Balkan airports. Swap German bases for Balkan bases and there you have it. Looks to me like the Russians have their Middle Eastern base firmly established in Syria now, and they're setting the conditions for working themselves into Africa. The fallout for allowing the Russians to help establish another Caliphate will be immense.'

'No shit. What's their motive?'

'As it's always been. Buying up influence, strangling corrupt governments and taking over the gold and diamond mines. Global stretch, and right now, they're looking to win the race for Africa by undercutting the Chinese who have bought up most of the land and the arms deals. That's all about to change. They're using mercenaries to inflict Kremlin power right into the heart of each nation. It can't be ignored, and the jihadi threat to the West is exactly what they want to foment. You're not playing the game well at all.'

'Right, get me some evidence and I'll run it through the Administration.'

'Tight hold though.'

'Don't worry. Just someone close to the President. But I need something to show them that this is tangible intelligence, I don't want to be made to look like a fucking clown. There's a big fight going on between the Defence Secretary and the Secretary of State about pulling out of Africa you know.'

'Yes, I heard. I'm putting it together. The message from my source tells me that weapons are being moved by the Russians between Bosnia and Herzegovina and Ghana where I suspect we'll find plenty of illicit activity going on. And that's where I need your help Laura. Here, have a look.'

Jack passed a small dossier to Laura and excused himself to use the restroom and leave a message for Sergei. The dossier was slim to say the least. But Jack figured there were enough intelligence leads that might, just might, get Laura to buy into his deception plan. Sergei's intelligence needed to be tight to get Laura to agree. The dossier was the first course and started with a short brief on the threat of the Sahel.

Mali is a sprawling country twice the size of Texas and sits next to seven countries with porous borders, located in the region of Africa known as the Sahel, an extremely arid area stretching from one shore of the continent to the other.

Many factors are driving the rise of the AQ and ISIS militants including grinding poverty, government neglect, pervasive insecurity and ethnic differences. The very same conditions that enabled the Islamic State in 2014 to amass a state-like system in Iraq and Syria until US-backed Iraqi and Syrian forces pushed them out in 2017.

In recent months, AQ and ISIS militants in Mali have been employing a new tactic to extend their control, trying to divide and conquer ethnic groups. Islamist militants who once tried to conquer Mali by force are striking again with the insidious strategy of provoking feuds between old neighbours - the Fulani and the Dogon.

When Jack returned, Laura gave him a look. The one that he'd seen all those years ago in Moscow. It turned into an irresistible smile. He watched her take her reading glasses off and place them into her purple Coach handbag. He sensed he could step the tempo up a little. The dossier might have been sparse, but it showed an ever-growing threat that would sooner or later snowball into an avalanche.

'Who are your sources on the weapons running I've just read about Jack?'

'Three sources. One in the Balkans, one Russian, and one British.'

'And this Moscow whisper you mentioned? All linked?'

'I think so, but I need to verify the intelligence I received today from my source here in London. My view is that the US should start having the same engagement in the Sahel as it does in the Middle East. Weapons are being smuggled from the Islamic State in Libya to their factions in Nigeria and Mali, and the rest now appear to be coming from Russian mercenaries. I need your Special Activities Division to help me harvest some more intelligence.'

'How?'

'We infiltrate the weapons dealers.'

'Jesus Christ Jack. With who? That takes years of work to embed someone into the heart of such gangs.'

'We have someone who's known on the circuit.'

'Go on.'

'Sean Richardson.'

'Good God. Yes. I didn't even think of him. But you're right. He's perfect.'

'I know. Now, listen to me. And you'll see my plan. Do you remember me telling you about Sergei? The Russian 'walk-in' I have been handling. He provided the inside intelligence for the Iranian takedown last year and he can get us into the Russian logistic chain. That way we can use Sean to infiltrate the network. We did it last time, we can do it again.'

'Really?'

'Yes. He's known now. We have first class evidence of him being arrested and jailed for illicit smuggling, as well as the weapons dealer linkages he made on the last job. He's deniable, known as a weapons smuggler, and perfect to drop into the maelstrom.'

'OK. I like it, but I'll need a lot more before we go hard on any plot you're scheming up. This needs to be watertight and fully deniable.' Jack watched Laura scrunch her face and take a sip of wine. 'What's the return on my investment if I give you the resources here Jack?'

'Insider intelligence on the *Peresvet* laser programme. A good head start towards your journey to becoming Director don't you think?'

'Neat. I like it.'

Jack chaperoned Laura to her waiting car that was parked a short distance from the hotel. Carlos Place looked glorious as they walked side by side past the tree shaded pond outside the hotel, and onwards to Grosvenor Square. The Mayfair village shone in its own world of terracotta hues, colourful window boxes and chic street-side coffee shops with pristine community squares. Jack was pleased Laura was on-side with his scheme but wondered how he could use this opportunity to verify Sergei wasn't batting for two sides, and he needed more collateral on the laser programme to help seal the deal with Laura.

'Why do you call it a sting though,' Laura asked casually as she tapped a message into her phone. 'Who else are you after?'

Jack stopped at a zebra crossing and turned to face Laura. 'I think one of our ministers might be involved somewhere along the line. He has a track record of being involved with the wrong people and he's now a minister who is able to sway influence on export licenses.'

'You think you can trap him?'

'Most certainly with your help. You see, we're currently investigating a small cabal associated with Le Cercle and the minister has been associated with them.'

'Le Cercle?'

'A very secretive bunch, a bit like Bilderberg but smaller and most definitely more secret. It seems from my inquiries that another group are competing with a small part of them, and now a feud has broken out. It resulted in a nasty explosion in Tuscany a couple of days ago with four of them killed. We presume it was planned by the competing group who call themselves the twenty-one-club.'

'But how does that link with your sting?'

'Well, we think both groups are involved in illicit weapons smuggling and are making a fortune from it. We were just getting into the intelligence collection when the man we were watching was killed in the explosion. A former MI6 officer. A high ranking one, codename SCARAB. Another was a former CIA officer, so you see, we're on the cusp of potentially uncovering something very big and very deep.'

'Goddamn it, Jack. I assume you were going to share all of this with me at some point.'

Jack smiled and turned to walk. 'You know I always will Laura, just at my pace. Keep up now.' He felt the shake of the head, the grimace, and then the warmth from Laura piercing his back as he strode ahead of her into the square. He knew she was probably smiling. Lots.

Jack felt Laura brush his shoulder and caught a smell of her perfume. 'What's the next move then Jack. This is too tricky to get wrong and we need to keep this on my track, and not yours.'

'Of course. That's why I bought you lunch. Sean and his team start the investigation tomorrow.'

'Good. What's he covering?'

'He's in Tuscany looking at the murder scene to try and track down the linkages before we can work out how and where to drop him into the arms network. It will take a bit of time. We need to know who the attack group is linked to. In the meantime, I'll meet with Sergei and delve deeper into the Balkans runners. This could be a long burn, but let's see where each stage gets us to.'

'Assuming I get the nod from Washington, what resources will you need from me? I know you well. That's what lunch was all about. A bit of British charm in exchange for the might of the CIA.'

'Oh, probably some satellites, a bit of cyber hacking into a foreign nation, and a small team from your Special Activities Division.'

.

Chapter 6

Tuscany

S ean stood above the fragmentation that had been collected from the bomb scene, and started looking for any obvious clues about the type of devices that had killed four retired officers from the five-eyes community.

He was stood in a small military hangar on the outskirts of Montepulciano that was being used as a temporary forensic retrieval station. A location where specialist forensic experts had based themselves to triage the initial findings of the bomb blast scene, before the exhibits would be processed and transported for further examination.

Jack had cleared the way for Sean to attend the forensic station and visit the scene of the blast, and he had been instructed by Laura to make sure a CIA officer attended the scene too. He wasn't happy with that but agreed to have a first look with the agent anyway. He wondered why Laura was involved again, but given that one of the dead was American, it seemed to make sense. Four deaths: one American, two Brits and a Canadian had ensured that someone had put pressure on the Italians to keep the scene very low profile, at least for the time being, and until Sean had managed to forage for some clues. The Italians had moved quickly to seal the area and retrieve the vital evidence, whilst keeping the villa discreetly secured. Sean knew something was amiss when Jack had told him he only had one discreet crack at this before the more formalised elements of international agencies became involved. Speed was of the essence to gain as much as he could, as quickly as possible.

Sean knelt to inspect what looked like the metallic remnants of the dining table legs, some warped in the heat of the blast, others fractured and twisted. It was a grim scene as he spotted small pieces of flesh welded to the metal, and copious amounts of splattered blood. He had been told that the seat of the explosion was not a single position or a single device, but multiple and synchronised explosions that had emanated from each of the six chairs around the table. He winced at the thought of dying from an improvised explosive device that had been placed below the buttocks and imagined the sheer destruction of the body parts from each of the men. His mind had already tuned into the murderers being highly sophisticated in their reconnaissance, their targeting and their eventual deployment of the IEDs. But what was the motivation? And who had murdered his best friend?

He felt queasy and angry as he stood to take a moment and walk around the hangar. Everywhere he looked were small piles of fragmentation that were being examined, recorded, photographed and placed into chalked squares with writing that gave a clue where they were situated on the terrace before the bomb blast. The efforts of trying to recreate the scene in a forensic shelter would allow the forensic explosive scientists to gain an immediate indication that could steer them to other lines of inquiry in an effort to track down the perpetrators quickly - and before the exhibits went further into the forensic chain for detailed analysis and assessment.

Sean sighed and ran his hands through his hair, gripping his skull angrily, before wandering over to a trestle table near the entrance where Phil 'the nose' Calhoun was chatting with the suited CIA officer and an Italian explosives expert. He watched Phil pat the Italian on the back before pointing and gesticulating enthusiastically. He was looking to build the trust and mutual understanding of two explosive engineers working together to solve a problem. It was how Phil worked. Every engagement included a beaming smile, and Sean knew how Phil would charm each and every one of the officers in the room that day. All in an effort to acquire as much intelligence as he could.

'What do you think then Phil?' Sean asked, placing a hand on his arm to steer him away from the table. 'We haven't got much time, and I need your ideas on what we should focus on.'

Sean sensed the presence of the CIA agent over his shoulder. He was following a short distance behind and keen to hear what these Brits were up to.

'He's promised to provide me with a sample of the explosive residue,' Phil whispered. 'His team have analysed the explosive as being PBX but I'll need lots more than that to try and track and trace who did this. I need to see if the bomber has a signature, and I'll match what I find here with similar incidents around the globe on our data base. It might give me a clue on his modus operandi.'

Sean noticed Phil touch his nose delicately as the CIA officer approached them. Phil was an explosives legend. Only 5'8, but well built with a distinguishable boxer's nose, wide shoulders and a trademark no 2 haircut. Phil 'the nose' Calhoun was not only the leading bomb disposal expert within The Court, he was also an accomplished forensic analyst used to conducting sensitive-site exploitation inside terrorist strongholds. His role was to make improvised explosive devices safe and collect the IED evidence after the bomb making cell had been killed in targeted strikes. Phil's forensic and high-risk search expertise would allow Sean to get an insight into the valuable forensic evidence from the site, which might lead to the next stage of the search for the bombers - and who was paying them.

'Mind telling me what your thoughts are gentlemen?' the CIA officer politely asked. 'I'm here to help, not hinder you know.' The man was tall and gangly, probably needed a damn good feed Sean thought, not warming to having an outsider looking over his shoulder day and night. He was used to running things his way with Court operators and the CIA in support, but Jack had been implicit that he had to work with the CIA on this one.

'I'm not sure yet. What was your name again, sorry I forgot.'

'Charlie. Charlie Alexander. You have my card.'

'Ah yes. Charlie. Forgive me, I must have lost it, and I don't use cards myself. But hey, I'll let you into a secret so we're clear on everything.'

'OK, I'm all ears buddy.'

'Well, Phil with the boxers nose will gather as much IED information as he can, and we've got a team back home in the UK analysing all the cell phone activity that took place on the day.

That's a Brit role that's been agreed from on high. You'll also meet Billy Phish in a moment to see what he thinks can be done with his assets. So, you see, I'll run the ops here, and you'll observe.'

'Billy Phish? Who's he? Some sort of cyber hacktivist? You guys are all mercenaries, right?'

'Veterans actually, professional veterans,' Phil replied strongly, taking offence to the intimation they were a rag tag bunch of amateurs.

'And yes, he is a cyber expert,' Sean chipped in calmly, 'But he's also our canine expert. He might just get us a lead from the fragmentation. He ran a case with the FBI some time back that he thinks he can replicate.'

'What, you guys think a bunch of dogs will just lead us straight to the terrorists? Jeez. We need something better than that.'

Sean and Phil looked at each other amused by the American's bravado, his passive aggressive sneering and brusque manner. Sean didn't like the man but smiled coyly. He pointed with a long arm towards the hangar entrance and the American turned.

'See that old man walking through the door? That my American friend, is Billy Phish - and he's about to make you look a mug unless you adjust the attitude and get a fresh bat. We can start again, and I'll ask Billy to explain.'

The American turned, shrugging his shoulders. Not long after, Billy Phish thrust his hand out to say hello. 'Eh up, I'm Billy,' he said, taking his pipe out of his mouth, tapping it on his palm, and placing it in his trouser pocket.'

'I'm Charlie. How ya doing.?'

'Aye, not bad for a Monday,' Billy Phish responded in a gruff Yorkshire accent. 'Don't worry, these pair get happier at the arse end of the week too. Now, are we going to get on with this then?'

Charlie looked bemused by the accents, the eccentricity and the Brits plan.

'Have you briefed Charlie?' Billy Phish continued.

'Kind of,' Sean said. 'He thinks you're mad. Best you explain it all to him.'

'Flippin 'eck. OK. First up Charlie, yes, I am a little wacky. A little old too, but my dogs keep me young and my pipe keeps me sane with these pair. They're just a bunch of jokers who probably think you're one too.'

Sean watched Phil howl with laughter, which began to ease the tension, and he saw Charlie smirk a little.

Billy Phish told a couple of jokes about Brits and Americans on operations and recounted how he had spent much of the last seven years with the FBI setting up their canine facility for advanced canine forensics. Billy Phish in his spare time was a forensic cyber-detective, which led to Phish being his nickname. But his real talent was training dogs: forensic dogs. Each was named after famous detectives, and trained to detect everything from buried corpses, to hidden weapons, to tracking people.

'Can we do this over a brew then,' Billy Phish asked, now tamping some tobacco into his pipe. 'I'm parched, and this plan will need some clever thinking. It might work, or it might not work, but we're bloody well going to give it a go.'

Sean led the way to the drinks station where they all grabbed a coffee before congregating around Billy Phish's Range Rover which was parked outside the shelter. Billy Phish grumbled about the lack of tea bags and grunted at Sean to fix that for the days ahead. They placed their mugs on the bonnet and Billy Phish reached in the rear part of the cab to bring out an odd-looking machine. It looked like a set of scales with a long conical container tapering off from the white plastic tray at the top, down to the base of the cone where it seemed to have a fitting for another part of the machine.

'Right, pin your ears back and I'll explain how this thing works,' Billy Phish began. He lit his pipe and checked he had everyone's attention. 'This is the STU-100 and it collects scent from pieces of evidence or fragmentation, or clothing. It's called a scent transfer unit and it's a portable forensic vacuum configured for scent collection on five-inch sterile gauze pads. I've used it on a few cases over the pond and we'll give it a go by transferring the scent of the frag onto the gauze, and then let Lewis track the scent.'

'Holy moly,' Charlie said grimacing. 'You're leading us on a wild goose chase here. Where the hell do you think it will lead us to, if it actually works anyway. We're wasting time here. Lots of time. Why don't I make a call and get us some real help.'

Sean and Phil ignored Charlie, and let Billy Phish deal with his interruption. Sean watched Billy Phish glare at the American before launching into him. 'If you pin those huge ears of yours back, and stop mithering me, you might, just might, learn something new. And if you keep interrupting me, I'll shove this pipe so far up your rectum, it'll roast your nuts.'

Sean watched Charlie harrumph like an adolescent clearing his throat after a scolding from an irate headmaster. Billy Phish was a gregarious, full-blooded ex-soldier turned canine specialist, with a distinctive mop of grey hair. Now in his late fifties, his edgy manner and 'say it as you see it' philosophy, shrouded a deep intellectual and wide thinking mind. Sean had listened to Billy Phish the previous night where he had explained how the FBI had captured a bomber by extracting the scent from a bomb scene using the STU-100, and then watched as a vapour trail dog led them to the very doorsteps of the bomber's house. Charlie needed to learn the legend of Billy Phish in an area of forensics he had little knowledge of.

Billy Phish puffed on his pipe and dunked a biscuit in the coffee. 'You may not know about the case Charlie, but it involved the conviction of a man called Sigmund who got thirty-two years for three felonies, including attempted murder. Have you heard about it?'

Charlie shook his head. 'No, I was never briefed on this kind of capability at all.'

'Well then, seventeen days after the bombing of a car, the FBI's human scent evidence team started the search from the bomb scene using a canine who had gained the scent from the frag of a pipe bomb. Without knowing where Sigmund lived, the dog trailed through car parks, in elevators, down streets, and alerted at bus stops before eventually leading the investigators to Sigmund's house where the dog alerted again. Right on the front door.'

'Jeez. That's impressive Billy. But what makes you think it will work here.'

'Because it's the exact same dog I'm using. And he's bloody nails at this. Come and meet Lewis.'

Sean watched the blood rise in Charlie's face and a facade of coyness swarm across his persona.

'On that day, Lewis had no difficulty differentiating the bomber's scent from that of thousands of other people on the streets of Washington DC. He can do it again here.'

'You mean to say the bomber's scent is amongst those fragments in there?' Charlie asked quizzically while pointing into the forensic station. Incredible.'

'It is,' Sean chipped in. 'But it's not a perfect science and it's not a given. Phil, can you grab the maps please. We need to work out how the bomber moved to the villa, what access routes and escape routes he may have used, and where he might have used a bolt hole to build the devices. My gut feel is that he would need a place close to the villa to conduct the surveillance first, and then find somewhere discreet to build the devices before laying them. Good old-fashioned kill-chain stuff.'

'First things first,' Billy Phish said. 'I need some of the fragmentation lying in that hangar, to collect the scent.'

'No problem,' Sean said. 'Phil's on the case, and his Italian friend inside has said he can let Phil have a few pieces for a short time.'

Sean had identified a few components of the IEDs that might be useful for the canine search. He had spotted what appeared to be a power cell and parts of a radio frequency transmitter board. His mind kept floating back to the images of Swartz's body that he had visited the day before, and the powerful emotions that had triggered his mind for revenge on whoever had murdered him.

It was the single shot to the back of the head, the cause of Swartz's death, that had haunted him the most. Swartz wouldn't have known that he'd probably been spotted conducting his surveillance operations on SCARAB, most likely by a brutal and sophisticated gang of thugs. They probably crept up to the hide and slotted him. He felt relieved that Samantha had escaped with her life. She had made her way to their Fiat 500 to grab some spare batteries, and by all accounts escaped with a volley of shots into the rear windscreen after taking a bullet in the shoulder.

Sean felt gutted that after all the years of Swartz evading terrorists trying to kill him, it was likely that a bunch of foreign criminals had got him. But who, and which nation he wondered?

Chapter 7

London

The prisoner transport vehicle making its way into London's Old Bailey courtrooms was a limited edition, ballistic proof and modular detention van, designed to transfer the highest and most dangerous category A prisoners across the UK.

Manufactured by Babcock, the special projects vehicle was fitted with GPS tracking technology, specially adapted cells with CCTV, modular full-length grills and a safety shield of Perspex, ensuring it provided the highest level of security for any prisoner transfer in the UK. The cells were fitted with LED lighting, air conditioning and a timed electromechanical handcuff restraint system.

Sat inside one of the two detention cells was a Russian SVR agent who had been captured and convicted of spying against Britain and had been designated as one of the most dangerous foreign nationals in the UK prison estate. Two prison officers sat opposite her as the vehicle sped along the A13 into central London, escorted by two police armed response units and four motorcycle outriders. The level of security for the journey to the courtroom was higher than that of the Prime Minister, and the details of the route, timings and destination were kept extremely tight. None the less, for a nation state with high end intelligence apparatus, getting access to such information was not just feasible to extract a high value agent, it was entirely plausible, but also highly unusual.

'Approaching Foxtrot five,' the commander of the vehicle said, as he provided a running commentary to his control room. He watched two motorcycle outriders zoom past the side of the van, each making their way to control traffic at the roundabout five hundred metres ahead of them. Little did he know what was about to happen.

Natalie Merritt had worked as a political advisor to British MPs and Lords at the Palace of Westminster for over five years before being uncovered as an agent of Russia's foreign intelligence service, the SVR. As an illegal sleeper agent in London, she was directed by her masters in the mysterious Directorate 'S' of the SVR to use her elegance and charisma to good effect in the male dominated world of Westminster. All that came to a juddering halt some years ago when she was duped and trapped by a British agent called Sean Richardson. His name was forever engraved in her mind, and the years of being incarcerated in a British high-security prison, with MI5 refusing to hand her over in a spy swap, had done nothing but create a drive to escape and kill him, and anyone associated with him.

Natalie Merritt was born Anna Katchalyna in the cosmopolitan city of Rostov-on-Don in September 1981. Her father, Andrey, came from Cossack heritage and had reared five well-to-do children. Natalie was his sixth, and destined to become his only child subsumed into the illegal programme. His enduring legacy to the Motherland.

Now a retired officer having spent his latter years in the internal security agency, the FSB, he had received approval from his masters, and put the plans in motion to free his daughter. A daughter who was once a calm, alluring, and cautious female with impeccable spy tradecraft. She was the perfect hidden mole within the British Parliament - but had now been utterly crushed by Richardson, and a man he had been told was called Jack.

The first thing Natalie heard was the screech of brakes as the vehicle came to a sudden halt. She gripped the seat hard, tensed her body, and knew what to expect next. One of the escort officers who had stood to stretch his legs was flung into the white tubular rails and crashed to the floor in front of her.

Outside, the rear ARV had been rammed from behind by a three-tonne truck and was slowly being squeezed into a roadside stanchion by a grey armoured Range Rover. Both police firearms officers were pinned inside the BMW X5 unable to open the doors and facing total submission. Ahead of them, two snipers located high above the roundabout pummelled high velocity armour piercing rounds into the motorcycle outriders who didn't stand a chance. Accurate volleys of 7.62mm calibre ammunition from the Finnish TRG 42, the sustained firepower, coupled with lethal surprise, meant that within less than forty seconds of persistent fire, the police were impotent. It was a complex ambush executed with simplistic precision, and brutal firepower that dominated the scene.

Two copper shaped charges were placed against the fabric of the prisoner vehicle, simultaneously detonating the explosives to rip the ballistic skin apart. The searing splinters of fragmentation killed the prison officers immediately. As the carnage unfolded within the prisoner transport vehicle, the front police escort vehicle was pinned down with heavy machine gun fire coming from a second armoured Range Rover angled accurately so the shots tore through the rear window of the police vehicle and cut off any chance of escape if the doors were opened. The officer's inside were helpless. A short, squat officer opened the passenger door and scrambled for cover with his carbine in his right hand. A hidden sniper with a perfectly solid elbow base made the adjustment in his crosshair, squeezed to feel the pressure on the trigger, and released a shot which struck the officer smack in the centre of the throat. The bullet tore through the flesh taking half of the neck with it, before the head flopped to one side, and the body folded in on itself on the tarmac.

A further volley of carefully aimed sniper shots saw the driver of the X5 eliminated within ninety seconds of the attack commencing, and within less than three minutes, Natalie had been hauled out of the transport vehicle, bundled onto a motorbike and whisked off out of the city.

Chapter 8

Tuscany

Sean watched Billy Phish take the gauze strip from the scent transfer unit and hold it close to the nose of Lewis, an eight year old English coonhound. The human scent evidence dog sniffed the gauze, wagged his tail and spun in a circle excited at the opportunity to win more food from his master if he could track the scent.

It was a cold morning with a swathe of layered fog creeping over the hills surrounding the villa where the explosion took place. Sean glanced across to the small dilapidated ruin which gave a perfect line of sight into the villa and its immaculate grounds. The location of the murder of Swartz. Sean gazed at it for a while. A bit too obvious as a hide he thought. A lone pimple on a hillside across the deep valley now being sown by a lone tractor scattering its seed.

'Come on, let's get on with it,' Billy Phish shouted impatiently. 'We only get one shot at this and if it doesn't work, I'm off home for some decent tea.'

Sean shook off his lingering trance, hoping that the human scent evidence dogs would lead to something tangible. 'OK, we're set. Just remember the 'actions on' a compromise, we need to be alive to the fact people could still be watching us.'

Sean had arranged for Jugsy to track the team from the air as they conducted the search, and he'd allocated Charlie and Phil to act as the backup team in Billy Phish's vehicle if they were compromised. Like the Washington case, he hoped Lewis might lead them straight to the bomber's bolt hole. Sean wasn't convinced they'd be successful, but the only other tangible lead he had was a few scraps of intelligence from the analysts back at The

Court, and the provenance of the explosives which might take days to identify.

Sean looked on as Lewis was released by Billy Phish to trail the lingering air at mid height, rather than with his nose to the ground where the scent of the explosives wouldn't remain. Sean watched the black and tan canine strain for a waft of the scent as he slowly exited the villa grounds, straining at the leash, nose high in the air.

'He's got the scent,' Billy Phish muttered grappling for his pipe, following a few metres behind Lewis on a long flexi-lead.

Sean walked alongside Billy Phish encouraged by the positive start. He admired the skill of Billy Phish, and how he'd spent hours on the North Wessex Downs training his dogs, interspersed with managing a large farm and conducting cyber-sleuth work for big amounts of money.

Sean gripped the radio pressel in his jacket pocket and transmitted his first radio message. 'All stations. Victor five is on lock, and across the start line. Acknowledge over.'

A moment of silence. 'Whisky three here. Roger that, I have eyes on and I'm tracking your movement now.' Jugsy's response came from his specially adapted transit van located a few kilometres away to the west of Montepulciano. 'Clear skies, a beautiful Tuscan day, go well. Out.'

'Echo four here. Roger your last message. We're in situ and moving now,' Phil said in his distinctive Welsh accent. Sean knew that he would be discreetly detached from the dog team, but able to respond within seconds if there was an incident that needed his backup. Phil was able to track the canine's route using a ruggedised tablet that displayed the live video imagery which was being beamed into him from the C-Astral airframe circling high above them.

Sean watched Lewis cover the first two hundred metres of the villa's exit route to a T junction, his head held high and his four-legged torso moving at a lively pace down the curving dirt track to the main road below. Lewis momentarily stood still at the junction before sniffing around in circles for a while. Billy Phish let a little more lead out, before Lewis suddenly headed right along a narrow road towards the city of Montepulciano.

'Great start,' Sean said, knowing immediately that Lewis had retained the scent, and unbelievably was taking them up a steep incline towards the mediaeval city, with a possibility of leading them to a lock-up or abode where the bomber may have stored and built his IEDs. Could it be a wild goose chase, as Charlie had cynically stated, and all for nothing? Only time would tell, but Sean wanted to keep the team sharp just in case any location that Lewis led them to was still inhabited. No point doing a job poorly.

Sean glanced at his map and eyeballed the small roads on the hillside feature that led to the city. It was now a two kilometre walk to the city walls on a route that had a few tracks leading to one or two small villas, and the odd farmstead. He wondered if Lewis might lead them to one of those estates, or if he'd steer them straight up the road that circled back on itself a number of times, before summitting the brow, and finally entering the city.

Sean strode powerfully up the hill, wiping his brow from the first beads of sweat that had accumulated on his forehead due to Lewis setting a fair pace. Sean was breathing heavily now, mulling all manner of things in his mind as he thought of Swartz and the clinical manner of his death. He started to think about the multiple ways that the bombing team would have completed their mission, convinced it would have been a small team, likely to be military trained, and capable of covering their forensic trail using different measures to safeguard their logistic chain. Where had they sourced the explosive? Who had provided the location intelligence, how did they carry out their reconnaissance, how did they assemble the IED componentry, and how did they manage to get unfettered access to the villa to place the devices inside the large void of the fabric chairs?

He then cast his mind back to the video coverage captured high above the villa of the moments leading up to the explosion, and finally the bloodshed itself. Jugsy had configured the replay of the aerial surveillance imagery in the back of his covert van and had talked to Sean at length about Swartz's end to end surveillance operation. He showed Sean the video footage of Swartz tracking SCARAB from the airport, his arrival at the villa, and the dinner on the terrace as well as the curious moments of the vocal entertainment on the terrace just before the final series of explosions. The hairs had stood up on the back of Sean's neck as he'd witnessed the vivid flashes of light, then the blast overpressure captured by the drone, and finally the blood splattered terrace that had emerged on the screen through the slowly dissipating clouds of dust.

'Look at where the bodies landed,' Jugsy had said. 'Phil reckons it was probably less than a half a kilo of explosives in the seats, but the body parts are scattered across a distance of fifty to a hundred metres.'

'Take me back to just before the explosion,' Sean asked, now leaning back in the chair to gaze across the four screens bolted to the inside of the Mercedes van.

'Here you go. This is the period during dinner where the female singer enters the stage.'

'Do we know who she is yet?'

'No. Bloody good singer though. Swartz was loving it at the time and beamed the sound straight into my van. A deep husky voice mate.'

'What about The Court analysts? Did they come back with anything on her? Hard to believe they've got nothing.'

'Diddly squat so far. Swartz sent the images back to RAF Bentwaters as it all happened. He tasked them to find out who she was, pretty much immediately.'

'Have you got the photographs he took of her on your systems?'

Jugsy nodded and tapped a few keys on his laptop, moved the mouse a few times, clicked some files and brought up a high-resolution face shot of the singer on the screen next to the rolling video imagery. 'Bloody good bone structure eh? Top quality surveillance pictures too.'

'A very attractive woman I agree. Very distinctive features,' Sean replied, edging closer to the screen. 'Hard to believe the analysts haven't found out who she is if she's a well known singer, she'll likely be plastered all over social media somewhere. I just don't get it.'

'I know. Very odd. Have a look at this though.' Jugsy pointed to the rolling video leading up to the explosion. 'I managed to capture the vehicle that collected the woman using split screen technology from the Avigilon software. The single sensor had one view of the dining table, and one view of the car that was collecting her.'

'Number plate?'

'Wait.'

Jugsy zoomed in using a toggle stick. It blurred in and out of focus until he settled for the most suitable view. Slightly blurred but showing the plate as PI 179 HH.

'Where's that plate from?'

'Pisa. Might be nothing but we're already looking into it.'

'OK. But look, the last person to see these men alive was that woman. That singer.' Sean watched the video of the black car leaving the villa, moving slowly over the brow of the hill and down the track, just as the explosion on the terrace happened.

Sean mumbled a few words and slid his hands through his hair. 'The bomber needed to have had a good line of sight all the way to the dining table to initiate the explosive using some sort of RF trigger. It couldn't have been a time delay device as the bomber would need to have been assured that the targets were all sat at the table. He'd had to have waited until they were all sat on their chairs and the singer had left. He'd have needed to have held his nerve for a long while.'

'I agree,' Jugsy said. 'I've done a bit of terrain analysis on the adjacent hills and I think these might well have been the perfect sites to fire the button and conduct the hit.' Jugsy passed a map to Sean with a series of circles and straight pencil lines that led directly from the potential firing points, across the valleys and onto the dining terrace.

Sean marvelled at Jugsy's work. Clear analysis, clear thinking and a man getting his mind into the psyche of how the murderers would have operated. Jugsy was now in his early fifties with swathes of grey hair, a thinning but noticeably radiant red face, and a prominent nose. His lean, strong figure gave some indication of a fit man of former special forces glory with the Special Boat Service, but his active social life had taken its toll on him. Hawkeye, as he was also known, was a leading expert in imagery analysis most often for highly sensitive and covert terrorist surveillance from helicopters and using drones.

Sean directed his eyes at the map again, admired the accurate work, and looked Jugsy right in the eye. 'You're looking older you know Jugsy. But you're still bloody good, if not a little hard to handle.'

Jugsy raised his middle finger, grunted, and scratched both his large ears. Sean had witnessed this habit over the eighteen years he had known him. One that stated he was not comfortable with such conversation.

'I'm never hard to handle. Except when you don't pay me. My wife thinks I'm still a saint I'll have you know.'

'I'll pay you after the next piece of work I want you to do.'

'What's that.'

'Search each and every single one of those potential firing points with Phil.'

'I knew you'd say that. I suppose you want me to search the likely escape routes too.'

'Yup. Might not find anything but they might have been sloppy and left us a clue. You never know.'

Sean glanced up the hill noticing that the dog was still straining at the leash and they were now within a hundred metres or so of the entrance to the walled city. The next junction was a crossroads and Sean hazarded a guess that Lewis might take them straight on and through the arch into the city. Lewis proved him right as he picked up the scent after about twenty seconds of sniffing around the cobbled roads. Sean was delighted. He had a trail, but for how long?

Sean grabbed a bottle of water, took a long drink, then used his radio to make sure each callsign was on point. 'We're moving into the city now, have you got eyes on?' A short delay before Jugsy and Phil both replied in the affirmative. Sean needed everyone to be sharp at this point. They approached the splendour of row after row of sumptuous residences and apartments making up the long narrow streets of the centre.

Confined within its ancient city walls and bastions, Montepulciano is crossed by a long and wide street called the Corso from which a series of angled passageways depart. Sean watched Lewis immediately strain his neck, pulling hard on the lead, before he swiftly departed down a small alley smashing the trail with vigour. Moving on at quite a pace, Lewis took them across a street and into a wider set of cobbles on an incline, where Sean was drawn to the sounds of the bells being struck on an imposing tower house. Sean stopped to take in the magnificent surroundings, curious to see the tower adorned with a metal figure that looked like Punch, from Punch and Judy. *'Pulcinella'* was striking the hours on the big clock dressed in white and wearing a black mask.

They continued down the incline for another two junctions before Lewis all of a sudden veered left into a narrow passageway. Sean watched Lewis stand rigid, breathing hard, arching and turning his neck to look for his 'Dad', Billy Phish. His tail wagged like a flag whipping in the wind and he clearly felt he had won his reward smelling the scent of the bomber. He didn't bark but Sean could hear the distant howl of dogs a few streets down, probably scavenging the conurbation for food. Sean studied the huge ancient wooden door that Lewis had parked next to. A silence engulfed him, and the gooseflesh tingled on the back of his neck.

'Shit, this is it,' Billy Phish muttered. 'He's only gone and brought us right to the building.'

'Unbelievable.' Sean replied, somewhat shocked he might have a lead on who had killed his friend and murdered the four men. 'Let's move on. Too conspicuous right now, I'll call Phil in to support us.'

Within minutes, Sean had moved to a rally point further down the passageway and was joined by Phil and Charlie, the CIA observer.

'Just as we said before, we do this in stages now,' Sean began. 'Charlie and Billy cover the exit routes outside, while me and Phil gain entry and see what's what. It looks like a set of apartments so when the coast is clear, I'll need Lewis to identify the exact door.'

Phil and Charlie nodded.

'Jugsy, can you hear me?' Sean whispered into his radio microphone.

'Loud and clear, and I can see you too. I'm right above the location.'

'Good, keep a close eye on who exits whilst we're on site. I have no idea which apartment is our target or if anyone will be at home. But let's have a look eh?'

'Roger that. Go well.'

With that Sean handed Phil a yellow jacket, white hard hat and a clipboard from his rucksack. He led Phil back to the door for a more detailed recce to see how they could get in. As they approached, Sean spotted that entry into the building was achieved using a proximity reader key fob, and a telecom for remote entry. Sean tried flat number seven first. Always his favourite number.

Sean held his clipboard high enough for any resident observing through the telecom to see he was a worker, conducting gas or electricity checks. Remarkably, within seconds, the sound of the lock disengaging was heard, and a piercing sound identified that the door was now open. Sean held the door open while Phil gave the signal for Billy Phish to bring Lewis forward.

Sean directed his eyes at the staircase. Not a normal staircase by any means, but one that steered a route dizzyingly around the huge marble stanchions, curving its way to each of the four floors. Majestically, each landing had ornate and glistening chandeliers indicating that this was not just any old apartment block. It was a luxurious one. It didn't take long for Lewis to identify that it was apartment number four on the first floor that was the end of his game. A game that would see him rewarded with a large bone once Billy Phish had extracted him carefully from the scene.

'And your plan is?' Phil asked.

'Simple,' Sean said, pulling his Glock pistol from the back of his jeans. 'We knock and see who comes, or we wait…'

'And see who comes. I get it,' Phil replied.

Even though two men could be seen on Jugsy's live imagery feeds, he didn't spot them. They were lurking near to the apartment Sean had entered and didn't look at all suspicious from the aerial imagery Jugsy was monitoring. Situated just around the corner from the apartment on the main street, a man with a black beard took out his phone. Neither tall, nor short, the man blended into the everyday life of Montepulciano. He kept his eyes on the large wooden door where Sean would at some point exit and spoke in

Russian to his masters. 'This is orange fifty-five,' the man said calmly into his phone. 'Richardson is inside the building and we'll watch and report.'

In a commercial building in London's Fleet Street, the commander of the Russian SVR unit responded. 'We have our teams at the airport and three mobile teams ready to follow them across Italy if we need to.'

The commander had already controlled the operation from the very first point that Sean had been identified by facial recognition CCTV in the airport at Pisa - his presence in the country was verified by the watchers who were in place around the villa that he had visited the day before.

The commander took his headphones off and turned to face a female who was dressed in black leather trousers and a white blouse. 'We have him, and we won't lose him now.'

Chapter 9

Tuscany

Yelena Hardy couldn't remember exactly what time her flight to London was, but felt sure it was around 8.10pm that evening. She had planned on a lazy day, some relaxation in the bath with a book, and a stroll out for some last-minute shopping.

'You must always keep a low profile,' her father had continually told her, 'And be available to them.' Those words had always haunted her. They never left her, and she had obeyed those instructions to this very day. Self-aware that she was being controlled and manipulated, but unable to rationalise why, or for how long she could continue this charade, she had led her life immersed in fear.

She knew those days of observance to her master were now coming to an end though, and it was just a case of working towards her exit plan and keeping her fingers crossed that she would be allowed to live. Her father was not one to forgive, and as a former Russian GRU officer, now re-badged as a mercenary working as a proxy for the GRU, he was eminently able to kill her and not regret it.

Yelena lived for her singing but also for her soul. She'd spend most of her days rigidly extending her vocal skills, looking forward to her next gig, and enjoyed shopping for wonderfully fitted dresses that would accentuate both her curves and her beauty. The immersion in her songs was the one thing in life that allowed her to soothe and reflect. A place she could transition to in her own peace and solitude, and one that allowed her to disassociate with the murky world she had been brought up in working for her father's dubious business associates.

Yelena started to undress before walking around the large open plan apartment, scattering her clothes as she went. At least her father ensured she lived abroad in luxury, even if she did on occasion have to work with some of his more shadowy colleagues. It was a small relief.

The oak floored apartment was home to three bedrooms, with a further two in a self-contained annex that seemed to Yelena to equate to a granny flat that had been built in the nineties, but was decked out with fifties style décor and furniture. This was a palatial home for a wealthy family of Tuscans who owned two of the local vineyards, famed for their Vino Nobile, considered one of the top Tuscan wines in the world.

Yelena switched on some music and danced her way around the dining room area pretending to dust everything she touched. She sang along to Isabel Leonard, the American born mezzo-soprano, singing 'Non piu mesta'. Yelena, at twenty-nine years of age, had the same striking features as the lady she was listening to, and her deep Latin tone was incredibly similar too. She turned the music up a little, the sound bounded across the room from the Bose speakers which caused gentle reverberations along the open windows. Yelena's brown flowing hair bounced generously as she sang out one of her favourite songs. She had the voice to sing classical opera, but felt she needed more training. She was however thrilled that she was now able to nail the higher notes after long bouts of training. For anyone looking in on her, they wouldn't expect such a tone-heavy voice to nail the lighter moments of the aria, but she did - with masterful artistry and style as she glided slowly across the airy room to land at the laptop situated on an antique desk.

Yelena hummed away as she brought up a piece of research that she had been working on for the last two months. Two months of her life that told a different story from the one that she'd been led to believe by her parents.

Sat in just a matching bra and knicker set, she tied her hair in a bun and fiddled with the software to zoom in on a family tree. Her family. She had spent many long nights researching everyone in the tree, trying to figure out exactly who her wider family was. She thought momentarily about taking a DNA test to help track and trace her relatives. She had known of no one, other than her parents, and a few close friends all her life. At twenty-nine, she was not only curious, but determined to find out why.

'Hear that music?' Phil said clutching his pistol close to his chest ready to respond at a moment's notice. 'Opera too. Someone has good taste.'

The moments before any house raid always filled Sean with a sense of being fully alive. It was the not knowing that gave him tremors of adrenalin and heightened anticipation. The surges of adrenaline were far better than any drug he'd ever taken, and the decades of living right on the edge always brought him to wonder if this might be his final moment. You never know, he'd often say to himself. Go out with a blast at least, he'd also say. The years had been unkind to him, and his service to the crown had left him with multiple traumas and a deep sense of longing for a peaceful, tranquil life. But he craved the risk and adventure. The power of operational missions. He often sensed when danger was rife, or when things might go wrong. Might this be the last hours of my life? No. On this occasion he felt secure. He didn't think this would lead to an armed terrorist lock-up with explosives inside, but who on earth had Lewis hit on inside this abode? There had to be something in it, surely? He'd soon find out.

'You knock, I'll go in first,' Sean said, moving to the side of the door, back up against the wall, and tensing himself up for the armed entry.

Sean watched Phil knock on the door using the small brass handle located just above the figure four. The music was too loud, so he knocked again. Much harder this time. A pause. Sean watched Phil roll his eyes, then knock again. Finally, the music was turned down.

'I hear someone coming, Standby,' Phil whispered, holding his clipboard up high, knowing the occupant would check through the spyhole first.

'*Ciao chi è,*' Came the voice from behind the door.

'*Ciao madam*, I am the plumber you asked for,' Phil replied in Italian, with a distinct Welsh accent.

The first thought in Yelena's mind when the door she had gently released burst open, was that she was going to be raped. She screamed immediately then felt a calloused hand thrust across her face before she was turned, bent over, and thrown to the ground. She felt the cold steel of a weapon held hard against the side of her head.

'Don't fucking move and do as we tell you. Then you'll be fine.'

She had dreaded this moment. Most of her life. One of the men was now picking her up and dragging her on her heels to the living room. What have I done wrong? Was it her father's men now wanting to kill her? In the moments that went by, a whole range of horrible thoughts flashed through her mind on how she'd be raped, assaulted and then probably killed. Too young, and life gone too early she thought. She should have run when she had the chance a week or so ago, before conducting this final job for her father at the Villa. Why didn't she blow the whistle on her father and hand over the documents to the British agent she had met in a pub in Camden when she had the chance. A man who had thought about recruiting her to provide insider information on her father. The documents that would have implicated her father in a raft of crime and corruption.

'Get her on that chair,' One of the men shouted to the other. 'Do a quick search before we bring the dog in.'

Yelena gazed around the room, trying not to look directly at the men. She felt nauseous and dizzy.

'Now, don't speak when I release my hand, do you understand?'

Yelena nodded, struggling to breathe. She clenched her thighs and closed her legs, a natural sense of protection. She had no idea what was going on and what might happen next.

The man slowly released his hand. She decided to shake a bit, shiver even. She needed to show she was weak and not likely to fight back. Unless she had to. And she would attack if she really had to. For now, she would see what would happen next.

'I need a shirt,' She said nervously.

The man with a bent nose and who looked like a Russian thug, started to look for her clothes. Maybe it was her father's men after all, and he'd found out about her secret?

The man with a ponytail knelt down in front of her. A rugged outdoor man, athletic looking, with a slight tan and greying brown hair.

'You're a singer, aren't you?' the man said, smiling now.

'How do you know?'

'Never mind. You won't be hurt, but you need to answer a lot of questions about this place and the murder at the Villa.'

'I told the Police what I know.'

'You may well have done. But we're not the Police, and we know you have information that can help us find those murderous bastards. So don't even try and bluff me.'

The eyes that were now piercing into hers, were ultramarine blue. The face was etched with an eagerness that told her he was very serious. And the half-bearded face was handsome, strong and exuded a fulsomeness that intrigued her. That kind of face that you need to look at again and again.

'Who are you?' She mustered not quite sure what she should say.

'I work for the British government and you're effectively under arrest as a British citizen involved in the murder of four men at that villa.'

'What? No, no - that's not right,' Yelena shouted harshly scrambling for some sense of understanding. Is he British Police, how does he know I live in London? Is he a secret agent? Or is this a con? 'I was not involved in any way in that explosion,' she shouted again.

'Oh, but you were, and I'll show you the evidence we have got right now.'

The blue-eyed man shouted to the thug with the boxer nose who was now rifling through her laptop and had bagged her two phones on the desk. He was humming to the music.

'Get the dog in and get a car at the ready to get us out of here once we're done.'

Chapter 10

Tuscany

Sean watched Billy Phish get to work to try and find any evidence within the apartment. This time he used Morse, a lively cocker spaniel who had been waiting patiently in the rear of the vehicle for his turn to search for what he had been trained to find. Explosives.

Morse took a few moments scuttling around the centre of the apartment, arched his neck, and headed straight for the small annex where he stood still at a locked set of double doors.

'Where's the keys,' Sean yelled at Yelena, who was now wearing a dressing gown with her hands bound in nylon cable ties.

'I've never had the keys. I've never been in there. What's the dog doing?'

'Never mind. Billy, get us in there quickly.'

Billy grabbed a multi-tool from his waistband and started to grapple with the single key lock. Realising such an attempt was likely to take time and be pretty useless, Sean urged him to use some brute force with his feet. Within seconds the doors buckled on the single lock and a second swift shoulder charge saw them spring open. Ungainly but effective.

'Come with me, and I'll show you the evidence,' Sean barked, taking hold of Yelena's elbow to steer her into the self-contained apartment. They followed Billy Phish into the complex where Morse scuttled into a small bathroom before standing rigidly still in front of the bath. His nose was three or four inches away from a central screw holding the panel in place. Sean noticed the paint had flaked away, giving an indication that the screws had been turned regularly. He stepped forward and released all four screws before bending the wooden casing to release it from its hinged grooves. Peering inside, his eyes were drawn immediately to a small carry on suitcase. A black one, full of dust and scratch marks. To the side of it were three round plastic containers, each one looking like it had the remnants of yellow slush at the bottom of the casing with drips of the same substance over the lid seals and down the side of the containers. Sean bent down, adjusted himself onto hands and knees, and asked Billy Phish for a torch.

Gently, he scraped the small pieces of cement rubble away from the base of the case. He didn't expect any of the contents in the void to be booby-trapped, it didn't make sense to do that. But he checked anyway for any obvious wires or explosives that might be hidden deep inside the void.

'Get Phil in here Billy, this is his bag now.'

'What about Charlie?'

'He may as well come in too. The apartment is secured but we'll need everyone to search the place thoroughly before we head back to London.'

Yelena spoke with a shaky voice. 'What do you mean head back to London?'

'You'll be coming back to London with us today where you'll be nicely tucked up in Paddington Green police station before being remanded in custody at Bronzefield prison.'

'But I haven't done anything. Nothing at all…' Yelena tried to get more words out, but broke down in tears, lurching sideways before sliding down the wall placing her head in her hands.

'You've got lots of explaining to do haven't you. You have about eight hours to tell me everything in the vehicle or on the private jet from Pisa airport.'

Sean reached down and helped Yelena to her feet. He nodded at Billy Phish as if to say you know what to do, and eased Yelena back into the living room.

'Do you want to start or shall I?' Sean held a glass of water to Yelena's lips. She moved her fringe out of her tear ridden eyes, wiped her cheeks, which were now full of black mascara, and struggled hard to stop shaking. Eventually she calmed down and drank some water.

'I'll tell you everything I know, but you have to protect me. My father will kill me the moment he knows you've met me. He has people everywhere, he pays people to watch over me, and has lots of East European thugs who do his dirty work.'

'Your father? Who exactly is he?' Sean pulled a chair close to Yelena who was hunched forward on the cream leather sofa. She looked as if she was praying with her hands tightly bound together.

'His name is Goran. Goran Dozich. He runs a Russian mercenary business from his home in The Republic of Srpska. He was born in Serbia but served in the Russian Army too.'

'Right.' Sean replied sitting back ready to listen. He thought it would have taken far longer to get her to talk. She was instrumental to his investigation, most probably a part of the organised crime group that had arranged the assassinations, and unlikely to spout everything she knew early on. He had thought he'd need to use a lot more guile, charisma and subtle threats to get her to talk. But here she was, the daughter of a Serbian warlord running Russian mercenaries as a business, about to spill the beans. He was guarded that it might be bluster from a highly trained agent. It made him wonder why no one at The Court could find out who she was.

'Before we go on, and in case you're spinning me some complex yarn, you need to know that my team will be collecting all your biometric data and transmitting it back to London in the next hour to verify who the hell you are. Iris scans, fingerprints, some swabs too. Do you understand?' As Sean spoke, Billy Phish arrived with a small black Pelco case and ripped open a small plastic bag. He started to swab Yelena's hands first.

'What's this for?' Yelena asked.

'Just checking to see if you've been handling any explosives.' Billy Phish replied, eager to get the work done. 'Open your mouth please, then I'll take some of your hairs close to your crown.'

Sean wanted tests conducted on her carbon thirteen readings which would be fully analysed in London using a mass spectrometer. It would provide an indication of where Yelena had travelled to in the last three months by analysing the food and drink content in her gut which could be achieved by looking at hair samples.

'Now, why on earth would your father put you at the scene of a crime? That just doesn't make sense at all.'

77

'It wasn't planned this way at all, but the British civil servant insisted I came along to sing.'

Sean took a moment to try and rationalise what was going on. He needed to conduct the interview in the right way to check if she was lying. 'Tell me the story line on this civil servant then? What's it all about?'

Sean studied Yelena's facial features carefully as she began to explain the detail. He looked at her eye movements, her posture, when she looked him in the eye, and when she didn't. It wasn't an exact science, but the training Sean had received in neuro-linguistic behaviours might allow him to sense the lie when it came.

'You see, my father only allowed me to sing for people he had targeted me to befriend. I was his route to the political elite, the hook he would use to get influential men to trust me and eventually him. I served him for his business needs, a prisoner to him. All he ever said to me was that I had to keep a low profile and always make myself available to them.'

'And who are these people? Can you name them?'

'Yes, but I want to know I'll be protected.'

'You will.'

'There weren't many. I knew the civil servant was corrupt and he gave me a lot of information about weapons deals he was involved in.'

'The former civil servant you mean. Now dead.'

'Yes, I know. It's horrible. I've never been close to anything resembling death at the hand of my father before. Another reason I'm happy to help.'

Sean still wasn't sure about this being the truth. 'How did you get close to these people then?'

'I became close to this man. Eventually I became his lover.'

'Bloody hell. Yelena, do you understand what the hell you've been doing here?'

'I know. I'm very ashamed.'

Sean stood up and glanced across the open plan abode. Phil was dealing with the suitcase, and Charlie and Billy Phish were conducting the rummage search of the rooms. He wasn't quite sure where this would all lead with Yelena but at least he now had a lead on who had killed Swartz. Plus, it seemed some intelligence on corrupt British officials funding weapons running and arms deals. He'd need to see where Jack wanted to take that. Sean just wanted the killers.

'Right. I need to know how that stuff got there in the bathroom.'

'He stayed across the road. An Albanian man. He only came occasionally into the annex. I was told to let him use the rooms.'

'Who?'

'I don't know his name. I sang at his club in London once.'

Sean handed her a pen and paper. 'I want you to write down his description, and the club in London where you met him, and everything related to him coming here. Do you understand? I'll be back in a moment.'

Sean rubbed his chin and felt himself grating his jaw again. He was itching to get at this man and find out who had killed Swartz. He walked into the bathroom where Phil had extracted the suitcase and was sat inspecting its contents. He was swabbing the inside of the suitcase and had started to cut the lining from its inner belly.

'What have we got then?'

'Nothing much really. A few containers that look as if they have a mixture of HMTD, a peroxide-based explosive. It fits with the small quantities of explosives they could fit into the chairs as this stuff is wicked. Seriously high explosives if made right.'

'Anything else?'

'Just this. Looks like it's been mislaid.'

Sean held his hand open to receive what looked like a small SD card.

Chapter 11

London

Sean gazed around the dim room before making his way down the short winding staircase that led to a plush but narrow lounge with a long cocktail bar. The seating was predominantly curved bay seats, elegantly decked out in red fabric, with an array of orchids placed in the centre of the large wooden tables. To his left were two well dressed women. They were sitting at the bar, legs crossed facing each other, and engaged in a deep conversation in between clinking their near empty glasses.

Beyond the end of the bar, the room tapered off into the darkness where a series of five high tables and comfy highchairs provided a more intimate setting. The club was quiet except for the dull thuds of the music, just how Sean had wanted it.

Sean guided Yelena to the bar where they took a seat. He ordered a Margarita for Yelena and a beer for himself. Then he started to study the room. He wasn't sure how this meeting would go and wanted to make sure he knew the layout of the room, the exits and the areas to avoid if things got strong. He turned from the bar to scan the room. On the far side was a small stage with a tall microphone, and to its right, near the staircase, were two women and two men who looked in a merry state, one of them seemingly exchanging some cash. Prostitutes maybe?

Sean caught Yelena's eye, wondering if the Albanian would show, with Sean hoping he'd arrive alone. The barman placed a small crock of olives next to their drinks.

'What will you do?' Yelena asked anxiously.

'I'm not sure yet, but just do as we said, and it'll all be fine. I need to see the man's eyes. It's important.

With that, a tall man in a dark grey suit and a pink open necked shirt walked confidently down the stairs. A smile and a glance of the eyes towards Yelena indicated it was the Albanian. Sean didn't expect this. A smart, well dressed man, not the gruff looking persona he'd expected. The only giveaway feature of a hardened man were two tattoos. A small bird on the base of the neck and an intricate drawing of a stag on his right-hand. The head was tattooed on the centre finger, with the sprawling antlers covering each knuckle, before curving upwards to meet at the wrist. It looked to Sean like a cultural sign: if you are able to withstand the pain of having a tattoo on the hand, it would show that you are strong. He wondered if he could test that pain threshold.

'Who's this,' the Albanian said to Yelena, surprised that she had company.

'Oh, this is Sam. He's my new guitarist and a good one too. He also paints watercolours, my new creative man you might say.'

The man took a pace back, posturing a little to give Sean a once over. Sean played the quiet, unassuming type. The introverted painter and musician.

'Can we sit down,' Yelena asked the man. 'I have something to ask you. Sam knows about this, but I really need your help.'

'Sure, follow me.'

Sean didn't like the way the man spoke, nor the way his arrogance matched his wide kneed stride. He smacked of egotism, had a condescending demeanour, and a smell of cheap aftershave that made him want to punch him right there and then. But he'd wait. He'd seen his eyes, he now wanted to know if this was the killer of Swartz.

They sat in one of the alcove seats that had its back to the bar. The Albanian sat in the middle of them both.

'You didn't just come here for a drink then did you?' the Albanian said with his elbows on the table. He eyed Sean first, and then sent a piercing look towards Yelena.

'No,' she said confidently. 'My father wants you to call him right now. He has something important for you. That's why he sent me and it's very sensitive.'

The Albanian sat back, somewhat shocked at something he clearly didn't expect. 'Oh. What right now?'

'Yes, he's waiting.'

'Where?'

'At his home. It's fine. Don't worry. He'll explain everything.'

With that the Albanian placed a hand into his trouser pocket, retrieved a large silver phone, and started tapping on the contacts page, his eye off the ball.

Sean was grateful for the loud music as he launched at the Albanian's right arm. He twisted it backwards with such ferocity that something cracked, causing the phone to fly out of the man's left-hand, before Sean pinned his right-hand to the wooden table. With a fierce blow, Sean stabbed a stiletto blade right between the stag's antlers, pinning the hand to the wooden table below. The man lurched forward before Sean punched him with a furious blow to the throat that muted the screams of pain. He watched the man's eyes juggle which was accompanied by the rasping sound of a man knowing he couldn't breathe. Sean followed up with a hefty stranglehold to make the man feel that he would soon die.

'Be quite sure I will kill you here and now if I have to. Or you can live.' Sean watched the man fight for air before nodding to Yelena to grab the phone.

'Open it and point to the contact who paid you to lay the explosives in Tuscany.'

Sean knew he only had one chance at finding the perpetrator who had paid for the assassinations at the Villa, including his best friend.

'Let me breathe,' was all the man could muster as he opened the phone with his left thumbprint. Yelena held the phone while the man scrolled down and pointed to an entry in green. The name shown was Bruno Golding and the number had a 00387 code. Bosnia and Herzegovina. Yelena checked the remaining number and nodded. It was the number of her father, Goran Dozich, who was now firmly in Sean's sights.

'You survived this one my friend,' Sean said sternly, watching two shadows arrive at the table. 'But let me tell you if you are lying, I'll kill you tomorrow. You'll go with these two men and tell them everything about this man and the assassinations in Tuscany, do you hear me?'

Groaning, the man nodded. 'OK, you're the boss man now.'

'That's right, and you're ours now. Our's to use as we like. Now, tell me who the bomber is.'

'I don't know. I was just the delivery man. Told how to place them.'

Sean eased more pressure onto his throat. 'Tell me who the bomber is.'

'Arghh. I don't - I don't know…'

Sean glanced at the two suited men straddling the table. No-nonsense ex-military men, and the enforcers from The Court who would take his interrogation to the next stages.

'Find out who the bomb maker is. It's important,' Sean instructed the veterans. A nod later, Sean released his grip and the Albanian slumped to the floor.

Sean and Yelena quickly left, flagging down a black cab with ease. 'I do like how your methods are not very conventional, but they do seem to work.'

'I was being polite to him. He may well have been the thug that killed my best friend, but the man I'm after is your father. And you're going to help me get to him.'

'I've been waiting for someone to tell me that all my life.'

'Yes, well don't get too excited. This is about building up a clear picture of linkages to his crime syndicates and everyone who is connected to your father. If it all comes off nicely, you can applaud me then.'

'I know you told me to say to the man that you're an artist, but is that true?'

'It is. Just as it's true that I'm a flamenco guitarist.'

Chapter 12

Sahara Desert

It was just before 2pm on a Friday in Timbuktu, and the intense desert heat was burning into the sand of the Sahara desert that surrounded the city.

People were browsing the huge outdoor market: an elderly lady waved her fan, as much to provide a breeze as to swot away the glut of flies swarming around the meat and cheese stalls. Above her, a Mali government soldier kept watch from the roof of a three-storey apartment building. He stood guard over the city and a large siren, ready to plunge the button at a moment's notice to warn the environs of any incoming rocket attacks from the Islamic State in the Greater Sahara. ISGS had attacked the market a few weeks ago with half a dozen mortars cutting through the hazy, sand-soaked sky, exploding in and around the streets next to the market.

Timbuktu was once the heart of the Mali Empire. The King, a fourteenth century multi-billionaire, was said to have been the richest man ever to have lived. When he went on the Hajj pilgrimage to Mecca, he took thousands of courtiers with him, and lavished so many gifts of Malian gold along the way that the price of the precious metal crashed across Arabia.

Mali was an empire built on gold, but it also grew rich on trade in metals, salt and mainly slaves. Traffickers have been making fortunes for centuries, moving their wares across the vast Saharan desert. Scholars from all over the Arab world travelled to the towns that clung to the river Niger as it arced through the desert. They came with wealth to Timbuktu, Djenne and Gao, where mud mosques were built, and beautiful Islamic scripts were painstakingly written and illustrated.

The soldier shielded his ageing eyes from the western sun as he watched five young children kicking a ball around the streets, laughing and sweating, having fun. A dog zipped around them barking wildly, and one boy bowed to his mother in response to being told off for not wearing his shirt. The soldier smiled. 'Thanks to God,' he mouthed, hoping and praying the terrorists would not come this day. He hoped that ISIS fighters from Syria would not come this way either, and he hoped the Malian government would one day buy him the equipment that he and his friends needed.

As he glanced towards the large expanse of desert beyond the city, he knew bad men were gathered there, somewhere amongst the dunes and rock outcrops, where the Sahara remained ungoverned and countries like Mali and Niger remained vulnerable to becoming a new, fully formed, Islamic State.

As he lit a cigarette and craved a coffee, he wondered about the future of his country, little knowing that bad men from the west were on their way to arm the terrorists he was defending the city from. Disguised as being friendly, with the promise of help to his government, these men were intent on creating the conditions of chaos by simultaneously arming the extremists.

Twelve Russian mercenaries boarded a specially adapted Antonov An-12 at an airstrip close to 10th GRU Special Forces Brigade near Molkino in the south of Russia. The veteran commander, an experienced battle-hardened hand of fifty-one summers, walked to the cockpit and told the pilots that there was a slight change to their flight plan.

After refuelling for a short stop in Qatar, they wouldn't be flying to Syria, but to a remote airport in the North of Mali. On board the aircraft were dozens of crates of Bulgarian made weapons and ammunition, destined to be delivered into the hands of a small group of Islamic terrorists led by the commander of ISIS in the Greater Sahara - Andooha al-Saqahrawi. He had amalgamated a number of Islamist groups into the ISIS militant faction known as Al-Mourabitoun, referred to in intelligence reports as 'The sentinels' or 'the masked men'. Included in the stash of weapons was high-grade componentry, designed with simple mechanisms, for powerful improvised explosive devices. The IEDs would be assembled by the terrorists following a short briefing by the mercenaries at the airstrip. The heart of each device was contained in a large cordless phone. Each of the casings had been stripped out and replaced with a blue and white wiring mechanism with a knot at the end of each wire. A curious set up. All of the devices were configured to detonate by an operator pressing the page button to trigger the relay mechanisms of the Chinese built phones. They would detonate specially manufactured, and high precision, explosively formed projectiles - EFPs.

During the flight, a uniformed Russian officer briefed them on the specially made devices and handed them a list of the components and a diagram of how to assemble the IEDs. Eight of the men practised assembling the power mechanisms, and configuring the EFPs, but leaving the wiring of the detonators until they were on the ground. They would be acting as mercenary mentors to train a small group of specially selected ISIS terrorists who would conduct the attacks. The Russian officer handed photographs and a list of the six designated targets around Timbuktu to the commander of the mercenaries. He briefed him on the French barracks, their armoured convoys, three hotels and a restaurant that the terrorists had to attack in exchange for the weaponry. He would disembark the aircraft in Qatar.

The mercenaries on board were all part of the Keystone Security Corps, a shadowy organisation stacked with Russian veterans waging secret wars across the globe on behalf of the Kremlin. The men on board the aircraft were making up to one million roubles a month, a mammoth sum for any Russian at home or abroad. Some of the men were fighting veterans acting as proxy forces for Moscow in Ukraine, Syria and the Central African Republic where they had a sprawling base that enabled them to fan their operations out into deepest Africa.

Born out of a need for plausible deniability in Moscow's military operations abroad, Keystone contractors were at the forefront of some of the heaviest fighting in eastern Ukraine and Syria in recent years, before exploding into the headlines with their brazen assault on a US military position in north-east Syria in February 2018. Keystone heralded a new reality, one in which it would form the spearhead of an aggressive new Russian policy abroad. Especially in Africa.

'*Mee dolzhny biyt' gotovy*,' the mercenary commander said, inspecting the work of the men on board. 'Be ready, be the best,' he said, switching to French, knowing they had all been selected as basic French speakers to converse with their clients in Mali. He had been told the terrorists were a mixture of Tuaregs, Nigerians, Mauritanians and a few Libyans. Like the rest of the mercenary team, he was dressed not in uniform, but in sand coloured fatigues with a bloated grey puffer jacket and a green bobble hat. The rest of the team wore a kaleidoscope of colours and brands, each with their own peculiarities as Russian combat veterans from multiple units. None of them carried ID, no photographs of their family were allowed, and they only had a smattering of US dollars to buy their way out of trouble should they come across it. They were deniable Moscow assets, neither attributable to Russia, nor a concern if they were killed.

The commander, a former GRU Major had some history to him. He was one of four unlucky fellows from the Keystone outfit who had been captured the previous year in eastern Syria and had been paraded before the camera. Had they been Russian servicemen, the outcry at home would have been deafening. Instead, their captivity was brushed aside, with the Kremlin simply saying they were probably volunteers. This allowed Russia to enter a foreign, hostile environment with minimal risk, and to exploit political and economic opportunities at will.

The jet struggled with the fierce Saharan crosswinds as it lurched and swayed before landing with a heavy thump on a makeshift runway to the north-east of Bourem. A recent sandstorm had left an orange fog swirling in the air and it was hard for the commander to make out the terrain as he dropped the aircraft steps. He knew he only had a maximum of thirty-six hours to impart the orders from up on high. He had to train the men that now stood in front of him, scattered in the back of half a dozen Mitsubishi pickup trucks.

He made the long lonely walk to introduce himself to the tall Islamist leader who was stood in front of the first vehicle cradling an AK47. He wore a traditional Tuareg turban and expensive sunglasses.

The commander thought momentarily of the second part of his mission given to him by the Russian GRU officer in Qatar. It puzzled him a bit. First, he was to arm the jihadis, and then he was to move to Niger awaiting orders to become bodyguards to the Mali President. He chuntered as he walked, dismissive of the quandary, content that he was getting paid well to make a good retirement for himself and his family. He didn't know, or want to know, but his Russian GRU handler would be the front man setting out to achieve Russia's three core aims for the country. To create chaos amongst the fighting factions, before making an offer to the beleaguered Mali President. The offer would be to provide close protection forces to his presidency, to provide training and arms to his armed forces, all in return for a stake in the gold mines of the country - and to undermine the French military dominance in the region.

'*I bisimila*,' the tall Tuareg said as the initial greeting using the Bambara language. '*I Jamu*?'

'*Merci*,' the Russian said, offering his hand. '*Je m'appelle Grigory*.'

The Russian handed his opposite commander a gift. A brand new, silver plated Makarov pistol direct from its Bulgarian factory.

So began the first step of a mercenary fighting force projecting a new wave of Russian dominance and influence across the Sahel.

Chapter 13

London

'Who would like to start,' Jack asked, from behind his desk on the first floor of The Court HQ in Devereux Court. 'We have a lot of intelligence now, and a lot to cover before we make any more plays.'

Sean looked around him. He gave a customary nod to each person, as if to say leave this one to me. He knew Jack would want this pitched clearly, with a steer as to what should happen next. But he needed to move through the stages before thrusting his recommendation on the table from a plan he had hatched the night before.

'Well, putting it simply, I now know who paid who to kill SCARAB and the three other men,' Sean began. 'But I'm not yet sure of the motive.'

'I can probably help with that,' Jack chipped in early. 'But let's share everything you have right now amongst all of us.'

Sean looked around the table, eyeing CIA Charlie first to check with Jack he was genuine. Jack smiled and nodded. Phil, Jugsy and CIA Charlie sat next to each other in a row. Each of them looking bemused at the retro fifty's office designed by D. It seemed strange for Sean to see Jack sitting in D's chair, commanding The Court in its entirety.

The Court was D's very own cabal of hand-picked officers who ran the office and its much larger intelligence fusion centre located out of the city. Together, with a set of core staff who ran what D used to call his own active-measures campaigns around the globe, it was a niche force for good. It employed a mixture of freelance ex-intelligence officers in the UK, as well as veteran special forces operators, and a mix of former MI6 and MI5 specialists, all highly vetted and sworn to keep The Court's operations fully secret.

'We've collected lots of forensic evidence that link the attack to the hand of a former Russian GRU officer of Serbian descent,' Sean began. 'The explosives were a mixture of Russian military explosives using peroxide-based detonators which disintegrated, leaving very little forensic evidence. We found the peroxide-based mixture in the bolt hole of the Serbian's daughter who had been singing at the villa that evening.'

Phil sat forward, eager to add more detail. 'We have the bomber's signature too. He used a Chinese built Senao mobile phone that our bomb database had seen being used in Syria. The bomber removed the plastic casing, ripped out the power cord, and replaced it with a battery before rewiring the phone's page function to an external relay switch. He'd connected the relay to a battery, and then the mix of violent TATP which acted as the detonator, and hey presto. Boom. The bomber simply pressed the page button, the relay flipped, and each bomb was triggered.'

'What about Swartz, how did they know about his covert location?' Jack asked, sitting behind the 1970s vintage President desk that was empty except for a large ink blotter and two pens standing to attention in a wooden stand. Jack's brown briefcase was propped up against the edge of the curved desk, with a light blue swivel chair contributing nicely to the vibrant colours of the room.

'Hard to say,' Sean answered. 'Jugsy searched the attacker's firing point and unfortunately for Swartz, he wouldn't have known that it had direct line of sight into the back of the ruined building he chose to conduct the surveillance. They'd quite probably have used it as their own firing point anyway, so they might have rumbled Swartz during their set up.'

'Or we have an insider who knew about the operation,' Jack proffered.

Sean found himself twiddling with the yarns on the pale green battered and beaten high-back chair. Its arms were decayed from years of guests gripping them and fiddling with its material. 'Is that what you think? You have a mole inside The Court?'

'Again, hard to tell, but if we have, this is where we hatch the plan to smoke them out. Give me some more information to work with.'

Sean could see Jack's brain was already hard at work trying to craft the next stages to his plot, and he wondered about the information that Jack had, but he didn't. 'I need to interrogate the singer a bit more, but she seems as if she wants to really nail her father. I need to find out why.'

'How on earth do you know she's not leading you into a trap?'

'Gut feeling as normal. She could be really useful for us to infiltrate his organisation.'

'Which we're already doing,' Jugsy chipped in. 'The contacts we've retrieved from the Albanian's phone has given us quite a network to investigate. The SD card found in the Tuscan apartment gave us intelligence on the arms manufacturers too, who are all probably under the threat of extinction if they don't cooperate with Dozich. A bloody good search all in all. Early indications from the analysts show his network was extensive in Sarajevo, and we've linked some of them to known weapons routes that have been used to smuggle arms from the Balkans and into Europe and Africa. It all begins in Bulgarian factories, and we've got a team of finance analysts looking at multiple transactions from Dozich's cover companies. One of them is just down the road at London Bridge.'

'Seems we've uncovered quite an operation and we can exploit it at will,' Sean said confidently. 'The data mining of the phone and SD card, the bomb forensics, and what we've gleaned so far from Yelena, gives us a few routes into the organisation and show that it's linked to Russian funders. With a bomber's signature too.'

'Blue and white wires, always with a knot at each end,' Phil contributed. 'He crimps his wires in a certain way, and our explosives analyst even reckons he's right-handed from the soldering. This bomber feels safe, uses the same devices time and time again, always uses his own signature. He'll also know that our databases have him down as a marked man. A massive ego who I'd love to find and kill.'

'You never know,' Sean said. 'Plenty more action to come I think.' He watched Jack reach for his briefcase and retrieve a buff coloured folder. Jack took a pair of varifocal lenses from his inside jacket pocket and opened the file before sitting back in his chair waiting for the quiet murmurings amongst the team to calm. Jack placed both hands on the arms of the seat and adjusted his tie so that it sat perfectly in the middle of his shirt.

'We are entering a new dimension with the Russians using mercenaries to conduct their active-measures campaigns,' he began. 'I've been working this case for a long time now, and I think we have enough intelligence to move forward. We'll mount an active operation against them in Africa. And it will all begin with Sean playing his Spanish guitar.'

Phil looked at Sean in bemusement, determined to lighten the air. 'We all know he's a bit of a strummer Jack, but a Spanish guitar? What the fuck's all that about?'

'He's gonna serenade some bird,' Jugsy piped up, grinning wildly at the mischievousness of it all. Sean rolled his eyes knowing what was coming next.

Jack smiled and let the banter continue for a short time. 'You're not far off the script there Jugsy. Very few of us knew Sean was an accomplished guitarist as well as an artist. It's all very useful, and it's the little things in life that help me craft the detailed plan I've been working on for many years.'

'Spill the beans then Jack. What are we gonna get up to?' Phil asked, eager as ever.

'All in good time. Firstly, Sean wanted to know the motivation for the assassinations. Thanks to Jugsy's airframe collecting information from their phones while it was monitoring the dinner from above, I have plenty of intelligence pointing to why this all happened. You see, each man was a member of Le Cercle, a secretive global organisation that included many former intelligence officers. SCARAB and his chums were targeted by a splinter group who are called the twenty-one-club. Their members felt the Cercle team were a threat to their own weapons smuggling empire. And they decided to take them out of the game and steal their clients.'

'Jeez.' Charlie said, speaking for the first time. 'Former intelligence officers you say.'

'Exactly right. And I'll need your help Charlie, at the right time. The twenty-one-club also includes a number of high net worth financiers, some of whom are politicians using their money and influence to support export license cheating.'

'Brits or who?' Sean murmured, eager to get as much from Jack as he could.

'Brits and French mainly, the odd American. All seemingly with connections to Russian organised crime syndicates. The motivation for them is greed and wealth with the main buyer of their services being the Russians. They provide secret government intelligence, political intelligence through their old contacts, and have established some very complex financial and geographic operations to move weapons into Africa and buy influence. Mainly by exchanging weapons for diamonds and gold, and propping up weak Presidents.'

'Ok. So, what's the plan?'

'I will ask an oligarch we have on our books to set up a deal with Yelena's father. His name is Leonard Berarnov. He's wealthy, under our protection, and influential with a few former Russian intelligence officers who will know the route into these operations. We'll run it as a lure to smoke out a few of the major financiers, and we'll run a new deal moving weapons through Nigeria and into Mali using a new route. All we need now is a Russian buyer for our services.

'Who exactly is this oligarch, Berarnov?' Sean asked.

'He's a donor to the Conservative party, quite a lively character, and very good friends with a number of MPs here in London, and one or two politicians in Paris.'

'But why a new deal? Are you going to bring Sergei into this too with his connections?'

'No, not Sergei. He's not needed on this. He's provided me with the leads here, but nothing else. You see, the reason that Dozich took out SCARAB is because he wanted his clients for financing the movement of weapons. And here we are. We're going to be one of those clients. And Leonard, our oligarch is going to set it all up.'

'Right. I see all that, but where's the route in?'

'Very simple. You are now Yelena's new guitarist. She's played across big London clubs, albeit with an Argentinean guitarist to make up the duo. We'll get rid of him, and let her explain to her father that you are her new guitarist - and you go everywhere as a couple when you play. She'll be at a meeting we'll set up to sing for the guests, and you'll be playing the flamenco guitar beside her.'

Chapter 14

London

Natalie Merritt's senses were electric as she strode into the Russian cyber operations room in Fleet street, excited that she was about to get her first big break in finding Sean Richardson before she would eventually torture and kill him.

Natalie had been informed by the cyber operations officer that the facial recognition cameras at Stansted airport had provided an exact match of the man who was her quarry.

'Where's he going?' Natalie demanded to know, her patience completely evaporated from three years of incarceration at the man's hand. She began to wonder how she would kill him, but first she wanted to know everything about his life. His family, his friends and girlfriends, children even. His handler, his accomplices, and even his parents were all in the sights of her assassination plans. She would make him, and everyone connected to him, suffer.

'We're tracking him now.' Boris, the cyber commander said. 'He's with a woman, here have a look, I'll bring all the cameras up on the screens.'

Natalie glanced up at the large bank of CCTV screens, eight monitors, all high definition, carefully configured on the operations room wall to provide high-resolution imagery at large-scale. She saw a man and a woman standing at the check-in counter of EasyJet. The man was dressed in a black T shirt, blue jeans and brown shoes carrying a guitar. The woman stood next to him was tall. Young too. Natalie leaned forward to get a better look at her. She felt an immediate attraction when the woman turned her head and swept her hair behind her ears that exposed the thin silver earrings she wore. The woman wore a black crop top showing off her midriff. Natalie's eyes were drawn to the female's lean and shapely figure whose expensive taste in clothing was set off with high heel boots and a grey Chanel bag.

'Are you sure it's him? What's he doing with a fucking guitar? It just looks like a couple going off on holiday together.'

'It's an exact match, here look.'

Boris pointed to a screen that showed Sean's full face with a series of small diamond dots interconnecting with blue lines to gauge the precise features and bone structure of the man. On the right of the screen in a small pop up was the original picture of Sean from his intelligence officer days. A picture that had been provided from the archival data banks of the GRU in Moscow. The software had churned out an alert and an audible alarm as Sean walked through the main entrance of the airport and Boris and his team swung into action to capture the imagery, and check the gait of the man they had been tasked to find.

'Brilliant. Now track and trace who that woman is. I want to know who she is and if he's shagging her.' Maybe she could kill them both in one fell swoop, together in bed perhaps, she mused.

'Do you want us to get a man on that flight? We can have someone there in an hour and boarding if there's any seats left.'

'Do it,' Natalie ordered, turning to sit down. 'You should have done that earlier. Now, zoom in on that board behind the check-in. Where are they going?'

Natalie was firm and committed. She sat at the rear of the CCTV console and began tapping her fingers on the table. She was eager to see where they were going and eager to kill them both. Within seconds the CCTV operator had zoomed onto the board.

'Looks like it's flight EA233, direct to Menorca.'

Chapter 15

Menorca

Nestled in a calm Mediterranean inlet, surrounded by a rugged coastline and hilltop fortresses, Cala Llonga is an enclave of understated wealth for elderly money bankers, oligarchs and oil tycoons. Palm trees and expensive motorboats line the coastline, and the residents tool around in golf carts. The median home price is three million dollars and someway north of that for the villa Sean was headed to.

Overlooking Mahon harbour, the views from its multitude of whitewashed villas are some of the world's best as it overlooks the entrance to one of the largest harbours in the world. With its waterfront location and commanding views of the port and marina, Sean was mesmerised by its beauty.

'It's only a ten-minute ride,' Yelena said as she grappled with her wind strewn hair, deciding in the end to tie it up. Sean sat close to her on a small vessel whose single engine chugged away harmoniously, while the sound of the blue canopy flapping above them provided a melodic backdrop to their journey.

'Are you sure your father didn't suspect anything when you mentioned me?'

'No. Not at all. He was curious why I had a new guitarist and interrogated me whether you were my lover or not. Other than that no. He's used to me singing with a guitarist.'

'At his home too?'

'Yes, a number of times before. He thought they were my lovers too. Some of my guitarists have had a dodgy background, so he checks them all out. He knows I like rebels.'

Sean grabbed a flask of cold water and raised his cap, watching Yelena lift her head to get the midday sun. She was dressed in denim shorts, a green sleeveless top and a wide brimmed sunhat with her brown hair now tied in a bun underneath. After only a day or two's practice playing as a duo with Yelena, he felt confident he could hold his own in front of the audience assembled to kick off Jack's sting operation.

The gentle murmur of the Honda outboard motor helped Sean think as they were slowly propelled towards the exclusive inlet. He marvelled at the huge forts and islands that formed the impressive backdrop to Menorca's capital city, all remnants of British naval power in the eighteenth century. He thought back to Jack's conversation that made him wonder where all this might lead.

'You need to use every opportunity to search the villa and get into his IT systems,' Jack had said. 'Berarnov will lead the discussions and you'll have time before and after your performance with Yelena to find everything you can from his office, his computers and his lock ups. Find out everything about this man and his operations. We've left plenty of information on your legend if he does background checks, and he'll find it's mostly unsavoury, but not a huge threat.'

'What's the wider picture Jack? You always hold stuff back from me, and if I'm going into this job, I'm going in with eyes wide open. I want to know more than just the background.'

'We had a whisper from Sergei's master in Moscow. The Russian GRU emphasis is now into Africa Sean. They are using mercenaries and Yelena's father is the maestro of a group called Keystone Security Corps. They're all ex Russian military mercenaries and her father runs the GRU elements of it. They're looking to arm Islamists in the greater Sahara and set the conditions for chaos in the region. There's every chance another Caliphate will be created in the region, and in my opinion, if the fighters turn up from Syria, the whole Sahel region will fall very quickly.'

'Not bloody good. So, what are we going to do?' Sean asked, bemused at Jack's nonchalance. 'Are we going to take this bloke and his outfit down?'

'Impossible Sean. It's too big, stealthily backed by the Kremlin, and impractical to do anything other than gather intelligence on their future plans in Africa and in Mali in particular. Moscow wants power there, and in Niger. This is where you come in to gather the intelligence and we can then see what we can do to disrupt them. We may not stop the place falling to the Islamists, but we can do our damned best. These bastards are arming them to create a Caliphate and sow the chaos that comes from that.'

Sean knew that he was Jack's fall guy. Using Sean, Jack had nothing to lose. He was a deniable asset. If he was caught lurking about the villa and its offices, he'd likely be killed by one of the Serbian's henchmen who protected the villa with automatic weapons and a bunch of vicious war dogs. Yelena had provided Sean with her knowledge of the layout of the villa, including the rough location of her father's office, his lock-up garage and where his IT server was located on the first floor. Little did Sean know this was only a small part of a much bigger operation that Jack was concocting with his friend from the CIA, Laura Creswell.

Sean stepped out of the boat onto a small white pier, his guitar neatly strapped to his back like a large rucksack. He stood to take in the huge grounds and mansion. It had a multi-elevated front-line position facing the shoreline with magnificent views across Mahón harbour from most aspects of the villa. He noticed what appeared to be an infinity swimming pool that dominated the centre of the grounds. The rolling lawns were immaculately tended, and a series of water sprinklers were dotted across the landscape spraying their feed.

In front of him were two men, both wearing what appeared to be the uniform of the Serbian's minders. Armed discreetly with small pistols under their black ultra-lightweight gilets, the men wore white sports polo shirts and dark grey tailored shorts, topped off with grey deck shoes and expensive sunglasses. As Yelena and Sean approached the grounds, he noticed one of the men with ultra-pumped muscles reach to touch his chest holster, as if to make a point to Sean. Muscles pumped with drugs, Sean thought, as he glanced across to the second pier where a twenty-three-metre Lagoon Seventy-Eight yacht was berthed. The two-million-dollar yacht cast a long shadow over the twinkling sea and onto the lawns.

Sean had plans to sit in the gardens later that afternoon to sketch and paint the stunning views across the harbour to El Castell. He spotted the perfect place to laze the afternoon out painting the terracotta red building of Spain's most easterly town and the most British of them all. It was built during the 18th century by British Royal Engineers and was formerly known as Georgetown in the honour of George III of Britain. But before that, he was due to meet Yelena's father and have a tour of the villa and its grounds.

Sean was escorted through the long, wide corridors of the expansive villa where the distinct odour of lavender caught the throat. Muscle man led the way, with the second tailing them at a distance. Sean felt the unease of them both but continued to scan the interior checking for security alarms, CCTV and movement sensors. Expensive modern art lined the walls and long Persian carpets led the way past a number of bronze sculptures sitting proudly on circular glass tables. A door was opened by the minder, who invited them with a long arm into an enormous reception room that gave access to an immaculate terrace with stunning views across the bay to Mahon.

Sean exchanged a glance with Yelena, and they entered. His eyes were first drawn to a tall elegant man who stood at the end of the room admiring the view. A split second later he eyed a second, more portly man who was sitting in a cream leather chair spying the same view. The tall man turned. 'Ah, at last. My daughter has arrived,' he said, holding his arms out with a lingering smile that provided the glint of a gold tooth. 'I've been waiting a lifetime for you.'

Sean noticed Yelena's slightly cold embrace for her father before she turned to the guest who had now stood to greet her. The first thing that struck Sean about this small squat man was the vast swathes of grey hair, swept back with Brylcreem, but immaculately trimmed to provide the perfect bouffant. The second thing Sean noticed was that his hands were trembling when he offered to shake. He looked pale, overweight and his skin badly scarred with purple patches. He seemed to delight in seeing Yelena and gazed at her for an embarrassingly long time.

'Father, this is Sam,' Yelena quietly stated, standing between the two men. 'Sam, this is my father, and this is his close friend Sir Rhys Eldridge from Great Britain.'

'Thank you for coming to see me,' Yelena's father said gripping Sean's hand and patting his shoulder. 'And thank you for looking after her on the music circuit. I've heard great things about your musical prowess which we will of course sample this evening. It's a fine gathering of my closest people.'

'Very pleased to meet you both and it's my pleasure to be here...' Sean was about to say more when he was interrupted by Yelena's father.

'Now please come along, we shall have lunch. We have a long day ahead. Please be seated everyone.'

Their imposing host was Goran Dozich, the fearsome former security chief of the Russian GRU and now the go-to man for the Keystone Security Corps when they needed complex weapons trade to support their missions across Africa and the Middle East. In a well-tailored light blue suit, the Serbian-born gangster eyed Sean across the table coldly, and told him that in another context they'd be trying to kill each other, if Sean had ever served in NATO. Indeed, Sean felt him trying to poke his own psyche about who he was and why he was here with his daughter. Sean ignored the numerous attempts to get him to bite, and just continued to act out his role as the quiet, insular guitarist he was.

Dozich, who said he was born in Serbia to Russian parents, maintained his long-standing connections in Russia as well as Bosnia and Herzegovina for his security businesses, and according to several reports Sean had read, he had lived in the Republic of Srpska for several years. Dozich often partied in Sarajevo with his close friend sat beside him, and according to one intelligence report, the men had known each other for over thirty years. They were an unlikely pairing, one a criminal gunrunner, and the other a Member of Parliament who had first met Dozich during a deal to provide high-tech security for energy clients in the Far East. According to the intelligence reports, one of the contracts Sir Rhys had given to Dozich in their early days of friendship, was for protection of ships drilling in Nigeria's offshore oil fields, which were often the targets for terrorist attacks.

Dozich, who wore a full greying beard and smoked Dunhill cigarettes in between courses, radiated enthusiasm. A good salesman is how one former MI6 officer had described him.

'I was lucky enough to be educated in France you know,' Dozich said, encouraging Sean to be more active in the conversation. 'I even joined the French Foreign Legion for a short time and served widely across Africa. Then I started winning security contracts and Sir Rhys was one of my first clients. What about your adventures?'

Sean remained unassertive, even boring, knowing that at the right time he'd get the chance to scour the property and search for intelligence in this man's computer systems and his office drawers. But for now, he needed to fake his lack of charisma. 'I rarely travel outside of London I'm afraid. My mother needs my attention quite a lot these days so it's nice to come away for a short time.'

'You appear to keep yourself fit though by the looks of it?'

'Hardly. No, I don't. I don't really like exercise, nor alcohol, but I do like weed.'

Sean noticed that Sir Rhys appeared irritated with having to suffer such boring company, especially as he himself was such a gregarious talker.

'Good God man, I'm glad you play such fine music, but you really need to travel a bit more and get excited about things you know.'

Yelena jumped to his defence, quietly, but purposefully making her point. 'He's a very kind soul, and we make such great music together. His talking is done with his guitar, and for our audiences, it's stirring stuff. They are fixated by his chatter.'

'Fine,' Sir Rhys said taking a lengthy drink of his Viognier wine and wiping his mouth with a napkin. 'Tonight is quite an important business event for your father and me, and we'd like you both to make a good impression on our potential client. He's a wealthy Russian living in London you know. His name is Leonard Berarnov. Have you heard of him?'

'No, I'm afraid I haven't.'

'Well, he's heard of you and is looking forward to a private performance my love.'

'It might just swing the deal,' Dozich chipped in, waving at the waitress to clear the course.

Jack had been unable to verify parts of Yelena's father's biography, including his military service with the French, but Jack's very own oligarch, Berarnov, and another Russian special operations veteran who had been with him in the field, said he was considered competent, ruthless and calculating. Another report from the CIA had stated that he was prone to exaggeration but for crazy shit, he's the kind of man you hire.

Jack had accrued intelligence from Berarnov explaining how Dozich's operatives had recently killed a Russian blogger who had been investigating his murky world, and apparently, he'd also tested poison on Syrian soldiers. He was also the likely assassin leader of three journalists who travelled to the Central African Republic to investigate the Keystone Corps and were shot to death. Sean knew he was in bad company but for the life of him, he couldn't work out why Sir Rhys maintained such a toxic friendship. As an MP he was taking huge risks. He felt there was more to this than met the eye, and made a mental note to delve into the depths of their historic relationship.

Sean tucked into a piece of pecan pie with a knob of cream, listening intently to the conversation but saying very little as the subject turned to family. Sunlight began streaming in from the outside terrace, and the two giant overhead fans pushed the fragrant air to provide a gentle breeze. He watched Sir Rhys rise, then snuggle into a cushioned wicker chair, before browsing through clippings of the day's news. Incongruously, Sir Rhys said he'd spend some time in the gym that afternoon, but Sean sensed he'd do nothing of the sort. Sean's afternoon would be spent scouting the grounds with his sketch pad, and confirming the security arrangements of the villa that he'd previously been shown on a series of black and white building plans.

'Now then Yelena, come over here and tell me what you've been up to,' Sir Rhys uttered. 'How is everything these days?'

Yelena looked discomfited. Offended even. But she chose to keep the peace and joined him for a private conversation. Recognising this, Dozich indicated to Sean to follow him onto the terrace.

'You're aware that we check everyone out before they're allowed here aren't you Sam?'

'What do you mean?'

'Let me tell you a story and then you'll understand.'

'OK, but I hope you don't think I've done anything wrong with your daughter.'

'Oh, I know you haven't - but let me tell you why you won't either. You see, I rose to riches in the eighties as an entrepreneur running a gang of thieves, something my daughter wouldn't have told you.'

Sean watched him light a cigarette and walk to the far end of the terrace to peer over the whitewashed stone wall. He blew a puff of smoke partially into Sean's face before he continued.

'As communism fell, I moved into a new world and I persuaded the heads of Belgrade's most prosperous crime groups to band together and form a single super-syndicate under my leadership. The group was called the Lozskaya and I needed to make sure the city's yobs knew I was in charge through killing them. It was how I survived to make wealth for my family and my children.'

Sean kept his eyes low and just listened, adopting a soft posture before placing a set of circular spectacles on his head to make out he needed a shield of security. He could see that Dozich was sending him a message and imagined how this man had probably shown his strength in a series of bloody skirmishes with the local mob, leaving the streets strewn with the mutilated bodies of rival gang bosses. Racketeering, extortion, robbery and contract killings were his stock-in-trade as well as arms smuggling that saw his trade skyrocket with the collapse of the Soviet Union. Sean could see he had an enterprising mind to match his wardrobe of well-cut suits and could easily blend in well with Europe's business elite. Sean wanted to kill the man there and then but strained every sinew in his body to hold himself back. His time would come.

'I have three children and Yelena is my youngest,' Dozich continued. 'If you've fucked with her mind or come here to get at me, you'll be taken out of the game.'

'I'm just her guitarist,' Sean said humbly but with strength of purpose. 'You've checked me out right?'

'I have, but just remind me of where you studied your craft.'

'Dulwich college and then the Royal Academy of Music.'

'What years?'

'I was at the Royal Academy from 1991-1993.'

'And a few criminal offences too, I see.'

'Oh, that was way back.'

'So, listen to me. There's something not quite right about you and I can't put my finger on it. But be warned, I'm going to watch you like a hawk and make sure you are who you say you are.'

Sean was pleased that Jack had done a good job making sure that his new legend of being a burnt out, but talented guitarist had held up to the scrutiny of Dozich's background checks by his people.

What Sean didn't know, was that two Russian SVR agents were watching his every move on that terrace from a carefully concealed surveillance hide in the undergrowth below.

Chapter 16

Madrid

The deal that brought a Russian Serbian mercenary to the streets of Madrid to hash out an initial transaction on the purchase of Balkan weapons, took place over a lavish lunch in the Ritz-Carlton situated on the magnificent Paseo Del Prado.

Leonard Berarnov, the London-based oligarch and a chiselled former Russian special forces officer, had flown in from the UK to make his pitch to Goran Dozich. It did not, as Berarnov had explained to Jack, begin well.

'Dozich suspected something was not right from the off when I mentioned we wanted the meeting to involve Sir Rhys Eldridge.'

'How so?'

'He challenged me on how I knew about Sir Rhys. He was about to get his coat and walk out when I explained how we knew that Sir Rhys was now funding some of the Keystone operation alongside his team from the twenty-one-club that had broken away from Le Cercle.'

'Good grief. How did you manage to convince him that this was all legitimate? The only way we know about Sir Rhys and his twenty-one-club is through our intelligence after Dozich had the intelligence officers murdered. They were Sir Rhys's natural competitors.'

'Ah, just a little GRU tale,' the oligarch said smugly. 'You really don't have all the inside information you know Jack. I have my own sources too, back in Russia.'

'You've been playing the field I see. You just better not be playing me Leonard.' Jack adjusted his tie and paused for a while before deciding to probe. 'It's fairly obvious why you pay the Conservative party all those millions of pounds every year which gives you access to ministers, but it's equally clear to me that you're a marked man as far as Moscow is concerned. You really need to be cautious you know, and if you're still fraternising with your old GRU chums I need to be kept fully in the picture.'

'Nothing so nefarious at all Jack, and you know my bread is now fully buttered in your marvellous kingdom. I simply used old intelligence from my special forces days in the Russian GRU - intelligence that I knew would keep Dozich interested because it came from the time he served in the GRU too. You see, we were both assigned to the KGB at one point in our youth, and we served under the same commanding officer, Major General Katchalyna. Once he'd sat down again, and we had some common ground, I told him that Sir Rhys and I had common political aims in the United Kingdom, and that we both had a hand in making sure our own wealth was being carefully invested. I explained how I knew that the return on investment for this old General was paying great dividends after he invested in Keystone operations. And that I could help with some smuggling routes he might want to use, alongside investing some of my wealth into Keystone.'

'The perfect partnership. You have the routes and the security of them tied down, you have a dealer linked to the Tuareg who can act as a jihadi broker, and he has the weapons to sell to a market of his choosing.'

'Exactly. It's an obvious alliance. We're both former GRU, both wealthy, and he wants to expand his business and make a few dollars beyond his paymasters in the Kremlin. A side-hustle.'

'Brilliant. So, you hit it off, and he agreed to meet again?'

'We didn't stop drinking vodka all afternoon. Quite a few toasts to our family, a chat about operations we had both taken part in, and finally setting a date for the meeting at his Villa in Menorca.'

'Did you manage to get any information about the operations he runs?'

'A little, but he was guarded on the detail of how he operates with Keystone. He obviously gets his instructions from Moscow, and he explained that it's not just Russian mercenaries he uses, but also Ukrainian and Serbian.'

'Interesting. My team have also tracked his recruitment activity and the salaries he pays out to his soldiers of fortune, which by the way, also include dozens of veterans from Belarus, Uzbekistan, Moldova, and even France.' Jack paused and thought carefully about what he would disclose to Leonard. Especially as Sean would at some point be dropped into the mix working as an arms runner with the Tuareg. 'What's more, our intelligence gathering on Dozich has revealed he takes supply orders from a few people outside of Russia to top up his own profits. A little bit on the side so to speak, which is why he probably liked your pitch.'

'Oh, he did. I assume he was making money from the original Le Cercle officers?'

'Indeed. Before they were murdered. Which is why I'm hoping Sir Rhys has bitten on this little deal we're putting together, because that was the plan he had hatched. To kill off his competitors and take their clients one by one.'

'It would seem you're right Jack. Dozich said he'd confirm the attendance of Sir Rhys, and he spoke to him by phone from the hotel lobby whilst we were there.'

'I know. We had a team standing right next to him as he spoke, who locked onto the conversation. Sir Rhys seemed interested. Very interested.'

'Well that fits as Dozich was very excitable at the table when he returned. As soon as I explained we had a fully operational smuggling route into our end-user clients in the Sahel, he was all ears, and wanted more detail on how they'd get the relevant export licences.'

'You explained to him about the investment, right?'

'Just as you instructed me Jack. Two million US dollars as a test of sale and delivery, followed by a further weapons purchase of around six million, with a large profit margin going to Dozich, and doubtless a big cut to Sir Rhys too.'

'Excellent. This is where we set the sting with Sir Rhys if he bites.'

Leonard took a sip of his tea that had been served in Chinese bone china. 'Are you going to tell me about it?'

'All in good time. You see, I need a perfectly aligned evidential trail for this operation, and I need you to play this out with Sir Rhys very tightly in Menorca. You'll have a wire on you, and I need Sir Rhys to agree to certain things you ask of him. Secondly,

I need to set up my Nigerian friends to support us on the tactical aspects of this sting.'

Sean spent the early evening relaxing with Yelena sitting at the poolside sketching the views across to Georgetown where he'd captured the Lagoon Seventy-Eight yacht in the foreground. He planned on converting the pencil sketch into a large oil painting one day, when he returned to France.

'Why don't you sketch me too?' Yelena asked sweeping her hair back behind her ears and giving Sean a look that he had seen all too often before.

Pheromones Sean thought. The scent and looks of sexual attraction were emanating from every feature of her body and Sean took more than a moment to look at her immaculately made up face. The evening light showed off her flawless skin, and her blue eyes glinted brightly with a look that said she wanted more attention from him. He watched her cross her legs, cutting a glance of thigh that promoted all the stimulus that a red-blooded man needed to provide such attention. Sean was hooked, and he knew it well at that small moment in time. He'd previously looked at her in a way that didn't initially show his attraction to her, and he'd eyed her perfect body on a few occasions, mindful that he had a job to do, but she was absolutely gorgeous in every manner. Something was missing though, and he couldn't put his finger on it. He needed to get to know her better. Those thoughts converged on the sexuality he now saw in front of him and he felt a few twinges of attraction that told him to take advantage of it, to find out more about her.

'You're driven by something,' Sean said glancing again at her thigh. 'I can't work out why, or what it is, but maybe you ought to tell me?'

Yelena smiled alluringly. 'You know exactly what's driving me, I'm sure.'

'I can tell yes. But I still can't work out why you turned against your father so quickly.'

'Like I said before, I wanted to share it much earlier and I tried. What more do you want from me?'

'I want to know about you, what drives you, where you want to be in a year, in ten years, and what your future might hold for you.'

Sean knew this was an opportunity to delve into her psyche deeper, and harness some trust too. But he genuinely wanted to know more about her life that had led ominously to this point.

'I'd like to be free of my father and maybe spend more time with my mother's family. I had a bloody awful childhood you know, and he still holds me as a prisoner of his whims.'

'But why though? How has he had this hold?'

'I really don't want to talk about it right now, and we have a performance to do in an hour or so. You just need to know I need your help to be free again.'

Sean placed his hand on hers and noticed how she was trying to hold her emotions in check, and the tears at bay. His time with her over the days had confirmed his thoughts that she was genuine in nearly all aspects of her story that her body language and her eye movements suggested. But she was still holding her own secrets deep within her. Like anybody else he surmised, knowing it took a lot of trust to enter those spaces. Two thoughts sprung to mind. Continue to bond with her and use a technique called neuro-linguistic programming to gently extract her thoughts using well-placed words and sentences. And secondly, to get closer to her in the time he had on the island. Something he didn't feel would be too difficult, as he already knew he liked her. A lot.

'Come on,' Sean announced standing up to take her hand. 'Let's get you fired up and ready for our duet and your masterpiece. This is a show where we both need to play a blinder. One last practice?'

Sean watched Yelena look up at him with a sense of surprise. 'But where? We've set the equipment up now.'

'My room. Let's go.'

Yelena stood up, looking a little shy, which acted as the trigger for Sean to hold her close to him. She stood in her training shoes, just a few inches shorter than him, and he noticed her pupils were widely dilated when he looked straight into her eyes. She was incredibly beautiful. He dropped his hands to her waist and kissed her. A short first kiss. Just to check. Her eyes were fixated on his, causing a perfect gaze before he felt her arms pull him close and tight to her. He felt her stomach and pelvis rub tight into his body before she clasped her arms around his neck. They exchanged the deepest of kisses, tongues exchanging rigorously, but gently. Within five minutes, Sean was undressing her in his bedroom and the pre-concert practice had begun.

Chapter 17

Menorca

Sometimes, covert search operations don't go to plan. Sometimes they fail entirely. Despite the detailed planning that Sean had been running through his mind for days, he knew there were too many known unknowns, and lots of things that could go wrong. It was highly risky, but vital to the next phase of Jack's plan.

His target was Dozich's secure computer system in his office. But so far, no one had shown him its exact location, Yelena had provided a few ideas, but the brief tour of the villa hadn't revealed any obvious office space. The plans of the house provided a couple of clues, and yes, there was an obvious lock-up he needed to check out. The mission critical information Jack sought were financial transactions stored on his computers, and the details of bank accounts being used to move funding through the various holding companies that Dozich operated. The golden ticket for Jack would be a connection that linked Sir Rhys and any other politicians to Dozich, and his murky underworld of money laundering and arms deals.

Sean lay on the bed with an arm around Yelena's waist. He had two jobs that needed completing. Deploying a high-performance audio bug in the dining room, and most importantly, acquiring evidence from a computer system that Billy Phish had suggested may be fully secure and not connected to the internet. Billy Phish had tried various ways to infiltrate the house systems, servers and network, all to no avail. His first stab at breaking into Dozich's devices involved brute force attacks, trying to crack the passwords with high-performance software. A simple eight-digit password could be cracked within two hours. But the software failed to crack the tight passwords. He had then tried attacking via the routers within the home, but again failed. Tight password management yet again. It was clear that the defences around Dozich's digital world were tight, and something he'd expected from an agent linked to the Kremlin. Next, he'd tried a few phishing attempts sending carefully crafted emails to Dozich's accounts which had been identified from the Albanian's phone. He had placed lures within the invoice attachments he'd sent to Dozich, hoping he'd open the attachment and then click on the embedded PDF letter. A trick to defeat email monitoring software that weeded out malicious mail. Dozich had done neither, and the malware hadn't deployed into his digital system. It was clear Dozich and his outfit were cyber savvy. It needed a ground operation to penetrate the devices, networks and applications held within Dozich's safe data havens.

Sean adjusted the pillow and lay on his back waiting for Yelena to wake from her afternoon slumber. What had confused him for so long, was how a well-trained singer had left virtually no digital footprint in her life. Yelena rolled over and strapped her arm over Sean's shoulders. Still wondering about the mysterious background of this woman, he rolled out of the embrace hearing a loud tut as he did so. He reached for his guitar and looked over to Yelena before throwing a smile at her. Yelena lay naked in bed with a crumpled cotton sheet now pulled tight into her chest. 'Where are you going?'

'I'll be back in a moment, I need to leave my guitar next to the speakers in the dining room. Do you need anything?'

'No thanks, just another cuddle. You'll have to be quick though. The guests will be arriving in an hour or so and I told you they always search the rooms and don't even allow me in there after that.'

'Until the performance, yes I know. Don't worry, I'll just play dumb.'

Sean made his way downstairs and navigated the labyrinth of long corridors leading to the long dining room, his mind still on Yelena. Yes, she was a real looker, and alluring for sure. But there was something else about her. Smart, compassionate, strong even. He found her mesmerising, but for now, he needed to focus on getting evidence back to The Court forensic team for analysis in the UK.

The double door entrance to the room was wide open with two minders dressed in dinner jackets stood outside denying access. Sean braced himself for the grilling he would get.

'You can't come in here Mr Sam,' the larger of the two minders said, holding his arms out to block the way. Sean leant over to peer behind the bearded piece of meat, all the time acting naïvely to the security needs of Dozich's crucial business transaction. Sean could see two men inside the room who were scanning the walls with what looked like non-linear junction detectors. He saw the array of flashing lights on each of the long, black detectors that had bulbous heads and were being swept in an arc to search for hidden bugs in the wall voids.

'I only want to place my guitar by the stage ready for the performance. It won't take a moment.' Sean pointed to the array of speakers and the velvet chair he would sit on while Yelena sang.

'Sorry no can do. The room is now secure, and nothing enters without being searched. You should have left it earlier.'

'Sorry. I didn't know. Here you go. Feel free to search it.'

'Just one moment, wait here.' The piece of meat growled and walked into the dining room to talk to the searchers. The second minder took a few paces to his right to block the way, and Sean caught a whiff of body odour as he'd stretched his arms out. He heard an exchange of Russian phrases inside the room before both the searchers came out to confront Sean.

'Why didn't you put this inside the room before, like you were instructed?'

'I know, my apologies. I didn't really understand what the man meant.'

The Russian searcher, dressed in a DJ that perfectly matched the other minders, grimaced, then tutted twice. 'OK, place it on the table and take your jacket off.'

Sean watched the second searcher examine the guitar with a handheld scanner that would alarm if any part of the guitar was emitting a radio frequency. He then arced a non-linear junction detector across the belly of the twenty-five-year-old instrument to sniff out any semiconductors or electronics that might be concealed inside. The guitar was pretty well worn, battered around the edges, and in need of restoration from years of neglect. It had been a gift of reconciliation from Sean's father after his many years of absence in the military, and during a period of Sean's life that had drawn him back to the only survivor in his family. When Sean played his guitar, he'd think of his mother. He'd play the tunes to reflect her passion, her love of life, and the extraordinary history she had created as an MI6 spy in the cold war. At fifteen years of age, living in Berlin, and listening to stories from his military mapmaker father, Sean had no idea that the real heroine in the family was his mother. A covert spy embedded into The British Commander-in-Chief's Mission to the Soviet Forces in Germany. BRIXMIS was a military liaison mission which operated behind the Iron Curtain in East Germany, and Sean hoped he didn't end up as his mother had. Murdered at the hand of a ruthless gangster.

Sean watched nervously as the machine alarmed with two red flashing lights indicating it had detected a junction of wires near the bridge of the guitar. Sean knew the guitar's mixture of six strings, the bridge pins and the saddle would create the conditions for it to alarm. He stepped forward to look closer at the instrument, hoping the searcher would put it down to a false positive. The searcher waved him away, put the machine down, and began a series of delicate search routines around the guitar. Had he been more attentive, he'd have seen that under the bridge of the guitar was a cleverly concealed semi-conductor that could be eased out with a sharp fingernail.

'Anything I can help with,' Sean whispered, being careful not to encroach too close to the man who now had his fingers inside the sound hole. Again, he was waved away. There was a real risk Sean's cover could be blown at this point, but if all went smoothly, he'd be able to deploy the audio bug inside the dining room allowing the operators at RAF Bentwaters to monitor every word of the business deal. The searcher was satisfied that the guitar was generating false positives on his RF equipment and conducted his final search by swabbing the guitar for any explosive residue. A thorough search inside an ostentatious venue that would soon host criminal negotiations between a Russian organised crime gang and a UK Minister of State. The search had included canines sweeping the room for explosives or weapons, and a high-tech team searching for hidden bugs that would incriminate three of the wealthiest men in the western world. A rigorous body search was completed before Sean was allowed inside the venue where he needed a quick sleight of hand to slot the semi-conductor into the PA mixer that had already been searched. It had been declared free of bugs.

'You can go inside now, but quickly please,' the searcher said in a throaty Russian accent. Sean collected his guitar and strummed it gently as he walked into the room. With the guitar shielded from the searchers, he carefully extracted the semi-conductor with his right-hand and clasped it in his palm to use it as a pick. He strummed a four-note tremolo for a few seconds which grabbed the attention of the searchers who were now immersed in the flamenco rhythm asking for more. They sat drinking their water and tapping their feet as Sean moved towards the speaker which he turned on. One of the men tapped his hand on the immaculate dining table that was shimmering with shiny goblets and large silver centrepieces. Sean nodded at both men and ramped the sound up to provide the resonance he needed for his impromptu performance. The rhythmic fandango was matched by the men clapping away in harmony creating a scene of masterly deception. It was a pitch perfect scenario: two of Dozich's security men now hypnotised by an expert aficionado of the flamenco guitar.

Sean knelt down and made a signal that he was adjusting the bass on the portable mixer system. He nudged open a slider which was discreetly located just above the feedback suppressor, and on his third staged adjustment, slotted the semi-conductor into position.

Job done, he turned the PA system off, played a few more chords, then leant the guitar next to the chair. He gave a brief bow to his audience and walked out of the room smiling.

Chapter 18

RAF Bentwaters, Suffolk

At five o'clock that evening, Jack sat alone at the head of the table in the conference room of The Court's operational HQ at RAF Bentwaters in Suffolk. The cold war bunker and its high-tech operations room was the central hub for its global operations and had been funded, in part, by the CIA: a legacy of D's vision. D had been able to see that the future of Britain's spy-craft required a close relationship with the CIA Special Activities Division, alongside other investment in offensive cyber operations, data mining and artificial intelligence.

Jack looked across to the five clocks on the buttermilk coloured wall. It was precisely 6pm in Menorca, and a few minutes before Jugsy would land his specially designed quadcopter on the roof of Dozich's multi-million-pound villa. Once the drone was in place, the signals intelligence payload would sniff around the property to latch onto the network that resided within the villa and install a Wi-Fi access point allowing him to listen in to the data traffic from the phones, devices and computers inside. Once the SIGINT had latched onto its targets, Billy Phish as the cyber-sleuth, would enable a digital bridge back to The Court's operators in the UK, who would be able to dump records, logs and data from any of the residential phones, devices and servers to analyse their contents. Meantime, Sean would commence his covert search of the villa looking for any of Dozich's computers that were standalone secured devices, and not connected to the internet or network.

Jack, dressed as usual in a Marks and Spencer's navy blue suit, reached below the table and flicked a switch. He heard the motors rev, before he turned to his right to watch the large oak panels divide and slowly open to reveal a data centre with a high-tech operations room taking centre stage. He walked towards the glazing, peering briefly into the dimly lit digital void where a dozen cyber operators were supporting the sting operation a thousand miles away in Menorca. Jack visualised the covert activity that would take place over the coming two to three hours before Sean would finally take centre stage in the dining room with Yelena performing her sets. He shivered a little knowing that anything could happen with Sean on the ground. He rarely stuck to the established plans. His mind tinkered with the memories of the Iranian operation that Sean had very nearly screwed up a year ago, and he shuddered at what might have happened if he had made the wrong call. Jack took some solace in that Sean had eventually won the day.

What could possibly go wrong this time he thought? The bugs were in place, the drone would soon be sniffing for access into all corners of the IT network, and the deal ought to go through thanks to his oligarch source. Laura was poised to support the ground operation smuggling the weapons into Mali, and the Nigerian General that he had kept on his books, was ready to support him with end-user export certificates.

Jack sat down and reached across the conference table to read the latest intelligence report from his analysts.

TOP SECRET STRAP 2 UK EYES ONLY

For C/Ops Circulation only

Reference: Intelligence Report: OPERATION BAMBARA

Cross border arms trafficking – Actors and Target Areas of Interest.
A subset of militia actors are deepening their involvement in a burgeoning protection economy within Mali. The so-called 'signatory armed groups' (Malian armed groups that signed up to the ongoing peace process) and ISIS jihadist elements, set up checkpoints and control sections of roadway in the north of the country, levying a fee for passage and assuring 'guaranteed protection' until the next checkpoint. Tribal militias control various routes and levy a tax on vehicles for

safe passage through their areas. These militias act as weapons brokers to arm the jihadists, and have been known to intercept convoys and steal their cargoes or kidnap individuals, releasing them for a fee or a portion of the goods. The widespread availability of arms and the absence of state control over these vast Sahel territories foment the growth of such actors in these areas, injecting new levels of arms trade competition and violence to safeguard illicit flows and illegal trade.

Intelligence from our sources across the Sahel and the region of ISGS reveals a complex cast of actors, including IS criminal networks with varying levels of organisation, armed Tuareg groups, tribes, border communities and a mix of government actors either directly or indirectly involved in smuggling activities including senior military officials. Some key informant interviews indicated that our best option is to recruit and pay a group of arms traffickers based at Talhandako.

The group is led by a former Algerian military officer, now a tribal lord, who has access to officials from Tamanrasset in Algeria, to local guides and buyers of weaponry in Tabankort – known as the intra-Malian trafficking hub. See maps and details attached.

Assessment: We can operate covertly in the region with the support and protection of <u>Mahani Al Traboun, a Tuareg and former Algerian commander</u>. His motivation is power and control of the sales hubs, and large financial compensation. Any operation will require contingency & solid logistic support in this remote, lawless area.

Jack's immediate thoughts were that any ground operation he mounted would need the might of the CIA Special Activities Division, satellite imagery intelligence, and operators like Sean able to conduct deniable operations to gather intelligence and disrupt the flow of Russian weapons to ISGS. He pondered the weakness of the Mali President and its government, and started to conjure up an idea of how he would deploy Sean as an arms dealer working with the Tuareg leader, Mahani Al Traboun. If everything went well in the next three or four hours in Menorca, he decided he'd set the ambush to lure Sir Rhys and his twenty-one-club into their own demise, and at the same time see who was responsible for any leak in his organisation. If there was one.

Jack didn't hear the boardroom door open as he sat deep in thought. But he did hear the American accent.

'Man is not what he thinks he is, but he is what he hides,' Laura said philosophically. 'What's behind that mind Jack. What are you hiding now?'

Jack sat bolt upright with a start. 'Bloody hell Laura. Don't do that.'

'I love to surprise people Jack. The nectar of living life you know.'

Jack often wondered what the hell would come next with Laura. She was one feisty woman. She stood gazing at him in a purple two-piece suit, with an open necked white blouse and her dark hair neatly tied in a bun. She was wearing killer heels that matched her vernacular and hard-core style. Jack watched her flick through the notes laid on the table.

'UK eyes only I'm afraid Laura. Not for yours.'

'Mmmm. Well I could say the same about me Jack. For US eyes only. But I do like to share sometimes you know. Especially with you Brits.'

Jack found it hard to deal with Laura's flirtation. But at the same time, he found it refreshing. He took a moment to compose himself. 'We'll find out soon if we can move to the next stages. You're still up for this right?'

'Oh, you know I'm up for it Jack. What's your plan?'

Jack stood and gave Laura a kiss on each cheek, then steered her towards the maps on the wall. 'If this all goes to plan, we can take down the Russian mercenary operation in Mali,' Jack began. 'The perfect start towards getting you the top job in Washington. It's a bit risky though.'

'I'm up for that. Risk is there to be grasped, cradled and loved. Live it, crave it, and hog the pain is my motto. We win big, if we go big. Plus, I've got the backing from Washington now to steer this my way, if I think it's all feasible. What have you got?'

Jack pointed to the map of the Sahara Desert. 'Well, if the negotiations go well tonight, we'll be running an arms smuggling operation from here in Algeria, across the border into Mali with the help of a Tuareg militia leader, before handing the weapons to the terrorists who have paid Dozich for them.'

Jack pointed to the arms smuggling routes on the map close to the Mali and Algerian border, then nudged his finger to the Tuareg villages that acted as weapons exchange hubs. 'We'll get right into the heart of the Russian plans to arm the jihadis across the Sahel, stop them taking over the Malian government, and you'll be left with an option to go to the President to convince him to make an American mark in the Sahel at long last. He'll be able to take down the second Caliphate and reap the political dividends from that.'

'Cheeky. I like it. But what about the French? This is their patch, right?'

'Yes, and I need to do some more thinking about them.'

'Look, I need an end game I can bet on Jack. Without treading on people's toes. The Defence Secretary has gone to war with the Secretary of State about Africa. He wants to reduce numbers, but my note from your intelligence went straight to the Chief of Staff who advised the President he needed to have a firmer strategy for the Sahel. The President agrees with my assessment and they're starting to move more quickly now with contingency being ramped up for ground operations. Your intelligence has led to the Secretary of State deploying a special envoy to the Sahel, all from the orders of the President. The Director of the CIA has also been ordered to beef up our operation from nearby Niger. We have a few secretive programmes in place there that are now receiving more investment too. So, you see, we have a good foot on the plate here, and I can bring lots to bear. But your thoughts and plans here need to be granite solid.'

'One step at a time. There are lots of moving parts to this one Laura. Firstly, I've got a Russian oligarch laying down the markers and the bait.'

'Who?'

'His name is Leonard Berarnov. A bit of an unruly one. A bit risqué. It's been a bit of a challenge to manage Leonard because he's on a number of hit lists right now. Lord only knows how he's still alive.'

'Go on, will he live to see this through for us?'

'I need your help with that. He's well protected, but there's the challenge of separating the Kremlin-sanctioned threats from those arising from his own risky business dealings. He's tangled often enough with organised crime to acquire some nasty private adversaries who tried to take him out before, and Moscow is equally capable of enlisting another oligarch to orchestrate his killing as a cut-out.'

'What do you need from me for this Jack?'

'Persistent protection on him. I need him alive for the duration of this operation and he's about to start phase one.'

'Interesting. How did you recruit him?'

'Oh, nothing too difficult, just as the Russians would do. A bit of Kompromat on him, and the promise of safety from Moscow's hitmen was all it took.'

Jack fielded one or two questions from Laura before sitting down to switch on the high-resolution speaker. He spoke briefly on the telephone to the operations officer whose team inside the ops room was about to monitor and transcribe the entire conversation in Dozich's dining room.

'Who's in the room Jack? Don't hold anything back now, I know what you're like. I want the full story before we make any further agreements to go forward as a full Third Avenue operation.'

'Three men - the key players - and a few of their aides, that include a financier for Dozich, and a young aide for Sir Rhys. Leonard has his own protection officer and is wired up with a video camera which they're unlikely to find. That's the first risk of many. Sean is in the villa and has placed a high-spec audio transmitter in the room too, so we should have good visuals and good sound to work from.'

'Sean? Mmm.'

Jack watched her lift her eyebrows. She walked to the one-way glass partition to study the high-tech operation room. 'Sir Rhys is the one you want to put the trap on, right?'

'Amongst other politicians and former intelligence officers in the twenty-one-club, yes.' Jack stood to join her observing the cyber operators at work. 'These men and women have done a great job gathering evidence on the activities of Sir Rhys, enough to get him charged and probably locked away for a long time. He's also led us to new criminal leads in the world he lives in, selling weapons, making corrupt deals, linkage with the Russian mafioso, and now, a major deal with the Keystone Corps.'

'Very neat Jack. How have they been watching him?'

'We've been tracking him, and a few other Westminster officials for some time now. The teams can easily use data sets from location tracking companies. We didn't need to mount complex surveillance operations, so we used the data sets to track his movement from the apps on his mobile phone. You see, most people don't realise you're only as safe as the weakest app on your phone. He used apps that he's unknowingly provided consent to track him - apps that show weather, local news, saver coupons, the lot. Like most people, he had no idea how his life is like an open book for anyone buying unregulated data from dozens of location data companies. We can track someone's movements for months, where they've been, who they visited, where they pray, if they visit a psychiatrist or a massage parlour.'

'Similar to some work we've done back home. Smartphone tracking is giving us a big advantage nowadays and we've used it to track military officials with high level security clearances who were under investigation, a few scientists on activist marches and even pop stars accused of major felonies.'

'That's why we've banned our intelligence officers from using these apps because it's too easy for the data to be sold to a hostile foreign power. The world of 24/7 mass surveillance has allowed me to connect the dots with Sir Rhys that would have taken months of traditional surveillance, and it allowed us to quickly open up a few new lines of inquiry. We've data mined the lot from his smartphone, and we've identified his Chairmanship connections to a new front company the twenty-one-club funds, and some former French intelligence officers who we think are part of the group.'

'The twenty-one-club. Have you got anything more on them?'

'Lots. Quite a few former intelligence officials within the group, funded we think, by illicit drugs and weapons smuggling across the globe. They also gather and sell intelligence'

'Sell to who?'

'Rogue governments, political groups who want to subvert their own nation for power, you know, people like the men who arranged for the Russian dossier to be used against your President.'

'So, we get to take down the club too?'

'We do. One at a time.'

Jack tapped on a console to start the live feed from Leonard's video camera.

The protection officer was a tall, elegant man with close-cropped silver hair and pale blue eyes. He was a shade more erudite than many of his security colleagues on Leonard Berarnov's team. He formed an easy rapport with Berarnov and had to make sure he was cautious about where he ate, and what he ate. The GRU assassins had already killed enough of Moscow's enemies on British soil, but he felt quite at ease chaperoning Berarnov to the dining room on a rare foray overseas.

The first to speak was Dozich whose deep-set eyes and grimacing expression set the tone for the negotiations. He looked around the table, then fixed his eyes on Berarnov. 'Gentlemen, this evening Mr Berarnov will present his deal to us and we will decide if we will act as the supplier.' He paused, before turning briefly to Sir Rhys. 'But before we agree, we need to be assured by Mr Berarnov about the security of the end-to-end supply chain, and the people who are involved in securing these new routes for us.'

Berarnov took the silence as his cue to begin. The atmosphere in the room was tense and brittle. 'Gentlemen, first of all thank you for inviting me here today. My group of Russian friends have been running these supply chains across West Africa for two years, and our routes are assured into the markets who will buy your weapons. My principal source is a man from Tripoli who previously stole Libyan government weapons to sell into the Sahel region.'

'But hasn't that stockpile all dried up now?' Sir Rhys inquired.

'That is indeed the case Sir Rhys, and that's why I'm here today. You see, the main buyers are the jihadis across the Sahel, especially Mali, Burkino Faso and Niger and they're paying top dollar for new weapons.'

'So you buy and sell as our broker but maintain security of the transit routes, is that right?' Dozich asked. 'Who does that for you?'

'A man called Mahani Al Traboun. We pay him to secure the routes using his tribal militia who operate mainly on the traditional nomadic routes from Niger and Algeria into the arms-selling hubs that are established in the desert villages of Mali. But my supply of arms is drying up, and the French military operations are now beginning to hinder some of the old routes.'

'Operation BARKHANE,' Sir Rhys chipped in, placing his bifocals on to read a small note he had made. 'The French counterterrorist operation in five of their former colonies across the Sahel. It must be constraining your operation and actually putting our stake at risk too?'

'Not really,' Berarnov stated. 'Their air operation is scant, and we have multiple routes and multiple officials that enable our business to continue. This is a long-term investment and a very good return for you both gentlemen. I am sure we will make perfect partners here for quite an enduring piece of business.'

'I agree,' Dozich said, waving an open hand. 'It fits our need, and it fits the need of an old General friend from our time in the GRU, Major General Katchalyna. He will be quite pleased that we can open up a new route into the jihadis.'

A long silence drew across the room as Dozich nodded to the maître d' to bring the first course. 'Mr Berarnov, I was very pleased to meet you in Madrid, and we have common ground with our past military careers. I do believe we can make a deal here today, and I also believe we can make a good return. But how do you expect us to arrange to get the weapons from the manufacturers?'

'Well I was rather hoping you could help with that as you have the relationship with the Bulgarians and Romanian manufacturers. Just as we discussed in Madrid, I propose that we use an intermediary in Nigeria to buy the weapons and acquire the export licenses for their Army as the end users.'

'I've discussed this proposition with Sir Rhys, and he thinks it's a perfectly feasible proposition.'

'Very good. In that case, I can assure you both that I have the buyer and a secure end-to-end route for you into the Sahel.'

'Wonderful. Before we look at the figures for a test run, I also want you to conduct some other business for us too. It is a non-negotiable part of this deal.'

The emergence of a new term and condition caught Berarnov by surprise. He'd thought the deal was all but done in Madrid. Berarnov adjusted his posture to make sure the hidden camera in his tie captured this new revelation. 'OK, what exactly is this new part of the deal?'

'A number of things which we can draft in our final agreement. Firstly, we want you to smuggle other weaponry into the sales hubs and we will arrange the buyers for these particular items.'

'That's fine, what are they?'

'Surface to air missiles.'

'Interesting. What else?'

'You'll need to escort a number of specially made bombs into the region. We'll give you the details over a secure communications system which we'll induct you on tomorrow morning. Now gentlemen, I suggest we toast our future and eat well.'

Chapter 19

Menorca

Wearing a white crew neck T shirt and laced with a thick gold chain, the man sat in a Volkswagen Beetle on the far side of the approach road to the villa and took out his phone. He spoke in Russian without taking his eyes off the exit route from the target building that held the man he was ordered to kidnap.

Two hundred metres away in the undergrowth close to the inlet, two other men sat patiently observing the villa's terraces through night sight binoculars, watching the armed guards perambulate the grounds. They had not sighted their target since late evening when they observed the man sketching a drawing on the terrace, and later, kissing a tall and slender lady before chaperoning her into the mansion.

'This is fifty-five,' gold chain man said into the phone. 'Richardson is inside the villa and no one has seen him since late evening. There are armed guards in place so we cannot get any closer.'

Two kilometres away, on the other end of the line, Natalie paced up and down the hotel room watching her tablet for any updates on the man she wanted to torture and kill. Natalie walked across the room to pull the curtains shut before reclining in a mesh chair. She tapped a few buttons on the desk mounted console and used a mouse to adjust the screen resolution of one of the sixteen images displayed on her laptop. The screen zoomed into the grounds of the villa using electro-optical imagery from a Russian Zenitt II satellite located some couple of hundred kilometres above the earth's surface. Natalie had all the technology of a nation state in front of her and was authorised to use any intelligence apparatus deemed necessary to kidnap Sean Richardson. But every element of her mission, and everyone she used on the ground were to be deniable. Whilst Moscow had approved her mission, they would distance themselves if it all went wrong.

Not long after Sean was seen boarding a flight at Stansted airport, she had booked a one-way ticket and flew to Menorca the very next morning. She was now awaiting further updates from her proxy soldiers in a hotel in the village of Cala Llonga, a short ride away from the villa. She could hardly control her urge to kill Richardson, make him suffer, and then embark on a lifelong mission to go after his own handler.

'Do nothing, just monitor and report hourly,' Natalie barked down the phone. 'We have information that the residents are our own friendly forces. So, we wait until Richardson leaves, probably tomorrow, but keep your eyes open through the night.'

Natalie at times could be a patient, shrewd woman. But she never liked it when she had to rely on proxies to fulfil what should be a simple task. These were not the highly trained SVR operatives that she had been used to commanding, Moscow wouldn't release any. These were locally recruited thugs, trained to the minimum levels of surveillance and kidnap operations, brought in to dish out a beating, and to make sure the target was captured and detained.

Each man was issued a syringe to quell their prey, and a small firearm in case it got messy. They had been instructed that a shot to the leg or arm was permissible but nothing to the torso. Natalie needed the man alive. The serum would be used as a sedative on the captured target to suppress any fightback, and the men had been told it will make Richardson feel very drunk within five minutes of administering it. The syringes held the notorious SP-117, a serum manufactured in a small, squat, beige building just outside Moscow, and known as Scientific Research Institute No 2, or NII-2 for short.

The man in the Volkswagen Beetle opened the window and lit a cigarette. 'I expect it'll happen tomorrow now, and we'll take him just after he leaves.'

Natalie blew hard trying to contain her anxiety. Three years of incarceration had taught her the art of pursed lip breathing to contain her hatred, anger and stress, and she felt herself about to burst again.

'Don't you dare fucking slack off tonight. I'll chop your testicles off if you fuck this up. Remember, Richardson is not the normal idiot you'd lift off the street. He's a highly trained intelligence agent, don't underestimate him at all.'

Natalie banged the desk and continued her tirade at the gold laden thug who was in no doubt that she'd kill him if he mucked this job up. 'You have your orders. When he moves, you contact me, and you detain him in any way you'd like.'

Gold chain took a long draw on his cigarette and smiled at what made his work most worthwhile.

Chapter 20

Menorca

At exactly eight o'clock in the evening, Dozich's internal CCTV system was infiltrated by The Court's hackers sitting at their dimly lit consoles somewhere in the quiet Suffolk countryside. Sean's phone began to vibrate - sure enough, right on time. Jack messaged him on TextSecure and the phone came alive with a green screen showing three dots flickering. *'Good to go. All stations on standby.'*

The Court's hackers had inserted a Trojan worm deep into the servers of the villa, which quickly propagated laterally to gain the privileged access rights to the CCTV system. The hackers took control of each of the internal cameras that would provide sight of Sean making his way to the rooms he would search.

'I'll be back in an hour,' he said to Yelena. 'If anyone comes and asks where I am, text me, and tell them I'm on the loo.'

'I can come along and keep an eye out for you while you're in the room you know. It's my father's house and if anything goes wrong, I'll be able to tell a story far better than you at being caught mooching around like a jewel thief.'

'Funny that, Jack set my legend up to show I was once an amateur thief.'

Had Sean seen the anxious look on Jack's face back at The Court, he may have taken her up on the offer to tag along. But no. he needed to do this work alone. He stepped outside the door knowing the corridor cameras were now under the control of The Court hackers who had digitally manipulated the imagery being seen by Dozich's security operators deep in the basement of the villa. He then sent a text to Jugsy: *'Land the drone on Dozich's balcony. Five minutes.'*

Within three minutes, Sean had turned a key to enter the spacious office which was located on the first floor of the villa. He'd memorised the plans of the villa and the layout of Dozich's office with the help of Yelena who had managed to coax the information from the housekeeper as well as the location of the spare key that her father always left in the vase opposite the door.

As Sean started to rummage the room, he still couldn't work out why Yelena had been so accommodating, so helpful. Almost from the very beginning when he first caught her half naked in that room in Tuscany. Since that moment, it had not been at all difficult to extract information from her. Indeed, she even steered him straight to the Albanian thug. Why, he wondered?

His phone began to ring. The signal that the drone was now inbound and imminent. Sean walked over to the terrace, released the latch on the sliding door, and stepped out to be confronted by a buzzing quadcopter two feet ahead of him at head height. He imagined Jugsy grinning at him through the onboard camera, so he decided to give him the finger. Following a smile at the ugly whirring beast, he grabbed a small black pouch from a cradle below the drone's belly. He gave a thumbs up into the eye of the onboard camera, and watched it lift quickly before silently peeling off into the night to land on the roof of the villa.

Sean pointed his penlight towards the large white desk that sat neatly in the corner of the room with two twenty-inch screens and a desktop computer. He gazed briefly at the three large pictures behind Dozich's desk. His gaze turned into serious study. Something had caught his eye. One picture had three men dressed in Spetsnaz fatigues and Dozich holding an AK47. It looked like it was taken in Afghanistan. Dozich was stood next to a man Sean recognised. It was a much younger Sergei. The Russian spy Jack had recruited and the man he had met only a year ago in the very conference room that Jack was now sat in. Sean's nape began to tingle. What if Sergei had played Jack all along? Surely this is too much of a coincidence for Sergei, the lead officer for a Russian illegals programme in the UK, to be a military friend of Dozich?

Sean took a photo of the wall mounted picture with his smartphone and beamed it back to Jack using the secure photo app specially designed for Court operations. He muttered a few words to himself about moles and how Swartz might have been compromised, before sitting at the desk. The computer screen was alive with a background picture of a mountain view. He tapped the return button to bring up the password box. He then stood up and walked around the room once more until he finally found what he was after. A small second desktop machine with a laptop beside it on a small table next to an open fireplace. Sean instinctively knew that Dozich would probably use the laptop for emails and internet transmissions, whilst he kept his main desktop machine isolated from any intruders who would hack into his machine via the internet. Operational security for organised crime lords in the digital world was a must, and one that Dozich would take seriously.

Sean tapped the number into his phone that he'd been given by Jack to speak to a Court operator in the operations room back in Suffolk. The hacker would help him get into the machine to search and retrieve all of the files of Dozich's illicit trade, his financial connections and any connecting evidence to Sir Rhys.

'Sean? Can you hear me? My name's Bill?'

'Yes, I can, I'm in front of the machine, go ahead.'

'OK, this won't take long. First off, there are two pensticks in the black pouch. Both will be required to perform this attack which should take less than five minutes. The blue stick will be used to create a live USB that will boot on the laptop while, the yellow stick holds the payload that will then be executed on the device. It will infiltrate the machine and search for the password hash. Place the blue one in now.'

Sean drew the blue pen drive from his jeans pocket and placed it into the USB drive. 'Done,' he said waiting impatiently for the next instruction.

'OK, now on the pen drive is a small switch. Turn it on so a green light flashes once before going solid after five seconds.'

'Done, what's next.'

'Just sit back for about three minutes or so. It'll boot on the laptop and also sniff for the drone sat above you on the roof, and once it's connected, we'll have a transmission frequency to extract the data we need.'

'OK, but why do you need me to get inside the machine if you can do all that remotely.'

'I need you to get inside so you can download another payload that will provide me with permanent access making it easy for us to maintain a long-term connection to the target device as it moves to different Wi-Fi networks around the world. There is just one click you need to make to download the malware that will initiate the kill-chain and weaponise the machine for me. Once that's done you can get out of there.'

'OK, how long now before I have a password.'

'Wait.'

Sean tapped his fingers on the desk, trying to keep calm. He only had an hour to search the office and then the lock-up in the basement where Yelena believed a second office was decked out.

'Just another thirty seconds Sean.'

'Roger,' he said, leaning back into the chair. He breathed deeply counting the seconds. 'Shit,' he muttered, hearing a sound outside the office. Was it a security man doing his rounds? He'd been told he'd receive a call if The Court operators saw any guards walking the corridor and the approaches to the office. He looked at his phone again. No second call and no vibrate.

'OK, we're in. Take the pen stick out and replace it with the yellow one. This will retrieve the password data I need for you to access the laptop.'

'Ok, inserting it now.'

Within less than a minute Bill's voice came back on the phone. 'Ok Sean, we have it. Tap this in.'

'Send,' Sean said eagerly.

'Victor, Romeo, two, four, upper case Yankee, five, lower case Golf.'

'Roger that, two seconds. Yay, I'm in!' Sean took a moment to take in the skills of Jack's team and leant forward to view the applications Dozich had kept open. He rubbed his eyes, then looked again to see which documents he'd last worked on. The latest PDF document looked like a contract. He scanned down the document, rolling the bevel on the mouse. There were no names that he recognised. It was a financial contract though, and it mentioned the figures $250,000. It looked to Sean as if it was a contract to pay a facilitator. The name of Blain-Sole consultancy was the recipient and indicated a percentage deal for providing business to Dozich. Nothing special Sean thought before moving onto a spreadsheet that was open.

The spreadsheet was intriguing. It had four tabs with the first showing row upon row of numbers and codes he didn't recognise. Except two. PG-9 he recognised as being a Romanian produced rocket-propelled grenade. He checked the numbers next to the designation. 12-11-456, which he assumed to be the lot number, and then the figure 2,300, presumably the quantity supplied. He reminded himself of how original equipment manufacturers code their weaponry, and the fact that this intelligence could be traced back to the original export license that Romania would have supplied to whoever bought the armaments. Nearly all military munitions, from rifle cartridges to aircraft bombs, regardless of the country of origin, are engraved and marked in some way. The arcane codes can identify the date of manufacture, the specific production factory, the type of explosive filler and the weapon's name, also known as the nomenclature.

Sean clicked on the second tab. A map. A large-scale map showing a small town with three long buildings identified by red arrows. The town's name was Bourem, an oasis town in the centre of the Sahara Desert.

'OK Sean one last thing please.' Bill's voice was crisp and sharp over the phone. Just as Bill finished the sentence, Sean's phone vibrated. He checked the screen which showed a red circle and the telephone number of The Court operator who was monitoring the corridor CCTV and had been primed to call if someone was approaching the office.

'Shit,' Sean muttered, his heartbeat rising rapidly now. 'Tell me quick Bill, I need to get out of here soon.'

'You should see a green box in the lower right-hand side of the screen. Just click OK to weaponise the malware and I can start extracting data.'

Sean clicked on the button, watched the box disappear and clicked control-alt-delete to log off the machine. As he removed the pen drive, he heard voices in the corridor - now getting a little louder but he couldn't make out what they were saying. To be caught now would be a travesty, having completed an almost perfect infiltration into the depths of Dozich's digital world.

Sean darted behind the door, ready to step out into the corridor if someone came into the office. Yelena didn't think that there were regular patrols by the security teams at the office, and Sean told himself it would all be fine. No one would step inside.

But they did, just after the door was opened with some gusto.

Chapter 21

Tabankort, Northern Mali

A wisp of smoke fluttered up from the soldering iron as the Algerian bomb maker dabbed the final touches of his circuit board to bond a complex set of wires to his time and power unit that he was in the throes of completing.

Circling above him was a drone being operated by a Tuareg fighter who was wearing a grey head wrap called a *cheche*. He had been instructed to capture video imagery of a group of Islamic State fighters who were preparing and rehearsing for a major attack on the Mali government forces. The video would be circulated as a marketing and recruiting tool across the Sahel states to inspire would be fighters to join the cause.

The foundations were being laid for an independent Islamic State across western Africa, and the attack that was being planned for the next morning would send shockwaves across the United Nations mission in Mali and the French led security forces in the region.

Walking amongst the men was a short portly man, dressed in a traditional Tuareg *bubus* gown. He was easily distinguishable as the commander of these forces. The only man amongst a strike force of men dressed from head to toe in brown.

'Commander, I want you to meet our head of training,' a moustached man said, leading him to the rehearsal area. He introduced the commander to a Syrian fighter who had brought the most recent skills and attack planning to the Sahel.

'This is Captain Mohammed al-Bahli, the finest soldier in the Syrian Al Qaeda teams from Hurras al-Din .'

The commander took off his sunglasses to greet his most recent recruit and his most battle-hardened officer. 'I have heard much about you captain. How close are we to completion?'

'Very close, please come and see the terrain model I have prepared.'

The captain, dressed in full war fighting fatigues, led the commander to a large-scale model that the fighters were being briefed on. It was the training model for a complex and multi-pronged attack he had planned.

The combat training area had been established in a large basin in the middle of the Sahara Desert, some fifty kilometres from the nearest town of Tabankort. The town had been the victim of multiple attacks on French and Mali forces in the north of the country.

At each end of the training area were two stolen Toyota Landcruisers still marked with the insignia of the UN, and acting as the guardians of the strike force from unwelcome eyes. Large bushy shrubs sporadically dotted the basin's deep orange sands, and alongside a cluster of these, a black Islamic State flag was draped on two bamboo sticks. In front of the flag, sitting cross-legged on a large wicker mat and being filmed, were four bomb makers. Spread around them were blue fifty-gallon drums, a couple of dozen 120mm mortars, yellow detonation cord, and a series of chemical containers.

'When did we receive these new explosive devices?' the commander asked as he was escorted around the areas. He was referring to the yellow detonating cord he was shown, the new arming devices, and boxes of military grade detonators.

'Courtesy of some Russians friends I made in Idlib,' the Syrian responded.

'GRU?'

'The Russian foreign military intelligence agency, yes. You may have heard of their Spetsnaz arm. I served with many of them who were in Syria before I swapped sides. My friends are all Russian veterans now.'

'So, it's true we have Russians amongst us then?'

'They are Russian mercenaries, and yes, they like to make money from amongst us commander.'

'Thanks be to God for your wisdom Captain. This is exceptional work.'

The Syrian captain, sporting a black balaclava on his head that matched the colour of his tightly trimmed beard, led the commander to the main rehearsal area. The men that were stood to attention in front of the terrain model wore a mixture of combat dress and webbing pouches. Some were wearing Burkino Faso fatigues, others wore camouflage from Niger forces, and a few wore odd-looking blue helmets, perhaps looking to act as UN imposters. Most had AK-74 rifles, and a few wore ammunition belts around their shoulders.

The terrain model had been crafted in the sand and showed huge long trenches that represented major tracks in the desert with a few model cars lined up along the route. Road barriers were made from twigs showing where the military checkpoints were established. The model was immaculately designed with the centrepiece being a well protected government compound which they would strike against, kill the enemy, and steal their weapons.

The commander smiled. He then hugged his new Syrian friend.

'*Que la paix soit avec vous*. Peace be with you my brother.'

'*Merci beaucoup*.'

'We will win this war, and my land will become the new home for our Islamic brothers across the world.'

Chapter 22

Menorca

Sean knew he was in trouble. As the door flung open, he was caught between the actions of bluffing it, or fighting his way out. Every strand of his DNA had always told him to fight, and his lifetime experiences that had offered him the choice of fight or flight, always ended in the former. Even as a seventeen-year-old kid, when he was cornered by four angry Irishmen in the top floor of an east end pool room, it had resulted in him fighting his way out, flooring two of them in the process. He'd soundly beaten the Irishmen at pool, winning eight games on the bounce, which gave him a healthy four-hundred-pound return. Needless to say, the men weren't happy with that, and the ensuing brawl taught him a big lesson in life. Watch your enemy's eyes, hit them hard when they come, and keep attacking.

He wondered whether deception was the better tool for this occasion but armed himself anyway. From behind the door, he leant across the bar bureau to grab a bottle of Jack Daniels that was just in reach. He snuck it behind his back in readiness for what might come next.

Just one man. With a torch. Easy enough to take down if he turns and spots me. Sean had nowhere to go except to sidle out of the door and into the corridor if the guard walked further into the room. Then it happened. Only a quiet noise but enough of a mistake. Sean accidentally tapped the bottle on the wall behind him. 'Shit.'

The guard turned with a jolt, his eyes wide and fierce as he stepped back to be faced by a man he didn't expect to see. In that split second, Sean had his chance to take the man down, but for some reason he hesitated. He went for the bluff to check the reaction first. 'I'm just looking for some spare guitar strings,' was all he could muster. Sean didn't have time to check the reaction. With a fierce burst of energy that caught Sean off guard, the heel of the guard's hand was rammed fiercely into his chin resulting in an upwards motion that nearly snapped his neck. The blow was mistimed, but there was enough force to send Sean plummeting headfirst into the wall. A few dark clouds exploded in the back of his brain, and the bottle dropped to the floor.

'Fuck you,' the man said in throaty English, his balled fists slamming into Sean's face and solar plexus. Reeling from the blows, Sean watched the man draw a leather strap from his waist before he twisted him around. Sean felt the sharp spike of a knee in the back of his spine, and the belt cutting into his neck. He tried to fight back, but the belt was being pulled so tight, he could only use his fingers to stop the constriction strangling him. He felt his eyes bulge, knowing he was moments away from certain death. Only instinct and fierce anger could save him now. The muscle memory of decades of street fighting kicked in and he spied his salvation. A silver pen, just in front of him on the floor.

Sean placed both hands on the inside of the leather strap, then spun his bodyweight with a dynamic hip jerk, causing the attacker to lose his balance. He twisted onto his back, with the man's body now underneath him, but the grip on his neck was still tight. With one last chance, he grabbed the pen, wiggled it to grasp the spine, then drove it behind his shoulder into the side of the man's face. Fighting for breath, Sean felt the grip loosen from his throat, and used both hands to snap the leather away from his attacker's hands.

'Fuck you too,' Sean snarled as the man grunted in pain. Within minutes the guard would be dead. Sean stood above his attacker, whose right eye was oozing deep red blood with the pen driven deeply inside its socket. He smashed his fist into the guard's throat before driving the pen further into the socket with the heel of his hand. He heard the man suck hard for air, saw the thick blood ooze from his nose, and watched the attacker's hands shake violently by his side. The body spasmed a few times before all movement finally stopped.

Breathing hard now, Sean strained to regain some sense of control and stability. He'd been fighting for his life, but somehow his lifelong training, and never say die mindset had saved him. He took a few moments to think through the consequences of his fuck up. This was not good. The whole operation was blown. Unless he could get rid of the body?

Sean peered around the corner of the door to check the corridor. All quiet. No signs of any emergency activity, and he still had a full forty-five minutes before he was due to accompany Yelena entertaining the diners. Why the fuck had the man come into the room? Was it a set up? He rushed into the bathroom at the far end of the office and started to splash cold water across his beaten face wondering where he could conceal the body.

Odd that he launched straight into me, Sean thought, speculating that Yelena may have tipped her father off? He checked the guard's pulse, just to be sure, then reached for his pocket-sized radio which had been flung to the floor during the melee. He turned the radio off, fighting a gag reflex as a sense of shock began to take hold. He never liked killing, though on each occasion it had happened, he had deemed it absolutely necessary. This caused him to remember that he still had a price on his own head, with the Russian SVR still deeming his death would be adequate compensation for him luring Natalie Merritt into a trap a few years ago.

Now what? He checked for activity over the balcony edge in the villa grounds. The first part would be easy to drop the body to the ground, but then there was the more difficult act of dragging the corpse to a small coppice at the edge of the grounds. He judged it to be about a hundred metres, noticing the four-metre stone clad wall just beyond the trees. He could conceal the body first, then return to bury the body surmising it would take days for them to find it, and he'd be long gone. The other option that flew across his mind was to call it a day. The team had infiltrated Dozich's digital systems, and Jack would have plenty of evidence to work through.

Sean returned to heave the body towards the balcony. The man was wearing a black gilet like all the other guards, which suggested there might be a weapon concealed inside. He patted the torso to check for a weapon, then the jacket. Sure enough, there was. A Zastava EZ9 pistol which he retrieved from the holster and stuffed it down the back of his jeans. He was more concerned about what else he had found. Attached to the holster was a small palm sized fob which had three buttons, one of which was flashing red. 'Shit,' he murmured, looking back at the door. He knew exactly what it was. A 'man down' device, linked to a tracking system. Dozich's words reverberated in his head as he grappled with what to do next. *'I'll be keeping a very close eye on you.'*

Sean punched a quick text to Jack on the secure app: *Aborted. Full compromise.* He stared at the camera located in the far corner of the office and signalled to the operators who were watching him: he swiped a straight hand across his neck. The stark sound of heavy footsteps and voices in the corridor forced his hand. There was no time to lose. He spun on his heels, his mind racing ahead to his next moves, reckoning that he had ten seconds at most before the men burst into the room. He could make for the sea and swim for it, but the guards would be patrolling the water's edge. No choices left. He had to get to safety through the coppice, and over the perimeter wall.

Sean sprinted for the balcony, his heart raging inside. He ripped across the balcony with a hefty bound and dropped the twelve feet to the ground, landing awkwardly. A jarring pain smashed through his body causing his legs to buckle. He clenched his left knee, cussing that he'd screwed it up, but knowing this was no time to scream injury on a field of play that was about to savage him.

He dug deep to fight the pain, managing to get to his feet before limping quickly towards the small copse, pushing through the pain to ease the injury into a canter. His only hope was the cover of the copse before scaling the perimeter wall and hiding in the undergrowth beyond.

Shouting from the balcony. A flurry of activity, and a long-barrelled weapon. Powerful torch beams scanning the lawns. Not far now, thirty metres, no, twenty. Not far to go he heard himself whisper. He strained every fibre in his body to make the last few yards knowing that death was imminent if he failed. Made it. He dropped to the ground behind the largest tree he could find but was shaken by the sounds of dogs barking. Bollocks. Sometimes, luck goes your way, sometimes it doesn't.

The sounds of barking and the hive of activity in the villa's grounds had sparked the gold chained Russian thug into action. He had been dozing in his vehicle when he heard the sound and was driven into panic when his binoculars presented a view of multiple armed guards scurrying across the villa lawns.

Meanwhile, a drone above the villa had locked onto the environment where Sean was trying to save his life. The infra-red imagery was being beamed back to The Court where Jack and Laura sat in disbelief at what they were witnessing. It looked like the entire mission had been compromised, even though the negotiations continued in the dining room. Jack spoke loudly into his phone to make sure The Court operators had initiated the backup plan to support Sean's bid for escape. Two operators were now haring towards the Villa in a battered old Peugeot, guided by the drone to the extraction zone.

The pain in Sean's knee caused him to feel sick, and the sound of dogs chasing him down made him retch. Groggily, he peered at the stone wall. He couldn't see clearly enough through the darkness, but he had very little choice now. Shit or bust it had to be the wall. Don't give up now, he mumbled, lurching to his feet to start jogging. He swept around the last of the trees, sweating heavily now, and spied a tree stump close to the wall. It was a foot or so away from the wall but with a good run and launch, he felt he could make it. There was a momentary lull from the barking as Sean increased his pace, all the time eyeing the tree stump. The closer he got, the more he felt he'd nail it. He urged himself on, five metres, four, three, two, one, jump!

Sean hands clamped onto the top of the wall like the teeth of a vice onto a metal bar. He shunted his right leg up the wall, grappling for a tiny foothold, then growled as he failed to find one. He felt his fingers slipping a little then lunged with his right hand to get a full grip over the back end of the wall. He was there. A few more long-armed tugs and he'd be over. For a terrifying moment he thought he would be shot, right there on the wall. Then he heaved twice, grunted hard, and cocked his right leg over the lip to get an ankle hold, before finally scuttling over the wall.

Sean didn't fuck about. He didn't care about his knee, he just wanted to save his life. He dropped to the ground, his landing cushioned by the soft plants of the undergrowth, then spotted a route through the forest and started an awkward jog through the bracken. His body was broken, his mouth tasted rancid, and his shirt was plastered to his back from the excessive sweat. But he couldn't stop now. He knew Jugsy would be watching him from above, and he knew he had to make his way to one of the four emergency RV points they'd discussed as an evacuation plan.

'How the fuck do I explain all this to Jack?' he asked himself. A dead Russian on the floor of Dozich's office, Yelena most likely compromised, and a failed operation likely to cause mayhem to The Court. Then he realised he was a deniable asset. They didn't have to pull out all the punches to save him. Something gained, something lost. They wouldn't care. The despair hit home. He had a small army hunting him down, he'd abandoned his rucksack that had a stash of Euros, he had a crocked knee, but what pained him most, was that he'd lost his father's guitar. Forever.

Something caught his peripheral vision as he jogged through the woods. It was brief and fleeting, a dark shadow and a chunk of mass. He jolted as he saw it come straight at him. For a moment he thought it was a large wolf lunging at him. But it wasn't. It was the muscled bulk of a large man who smashed Sean to the ground with a brutal rugby tackle, the likes of which crowds scream at.

The last thing Sean felt, was the wind being knocked out of him, then the horrific thud of a baton smashing him over the head. Within seconds he was unconscious.

Chapter 23

Menorca

The first feeling Sean had when he came to, was an agonising pain at the back of his head. Through the painful ringing in his ears, he could make out the faint decibels of Russian accents around him, each sound dulled by the rusty steel door in front of him. A halo of bright light was playing havoc with his vision and he couldn't focus on anything, not least the black handcuffs that he held in front of his eyes trying hard to see if his eyes might clear the double vision to focus correctly. The fear of losing his sight was real, and the shock of capture hit home once again to bite hard into his very soul.

The sounds disappeared and he was left alone with his thoughts, his pain and his fear. A passage of dark, bleak and submissive thoughts started to enter his mind. He had fallen short on this job in every single way, and somehow, he was yet again incarcerated with little chance of escape. Who was it that had smashed him over the head? Dozich's thugs? He had the feeling that Dozich himself would dish out the beating to terrorise him into revealing who he was working for. What the hell had happened to the emergency plan for God's sake? Had they hung him out to dry?

The minutes and hours whiled away, which he used to good effect exercising his legs and moving around vigorously in the hope that the blood flow would improve his vision and hearing. His balance was peculiar and the throbbing in his skull wouldn't go away, but at least the double vision had gone. The loneliness and the pungent smell of the stale urine reminded him of Swartz's reply when he'd asked who it was outside his Kuwaiti cell. 'Who the fuck do you think? There's only one bloke who ever breaks you out of jail, for fuck sake.'

Sean managed a painful smile from those words, and the memory of Swartz breaking him out of jail, not once, but twice in the last few years gave him some comfort that there was always hope. Hearing Swartz talk made Sean all the more determined not to plummet into a deep trauma, and to keep fighting, keep attacking.

Sean had been dozing in the corner of the cell when mayhem broke loose. He hadn't seen the grenade thrown through the sliding partition and into the cell from the hands of his captors. But by Christ he felt it. The flash bang was designed to shock him, allowing his interrogators time to brutalise him, and let him know that the time had come. The blinding flash and series of deafening explosions annihilated any sense of fight Sean had left as two burly men stormed into the cell. His head was spinning again, and he rolled into the foetal position to save himself from whatever beating he was about to get. The next thing he felt was a boot smashing into his kidneys before he felt the cold steel of a weapon being prodded forcefully into his neck. He was hauled to his feet and dragged from the cell.

'Come on guys, I've got a small stash of gold sovereigns my friend can give you if you let me go. I'll call him now.'

The taller of the two skinheads, smiled back at him, but said nothing. The other man laughed before giving him a dig in the side again for his troubles.

'Where are you taking me? Back to Dozich' s house?'

'Don't know what you're talking about, now shut the fuck up and get yourself in there?'

Sean was bemused. In front of him was a fully enclosed steel mortuary box, the type they shoved into a freezer cabinet with row after row of bodies. The box was on wheels and had four handles, all readied to be pushed across a gangplank onto a small cabin cruiser.

'Do you mind if I take in the sea views instead?' Sean ducked as he saw the incoming blow and decided he would after all fight. Fuck it, he thought. He tensed his shoulders and swung his handcuffed wrists at the skinhead who had fleetingly lost his balance trying to punch Sean. He caught him square on the chin as he ripped the handcuffs upwards with as much might as he could muster. He felt the metal rip across the man's cheek leaving a three-inch gash that saw him step back grasping for air, screaming. A metal pole. A Thud. Sean was smashed across the back of the legs by the second skinhead and fell with such force that he heard his wrist crack. 'Fuck,' he shouted rolling in pain on the floor. Within seconds he'd been jostled and bundled into the mortuary box and was quickly hauled onto the boat.

The agony Sean was in was unbearable until he calmed his breathing and stopped thrashing around in the box. It was pitch black with hardly enough room to fit his bulk, and the size of the box was way too small. Whoever the undertaker was who measured him up for his death, had fallen way short. He knew he had to wrestle back control of his anxiety and started to calm himself with breathing exercises to quell his mind of the pain. The boat trip was bumpy, and the monotonous drone of the engine was all he could hear apart from his own occasional groans. He had no idea where he was going, and the ringing in his ears from the flash bang seemed to be getting worse.

The boat slowed to a crawl, and eventually he felt the box being manoeuvred across the gangplank, before hearing the scrunch of gravel beneath the four wheels. The hatch was released, and he flinched at the sudden sunlight. The silhouette of a person grew larger as he felt four hands grab his shirt to force him upright. He couldn't make out who it was, but the silhouette of long hair accompanied by the smell of perfume gave him a jolt. His eyes focussed on the long golden hair, then the jawline, then the piercing eyes. It was Natalie. Natalie fucking Merritt. 'Jesus Christ,' he uttered.

'Not yet,' Natalie said, 'But yes, you might meet him on the way to your maker you horrible fucking man. Get him out of there.'

Sean was manhandled out of the box and on to his feet. The strength in his knee had completely gone and he found his body arched like an old man, just as if he was already praying for mercy.

'What the fuck do you want, I thought you'd have been dead by now.'

'Oh, I was dead, and you damn well know it. Murdered by you, and whoever that other bastard was that caught me.'

'You're living, you're free, why don't you go home to Moscow for fuck sake?'

Natalie's eyes narrowed and Sean could see she was about to explode.'

'I'm not sure where you've been over the years, but you should have known by now that your handler bastard wouldn't let me go back. I'm *persona non grata* in Moscow, shamed, can never go back, and I'm somewhat fucked. So, I have nothing to lose now.'

'Don't tell me, you're now hell bent on revenge and will live your life seeking retribution. Come on Natalie, you fucked yourself over. It was you who failed on the mission, you who got yourself caught, not me.'

Sean dropped to his knees unable to fight the pain in his knees. He felt weak, needed water, and didn't know how long he'd stay conscious, but he wouldn't be bullied into submission by a Russian megalomaniac. He'd had first-hand experience of her sociopathic tendencies in France a few years ago.

'You sucked the life out of me you little bastard. Do you have any idea of what it was like to be banged up in a cell twenty-three hours a day, beaten and psychologically assaulted by MI5 interrogators?'

'I do actually. Yes, I bloody well do. Now enough of your heartache, get this over and done with and lets just call it quits and go our separate ways.'

Bizarrely, Sean thought momentarily of the crazy sex they'd had before he tricked her into incriminating herself. Maybe he could work that soft spot she had for him? Weakness and appeasement would most definitely not work. Strength, guile and manipulation might give him a fighting chance.

'Stand up, you piece of shit,' Natalie shouted. 'I have some work to be done.' Natalie was dressed just as Sean remembered her. Black patent leather heels, tanned legs and a red dress. He looked around at the environment. He was in a gravel yard of some kind. He could just make out some white revetments and what looked like military fort walls, painted red at their base. The fort looked like it may have once been a prison or a military hospital, particularly as the white building in front of him had the patchwork of a large red cross above its entrance.

Sean was hauled to his feet and frogmarched towards the red cross with the words of Natalie ringing in his ears. 'You will either die and be buried here on this island, or you will tell me everything I want to know. It really is that simple.'

He glanced around at the buildings trying to make sense of it all. This part of the old military hospital was totally deserted and one of the last bastions of British military history in the Balearics. He was on an island known as 'bloody island' and the hospital had been built in the eighteenth century by British military engineers before being finally abandoned in the 1960s having returned to Spanish control.

Sean was forcibly steered into an old ward that still had a few wooden beds inside a tunnel like enclosure, with a single window at the end of the room. The once whitewashed walls were now in a state of disrepair and the musty smell of rotten grout made it feel like a mediaeval place of torture that had been mothballed for some time. He didn't know it, but the ward had once been home to sailors who were classed as mentally retarded and who had endured all manner of barbaric practice to cleanse them of their illnesses. Sean spotted a few old anchor points with chains on the wall, and could only imagine how the ward's incumbents had suffered before their death. He had to find a way to avoid the same fate at the hand of a female assassin who had gone mad.

'First I will talk, and you will answer all my questions,' Natalie explained in a condescending manner. Sean was made to sit on the floor, bent forward, hands around his ankles.

'What exactly do you want to know. There really isn't much to tell you know.'

An uncomfortable silence. Sean watched the two skinheads attach strips of blankets to his wrists and ankles, before nautical ropes were placed around them, presumably to prevent lasting scars. He felt the ropes tighten and watched as a steel pole was passed under his knees and elbows. He was then lifted four feet off the ground and the pole's ends were placed on two stools that had been placed on the flat wooden beds. Sean's body swung like a pendulum, before settling into a position where the entire weight of his body was being borne by his knee and elbow joints.

Natalie strode back across the room to sit just below Sean on a stool with two oddities in front of her. An old military telephone that included an electric generator wired in sequence to two dry cell batteries, and a bamboo stick. She held an open laptop in her hands.

Natalie gave a nod to her minder who began the process of wiring Sean up. The ground wire was wrapped around his big toe and the hot wire was wrapped a few times around his ear. Sean was grateful that the node hadn't been attached to his testicles, but he felt sure that would come later.

'You want to make a long-distance telephone call then I assume?' Sean couldn't help himself. He just had to keep fighting.

Her face drew back in a mirthless stage of fury. 'You won't be making jokes in a moment I can assure you.' Natalie prodded his testicles with the long bamboo stick. 'If this doesn't work, I have plan B with this little beauty.' Natalie leant over to retract a syringe from her handbag and placed it on the small wooden stool next to her.

'I always had fantasies of doing it with you in a nurse's outfit,' Sean joked, now laughing intolerably. 'Come on Natalie, look at all this bollocks. You really don't need to do this you know. You were not like this as a kid, there is some goodness inside you somewhere, you know.'

'It was burnt out of me, and you helped that process. Now, tell me Sean, who was your handler who set me up to be detained? I want his name, where he lives, his children, their schools, where his wife works, the lot.'

'His name is Jack, and that's all I know about him.'

'Oh, good you will talk to me,' Natalie said faintly amused. 'But that's not a great start. I already know his name is Jack, but where does he work, what does he look like? I have plenty of time, tell me his story Sean.'

'That's all I have, you know the score. He's a blank canvas to me, he's my handler, not my friend, and MI5 handlers, just like yours, don't go telling the likes of me their fucking life story do they. Get real Natalie. It's not even his real name.'

Sean had never seen a female look so demented, her wildness now forged across her steely face which went pink, then red, as her eyes flickered in a type of craziness he'd never before witnessed. With a single whip of the bamboo cane, she wacked Sean with all her might up, and into his exposed bollocks. She followed it up with a crank of the telephone handle.

'Oof,' came the deep groan, right from the bottom of Sean's lungs, followed by an involuntary muscle spasm that made his body reflex on the pole. The sharp sensation of piercing pain shot right into the very bowels of his body, and he felt they would open up with the next burst that was shot into him. Natalie was now cranking the telephone sporadically, and then faster. The electric current shot straight into Sean's body. 'Aaaarghh,' came the high-pitched response as a sound that could never be easily reproduced, but anyone hearing such a groan, would never forget. The skinheads were now wincing.

'Come on Sean, you know you can tell me.'

Sean noticed that when the machine stopped for a moment, which was accompanied by Natalie's beaming grin, his muscles relaxed, and his body dropped back to its original position. He also felt his tongue shrinking and had now lost control of his bladder. While he was hanging from the steel pole, he couldn't feel his legs or clench his stomach. He'd been reduced to a terribly painful mass that no longer obeyed any orders from his mind.

Then Sean spotted one of the men was pouring water into a bucket. 'Fuck,' was all he could muster.

.

Chapter 24

Menorca

'What the hell's the plan now Jack,' Laura shouted across the conference room, aghast at what she had just witnessed on the screens in front of her.

Jack and Laura had watched the entire compromise of Sean's operation in high definition imagery from the drone circling above the villa as Sean made his escape. They had watched Sean kill the minder on the imagery feed from the CCTV camera in Dozich's office, saw him signal to them that the mission was over, and finally watched him disappear into the woods.

'We switch to plan B, that's what,' Jack said, with an inscrutable smile. With every cock-up comes opportunity, and what we have achieved so far is not completely blown.'

Laura walked towards the large sideboard and poured herself a cold coffee before turning. 'Jack, I know he's a good operator, but this is a cock-up of mammoth proportion. How the hell can you stay so fucking calm all the time.'

'Very simple my dear lady. Flexibility on operations is key. And I built flexibility into this operation with a few friends I could call upon, if, and when the need would arise. As we always say, no plan survives contact with the enemy, so think a few steps ahead, and think *what if*.'

'You mean to tell me you planned for this?'

'To the extent it might all go wrong, yes. There are a few more strings to this operation that play in tune together, but apart from those, Sean is vital to the next one.'

'So, come on Jack how? How do we get to him now?'

For all the display of Jack's smooth, calm, confidence in front of Laura, underneath he was fuming. He now had a rescue operation to mount, and the safety of an important oligarch to think about. Everything he had heard from the hidden bugs in the dining room had so far told him that everything was calm, no deviation from the negotiations had occurred, and no suspicion had been placed on Berarnov. Jack was wondering how Yelena would explain this away to her father, and he was concerned for her fate too. But first, he needed to get Sean out of there.

'Do you want my team involved in the extraction Jack?'

'Yes, I think that would be sensible.'

'I have them on standby. How do you want to play it? The only lead we have is the drone footage of Sean being bundled into the Volkswagen Beetle boot.'

'Well, that, and the tracker that's been inserted into his shoe. Quite useful when you have high-risk agents continually being lifted don't you think?'

'Or absconding.'

'Precisely.'

'I can't imagine why he'd have agreed to it though. I wouldn't.'

'It was all part of the deal to keep him on the books of The Court after the psychiatrist had assessed his state of mind. Essentially, he's still carrying a lot of trauma and was as likely to abscond now as he was after the last fiasco in Istanbul.'

'Ah, when he went AWOL with the hookers you mean? You do have a soft spot for him though Jack. You never told me why?'

'He's a vital part of my machinery, and yes I do have a soft spot for him. He was stitched up all those years ago by a corrupt copper who had him arrested in Kabul. But up to that point he was recognised as one of the best agents we had. It could happen to any of us, and I felt we needed to give him some sanctuary from himself as much as anything else. D agreed with me. And apart from that, D somehow knew that his mother was a legend in the secret intelligence service who would have wanted someone to keep an eye on him. Sean feels he's tied to us as family now. He's had nothing, and no one, except his son whom he sees occasionally.'

'A hell of a backstory Jack. He's a good man, let's get him out of there and find out who lifted him.'

'I have a funny feeling I already know who that might be.'

Jack kept his counsel and sent a text to his wife. The breakout of Natalie a few weeks earlier had forced him into making sure he had protection placed on his family home. Just in case.

Chapter 25

Menorca

A small size drain. A set of rusting bars above it. A stench of rotting flesh. That was all Sean could see and smell as he felt the last breaths of his life draining from him. He was kneeling, trapped inside the drain, naked and drenched in his own blood. He could hardly focus but felt the pain of his handcuffed hands in front of him. He seemed to remember her talking about Jack before she hacked at his finger, and then he'd passed out.

For now, he was awake. He knew he'd been dropping in and out of consciousness for a long time but couldn't remember how he'd ended up in this hellhole with his shoulders wedged solid against the brick work. He tried to look up at the bars above him. Four feet perhaps? Maybe five. He winced at the searing light pouring into the drain and dropped his chin again feeling utterly ruined. There was nothing left. He'd been wiped out. All he could hear was the echo of draining water inside the void, and the only thing he felt below him was the mass of a black rodent as it swept around his feet. He tried to swot it with his right foot, but the energy he needed for a simple move just caused more pain. No energy. No will. Nothing left but the thoughts of death.

'Thanks for all the information Sean,' he heard from above. 'I'm off now but I'll forever have your finger on the pulse.' He heard a burst of sickening laughter but couldn't strain himself to look up, where Natalie was peering into the drain, drooling with hate.

'I'd say you have around four to five minutes to live, make it the best you've ever had.'

With that, Sean heard the rasp of gravel straining under walking feet and then he heard it. The gush of water around his feet, signifying that a valve had been opened to flood the void and send Sean to his death by drowning. What the actual fuck was all this about, he thought. He had no energy to even shout out loud and couldn't be bothered to struggle anymore. It was fruitless. He felt the force of the water across his feet, then his thighs, and quickly the water level began approaching his chest. He started to say a final prayer and he seemed to spin, falling through the water, into a dazzling dream…

They say that the last moments of your life show you a kaleidoscope of dreams, merged with explosive bursts of images from different periods of your past, almost like a slideshow on overdrive.

Sean could feel that he had entered the borderland between wakefulness and final rest, slumbering into a strange and fascinating state of consciousness characterised by dream-like visions and strange sensory occurrences. He could see his hands above him as he spiralled away in a vortex of clear water with odd looking faces smiling down on him. It seemed like they were saying their final farewells, and the most prominent image was that of his wife. It was Katy. She was kissing him on his cheek waving at him. He tried as he might to grasp for her fair hair, but she slipped through the three fingers he could see. He longed for her, he'd lived for her. But then came his mother. The image of Katy dissolved, and he witnessed his mother shouting at him. Telling him to stay away and to find his father. No, she was telling him to be like his father. Then the images turned dark, the spiralling water turned murky and dense. She was being dragged away and killed. A gun against her head. Bang!

The state of mind that Sean was in, was fluid and hyper-associative, giving rise to images that expressed layers of memories and sensations. He had entered a phenomenon somewhere between sleep and death, where the alpha and theta waves were playing havoc with the brain, but he was in harmony with his subconscious mind. He felt his shoulders twisting as he plummeted gracefully to his death. He was passing the faces that came in and out of focus intermittently. There was Jugsy, *'Bye, bye, mate, see you at the big bar in the sky,'* were the words he could hear in an echo chamber. Billy Phish, with his pipe. Billy nodded at Sean as he passed by. Taking his pipe from his mouth and raising it to gesture *'farewell'* my good friend. Then Samantha, Jack and D. They were all waving to him. Then Phil. What was he doing? He had a bomb in his hand. A timer. He was switching it on, then he was shouting. *'Three, two, one, firing now.'* Then he threw the bomb right at Sean as he was falling...no, no, no - bang!

'Oh, God, I'm going...' Sean's body was closing down, just like a computer shuts down. It's known that after motor, the sound, and the visual brain cells all turn off in stages. The very last feeling Sean had witnessed was an exploding head as he caught the bomb. Scientists have proffered that during death, instead of the brain shutting down properly in one go, the brain cells responsible for such sound and vision are thought to fire all at once, creating a blast of energy that the brain interprets as a loud noise. Boom!

He heard it again. Loud bangs and gunfire. Then very slowly, the bizarre slideshow came to an end. Just as the last white dot appears on a screen in the cinema. There was a calming hush. Then the final words from his murderer. *'Your mortal remains will be left in a pit to rot away slowly.'*

'Jesus, get him out of there quickly,' she shouted. 'Get him out.' Yelena Hardy stood above the rusting grille and could just see a mop of greying hair above the water line.

'How long do you think he's been there,' a voice shouted back, taking aim with a pistol at the silver lock.

'Je ne sais pas,' Yelena replied trying desperately to hold her fear at bay. *'Vite, vite, il faut le sauver.'*

'Stand back.' Bang! The lock flew off the grille and the bullet ricocheted into the hospital wall. The ageing Frenchman dropped to his stomach and leant over the edge of the drain to grab the body out of the hole. He couldn't get a grip on the slimy body and needed help. *'J'ai besoin d'aide,'* he shouted across to a second man who had rigged up a pulley system onto the black jeep that had skidded to a halt moments earlier. Between them, they wove a wide leather strap between Sean's arms and began to heave his body out. Within seconds Yelena watched the men get to work on the body using a portable defibrillator.

She dropped to the floor and sat cross legged, holding her head in the palms of her hands wishing this wasn't true. She had fallen in love with Sean, the first man in her life to show her any tenderness and care. How was it possible after all these years to find a man that truly cared and had no hidden desire to control her? No coercion, no hatred behind the mask. She prayed they could save him, but how would she explain the circumstances to him if he survived?

Yelena Hardy was a spy. A French spy. Like everything in life that ends up being complicated, Yelena's story had begun in a simple manner. She was born as Marijana Dozich, the youngest of three children who rarely saw their father during his service in the Russian military. She adored her mother and had a happy childhood in the southern Russian city Krasnador before they eventually moved back to Belgrade where her grandfather had served as a Russian defence attaché during the cold war.

It took a lot for Yelena to eventually betray her father to the French intelligence services. It took her a decade to overcome the constant fear, the stomach-churning panic, the never-ending emotional abuse. But she had chosen to break free eighteen months ago to the day.

It had all begun in her early teenage years when she'd caught Dozich cheating on her mother, and not long after that she'd become the victim of his own sexual abuse. Everything about her father was control. Exerting power and fear. As the only daughter, her mother had tried her best to protect her in those early teenage years, and she made sure that Yelena attended her drama and singing lessons in the opera house of Belgrade where they had a youth programme in place. Music became Yelena's escape, a safe space, particularly after her mother took her own life in 2004.

With her head in her hands, unable to watch Sean being worked on with the defibrillator, she started to cry. Her mind splintering with bursts of memories of her life before it centred on a moment in time when she seemed to be at her happiest: as a seventeen-year-old girl whose voice had finally been recognised for what it was. Utterly outstanding.

'Your voice is dark, but voluminous,' her amateur opera producer had said as she sat at the end of the stage, her legs dangling over the side. 'I think you have a wonderful professional career ahead of you if you get this performance right my dear. You might one day become a huge star.'

No one had ever said that to her. Everyone had marvelled at her very rare contralto voice, but never had anyone said that she could become a star of the opera. I can become famous, I can, she had said to herself, wandering back to the centre of the stage to sing Olga's aria from the opera Eugene Onegin. Her confidence visibly grew for the second rendition, one of the toughest solo contralto arias of any opera. She was playing the daughter of Madame Larina, now engaged to Lensky. Her voice was enough to rupture any man's heart as she belted out the aria. She was one of the very few singers in the world who could sing the low ranges needed to be designated a contralto, a rare case of exuding a deep voice with spectacularly dark colour, but laced with a slender and pure tone. Think Cher. Think Amy Winehouse, or Tina Turner, but in opera mode. Yelena's voice had grown and matured like a fine wine that should never be served before decanting first.

'The only problem as a contralto,' her producer had said, 'Is that you will always be playing tarts, villains or witches.' She had chuckled at that, but a career in music was not only her dream, but the route to escape her abusive father.

'He's a Russian attaché,' she had said, when her introvert friend in London asked about her family. 'We lived in Russia, Serbia and Bosnia and we visited France a lot where my mother was born. She passed away from cancer and I hardly ever see my father nowadays.' But the truth was much deeper and darker. Her mother had never ever recovered from the death of her eldest son when Yelena was only fourteen. It was a tragedy of epic proportions for any family, but to have your brother stabbed to death by a drug gang in the Palilula district of Belgrade was the catalyst that led to her mother's death, and for Yelena a lifetime of mourning. He was only nineteen. The complex truth about her father provided a level of shame that she carried deep in her soul. Something no child should ever have to live with. He was a killer, a criminal and a spy for the Russians who had risen to fame by establishing his own mercenary outfit to support Russian interests in the Balkans and overseas. What was equally hard to suffer, was her father's infidelity, and his betrayal of her mother. A memory that still hurt her deeply.

Her entire understanding of family life had been obliterated through trauma after trauma, yet she was a survivor. A victim yes, but a victim with a sense of having to survive by creating coping mechanisms to deal with her angst, and an innate survival instinct to deceive her father, and stay alive. His affection for her was meaningless and chillingly sinister. 'You do as I say, and you will have everything you will ever need in your life,' he had said on countless occasions. It was only in recent years that she realised that she was the victim of emotional manipulation and effectively a prisoner to his every demand, even though she lived a wealthy life centred on London. She didn't see it initially as punishment, but then she had read about Stockholm Syndrome, and how victims can never seem to break away from their abusers.

Her childhood and her suffering over the years meant that she could not hold down a relationship with a man, and her default was to view them with suspicion, with fear and with loathing, Sometimes, she played games with prospective lovers. Manipulating them using defensive coping mechanisms that had become instinctive to her survival. The years of emotional blackmail and grooming by her father had eventually led to her developing skills that she would put to great use for his business connections. She had become a master of deception. Her raw instincts for survival had turned her into a young woman who could trick and deceive elder men into leaking secrets that she'd been ordered to pass onto her father. Government officials, captains of industry, military officers. And yes, she did sleep with them all.

The gut-wrenching shock of her mother's death led her to a journey that she'd hoped would see her become an opera star. It never happened. Her father moved what was left of the family to the dense forests, mountains and rivers of the republic of Srpska, a confederal entity predominantly comprising Serbs, and there he expanded his new mercenary business.

At twenty-nine years of age, Yelena was no moralist, and she had worked the circuit for her father to act as a spy for his gains. Never hers. She had been groomed to live this tortuous life but had kept her singing as a way of disassociating from real life, working the circuits. This acted as her natural cover to trap the targets she'd been fed.

That was her life, until one day, she spent her father's money on psychotherapy, dialectal behavioural treatment and years of self-analysis to diagnose her own mental health condition.

Then the journey towards retribution began. She met the British agent first but heard nothing back. Then she met a Frenchman. The training and the leaks of information to the French General Directorate for External Security had begun. The DGSE were delighted with their new agent.

Chapter 26

London

Jack strolled along Millbank heading for a meeting that would either make or break his plot. He was scheduled to attend an informal and unminuted meeting with the cabinet secretary who also doubled as the national security advisor to the UK. Sir Justin Darbyshire was one of the Prime Minister's core advisors, and the only senior civil servant who knew of the existence of The Court.

Jack arrived in good time to meet with Laura who was inspecting the maps on the cabinet secretary's wall. She was studying a silk escape and evasion map of occupied France in 1944 when Jack strode into the office.

'Ah, nice tie Jack.' Laura began. She threw a cheeky smile across the room. 'I thought you might like the colour.'

'Very kind of you to send me such a gift. How are you?'

'Couldn't be better. You know, if ever you want to get me a present, one of these would be great!'

'I think the one next to it is probably more interesting, and quite a rarity. That's the original map of the Dayton accord, signed by the US and Serbian Presidents when they agreed the re-alignment of the Bosnia and Herzegovinian border in 1995.'

'Very good. I had no idea he liked maps so much.'

'Well, Sir Justin started his career as a Military Surveyor you know. Long before he became a civil servant.'

Sir Justin Darbyshire walked in to greet them both, apologising for his absence due to a short notice meeting. He was a man of real stature with impeccable manners but known to swear often. He had represented his country at rugby and athletics in the '70s and was a rare civil servant who had previously served with distinction in the Army. His government role was comparable in rank to that of a military General or a High Court judge, and his political acumen saw him quickly promoted to become the UK's highest ranking civil servant within an impressive twenty-two year period.

Sir Justin wore a dark blue suit partnered in masterly fashion with a dazzling emerald green tie set against a pristine white shirt. Powerful, wise, and a friend of the new Prime Minister, he carried considerable influence far beyond administrative matters, reaching deep into the very heart of the political decision-making process. His unelected role also provided some authority over elected ministers, although his constitutional authority was somewhat ambiguous, but noticeably stronger with a new PM in town.

'Jack, Laura, so good to see you both. Sorry I'm late, do please take a seat. I've just been having a chat with the Chief of Defence Intelligence and he'll be joining us a bit later. Now, tuck into some of that grub, take a seat and we can start.'

Jack helped himself to a few cheese and pickle doorstops, and a glass of orange juice. He noticed Laura fleetingly wince at the spread that Sir Justin had ordered for their informal chat which was the precursor to a more formal arrangement at a later stage.

'Nothing fancy food wise I'm afraid Laura. Just the good Lord Sandwich.' Sir Justin took his jacket off throwing it onto the leather chesterfield. 'One of the best British inventions ever my good lady, alongside Branston pickle of course.'

Jack watched Laura mouth the words Branston pickle back at him, before making a face. She grinned at the simplicity of a British government official's lunch. The CIA would have had rare roast beef, chicken goujons and a vegan selection, all followed up with Key Lime pie, Jack thought.

'Jack, where are we with all this? Is it looking good?'

Jack took a moment to chew a mouthful of the thick sandwich, pausing to swot away a few crumbs. He nodded eagerly before placing his tie in the centre of his shirt. 'I would say it's OK sir, but not fantastic. I would, however, like to propose a plan to take us to the next stages in Africa.'

'Good. Laura, what's the American take on Jack's plan. Will you support us?'

'We will Sir Justin. The President feels it's worth putting some effort into. Importantly, his Special Envoy to the Sahel has now arrived in the region and is making himself known. But I have to tell you it's been a tough sell. The President wants to reign in global interference, and he wants to be certain that anything we do in the future for the Sahel is collaborative and worthy.'

'Well, I'd say it's certainly going to be worthy. He could be the first US President to stop the formation of a Caliphate dead in its tracks from what Jack has sent to me. I do appreciate though, that he'll need to condition the media and his opponents on the hill and lean gently into this one.'

Laura fiddled with a piece of Branston Pickle using a knife to extract it from the remains of her sandwich. 'We can never let another Caliphate happen ever again Sir Justin. Take that as an American position. The fear of that notion sends shivers down the spines of many people in the administration. It's bloody awkward right now though, especially with the Chinese relationship worsening, and the Iranians agitating in the Gulf. The American embassy siege at the beginning of the year is still taking its toll, and Americans everywhere are thinking that he'll be goaded into attacking Iran.'

'I agree. A simple spark in the Gulf, or a misplaced kidnapping, or even another embassy siege or Al Quds assassination will most certainly result in one side going too far, that's for sure. Much as the President has his hands full globally, our new Prime Minister has exactly the same. He wants to steer a course of a closer relationship with your fine people, and wants to show the Europeans we are indeed a fine neighbour too. An awkward stance to reconcile.'

Laura nodded and took a sip of water. 'My assessment from a CIA perspective is that we need to set the right conditions for US action in the Sahel. But it will need to be achieved in small steps which Jack and I have talked about. All avenues will need to lead eventually to US intervention which the President has agreed upon. We'll need to stage the intelligence findings in a phased way, not a big burst.'

'Quite right Laura. I was at a cabinet office intelligence briefing today where we received formal notification that the

French want us to provide another two squadrons of armoured infantry, more counter IED specialists, and more Chinook helicopters for their operations in Mali. They're taking casualties in a big way now, especially from IED attacks on Operation BARKHANE, as well as complex attacks using ambush tactics on their convoys and desert barracks. The government forces are all but defeated after the last six months of fighting which has accelerated at such a pace that the dangers of a new Caliphate are very real.'

'And we now know why,' Jack chipped in. 'The influx of Russian weaponry and mercenaries who are supplying and mentoring the jihadis is having a devastating effect now. The latest intelligence suggest that Keystone Corps teams are planning to infiltrate the government of Mali, offer the President and senior officials close protection, and win a cut in the gold and diamond mines, as well as the lithium industry too.'

'Yes. And what was clear from this morning's briefings is that the French are fucking fuming,' Sir Justin explained. 'While the intelligence on Russian weapons interference is not known in Paris, the Russian influence on what they see as French territory is quite obvious to them, and there's a huge risk that Moscow can cajole their way into controlling the entire Sahel and Sub-Saharan Africa. The PM knows this, and he's asked the Chief of Defence Intelligence and myself for some answers on how we can support the French, and all of our western interests in the region.'

'Collaboration is the answer,' Laura replied.

Sir Justin smiled in agreement. 'Jack, what's your view on the next stages then?'

'It will need to be quite a lengthy plan to shape the way we will operate with the French and the Americans. But there are some real benefits to such a long-term goal of securing the Sahel. First, we get to show the world the collaborative strength of NATO's three most potent military nations operating together, which I'm sure the PM and US President will be pleased about. Secondly, it shows our national support of French and European operations, and lastly, we have a common foe to put the boot into. Russia's ultimate aim is to influence and control all African nations as part of their global strategy.'

'It's a no brainer then Jack. How do we channel each nation where we want them?'

Jack stood and walked to the white board at the end of the table. He grabbed a black marker and began to draw the linkage map that had been tattooed into his mind. 'I'll draw the intelligence picture of the linkages we've formed over the last six months of all the key players on the stage. But to answer your question sir, we infiltrate the weapons stores, collect the intelligence of Russian mercenary supply chains, link it back to the Russian GRU, and show Washington and Paris how the situation needs a massive overhaul of strategy, and a new injection of boots on the ground to sabotage the Russian supply chains and take the jihadis down.'

'I assume you don't think we have enough to go with right now?'

Jack took a deep breath and paused. 'No, not enough to get the Americans to move troops quickly. We need to present the evidence on a plate.'

Laura pitched in to support Jack's assessment. 'The problem is this. We need more intelligence on the smuggling activity, and it will need to be covert operators collecting it. No one will sanction formal operations on what they'd see as a wild goose chase. I can provide the top cover using my teams, but this is Jack's operation, and he'll need to find the weapon and bomb caches. Then we can present the evidence as a fait accompli.'

Jack drew a few circles on the white board and linked them with dotted lines. He explained to Sir Justin how Dozich was the centre of the Keystone Corps logistics operation for smuggling the weapons and how a sting operation had been set to gather the intelligence.

'You see,' Jack began, fiddling with his tie, 'Dozich likes to run side-hustles too, and it seems his masters are OK with that. His greed will be his downfall. It's a curious relationship where Moscow encourages organised crime gangs to work for them, and for other outlets too. The Kremlin will recruit cyber and mercenary gangs who can fulfil their national interests, but they allow them to self-fund their businesses turning a blind eye to illicit dealings that are going on - so long as they don't interfere with the state apparatus, or their core missions. For the bait, I used this man here, a London based oligarch, called Leonard Berarnov.'

'How? What's the link here?'

'A gentleman you know very well sir. Sir Rhys Eldridge.'

'Bloody hell. What's his involvement? He punches heavily in government you know.'

'Yes, I know. I'll brief you on the detail later, but in short, he is the Chairman and figurehead of a corrupt cabal known as the twenty-one-club which we have infiltrated.'

'Magnificent Jack. I'm with you so far, but what exactly is the catch? This is a very complex web of deceit you are about to jump into.'

'No catch. But a good rub. We can offer the French our intelligence on their officials who are part of the twenty-one-club. I've been worried for some time about how we can entice the French to play ball with us, but something came up recently to help nudge that thought. We need the French on-side with all of this.'

'They're stubborn bastards, I know,' Sir Justin exclaimed throwing his hands in the air. 'Especially when it's their former colonial territories that are at stake.'

'Exactly sir. You see, my team have been conducting SIGINT operations in France as well as hacking into some very senior French minister accounts. Certain members of the twenty-one-club. What we've put together is a great package for them.'

'Jesus Christ, Jack, this better not come back and bite us on the arse?'

'On the contrary. The French will come back for more. They will trust us to operate as a triumvirate, and together, we can take down all Russian operations in the Sahel.'

'Extraordinary thinking Jack. Very well done. A riddle wrapped in a mystery, inside an enigma. It would be for the best if we don't fuck this up, but tell me, how on earth did you get this information?'

'It all began as a whisper from one of my sources, but now we pretty much know the whole story with the Russian mercenaries. As for the French, Sir Rhys had recruited former DGSE agents, ministers of state and a handful of military officers into his twenty-one-club, all working towards the same aim. To run an off-the-books intelligence agency, probe into weak states across Africa and the Far East, bribe the corporates and then reap their rewards on a scale we've never seen before. They fund their activity from drugs and weapons smuggling.'

'Bloody hell. A rogue intelligence operation? You mean to say they're bribing governments?'

'I was astonished at the extent of Jack's intelligence collection,' Laura interjected, tying her hair in a ponytail. 'All with a bit of CIA funding of course,' she joshed. 'The value of political intelligence on weak governments, fused with veteran intelligence officer collection techniques, has provided them with some potent collateral. The power of bribery is their tool to go big. Very big.'

'Good God,' Sir Justin said, leaning back in his chair. 'So, let me get this straight. We can offer intelligence to the French to get them to accept American intervention, and we can get the Americans to play on this wicket by simply showing that they can take down a new Caliphate?'

'Yes,' Laura quietly clarified. 'But the best bit is this. Two previous presidents allowed the incubation of AQ and ISIS to take place, allowing them to grow. Can you imagine how this will look to our new President? He has an ego the size of a planet, and this will be too much for him to pass on.'

'OK, what do you pair need from me now? I'll authorise some action and have a discreet chat with the Chief of Defence Intelligence when he comes along shortly.'

Jack looked across at Laura looking for inspiration and support. She nodded for him to go ahead. 'Well, there is one slight complication sir.'

'I fucking knew it Jack. Just like the last one. Go on what is it?'

Jack watched Sir Justin place his elbows on the table. He noticed a slight twitch below his left eye. He was anxious. 'Well, we have a slight cock-up in play right now, but I think I may have solved it.'

Sir Justin waved an arm and rolled his eyes. 'Go on. I'm ready.'

Jack drew another two circles on the white board. 'It's a bit complicated, but the essence is that we've steamrollered a French intelligence operation. They're, erm, not very happy with us at the moment and I thought you might be able to make a few calls.'

'For fuck sake.'

'I know. I'm sorry. We really didn't know. You see, this woman here - her name is Yelena Hardy, is a French DGSE agent. We lifted her in our own operation that was led by Sean Richardson.'

'I somehow knew his name would crop up. A good man, but a bit of a maverick at times.'

'Indeed sir, but he gets things done. So, we only just found out that Yelena was a French agent, the daughter of Goran Dozich, and she'd been supplying intelligence on his operations to the French DGSE for just over a year. They've trained her well, and by all accounts she's very good in the tradecraft.'

'I see. Now you need me to calm them down a bit and tempt them into our little plan. How did all this happen?'

'She rescued Sean from a rather delicate situation in the Balearics. He's alive, but in a bad way. I've been in touch with my French counterpart to explain that we were running an operation against Dozich too.'

'But why didn't Yelena explain that she was working for the French when you got to her?

'Apparently, she was intrigued about Sean, and didn't want to expose herself until she felt he was trusted and operating for a British agency that she could switch to. She thinks the French have been pretty useless.'

Laura stood and walked to the whiteboard where the names, circles and dotted lines were now filling up. 'I actually think she is a very clever agent. She played an excellent stage role with Sean, is a good actress, never gave so much as a whisper away as to who she was working for, and ultimately knows her game well. She's a tough and very bright operator. She'd have to be, to win Sean over and hide her own persona.'

'This is quite an incredible turn of events. You say you have it under control then Jack, and Sean is safe. Can the next phases go ahead?'

'We think so, yes. We need to debrief Sean and Yelena, but the word from Berarnov is that the trap has not been compromised. We had a big scare, yes. They'll be very wary, but I think the greed of Dozich and Sir Rhys has driven them on. When Dozich conducted background checks on Sean's alias, he'll have found that he had a record of burglary.'

'Good work Jack. I must say, I'm surprised we didn't know much about this woman...' Sir Justin struggled with the name and opened his palm.

'Yelena Hardy.'

'That's the one.'

'We know much more about her now. Our original searches revealed nothing. She was squeaky clean. Nothing on the national database, nothing from Interpol. It was as if she didn't really exist outside of her passport and retinal scans. Not even a parking ticket. She's been listed as a singer and songwriter, resident here on an exceptional talent visa with a Bosnian passport but has never come under any of the law enforcement or security service noses. Until now.'

'What have you found?'

'Her real name is Marijana. Marijana Dozich. Her DNA has provided us with some quite clear links to her family ancestry.' Jack passed an A4 report on the DNA analysis and the carbon thirteen analysis of where she had recently travelled in the world.

'Good God, this is quite remarkable Jack. Whatever next.'

'I know sir. Quite remarkable, and something to be used at a later date.'

'Absolutely.'

'We checked her bank records, tax records, health records, and they're all squeaky clean. It seems that Dozich provided her wealth through regular payments to a Jersey bank account which also feeds money into the twenty-one-club. The financial evidence and all the connections with Sir Rhys and Dozich are now joining up to form quite an explosive mix.'

Sir Justin edged towards the window before turning sharply on his heels. 'You know, you are a devious pair of bastards and I'm guessing you've got more up your sleeves with this?'

Jack waited for the natural pause to end, knowing he'd have to declare his hand.

'Come on then Jack. Tell me the next moves you want me to authorise.'

'I want to send Sean and Yelena together on a joint mission right into the heart of the problem. Into Mali as a duo.'

'Good grief. You're really stretching my patience Jack. That will never work.'

'I think it will sir.'

'Why?'

'The French will feel they have a stake in the operation.'

'Mmmm. OK. But there's always a 'but' Jack. Where is it?'

'I suppose the 'but' is this. I need to make it look like the French DGSE will get the intelligence glory when we pull it off. I'll feed them their bit. But not the full works. We'll use this as a real opportunity for a joint Anglo-French intelligence mission, but the rewards will be for us as a joint US/UK mission.'

'How?'

'Well, firstly I'm convinced I can convert Yelena to come onto our side with all the intelligence she brings against Sir Rhys, and Dozich, who we will take down. It's not for the French. I'll give them their ministers and the other lizards in their system on a plate.'

'I like that. Go on.'

'And the Americans win control of the Sahel, including placing new government figureheads that it wants across the region, all in return for safety, security and investment. This will lead to decades of influence for Anglo-American interests, right into the very heart of Africa.'

'By golly Jack, you're a cunning old spy.' Sir Justin was now grinning like a Cheshire cat. 'So, we take down an illicit intelligence network with Sir Rhys, nail Dozich and the Russian mercenary outfits, shaft the French out of their territory, and elevate the Yanks into central influence over Africa pissing the Chinese off too?'

'That's about the gist of it, sir. *Perfidious Albion* I believe we call it.'

Sir Justin roared with laughter. '*Perfidious Albion* it is young man. By Jove, it's sheer genius Jack, the PM is going to love this.'

Chapter 27

Private Clinic, Marylebone, London

Jack watched Sean fiddle with the nasal cannula which was causing him some discomfort as it delivered the supplemental oxygen he needed to help his lungs recover. The pain Sean had endured resulted in his left lung collapsing, but despite his ordeal, the doctor had insisted he was actually in good shape and recovering well.

'Can I get you anything Sean? Anything to help?'

'You can get me the fuck out of here Jack, and quick too. I hate these places.'

Jack watched Sean wince as he tried to sit up. Sean had endured horrific periods of torture and was struggling to remember everything that had happened.

'You need to watch out for that bitch Jack. She's after you now, probably your family too, and I can't for the life of me remember what I told her.'

'Natalie, you mean? You don't know enough about me to have revealed anything critical. Don't even worry yourself about that. We have enough people that can help me on that score.'

'You did once tell me about your local pub in Marlow though. I can't remember what else I told her.'

'There is that, I agree. But hey, that's the life of an ageing MI5 counterterrorist officer. We've both got plenty of other enemies who would do the dirty on us, even if she doesn't.'

'Did you find her?'

'No.'

'Fuck, Jack. She's a walking lunatic. A sociopathic robot intent on killing both of us.'

'We didn't have enough assets on the ground to track her but fear not, we'll spot her if she returns to the UK. We've got facial recognition pretty much everywhere at ports of entry, and the team are onto it now. We'll find her and take her down.'

Jack watched Sean struggle for breath and begin to fiddle with the cannula again. He took a step forward to check Sean's pulse-oximeter readings. Blood oxygen at ninety-two percent, pulse rate of seventy-eight.

'Let's go,' Sean demanded. 'I'm fine. Physically that is. My mind is fucked up a bit, but hey, that's another drawer to shut another memory on. Anyway, I need a cigarette. In fact, let's do a beer or two too while we're at it. There's some great boozers down Marylebone high road.'

'Very funny, Jack said, reaching for Sean's medical notes and chuckling at the very notion of Sean going on another bender. 'You need to be at ninety-six percent oxygen, and our own doctors will check you tomorrow morning to see how you've improved. Then I'll get you to a safe house before we decide on how to proceed.'

'We'll see about that,' Sean retaliated. 'I'll discharge myself later, walk out the door and go drinking by myself if you want to play that fucking game.'

Jack smiled but ignored the response. He could tell that morphine was still lingering in Sean's body, his pupils were heavily dilated, and he looked as if he was on a high. 'Listen, I can get you out of here tomorrow if you're well enough, and then we can work on the next phase of my plan. That is, if you're up for it?'

'Seriously?'

Jack sensed he might get his way, given time. But he never could tell with Sean. In this state, he was a live cannon, and could do anything, including ripping out the cannula and just walking off to get pissed. Jack had considerable empathy for Sean's traumas and near-death life experiences and needed him to get things done on the ground. There was no one better at making things happen. No one quite like Sean who could turn his own scheming plots into reality and success. There were always risks that Sean would go off the edge of a cliff on operations - such was his fragile mindset. But Jack believed in him.

Jack took a moment to check his phone, while Sean blew bubbles into a covered plastic bottle through a plastic pipe. He was trying to raise his blood oxygen levels and improve his lung function by increasing their collateral ventilation. A tip that the young pulmonary doctor had shown him.

Jack watched the percentage oxygen rise to ninety-three percent and wondered how he'd break the news about Yelena to Sean. The least of his problems he thought. Jack tapped a few buttons on his smartphone and expanded the photograph that Sean had sent him from Menorca. He still couldn't shift the niggling thought that Swartz's surveillance operation may have been compromised by Sergei leaking information. And now Sean had provided him with first-hand evidence of Sergei and Dozich having served together in Afghanistan. This was not good. He needed to set a trap to see if Sergei would bite. Would he leak information to Dozich?

'There you go, I'm up to ninety-four percent already,' Sean muttered, breathing heavily now. 'We'll be out of here in an hour.'

'You won't. Now, are you up for it Sean? Do you want to take this on?'

Jack watched Sean roll his eyes, noticing that he was also grating his jaw. The tell-tale sign that Sean was feeling stressed.

'Look Jack. Let me be pretty clear about this. You can be an utter bastard at times, and don't for one moment think I can't see the guilt in your eyes. You're about to send me into the abyss, again aren't you?'

'I really don't know,' Jack calmly stated.

'Don't pull the fucking wool over my eyes Jack. I can tell when you're lying or stressed. You fiddle incessantly with that bloody tie of yours. Can't you ever dress down? Maybe just once in your life.'

'No, not really, and yes you're right I am stressed. This is too big to get it wrong. We're on the cusp of setting something up that is very bloody big.'

'So why don't you use someone else to do this next part?'

Jack felt a slight swell in his temple and began to feel feverish. He loosened his tie, as much to put Sean at ease, as well as give himself some air. He knew Sean would not be happy with the next part of his plan. 'Two reasons,' Jack began. 'Firstly, The Court does not quite have anyone of your calibre on the ground. Yes, we've got great intelligence officers, veterans with fine pedigree, but we don't have anyone with your skill set to conduct covert searches, gel a tech team in high threat environments, or charm the pants off an adversary when needed.'

'All in the name of plausible deniability eh Jack.' Sean started blowing into the bottle again. 'What's the second reason.'

'Ah, well…' Jack coughed. 'I've agreed it will be a joint operation with the French. You'll go into the desert with one of their agents.'

Sean looked startled and banged the bottle onto the overbed table. 'You're fucking kidding me? What the hell. This had better be good Jack, I only work well with my team and you know that.'

'I know, but it seems you've struck a chord or two with this one. It's your singing partner, Yelena.'

'Jesus Christ,' Sean shouted, before standing up and walking to the window, trailing the intravenous stand behind him. 'She's a French spy?'

'Well, yes. One of their agents they enlisted, and one we failed to recruit.'

'Bloody hell Jack, you've got some explaining to do here you know.'

'Yes, I know, but I thought I'd let her explain it all to you face to face. She'll be here soon, and she has really taken to you in a big way. You'll need to manage that. Before she arrives, I want you to read this note.

Jack handed a brown envelope with a single A4 sheet of paper in it. It was the most recent intelligence report compiled by The Court operators.

TOP SECRET STRAP 2 SIGINT UK EYES ONLY

For C/Ops Circulation only

Reference: C/Ops RF/248345

Intelligence Report: Operation BAMBARA

Andooha al-Saqahrawi *is the U.S.-designated leader of the ISIS-affiliated* <u>Islamic State in the Greater Sahara</u> *(ISGS). He was the former senior spokesman for, and self-proclaimed emir (leader), of the Sahara-based, Al-Qaeda-linked group al-Mourabitoun known as* "<u>The Sentinels</u>". *In May of 2015, Saqahrawi pledged al-Mourabitoun's allegiance to ISIS and its Caliph, Abu Bakr al-Baghdadi, urging "other jihadi groups to do likewise." Saqahrawi then split from al-Mourabitoun to form ISGS.*

*Saqahrawi is a member of the Sahrawi people, who are spread across southern Morocco, Mauritania, Mali and parts of Algeria. He is the former spokesman of Mali's Movement for Unity and Jihad in West Africa (MUJAO), formed in 2011 as an offshoot of al-Qaeda in the Islamic Maghreb (AQIM). In August 2013, MUJAO merged with Moktar Belmokhtar's al-Mulathamun (**"The Masked Men"**) Battalion - another AQIM offshoot—to form al-Mourabitoun. The group released a statement that the region's jihadist movement is "stronger than ever," and al-Mourabitoun would "rout" France and its allies in the region.*

<u>Assessment</u>: *Al-Saqahrawi is the glue that binds together all the ISIS and AQ factions and he has had considerable success in putting tribal competition to one side in order to create a cohesive force that can form the basis of the second Caliphate. Islamic fighters have now been trickling through to Mali from Syria, supported by funding and payments for fighters to join the new cause. The funding is assessed, with some degree of verification, as coming from Russian mercenaries who are paying the fighters and providing their reporting orders in Idlib.*

Support: We have credible weapons intelligence and HUMINT reports that suggest Al-Saqahrawi is being supplied with high-grade IEDs and telemetry from Russian mercenaries. We believe component parts that have been tracked and traced from Syria include explosively formed projectiles (EFPs) which will provide a considerable advantage to ISGS in attacks against French and G5-Sahel armoured vehicles.

Jack could see the wheels of cognitive thought rumbling through Sean's mind. He was grating his jaw even more now, to the extent that his cheeks were intermittently twitching.

'What's the plan then Jack?'

'In big brush strokes, you work with Yelena to make contact with a militant Tuareg called Mahani Al Traboun. He's a weapons broker who has been feeding Andooha al-Saqahrawi and can provide you with a market to sell a consignment of weapons that will cross the border into Mali courtesy of Dozich and Sir Rhys Eldridge.'

'Presumably you want me to get the evidence of these being sold on to ISIS then?'

'Yes, and then track them to their storage areas. Evidence from Dozich's computer suggests he uses a storage facility in Bourem. I want you to find where the weapons are coming from, where they're stored, link the evidential chain so we have attributability to Dozich, and then we'll take them down.'

'How?'

'Special Activities Division of the CIA and a few snippets thrown to the French to let them play on a small piece of the pitch.'

'Masterful as ever Jack. Sounds adventurous, that's for sure. I'll need backup, oh, and Jugsy and Phil 'the nose' to play in this team as well.'

'Of course. Now, how's your French?'

'It's got better, I've been living there for years now as you well know. How's Yelena's French?'

'Very good by all accounts, it seems she's been to the region before too. You'll need to extract that kind of information from her. She's trustworthy, motivated and quite capable.'

'But why do we need to use her?

'It's the only way the French would allow this to go forward. You see, we stood on their toes a bit, crossing into an operation they were running against Dozich too.'

'Shit. So that's how Yelena got involved and why we couldn't get much out of her. Something always struck me as being strange about her.'

'The French will be providing tracking cover using their Reaper unmanned aerial systems. They're fitted with laser-guided missiles which may come in handy when we want to take out the caches. The CIA will be available for tasking once you've collected the ground intelligence and have enhanced their teams on the ground. Laura has arranged that they'll be based at a forward operating site in Niger, with Charlie leading their teams.'

'A two-eyes operation then, with the French in play. We'll have to be bloody careful Jack, the French leak like sieves.'

'Exactly. Which is why you're going to gently coerce Yelena to fully switch to our side. We'll feed the French what they need, but we need her to feed everything to us from this point onwards. Have a chat with her when she arrives.'

'OK, I'm in. I assume you've got all the logistics sorted out?'

'Yes, you leave on Wednesday evening on a CIA flight from our HQ at RAF Bentwaters. Oh, and there's one more thing.'

'Go on.'

'One of your objectives is to kill the ISIS commander, Andooha al-Saqahrawi.'

Chapter 28

Private Clinic, Marylebone, London

Sean watched the door slowly open before Yelena stepped in to the private ward carrying a box of chocolates. He watched her smile and it looked as if she was blushing a little. Her long black hair looked immaculate with sweeping curls that he was sure she'd just attended to outside. Her piercing blue eyes hit him like a bolt.

Yelena wrapped her arms around Sean's neck so tightly he had to take a step back causing the cannula to rip the tape from his hand. It felt good to have her in his arms again, and she smelt divine.

'It's amazing to see you looking so well so soon,' she said rising on her tip toes. 'I missed you lots, and I was frightened to death you'd die in front of me.'

Sean felt an inner warmth as she kissed him tenderly. But he was also mired by the fact that she was a French spy and he'd soon be embarking on a mission with her. That made him immediately feel uncomfortable and confused about his feelings for her. He needed to find out lots more about her, separate truth from deception, and get a hell of a lot more comfortable trusting that this was the right way forward with the mission Jack had given him.

'Jack has told you right?' Sean asked.

'Told me what?'

'That we're doing a job together.'

'Yes, he did. Did he tell you about me?'

'He did, and I'm shocked.' Sean watched Yelena step away and take a seat on the end of the bed looking somewhat ashamed.

'I wanted to tell you everything Sean. From the very first time I met you in that room in Montepulciano. I was trapped from all angles: by my father, by the French, by very nasty people. But I didn't know who you were and if you were more of a danger to me than a friend.'

'Have you got any nicotine gum on you?' Sean asked. 'You know, the ones you always seem to have when you're stressed.'

'Yes, I've got vapes too. Shall we walk?'

'No, gum will be fine.' Sean popped a stick into his mouth not knowing what to say next. He walked to the window wheeling the intravenous stand behind him before opening it.

He took a moment to look at his phone. He noticed he had a text from 'One-eyed' Damon, a veteran friend who was the go-to man whenever Sean needed dubious work undertaken in London.

'Got your message. What are you doing in town? Have you fucked up again?'

Sean smiled and walked back to stand in front of Yelena.

'Look, there's some very bad stuff going down right now, and I know you're caught up in the centre of a lot of your own shit too. I need to know everything about you before I agree to take you with me.'

'I know, and I've told Jack everything too. I tried you know. I tried to tell you, and I tried to tell a British agent years ago, but no one ever contacted me again. That is, until a Frenchman latched on to me in a bar in Soho, and before I knew it, I'd been recruited by the DGSC. It was a relief to me. They trained me, they trusted me, and they set me to work against my father. They told me my information had led to convictions, but I never saw any evidence of that, and after a while they seemed to go quiet. I felt, and still feel it was right for me to do this. He's evil. A torturer that has left my soul in pieces. Surely you can see that.'

Sean could see the anguish in her eyes. Her body language, her fear and her vulnerability all came through in that one moment before he watched her cry. Here was a woman that had been used by everyone. Her father, his accomplices, his friends, his criminal gangs, and now the world of spy agencies. He sat beside her and gave her a hug.

'There's lots you don't know about me, but the one thing you need to know is that I do care, and I can see what's happened to you over the years. It's clear as day.'

Sean handed her a tissue and started to punch a text to 'one-eyed' Damon.

'Meet me in an hour in the blue posts, Fitzrovia. I need a job doing. Bring your drinking boots.'

Sean was beginning to form a plan in his head for two courses of action. Two simultaneous plans that needed some very careful choreography. He'd already checked where the emergency exits were in the hospital, and the best way to get back in late at night without being detected. One-eyed Damon was exactly the man he needed for two things. A kill. And a night out drinking beer.

'I wanted to show you this Sean. If you don't mind, I'd like to start here.'

'Sean took the sepia stained photo which had a few rips along its sides. It was a picture of three children and a mother sitting around a picnic blanket next to a river. There were two men sat at a bench behind them. They seemed to be drinking beer.

'I'm the smallest, the one in the front with a red dress and a headscarf on.'

Sean spent the next forty-five minutes listening to Yelena's story. It was harrowing. Either she was a highly trained spy providing yet more deception, or she was pouring out her heart to a man she finally felt she could trust. Sean instinctively knew it was the latter. And it brought a tear to his eye.

Sean studied her face. He loved her ebullience when they had spent their quiet time getting to know each other in Menorca, and he adored her resilience. She stood and walked around the room, advancing the story to London where she had been placed as a spy to trap the wealthy on behalf of her father.

Yelena was lifting his spirits after the drama of the last few days and he could see how she'd been abused through coercive control by everybody she'd ever lived and worked with.

'Tell me some more about this man here.' Sean held the photo in front of her pointing to the man sat opposite her father.

Yelena stood and walked to the window before turning. She wore white gold earrings which glistened from the sunlight pouring through the vertical blinds. 'A much younger Sir Rhys. They worked on oil security together in those days.'

Sir Rhys looked strong and fit, hardly anything he had seen of the man reflected the photograph of him smiling broadly with quite a tan. Sean began to wonder how much of this story she'd relayed to Jack and how much she'd only revealed to Sean. Normally, he'd have grilled Yelena in more depth, but he was feeling frustrated, hungry for a drink, and needed some time-out to think everything through.

'Can you pass me my jeans and jumper from the locker please? I find it hard to lean down at the moment.'

'Why, where are you going?'

'To meet a friend and get some thinking done. Come back in the morning and we'll talk some more. I need you to put my clothes in your bag and accompany me to the shower.'

Within fifteen minutes Sean had hailed a cab and was headed towards Fitzrovia.

Chapter 29

The Blue Posts, Fitzrovia, London

The taxi driver looked in his rear view mirror and told Sean all about the days of London's black cab drivers migrating out of the east end, and into the pleasant pastures of Essex. The driver, a portly man in his late fifties was pleased with himself. Sean had asked him how the trade was surviving with the online competition of Uber, and the man smiled before going into his lifelong story of how he'd saved wisely for retirement in the good old days. He only needed to keep things ticking over to make a living.

Sean admired the man's positivity, how he grasped change, and how he'd make sure his family would always be OK. His exchange brought back memories of how he had always wanted to be that family man himself, to play with his kids, and to sit around the dinner table telling stories of derring-do, but safely away from his manic world of risk and terror. It was never to be, he told himself, but he felt heartened that he did at least have a child he hoped to coach into his teenage years and beyond.

Sean asked the driver to drop him off at the corner of Fitzroy and Charlotte Street deciding that he needed a walk to test his lungs, and to do some thinking before he met with one-eyed Damon. He passed the man a twenty-pound note, telling him to keep the ten-pound change, wished him well in his retirement, and stepped out into the early evening sunshine. He had lots on his mind, and he felt drunk with all the goings-on of late, but one thing kept worrying him more than the others. The fact that Jack went into detail about Sergei being the likely mole in The Court gave him real cause for concern. Jack had planned to leak elements of this job to Sergei, and that put Sean in the firing line once again.

Jack was using a barium meal test: an espionage trick used to find the source of a leak where he'd feed each person in his organisation a slightly different piece of information, and would see who talked. Sean knew his mission would be the bait where Jack would issue everyone a piece of vital intelligence, and the double-agent, if he existed, would have to relay it back to the Russians. He'd then watch for their counteractions in the desert, knowing if it came, he'd realise exactly who the mole was.

Sean's knee was giving him a bit of gip as he strode gently down Charlotte Street, but he knew his own body, knowing it would be fine with some more ice and heat treatment, and that it would be good to go before he hit the deserts of Mali. He ramped up the pace and started deep breathing exercises to exhale as much carbon dioxide as he could from his damaged lungs. He felt good, the cold fresh air made him feel alive and motivated, though the sad words Jack had used in his meeting came back into his mind.

'I just don't get it Sean,' Jack had stated with a quivering hand. 'I have never ever, in all of my career and operations had a leak or a mole inside my teams.'

Sean had carefully studied Jack's demeanour and was surprised at his ashen face. He could see that Jack was genuinely in shock at the very thought that Sergei, The Court's top spy, whom he had recruited and mentored himself, could be the mole inside Britain's most ultra-secretive intelligence operation. It was the moment every spy dreaded, and it was written all over Jack's face. Total fear. Even with the mutual but professional friendship Jack had with Sean, there was always a distance that Jack kept, but his ice was melting now. In the past, Jack would never disclose anything more than was absolutely necessary. Yes, Jack had hidden plenty from him, yes, he had been at the mercy of a stream of nemeses because of it, and yes Sean knew that was the way it had to be. Sean had never liked it though - being kept in the dark, treated like a poisonous mushroom that would grow well in the dark, told of only the meagre details that he needed, and never trusted to be told the whole lock, stock and barrel that would have armed him far better for the jobs that had nearly had him killed on each and every occasion.

But this time Jack was opening up to him. Not about what he needed to fear most - Natalie on the rampage intent on killing them both. But fraught with worry over a mole at the heart of his beloved Court.

'Who else could it have been then?' Sean had asked realising the powerful emotion of knowing a traitor was within their midst.

Jack had acknowledged the question with a shrug and Sean could see he wanted to tell him more. Maybe for once he might just open up.

'You mustn't discuss this with anyone Sean, but it's not just Swartz that we've lost.'

'What do you mean?'

'Well, I'd been monitoring things for a long while before SCARAB came onto my radar, and before Swartz had been killed. I had an inkling something was going on, it was just a gut feel. So I checked and double-checked every operation I had on the go. Emails, reports, human intelligence, and I sat back looking at who we were communicating top-secret intelligence with.'

'And? Go on.'

'Well it gave me the shivers when I thought about it. We're a tight team of veterans Sean, loyalty running deep into our organisation, good people, heavily vetted with an ethical edge believing in what D had created. So you see, I think the core is safe. And we're bloody careful who we share information with, never disclosing our full hand unless it's necessary.'

'Oh, I bloody well know that Jack. I know what it's like to be treated like a second-class citizen not worthy of being given the full picture.' He watched Jack take a deep breath and throw his head back. This was a man who was suffering badly inside.

'I'm sorry about that Sean, but you can see why it's dangerous to give you too much.'

'I know. I'm still worried you told me where you drink in Marlow. And that could lead to serious danger with Natalie out there somewhere, ready to kill you. She won't just shoot you either. She'll make you suffer.'

Sean watched Jack shrug his shoulders and pass a hand through his hair. He had the beginnings of sweat dripping from his brow. 'Who else did you lose then? Who could it be if it's not Sergei?'

All of a sudden Jack opened up and Sean felt he'd never stop. 'We lost a scientist at the very heart of this operation Sean. An ISIS engineer who had been recruited by the Russians in Syria, before deploying him into Mali to set up a manufacturing operation. He was the Islamic State's top engineer who had set up manufacturing plants in Raqqa to convert weaponry and build attack drones. He was an important source that we had groomed through his family who live in Slough, and we had just agreed a deal with him to come over to our side in return for repatriating everyone back to Pakistan with a large sum of money. He was assassinated in Senegal, just as we tried to get him out.'

'Jesus, well that fucks up my mission then doesn't it. Who the fuck knows all this stuff? Who's in the know? Who's been passed this information?'

'Sergei gave us the connection from his contacts in the Russian SVR in Syria, so he obviously knew, and it was his lead for us to work on. He fed us the intelligence and we worked it. Exactly as the deal had been arranged. I always thought that it was a tight plan, but I think I'm wrong. Or am I? I really don't know anymore. I have the names of everyone who saw the details of both operations, who attended operational meetings, and I've checked them all, and checked them again.'

Jack now had his head in his hands and took his jacket off indicating that this would be a long meeting, and he needed someone to bounce his ideas off. It was a lonely furrow that Jack ploughed, and he needed a friend to talk it through with. Sean felt privileged that he'd been chosen. Sweat patches under Jack's armpits told Sean everything he needed to know. His entire raison d'être was at huge risk. 'And what have you come up with?' Sean asked passing Jack a glass of water.

'One possibility is Ryan Galloway. He's been used occasionally on Court operations for agent running where we have a need for experienced officers from D branch when we have too many things going on at once. He's a backup for us. Seemed like a safe pair of hands, worked on the SCARAB case from the outset, and ran a source that provided us with an insight into the operations of Le Cercle and Sir Rhys. I've got Samantha looking into him for me.'

'Samantha. Is she OK? She's gone very quiet on me for once. Probably still shaken up from the SCARAB task. She was lucky to get out alive.'

'She's fine now, but I wanted to keep her on light stuff for now, and investigating Galloway is perfect for her.'

'OK, who else then?'

'Apart from Sergei you mean? This is where it gets very tricky. And very political too. You see, I have no idea what happens when our intelligence is in the hands of the CIA.'

'Shit. That will be curtains for us if the leak is inside there.'

'Quite. Laura assures me it's tight within the Special Activities Division, but we were looking to bring more of their operators into the HQ. They're funding a lot of what we do you know.'

'No, I didn't know that, you don't reveal much at all about the setup, before today that is.' Sean appreciated the nod from Jack. 'Come on then, let's work this through right here and now. I need an assurance that my operation isn't compromised, and I can bring others into play where we need to smoke the bastard out.'

It took them both around twenty-five minutes to set the barium meal test. The trap to smoke out the mole.

Sean turned down a narrow alleyway next to the Newman Arms which was heaving at 5.30pm as the local high-tech crowds spilled out into the streets, heading for one of the many historic pubs in the village area. He kicked a can with some gusto as he thought back to Jack's hopes and fears.

He liked the idea to feed a snippet of intelligence to Sergei and Galloway as a test of their loyalty. And he appreciated that Jack had for once invested in him by telling him straight that he would be the lure. Dangerous, yes, but workable to trap the bastard if indeed it was either of them. It all became clear to Sean now after Jack had explained the potential significance of Sergei and Dozich serving together in the GRU, verified by the photo Sean had seen on the wall in Dozich's office. As for Galloway, he had a plan to find out more on him.

Sean glanced up at the immaculate pub sign that hung on two chains above the hostelry. He remembered a pub crawl with his father who had told him about the legend of the Blue Post pubs in

Soho, St James and Fitzrovia. The sign showed two blue posts that acted as the forerunners for taxi ranks. Sedan chairs could be hired from any location sporting an azure bollard and sure enough, the sign had a wealthy Georgian miss sat in the sedan chair being carried by two smartly uniformed men past the two blue posts.

Sean pulled the ornate wooden door by its brass handle to enter the pub and made for the bar. He ordered a pint of Sam Smiths bitter and scanned the room while he waited, as much to check the entry and exit points, as it was to check if one-eyed Damon was lurking in a corner somewhere. Two young men were playing darts in the corner, and a group of hipster nerds were gracing the central high table laughing and shouting at each other while taking selfies. Sean watched one of the youths who had started on the shots early and had begun to make an arse of himself with the arm hardly past 6pm.

As he turned to make his way towards a couple of high stools with a ledge, one-eyed Damon entered. A man mountain, with multiple scars on his face and a glass eye, he was hardly the most inconspicuous bloke to quietly enter any London bar scene, and the gang of hipsters went a little quiet when he walked past them. Sean heard one-eyed Damon speak a few words as he passed their congregation. 'Eh up laddies. I've got my eye on you lot.' The youths chuckled cautiously, not knowing what to make of a face that had seen the surgeon's blade on over a dozen occasions. Sean smiled and nodded towards the ledge. One-eyed Damon lifted his white stick indicating he'd grab a couple of pints at the bar and see him there.

One-eyed Damon placed his two pints of Sam Smiths next to Sean's single pint, retracted his telescopic pole placing it on the ledge, and gave Sean a beast of a man hug.

'You'll notice I have my drinking boots on which are double the size of your little ones,' one-eyed Damon said with a huge Yorkshire grin. 'You look fucked again mate, you been tortured or something?'

'Very fucking funny, but yes I have.'

'Really? Jeez.' One-eyed Damon had a look of concern knowing Sean didn't lie about such things.

'And I thought I'd had a shit time of it. Bloody hell.'

They chinked pints. 'What's been happening with you then mate?' Sean asked swigging a full half pint to get going.

'Oh, nothing much really. Normal shit except I just lost my box of eyes a week ago. Got pissed, hopped on the tube, then a train, and realised the next day I'd lost the box. I couldn't remember a fucking thing. Twelve eyes at £120 a pop pissed me off a bit to be fair.'

'Wow. And no one has found them yet?'

'Nope. Blind Veterans have been bloody great though, pushed out an all-points bulletin everywhere on social media, even got it on BBC news and web sites. Fingers crossed eh.'

Sean handed one-eyed Damon a photo. He watched him pull out a magnifying glass from his inside jacket pocket and begin to inspect the image with his stronger right eye. Sean admired the man immensely, and enjoyed drinking with him, though he could never keep up with the man's propensity for doubling whatever he drank. On the day of his injury, Damon had successfully rescued six of his colleagues whose vehicle had broken down in Iraq. As he was withdrawing from the area, he was hit by sniper fire. A bullet entered his left cheek and exited through his right, shattering both cheekbones, destroying his left eye and severely damaging his right eye. He was rushed to emergency treatment at nearby Basra Palace, where he was given a lifesaving tracheotomy to let him breathe before being airlifted by helicopter to the base hospital where he had the first of many operations to rebuild his face. His cheekbones and nose were reconstructed using titanium, his jaw broken and remoulded, and a prosthetic eye fitted. His favourite eye, Sean recalled, was his Yorkshire rose, closely followed by his Blind Veterans UK logo.

'Who is she?'

'Her name is Natalie Merritt, aka Anna Katchalyna. She's a former SVR illegal and a fucking sociopath who nearly killed me last week.'

'She looks nice mate, your sort too. Bet she tortured you with her knickers off eh?' One-eyed Damon snorted loudly as he laughed.

'Mate, she's a psychopath. Tried to bloody drown me and is now looking to kill my handler too.'

'OK, I see what's coming. Fifty percent up front cash, and I'll need to pay out for a few blokes on this one.'

'You don't even know what I want you to do.'

'Course I do. I can read you like a book. It's bloody obvious. Slot the bird whenever we find her, protect your handler in the meantime.'

'Close, but no cigar,' Sean said, watching one-eyed Damon sink his second pint. He noticed a man approach from behind him with a pint of beer.

'This is for you sir,' the middle-aged suit said quietly to one-eyed Damon. 'Thank you for your service. I've read all about you. Respect to you.'

'Thank you kindly, Sir,' one-eyed Damon said, making a gesture to tip his cap. 'You are a gentleman of gentlemen.'

'Did you serve too?' the man asked, looking at Sean. 'I'd be delighted to get you one too if that's OK?'

Sean was caught off guard. He'd never normally confess to such a question and would answer by saying he was an artist.

'That's very kind sir, but no I didn't. Damon is a rugby friend of mine. He was a bastard of a second row you know.'

'Ah, happy to oblige then, that's good enough for me,' the man said heading back to the bar which was by now getting very crowded.

'Nice place Sean. Now tell me what I missed.'

'I need you to keep an eye on a pub near Marlow. She's likely to head there to try and take him out, rather than risk it in town where he's better protected. She doesn't know what he looks like, but I'm sure that I gave her a good indication under duress, and the trouble is, he dresses the same every bloody day.'

'Well that's a bonus. Are you sure you can't remember what you said to her?'

'Not a bloody thing. Jack is careful not to set patterns with his routes into work, it's inbuilt into him, and he'll mix it up, plus in town he'll have minders watching his moves now that he knows he's a target of hers. But I worry about him and his family out in Marlow. She won't just kill him, she'll look to kidnap him and torture him first. Can you do this for me?'

'Of course I can. I'll use my Bulgarian mates for surveillance. They're disciplined and well drilled particularly if the money's right. This could go on for weeks though mate. I'll work out a day rate now.'

'That's fine, I'm going overseas for a while, but I'll keep in touch. No messing about, if you see her, take her down. Samantha will provide any intelligence we find on Natalie's movements, if indeed we ever get any. She's a sharp cookie so play safe.'

'Are you and Samantha not an item yet?'

'Nope. We're just good friends, as well you know.'

'She's still mad on you though, right?'

Sean nodded, thinking back to the times they'd both had on surveillance operations and the closeness they'd had on the Iranian operation the previous year. An accomplished SIGINT operator, Samantha was one of The Court's most seasoned ground operators and forever chasing Sean to marry her. He'd come close on many occasions in buckling to her charm, but each time he fought it off to go on yet another direction in his personal life.

One-eyed Damon pushed his beer glass to the side of the ledge which was immediately whisked away by the passing barman. 'OK, tell me more about this mad Russian woman,' he said in his serious Yorkshire tone. 'I need the full SP, no short-changing, and give me everything you have. We'll start tomorrow.'

Five hours later, Sean staggered back into the hospital, where the CCTV captured every step of his entry back into his private ward.

Chapter 30

London

Sean woke to a hazy view of his private ward in Marylebone with a thumping headache trying to remember what the hell had happened last night.

He groaned as he lifted his torso to reach for the jug of stale water which was too far to reach. A long groan. He had a rampant thirst and his face felt as if it had been through an orange squeezer. He cursed his stupid idea of having a full-on session with one-eyed Damon knowing such things always got too messy, and never ended up well.

He had a fleeting memory of being hauled out of a strip bar in Liverpool Street, but he wasn't quite sure if it was a dream. What wasn't a dream was the angry looking matron now stood over him pouring the water.

'You were a disgrace last night Mr Richardson and I've had a number of complaints you know?'

'Oh,' Sean said wheezing. 'I don't suppose you can give me a shot of morphine can you nurse?' He raised his head to see the redness filter down the elderly lady's face, fuming at such a quip.

'I have never in my career had anyone jump out of my hospital to go drinking and think they can return singing 'When the saints go marching in,' using a bedpan as a drum set. I have reported you to your boss and you are lucky we didn't call the police.'

'Oh shit - I'm ever so…' Sean couldn't get the words out before the nurse was berating him again in a raised voice telling him never to swear in front of her. He wasn't quite sure who was more fearsome - Natalie or Nurse Daphne. Sean made numerous apologies before she left, telling him the place stunk of alcohol, but that she was also a Northampton saints rugby fan. Sean was sure there was a glimpse of a smile on her face as she left.

'Thanks Matron,' I'll make it up to you one day,' Sean said, lurching onto his side to grab the water, closely followed by his phone. Shit. Fifteen text messages he'd rather not look at. He snuck a peek at one text from one-eyed Damon. A photo. A photo of Sean wearing a baseball cap straddled by two topless women and the text on the hat stating '*time to drink*' with the clock showing 9.30 and one-eyed Damon holding a shot of tequila to his mouth. He snorted, coughed up some phlegm and groaned again.

A couple of pints of water and a mixture of two Paracetamol and two Ibuprofen later, he had grabbed his clothes and discharged himself, apologising to everyone he met on the way out. His shame was only worsened by the ringing tune in his head that he couldn't get rid of. He started to mouth it as he hailed a taxi. *'Oh when the saints go marching in, I want to be in that number…'*

He quickly texted Yelena, explaining he'd meet her that evening before moving to Suffolk to catch their flight the following day. Then he texted Samantha. The only other person in London other than one-eyed Damon who would give him a place to recover for the day. He hoped she was in town knowing that she didn't live far from Millbank where she worked in her MI5 liaison role with GCHQ.

Samantha was a signals intelligence specialist. An expert surveillance officer, as well as a handy cryptographer. Sean had met her when she started her career in the Intelligence Corps in Northern Ireland. She had come a long way since those heady days of the nineties. Speaking five languages, with fluent Russian, she could also turn her hand to managing the logistics of any major intelligence operation with boots on the ground. She liked to be in charge too. She was a major asset to Jack's Court operations and played a massive role in collecting the SIGINT for each operation.

Sean wondered how she'd react to him again after the last job when he'd been rather too blunt in turning down her advances in a shared cabin they had on a luxury cruise liner conducting surveillance on a Pakistani nuclear scientist. They were great friends, but Sean had always felt hunted by her. Chased. Her quarry. He wondered now if she'd just tell him to leg it. One thing that generally remained the same between them forever, was that she liked to be the boss.

Just as that thought crossed his mind, a reply arrived from Samantha. *'I'm at the dry cleaners but working from home. Jack put me on light duties. I'm free in fifteen minutes. But not available.'*

Sean felt relieved. Though her last sentence clearly told him what she now thought of him. At least he could bunk down for the afternoon before heading to RAF Bentwaters. He was a bit confused though by the text. Samantha would normally wrap the text with kisses and emojis. Nothing on this occasion. Maybe she really was pissed off with him.

Ten minutes later, Sean stood at the base of the front door that led into her Georgian style townhouse on the outskirts of Victoria. He watched her approach the steps with her head down. She was looking weary. She was carrying some flowers which were dripping beads of water onto her tight-fitting black jeans, which were matched with a chunky cable-knit jumper. Sean always liked her in green. She looked up and threw Sean a smile. Not her normal one, that was for sure.

'Are you OK Sam?' Sean inquired sympathetically.

'No, not really, but it is nice to see you again.' She stepped forward and flung her arms around him. Ordinarily, Samantha would be beaming with life and her piercing green eyes would shoot out as if to touch Sean right on the chin. But her feisty and impish character had been dulled. Sean was worried about her.

'It's Swartz isn't it?' Sean said quizzically. 'Come on let's go and have a chat about it.'

Samantha made Sean a double espresso to settle his stomach, and having showered and taken another four pills, Sean sat down on the sofa with Samantha to walk and talk through what had happened to Swartz in Tuscany. It was clear she was still suffering the effects of post-traumatic stress, and she needed someone to talk to who knew Swartz as well as her. It became an afternoon of soothing and sorrow. An afternoon of sharing the burdens of forever being close to death, knowing one day it could come to either of them, or their beloved team members. Samantha seemed genuinely shocked that she'd been spared that day, and felt the guilt of a survivor. Guilt and shame that Sean knew all too well. They held hands for a while. As friends. The warmth of her hand reminded Sean of how they had become lovers for only a short while, but close friends forever. He wished he could make her life what she wanted of it with him, and she'd told him how she wished she could be different for him - their own silent guilt was shared between them by their own tight bond on the sofa that afternoon.

'Are you still investigating this case for Jack?' Sean asked, standing up to put the kettle on. 'I need to know everything you've found out before I depart tonight.'

'Where are you going?'

'Hasn't Jack told you?'

'No he hasn't. He's keeping everything very tight now, and made me his very own molehunter.'

'I know.'

'Oh? Jack doesn't normally share such details you know.'

'I know he doesn't, but in truth we're all suffering now Samantha. The whole team. Jugsy, Billy Phish, you, me, Phil and Jack - well, Jack is really suffering and opened up to me yesterday for the first time ever. Swartz was a part of us, the hub of the team. He feels responsible for his death and now he sees his own pride and joy in The Court about to implode. It's not good.'

'I know. I'm not sleeping well, and I know I should try harder, but it has given me time to get deep into the investigation.'

'What have you found out then?'

'Lots to be fair. I've been looking at this bloke called Galloway. D branch bloke. Works only occasionally for The Court. Once I targeted him and started a deep dive on him, it never stopped. I think it might be him. I think he's our mole.'

'How? Come on let's draw this up so I can work it through.' All of a sudden Sean got the sensation he craved. A chance for revenge maybe? To get the bastard who had set Swartz up for his murder?

Samantha led Sean to the large white oak dining table and began to draw on an A3 piece of paper her own intelligence picture that she had gathered through hacking, SIGINT, and surreptitiously loading a piece of malware onto Galloway's private phone. She explained to Sean how she'd done it. She'd sent him a

WhatsApp message with a video purporting to be a video of a new terrorist drone dropping bomblets. She knew he was fascinated with the techniques of ISIS, and she'd said she had just seen this on open source media from twitter. He opened the file and bam! The malware was downloaded onto his phone and she then had access to all his WhatsApp files.

'You'd have thought a seasoned spook wouldn't have fallen for it, but he did.'

'Great work Sam. And?'

'Well you know he's indirectly linked to Sir Rhys, right?'

Sean didn't disguise his surprise. 'What the hell? No, I bloody well didn't.'

'Jack didn't tell you?'

'I think he bloody well forgot. Or decided, like he does, to keep that nugget from me.'

'He probably thought you'd go and slot him straight away,' Samantha said knowingly. 'Jack doesn't want to move on him until I've got more evidence that incriminates him, and not until I verify the link to Sir Rhys. He's not yet convinced it's him. But it is. I know it. And this is why.' Samantha drew another circle. She named it FCO Dan.

'You see Sean, Yelena was shagging this bloke. Mid-forties, right in the heart of the FCO.'

Sean tapped at the circle right on the word Dan. 'But why?'

'I thought maybe you could tell me that seeing as you've been getting pretty bloody friendly with her too.' Sean felt the heat of Samantha's piercing finger stab right into his solar plexus. Then it came again. A long finger. Hard jabs.

'How'd you know?'

'I was the case officer for this operation, that's how. I know everything there is to know now about this operation. Except the next phase, which Jack has demanded is kept very tight hold. Just so you know.'

Sean felt as if he'd just been delivered a left hook to the chin, followed by one of Samantha's high heels right into his heart. The intensity of Sam's gnawing face told him everything he needed to know. She was pained. She was jealous. And she hated him for not loving her. He wondered when the next knockout blow would be delivered. She had all the answers.

'Dan the man is a grade two senior civil servant and Policy Director who reports solely to the Minister of State for the Middle East and North Africa. The minister's nickname is Hoover, Jack tells me it's because he charms everyone of any importance in the FCO into his own social party clubs. His real name is Vincent. He's also responsible for national security, defence and international security - so he's a key target for espionage. As his Policy Director, Dan the man was clearly the target for your young lady to extract secrets, but for why, I don't quite know. All I know is that the hacks and texts I've seen all state that he was her lover. She was milking him for secrets.'

Sean wondered if Samantha knew she was a French agent too when he lined up his next question. 'Well, I know she was acting for her father to lay men, and get their secrets, if that's what you mean. She was also a lover of the murdered civil servant and that was a good way in. I assume you think she was milking Dan and he was in turn providing information from the offices of this bloke called Hoover? And Hoover is a close friend of Sir Rhys, so there's a bit of a serious link here. Probably the twenty-one-club.'

'Mmmm. That's how I see it. But something is a bit odd. Jack has implicitly told me not to go too deeply into Hoover. I think Jack is using compartments on this mission. I've only been given specific authority to target certain people using SIGINT and cyber tactics, but I think Jack has someone else in another compartment looking at both ministers. A bit odd eh?'

'Not so odd given the ultra-secrecy of this. You know how Jack schemes up his plots and then puts each of us in tight compartments, so that only he has the full aggregation of the intelligence.'

'True, but I think he's panicking now with the mole issue. It might be clouding his judgements. I could easily wrap all of this up if I had wider authority to infiltrate who I want.'

Sean pondered her wise words. What exactly was Jack up to? He and Samantha were getting close to putting together the full puzzle but there were one or two vital pieces missing.

'It's curious I agree,' Sean said squeezing his chin. 'But tell me, how's this all now linked to Galloway, your suspected mole in MI5?'

'Simple. Galloway is gay. And Dan the man is his lover. Dan was batting on both sides.'

'This is all now beginning to make sense. Sir Rhys is the current Minister of State for the FCO responsible for Europe and the Americas. And we can easily assume he's good friends with your Hoover minister who between them could easily influence British export sales into African nations. British weapons exports for example destined for an end-user like Nigeria, Ghana or Sierra Leone …'

'Which never ever arrive into those countries but instead are diverted into some other African state,' Samantha chipped in finishing the sentence.

'Like Mali for example.'

'Bingo.'

'And what's more,' Sean proffered, 'Sir Rhys could easily introduce a lady like Yelena into the mix at cocktail parties to trap the likes of Dan the man, bed him, sex him up for months on end, and extract secrets that could be passed to foreign states.'

'Or serious organised criminals like Dozich who is operating as a proxy for the Russian GRU.'

Sean's brain went into overdrive as he tried to figure it all out. He stood, clasped his injured knee, and walked around the table trying to warm the muscles. 'Bloody hell, you're right. This is messy and very murky. Deep foreign office murky. It seems Sir Rhys is the kingpin, acting as the conductor of the opera enabling secrets and weapons to be passed indirectly to the Russian cause and their mercenaries. All the while making a fortune but remaining hidden behind his ministerial cloak. A hive of traitors.'

'Indeed,' Sam said passing Sean a vape which he appreciated. 'I can see how Yelena has been played, used, and told to pass everything back to her father via secret runners. The hacks and texts show me that. But why did Galloway get involved? Risking his MI5 career and pension when he retires next year.'

'Easy. Money and wealth,' Sean suggested. 'I'd imagine he was promised entry into the twenty-one-club somewhere along the line. Probably when he retired.'

'Well that does fit with what I've found. He had a stash of cash in a number of bank accounts which I need to complete some checks on, just to verify its provenance.' Samantha paused scribbling on the paper. 'I'd say that Dan the man may have offered him the deal on behalf of one of the ministers. It certainly looks that way as Galloway had lots of cash periodically ploughed into a Zurich account which I've traced. For me, it looks like Galloway gave this information to Dan the man, who gave it to Yelena. It's still not solid at all, but the links are there.'

'Exactly. Let me see if I've got this right,' Sean mulled. 'Galloway knew about SCARAB meeting his people in Tuscany and then he told Dan the man in the FCO, his lover. Maybe they were all part of Hoover's and Sir Rhys's syndicate? I don't know. Either way, the only legitimate way that Dozich would have found out, is if Dan the man told Yelena. Probably after they'd had a sugar daddy shag, right?'

'It's plausible yes. The only man who knew Swartz would be leading the surveillance with me, would have been Galloway. The only route for that information to get to Dozich would have been from Yelena, who would have been told about the Tuscan meeting by Dan the FCO man.'

Sean was mesmerised by the depth of the deceit. Two cabals fighting against each other, both with ministers and intelligence officials, one trying to knock the other off, and the link to the Russians and their mercenaries all via Yelena's father: Goran Dozich. And he was linked to Sergei, Jack's top Russian spy. Sean's head was spinning as he began to draw all the connections on the piece of paper.

'OK, I've heard enough. Here's what we do. We need to protect Jack as this has already gone too far. I can't allow anything to jeopardise the next phase in Algeria and Mali. No leaks. Where does this bloke Galloway live?'

Sean watched Samantha go white with fear. 'You can't Sean. You simply can't.'

'I bloody well can - and I bloody well will.'

'But Jack has got all this lined up to take them down one at a time. You know what he's like. He's thought it through like a top-class piano tuner.'

'I know. And I know what his end game is. And his route to it. Trust me, doing this will not harm that plan and I need it as an insurance for what he's tasked me to do next. Show me where he lives, and I'll get one-eyed Damon on the case.'

Chapter 31

Algeria

Sean felt the Toyota Landcruiser lurch lazily to the right as he shifted down a gear to get more traction across the shallow sand dunes of the Algerian desert. He checked the four-wheel drive was still engaged, dropped the revs a little, then slammed the accelerator to speed quickly across the fractured crust of the sun-drenched sand.

He watched the white vehicle ahead of him bank to the right before it entered a small ravine. Using all his efforts and concentration, he tried to steady the juddering of the steering wheel to stay in the vehicle tracks, before gently navigating the lip of the sand cornice to roll gently into the broad gully.

The four-vehicle convoy was heading south towards the Mali border, deep into the unchartered territory of the Sahara, and skilfully navigated by his escorts: Tuareg tribesmen who had been paid a handsome sum to protect Sean, Yelena and Phil Calhoun from the many threats of attack across the ungoverned area of the Sahel.

The Sahara is the largest hot desert in the world, and the third largest desert behind the cold deserts of Antarctica and the Arctic. It's one of the harshest environments on earth, covering nearly four million square miles, and its name comes from the Arabic word ṣaḥrā, meaning 'desert'. Sean was mesmerised by the beauty of the landscape, safe in the knowledge the convoy was being monitored from above by a French unmanned aerial vehicle, all part of the deal Jack had hatched with the French DGSG. Jugsy had been dispatched to a joint French and US airbase in the Sahel where the imagery analysts were based. He'd act as the ground liaison officer relaying situation reports to Jack and the CIA teams that Laura had assigned to the mission. Sean had been informed that the Special Activities Division could react to any incidents he encountered within less than thirty minutes, but he dismissed that as simple comfort talk to keep him on-side.

The mission that Jack had given him was complex and highly risky. Make contact with Mahani Al Traboun, a militant Tuareg acting as a weapons broker feeding weapons into the ISIS commander Andooha al-Saqahrawi, deliver Dozich's weapons consignment, then track and trace where the weapons are being stored with the intent of destroying them. Jack made it all sound so bloody simple, but this was an odyssey fraught with danger: multiple jihadi groups vying for control across the Sahara, and Russian mercenaries with embedded spies within the militant groups, ready to assassinate any outsiders who became a threat to their mission. A bullet in the back of the head, with no discussion, was a simple outcome that Sean was alive to. Phil had been tasked with collecting forensic evidence on the weapons and the IEDs, and Yelena was the bolt on he really could do without. What the hell was Jack thinking? He couldn't reconcile the story that the French had demanded she was part of the mission, it didn't make sense to him. Unless Jack was hiding something from him again?

Sean revelled in travelling in some of the most remote parts of the world and the Sahara Desert was no different. It made him feel alive, living life right on the edge, and a challenge that he lived for: high-risk adventure. He'd been told that it was too dangerous to follow the regular border crossing into Mali, and his minders were taking him on a circuitous, but little known smuggling route that skirted any areas of conflict or checkpoints manned by militant tribes seeking to dominate the territory. Kidnappings were rife for the unwary, as were ambushes on lone vehicles and even large convoys. Life had little value out here, but smuggling drugs, weapons and women was where the top dollar was made.

The vehicle ahead of them skidded in the sand before slowing and coming to a halt in a deep sand basin between three rolling dunes. Sean watched a tall Tuareg step out of the passenger seat and wave an arm signifying for Sean to slow down. He then raised a clenched fist four times, releasing his fist and spreading his fingers, to signify they'd take a twenty-minute break.

The Tuareg warrior was Mahani Al Traboun, but his friends called him Maku. He was a thirty-six-year-old veteran of many battles who was born in the oasis sands of Tamanrasset in southern Algeria. He was a man who was equally at home in the cities of Marseille and Nice where he had a penchant for purchasing expensive watches and jewellery in return for the large wads of dollars that had been thrust into his hands for the work he accomplished across the desert. Sean had been introduced to Maku in Algeria by a French agent who acted as a trusted facilitator for The Court, and the man who had vetted Maku for this task, with the final approval of Jack. The agent explained that Maku's desert wealth had come from connecting people, selling information to the French, and on occasion helping MI6 for the covert extraction of agents.

Maku was also an insider that the French had nurtured to pay for information on a new charity that had set itself up across all the towns and cities of Mali. The Islamic charity, known as Al-Farouk, had been channelling millions of dollars a year from donors in the Gulf Arab states and Turkey to open mosques, Koranic schools and health clinics in rural areas starved of social services. Maku had explained that these charities and other groups were there to push an enduring hard sell on the stricter Wahhabi school of Islam that inspired Al-Qaeda and Islamic State-affiliated militants, who were creating chaos across the region as AQ and ISGS grew exponentially each year. Sean could see this was becoming a tipping point for the region and needed intervention on a much larger scale than his own mission could ever achieve - but this mission was Jack's catalyst for a much deeper involvement from the Americans. It felt strange to him, that he was forging a route that could see the course of history change within weeks.

'We need you to change into local dress,' Maku exclaimed with a beaming smile. 'This is the most dangerous part of the journey and there are plenty of people who will be watching our travels.'

Sean liked the man. He had a quiet, confident charm about him, and he was anything but overbearing. Maku was dressed in a traditional Tuareg *bubus*, a flowing gown that had been dyed in striking azure blue, the same colour as his headwrap called a *cheche*. Sean watched Maku prepare the *cheche* that he would wear himself. A long flowing headwrap whose fabric was about eighteen feet long and designed to provide protection from the sun as well as help conserve body water by limiting sweat.

As Sean completed his new disguise, he felt a sense of security in the confinement of such splendour. Maku tossed a few silver bracelets on Sean's wrists, and topped him off with a set of distinctive sunglasses.

'You look like a sartorial king of the desert,' Maku said, pleased with his work. 'As good as any power suit you wear in London my friend.'

'I like it. Can you show me how I pull it across my face?' Sean asked, checking his image in the blacked-out windows of the Toyota.

'Easy. Here pull this. You should know that when two Tuaregs meet in the desert for the first time, we use our fearsome and anonymous image by covering our entire face with the free end of the *cheche,* so only our sunglasses show.'

'Brilliant. This works well for this job, that's for sure.'

'When we meet as strangers, we start with a handshake. Three fake out touches followed by a firm grip. Only after a few minutes of traditional greetings perhaps talking of our livestock and our wealth, can we establish who is the more eminent.'

'What happens then?'

'The more powerful man will remove this portion of the headwrap showing his mouth.' Maku grasped the end of the headscarf, placing it across Sean's chin. 'With this act of exposing the lower part of your face, things are then allowed. We can then talk and barter. I've always been the most powerful,' Maku said, laughing loudly into the light desert wind.

Sean took a bit of time to walk around the dune basin getting used to the robes. The wind was sweeping through the dunes causing the most amazing sounds. 'The songs of the desert have many verses my friend, and the most expressive is made by the wind,' Maku had philosophised when they had first met. Sean felt the dunes were making their own sounds. Their own hums, their own whispers, like a finely harmonised violin quartet. He respected the singing sands that provided him with an imagination of life and images of the Tuareg legends that had walked before him. He sat for a few moments on the crest of a dune and sketched a quick and simple painting of the warriors, the vehicles and his surroundings. He'd turn it into a painting one day.

'Come on Sean,' came the shout from below him. 'Work to do my boy, guns to sell and bombs to find,' Phil shouted. Sean couldn't help but laugh at his boxer's nose that defined his odd image. Phil 'the nose' was now dressed in a slightly greying set of gowns, with a black *cheche*.

'Get the map out, Sean shouted down the hill. 'I'll be there in five minutes and I want to know everything about the next part of the route.'

Sean started to complete his sketch of an armed Tuareg warrior who was stood on the furthest dune, a small sandstorm swirling around his torso that was gliding gently up into the thermals of the hot desert air. His concentration was broken by two fully adorned Tuareg women breaking cover from behind the last vehicle. He looked closer at the first female. It was Yelena. As he skidded down the dune getting closer to the vehicles, he could make out more clearly what she was wearing.

'You look stunning,' Sean said, taking his sunglasses off to admire her striking new look. She wore a deep indigo headdress and robe that was accompanied by a gold necklace with three patterned plates that sat astride her décolletage. The vintage Tuareg necklace had tribal charms hanging from the plates, completing the image of a woman of high caste nobility. The expensive designer sunglasses added the final touch.

'I'm impressed you brought your woman here to negotiate with the brokers,' Maku said tapping Sean on the shoulder. 'We are a matriarchal society, and our society is run by women. Women of power and wealth.'

'I didn't know that. Will it help?'

'Oh, it will. Especially with this gorgeous woman leading the talks. We love our women and they never ever wear the veil. It is we men who cover up.'

Maku passed Sean a small glass of tea before proudly explaining the ways of the Tuareg, and how their women are powerful and revered. 'Tuareg women have great privilege. Their private parts are unharmed, their childhood free from marriage, and their husband's dowry and tent is entirely their prerogative. As is divorce, which unlike our middle eastern neighbours, they can call for. Tuareg women are also free to flirt and do so without fear Mr Sean. They can of course also have sexual relations outside of marriage, and similar toleration is given to us.'

'I really like your people and your culture Maku,' Yelena chipped in politely. 'Your wife told me how men have the social and political positions, but it all rests on female patronage that can easily be retracted.'

'That is very true Miss Yelena. But sadly, things are changing, and we fight, my men fight, and our women fight to preserve our way of life. You see, we rebel against any colonisation whether from the French or from ISIS. Now the Islamist foreigners want to hijack our lands into a Shariah governed state. We are slowly being dragged into a patriarchy that our women have never before seen.'

Maku paused to point across the dunes towards Mali, the smile long gone. 'You will see over there, where we are going, our women are being forced to wear veils, banished from the political sphere, stripped of their ancient privileges and prerogatives, and punished for their sexual lifestyle in a way that kills our soul.'

Sean put a hand on Maku's arm. 'Thank you for telling us this Maku. You are a fine man and I only hope that some of our work can help you for the future. It will be a long struggle, but I sense a change is coming.'

'I hope so Mr Sean. Now, let me explain what we do from here.'

Maku coaxed them around a map which had been spread out onto the bonnet of the Landcruiser. He took a pencil from his *cheche*. 'The route I will take is an old caravan route which follows a string of reliable wells, while we avoid the larger sand seas and some checkpoints of the Islamic State in the Greater Sahara.'

'Have you used this route lately,' Phil chipped in. Sean could see he was wary about patterns being set that would give the desert terrorists an advantage.

'Not for a long time,' Maku replied pointing to his eyes. 'I have many people who just watch the traffic moving through the desert and I know which ones are the safest to get you to Bamba. Just like a hundred years ago, the safest routes change according to political alliances and the activities of fighters who will either offer to guide a caravan across the desert for a fee, pillage it, or do a bit of both. Remember, we are entering a war zone with many enemies now.'

Sean took a moment to study Maku's face. It had a few small patches of blue dye on his dark skin from the fabric of the headdress, and his steely eyes showed a level of confidence he had seen before in seasoned warriors. Sean felt he was amongst good fighting men with a leader who exuded strength and conviction.

'How long is the drive Maku?' Sean asked, keen to keep an eye on the navigation throughout the journey.

'Two full days. If the weather and the Gods are good to us.'

Sean watched Maku point out the circuitous journey that took them from Algeria right into the heart of the Sahara through the Mali regions of Kindal and Gao. Sean noticed the text on the map was in French, but more curious for him, was the straight-line border on the map which had no feature on the ground that it could physically represent - yet it ran for 750 kilometres from Mauritania before dipping southwards at the 21st parallel towards Niger. The scramble for Africa by European powers in the 1880's had seen the French finally draw that line on the map in 1909 as part of the Niamey convention that delineated French Sudan, now Mali, and French Algeria.

As the sun was approaching its apex, the convoy set off for the border, crossing without any trouble, before making headway into the deepest part of the desert. Maku was navigating by knowledge with the backup of a Magellan GPS receiver but Sean was taking no chances. He started to draw the route on a blank piece of paper using a technique he had been taught many years ago at the Royal School of Military Survey. A desert navigation skill called dead reckoning. He trusted no one and he never trusted hi-tech equipment which could fail at any time, so he always went for the belt and braces of reversionary mode skills, just to keep an edge. He fondly remembered his days of being taught desert navigation by an unconventional gentleman called Boris Borkowski. A British Royal Engineer of Polish descent who had taught him astro-navigation by aiming a theodolite at the sun and stars, and steering a course through the sands using a Coles sun compass - a large silver instrument that was used by the British Long Range Desert Group in the second world war.

'I love the generosity of the Tuareg,' Yelena said tapping Sean's knee enjoying her time driving. 'All this power for the women, it's something I never thought I'd see.'

'Well, get this. Maku told me that it's a matri-lineal society which means the families trace their lines through the women, rather than the men, right the way back to their first Queen. Some family tree eh?'

'Probably why their welcome is legendary. They never forget to offer water, and visitors always seem to be treated like royalty.'

Sean drew a line on his blank map. By monitoring the speed and bearing that they were travelling on, he was able to estimate his position relative to where they had started from. 'Talking of lineal ancestry, you have a lot of stuff to tell me that you've kept to yourself.'

Sean watched Yelena's face tighten as he changed his tone to start probing her. He sensed the nervousness in her reply.

'What do you mean? I've told you everything, you know I have.'

'I know you haven't. There's a lot I've found out about you that I know you hid from me. I don't like that one bloody bit.'

'Like what?'

'Like you travelled to Ghana a few months ago.'

Sean kept looking at her face as the silence drew them both into an impasse. Yelena looked back and forth at him struggling to maintain her concentration. He left it for a while knowing she would eventually talk. He'd landed the hook, and it was up to her now to explain herself. He needed to be fully sure she was batting only on one side, and not for her father anymore.

'I suppose you got all that from checking my DNA,' she eventually said with a croaky voice.

'Kind of. Carbon thirteen actually.'

'I don't know what to believe or who to trust anymore Sean. I took a DNA test myself to check my ancestry. The results shocked me. Horrified me in fact.'

'Why?'

Sean noticed the tears in her eyes as she replied fretfully. 'He's not my father. It's not him. I don't know who my father is.'

'What do you mean. How can you be sure?'

'The DNA tests don't correlate to my father. Goran Dozich is not my dad, and I have no idea who is.'

'But your mother…'

'Is definitely my mother.'

'But how did you test your dad's DNA?'

'My French handler told me how to do it. We collected it from his used tissues, and a few dried blood stains on his shirts. They've linked him to various murder scenes with it, and I found out we are not linked at all, in any way. Not through any family lineage.'

'Bloody hell. Have you asked your mother who your father is?'

'No. She passed away sixteen years ago. I'm frightened. I'm frightened he'll find out too and come after me.'

Sean took a moment and fired up a vape. 'I'm sorry about your mother and don't worry, you'll be safe now. What about Ghana? You need to tell me everything about your work with the French and your father. Sorry, I mean Dozich.'

'I travelled with him to Ghana. He wanted me to help on a deal he was striking with a Ghanaian General. I'd been told to sing for him at his Embassy in London, befriend him, then suggest he met with Dozich in Paris for mutual business benefits.'

'Do you remember his name?'

'General Boateng?'

'Oh, great, there's hundreds of those in Ghana's Army. Bloody hell.'

'His nickname was General Elvis.'

'That's better. Certainly distinctive. Did Dozich make you sleep with him?'

'No, thankfully I managed to avoid that. But he took the bait and met with him.'

The link to the General fitted with what Sean and Samantha had suspected, and he began to believe that Sir Rhys and Minister Hoover were the link men to the deal Dozich was working on with the Ghanaians. Balkan provenanced weaponry coming into

Ghana, and then onwards into Burkino Faso, and then Mali. He probably had deals with both nations. He couldn't be sure.

The deal that Jack had arranged as part of the plot, involved a Nigerian General who would ensure the consignment Sean had in the convoy vehicles, was registered as being for Nigerian military end-use.

'There is one other thing I haven't told you yet. And I'm sorry I didn't mention the General before,' Yelena added.

'Go on. I'm all ears for the next two days and you're going to tell me everything.'

'I think I've fallen in love with you.'

Chapter 32

Bamako, Mali

President Abel sat at the head of the table in the long room of the Presidential Palace which bestrode limestone cliffs overlooking the centre of Bamako. It was just past eleven in the morning and his future as the head of state of the beleaguered country sat in the hands of his guests.

Lining both sides of the conference table sat several foreign Emirs who had been dispatched to sell a story and extort a nation. The President knew he was in the last months of his seven-year reign and had very few strong cards left to play as he sought to roll back a jihadist insurgency and mounting public discontent. The failure of Mali's poorly equipped and demoralised military had now sparked an outcry, shaking confidence in President Abel's government. It was only a matter of time before he was overthrown in a military coup - and his guests knew that.

His only aide that morning sat at the end of the conference table. His military friend and army General, the ageing but legendary warrior of the battle of Gao in 2012, now a sliver of his former self.

A grey suited man sat to the left of Abel and it was he who had requested the meeting on behalf of his government. It was clear he was in no mood to deal in small talk. Grey suit was the Head of the GRU assigned to lead all mercenary operations on the African continent, and Mali was top of his list for bringing them to heel. He wore a black patch over his right eye, a legacy of recent times where he had been shot in Syria, unluckily from a ricochet from one of his own soldiers in the close confines of street fighting in Kobane against Kurdish forces.

The grey suit adjusted his eyepatch which caused him some discomfort to wear. He frowned. He waited for complete silence. 'We cannot allow your government to continue its own suicide,' he began. 'We will now prepare our formal engagement to save not just your Presidency, but your life. Of course, Mr President, this is not a request, but an order.'

The silence that followed that statement was only broken by the next comment from a man who spoke with a quiet confidence. Goran Dozich explained to the President that this was his very last chance to save his life, his legacy and the life of his youngest granddaughter who was now being entertained by two of his strongmen in her mother's home a few kilometres away.

'Your granddaughter wishes to talk to you Mr President,' Dozich said, passing the phone which had its Skype app open.

The picture of his seven-year-old granddaughter being held by a Russian foreigner caused Abel to gag. His friend at the end of the table had a face of thunder, wishing he'd never ever invited this man Dozich to help him supply arms to his army.

President Abel pushed the phone back to Dozich and placed his hand on his heart. 'The deal will be done, and so long as you remain my guest, I would ask you to honour my word, and honour my loyalty to this nation. What I ask for is very simple. I remain in power for five years, my family remain untouched, and you support the wishes of my Generals to ensure our army remains in control.'

The grey suit shuffled in his chair. He scratched his shaven head. The gold cufflinks told Abel everything he needed to know. His guests would rape and pillage his country of its gold and diamonds, but he no longer had a choice. Better to stay in power and find a way to salvation, than die a besieged President and watch a nation die through jihadism. Maybe these people could stop those Gulf states peddling their version of extremist Salafism into his country, maybe their culture could be preserved. Or maybe he was being tricked? He sensed that the Russians would let the northern Badlands go to the jihadis, whilst they protected the enclaves of the south where the country was rich in its mineral wealth.

'My president wishes this to be a formal agreement, a treaty, and an enduring friendship Mr President,' grey suit announced. 'We will provide your army with hardware, good quality clothing for your soldiers, a regime of looking after their families, and we will provide technical support and military advisors on the ground. My officer here, Mr Dozich, shall remain here to make it so.'

Abel nodded and shuffled the papers in front of him. 'I have read this agreement in detail, and I will agree if you double the military advisors and weapons at our disposal. I need large acts of retribution to stop this war and push them back to the Middle East. They are engineering a new Caliphate and that must be my single aim. To stop it being the cancer of our nation.'

'We will see. I shall relay your messages to my president's emissaries and ministers. But you must agree to the brokering of your gold and diamond mines into our hands as a share set out in the treaty. We may be able to help you save your cities and perhaps in the longer term your nation. This will not be a quick victory, but we will protect you, your Generals and your presidency so that there will never be a military coup against you.'

'You may start that process now. We need help quickly.'

'A fine assessment. Mr Dozich will work with your Generals and start bringing a small cadre of his men into the capital, and we shall commence the supply of the weapons and training to the Presidential guards.'

The ageing president nodded again and looked across the table to his friend for his agreement. The General was now in a state of emotional rage. The President watched his friend of five decades slowly stand, raise his pistol, and with a shaking arm, aim it at the grey suit. Milliseconds later, Dozich had beaten the elderly General to the draw, and pumped a single shot from his Makarov pistol right through his heart.

Chapter 33

Sahara Desert

Empty field myopia is a condition where the horizon blurs away into the distant sky, where the eyes have nothing specific on which to focus. This results in them focussing automatically at a range of nothing more than a few metres ahead. Dangerous for aviators, and more so for desert travel, especially when you're following a vehicle which has disappeared into an indistinguishable horizon.

Sean had begun to witness this curious phenomenon and helped Yelena focus on the sands by flashing a strong beam of torchlight about ten metres ahead of them. 'Your eyes get tricked into going into a resting state,' Sean shouted above the hum of the engine. 'If you haven't got anything to simulate the lens, they go passive and retract to focus just ahead of you.'

'This is bloody frightening,' she replied trying hard to stabilise the bouncing cab, and at the same time focus on the beam of light ahead.

'Just relax, I'll tell you when to shift focus if we see the vehicle come back into view.' Sean provided a running commentary to keep her sharp. He shouted out the number of handspans to turn the wheel and provided strict instructions for her to keep at a steady twenty-five miles per hour, telling her to speed up or down as necessary. They had started the afternoon with a deep blue sky, yellow sands and the vista of occasional rock bushes, but had soon transited into the deep orange hues of the Malian desert where the wind whipped up the sand to create the condition of virtual blindness.

Sean had fought to stay alert, but it wasn't an easy battle. Mile after mile of nothing but sand and empty field myopia amidst the monotonous hum of the engine, all worked against him to dull his senses. His eyes grew heavy, and a dream-like state came over him before he nudged himself back to reality. They travelled in silence for the next twenty minutes or so, praying that the horizon would come back into view and lift them out of one of the most mesmerising experiences he had ever experienced. He heard the melodic tunes and songs of the desert again, battling for prominence over the hum of the vehicle.

Fifty minutes later the haze began to lift a little, and Sean heard Maku's booming voice across the VHF radio. 'Make your way to the following grid reference. We'll have to stop for the night.'

Sean couldn't see further than forty odd metres and he didn't know how far apart each vehicle was in the convoy. But to his amazement, when he arrived at a small rock outcrop, every single vehicle was there, and a small fire was burning in the middle of the pack. It was close to 6pm and the sun was barely visible through the desert smog and he reckoned it was only a handspan from falling over the horizon. An hour maximum.

The chill had begun to set in by the time Sean watched the activity around the fire and a cold breeze greeted him as he stepped out of the vehicle. He smelt the smoke of charcoal and heard patches of conversation, pausing to take in the scene of five or six men, their indigo *cheches* wrapped around their heads, chatting with glasses of tea around the fire. Maku had posted three guards covering a 360-degree arc around the RV point, and Sean wondered if the unmanned aerial vehicle could see them through the smog. He didn't know it, but Jugsy was instructing a French imagery analyst to zoom in on Sean as he walked across the small dip towards the fire. Jugsy had been tracking them across the desert, and now had a perfect view of the stationary convoy using the infra-red and radar payloads in the French Reaper's nosecone.

Sean was tired, a little narky from the journey, and could eat a horse. His stomach never betrayed him. And he was never fussy about food to keep it happy. He spotted two of the Tuareg warriors carry the carcass of a goat to the open fire and watched them hack off the meat in large chunks using a machete. He'd been briefed about this before. Tuareg nomads usually eat cooked goat meat. They slaughter a goat and then they boil the meat together with bones, innards and tomatoes in a pot. Sean watched the two men start by cutting the organs into small cubes and wrap the pieces in netlike peritoneum before placing them on a skewer to hold them above the fire for grilling.

'What's your wife making?' Sean asked Maku, noticing that Yelena had walked over to sit beside her.

'It's called Taguella. Our sand bread. Come, watch how she makes it. We have an old Tuareg proverb I think you'd like. Women are for the eyes and ears, not solely the bed.'

Sean watched Maku's wife skilfully mix the disc shaped bread which was made from mixing wheat flour and semolina before being placed under the searing hot embers of a charcoal fire.

'It's our staple food,' Maku said, handing Sean a piece. 'Made from within the sand. Our tradition is that the women will prepare the Taguella, while our men select the pieces of meat. They will make sure that our guests get the best pieces. I like my Taguella fiery with chillies and tomatoes, and you and I shall have a competition - to eat the hottest.'

Sean laughed, feeling humbled by the hospitality. He watched Maku's wife knead the bread with her dextrous fingers. She flipped the dough nonchalantly to Yelena, who placed the discs in the embers using only her right hand as she'd been instructed.

An hour later after a desert dweller's feast, Sean took Yelena for a walk around the vehicles which were laid out in a circle for protection. Sean kept his AK47 close to hand, and Phil was eager to check the security around the perimeter to make sure the guards were awake, and not lazing around.

'We need to talk a bit, Sean started catching Yelena by surprise with his tone.

A long pause as they walked. 'I know. But can we just savour the moment for a bit? It's such a wonderful place and wonderful people. I feel honoured.'

Sean let her take in the moment for a few minutes, but he was in no mood for too much prevarication, reminding her they were right in the middle of a war zone, not a romantic holiday destination. 'I've been meaning to ask you. You were a lover to a bloke in the foreign office. A man nicknamed Dan the man, right?'

He heard Yelena gasp before she stood rigid to face him. 'Oh, my God, how did you know that?'

Sean put his hands on his hips. 'I didn't, but you just confirmed it. I had a snippet of information that you'd been sleeping with this bloke for money.'

'I'm not a fucking hooker you know,' Yelena shouted in fury. 'I was doing what my job was, as an agent. Collecting information.'

'An agent for your father as a gangster is completely different from being an agent for people like me who believe in good things. I'm beginning to see you for what you are.'

'And what's that then Sean? A tart, a slapper as you Brits say, or a slut? Fuck you, you bastard.'

A silence. But Yelena wanted more. 'I'm sorry, I have to reply to your horrible assertions and your judgements. I'm not a prostitute, nor easy meat, nor have I ever been banged over a wheelie bin. So, fuck you again. You can fuck right off.'

Sean drew his eyes back to hers. He felt he'd pushed his luck far enough but needed to know more. He had feelings for this woman, but he couldn't realise them fully until he knew everything about her - and so far, she'd been caught lying, hiding information, or skewing the facts. He didn't like that.

'Did you know he was gay?'

'Who.'

'Dan the man?'

'I didn't - no. What the fuck's that got to do with this. Every time I open myself to a man, they shit all over me. Why is that Sean, why are you doing this to me when I've told you I love you? Does it make you feel powerful? Fuck off.'

Sean tried to make himself less tense, less angry. But Yelena interjected again. 'Tell me about you? You've been just as tight with the truth. Do you have a wife?'

'I did. She died.'

Yelena scrunched her eyebrows. Sean felt uneasy being on the other end of a grilling, but knew he needed to take some, as well as give some, if he was to get to the truth and prise out more information on Dan the man and the minister nicknamed Hoover. 'She was my best friend,' Sean muttered. 'We wanted kids, she died, and I ended up on a branch of life that took me into some very dark places, as well as jail.'

'Good grief. I'm so sorry.'

'Listen, my life has been one long spiral into dark murky places, I've been betrayed, shat on by my employers, put under the curse of death with a price on my head, and used by lots of people. Exactly the same as you, so I understand what you've been through.'

'Do you? Do you really? I very much fucking doubt it, Sean. Your life and mine are polar opposites. Have you been sexually abused, told who to sleep with, treated not like a daughter, but emotionally abused like a slave? He controlled my money, where I lived, my inheritance, who I slept with, and turned me into a fucked up moron. No, you fucking well haven't. You ask me your questions and I'll tell you what I know, but don't ever fucking judge me again.'

Sean avoided any more talk of his own traumas. That wouldn't help now. What Yelena needed was assurance. Some adoration. Some trust. But he couldn't quite bring himself to that point. Yet. 'Did you know Hoover?'

'Who's that?'

'The minister Dan worked for?'

'I know the minister but didn't know his nickname was Hoover. And yes, I got lots of information from Dan on him.'

'Like what?'

'He told me that Hoover had been asked to join an exclusive club, called the twenty-one-club. Does it mean anything to you?'

'Yes. But why?'

'Sir Rhys had just become the leader of this group a year ago and that's how my father and he had become reconnected, and why I was tasked to smooth the way for Hoover to become involved in it.'

'You know why they told you to do this, right?'

'Of course. My dad wanted everyone who could influence export sales of weapons into this new circle of bastards called the twenty-one-club.'

Just as he was deep in thought, he heard a weird noise. A loud noise in the desert. A backfire? Was that the backfire of an engine?

It was. Then came the first of a volley of automatic fire. He then heard the crack and thump of a high calibre sniper weapon, before hearing machine gun fire smashing out a hundred rounds a minute from a position somewhere to the south. They were under serious and sustained fire.

He grabbed Yelena and darted for cover below the nearest Toyota watching the sky come alive with tracer fire, and the pounding of rounds into the sand in front of him.

Chapter 34

Marlow

Just outside Marlow, you'll find the Royal Oak, a rustic country pub whose motto for food is: *'If we don't know who grew it, or where they grew it, we just don't use it...'*

The legendary Rebellion beer is a hook for all the locals, and it was particularly appealing to one-eyed Damon who would partake of a hefty few after he'd conducted his recce of the area with three former Bulgarian Spetsnaz officers. They would provide twenty-four-hour surveillance on the quaint public house to wait until Jack came for his single quiet pleasure in life. A walk with the dog and a couple of IPA beers, perhaps with a single shot of Isle of Jura whisky for the walk home.

Jack only frequented the pub occasionally, according to Sean. Once or twice a week when he had time. All one-eyed Damon knew, was that he and his team had to monitor the pub for any 'dickers' that were watching the pub. Acting as the eyes on the ground, the dickers would likely be Russian agents operating on behalf of Natalie who planned to kidnap and torture him, much the same as she had done with Sean.

With a large garden, the Royal Oak was a perfect pub to visit after a walk in the warmer months or enjoy the warm and cosy interior when the days were short and colder. Jack enjoyed both, according to Sean, and he also liked to sit in the huge Indian teepee in the garden which was decked out with colourful native American sofas and stools.

With a narrow road and two entrances to the pub, there were very few areas that 'dickers' could use to get a perfect view of people entering one of the two entrances to the pub. One-eyed Damon put himself in the mind of the kidnappers. He'd been assured they wouldn't lift Jack in London due to the protection they'd put in place, and they wouldn't target his own house, if indeed they'd ever been successful in following him from his London offices where he was transported by different routes each day in a specially protected car. Add to that, the security and panic alarms in his house, and a secure panic room, it simply didn't make sense for the Russians to take any chances that they really didn't have to take. They'd have to be very careful that MI5 close protection officers didn't spot them.

Sean had surmised that the only suitable place to kidnap Jack was when he went for a walk to the pub - the only location that Sean could possibly have disclosed under torture. It was the only piece of personal information Jack had ever revealed to him in the years he'd known him.

One-eyed Damon used the limited sight of his one useful eye to have a walk around the pub looking for the optimum 'dicking' spots. Surveillance locations that he would describe in his former years of being a counterterrorist surveillance officer, as being dicking observation posts. OP's used by terrorists to spy on their prey.

There were only two suitable OP's. A clearing in the bushes opposite the pub, and a small ditch about fifteen metres to its left with excellent access routes from the fields behind the high treeline.

It took his highly disciplined Spetsnaz friends around an hour to establish their equipment in the area. Two field camouflaged covert cameras, normally used for imaging wildlife, but this time set up in trees to capture both ends of the road - and a series of passive infra-red motion detectors in the field behind. Each covert motion detector was covered by small camouflaged cameras to detect anyone approaching the OP's to watch the pub entrances.

Chapter 35

Mali

The bullets kept flying. Accurate automatic volleys of fire. Sean looked across to the remnants of the bushfire where they had been feasting. He spotted two dead Tuareg warriors lying in the sand and heard the piercing screams from another who had been shot through the jaw.

Sean had grabbed Yelena and had thrown her to the ground pushing her under the Toyota when the incoming fire had struck. The vehicle was in a basin and shielding them both from the incoming fire, which was now striking the rear of the cab.

'Five o'clock, two vehicles,' he had heard Phil shout before he released bursts of fire from his M16 semi-automatic rifle. 'Get over here Maku, I need more firepower.'

Sean was pinned down, and couldn't get across to Phil, but Maku had run with another Tuareg to join him behind the forward most Landcruiser. Phil was using precise shots to keep the aggressors from advancing quickly onto their location. As the sun was going down with the Tuaregs returning fire, he provided loud and fierce instruction where to target their fire on an enemy that Sean couldn't yet see.

More often than not, covert operations involving high-grade intelligence apparatus and paramilitary forces will not go strictly to plan - and this was one such occasion. Sean immediately knew it was going to rat shit and they'd be lucky to get out alive from the ambush. But how? Who was it? Had they been compromised again? And where the hell was the overhead cover from Jugsy who had been monitoring their every move from the comfort of an airbase somewhere to the east? Fleetingly he thought about if this all went wrong. What would come next? No plan survives contact with the enemy, and everything Jack had put together was unlikely to succeed at all now. Flexibility and failsafe plans were everything on covert operations, but first, they all had to save their lives.

Then it happened. As if out of nowhere, Sean heard the unmistakable sound of high explosives detonating somewhere near the enemy ambushers, followed by a fireball lighting up the sky. It was a 250kg laser-guided bomb that had been remotely fired by an operator at the American base in Niger. It was a direct hit on the lead enemy vehicle killing all four terrorists immediately. Sean didn't know it at the time, but the CIA and the French were operating as a joint force to provide the full spectrum of defence for Sean's mission in the desert, and it now looked like the actions on compromise were now being put into place.

The *pièce de résistance* of American military engagement in the Sahel was a $110 million drone base that the US had recently built in Agadez, a city that for centuries had served as a trade hub on the southern edge of the Sahara Desert in Niger, not far from Mali. One of America's largest ever military investments in Africa, it was the hub of secrecy for CIA covert operations with the latest incumbents being their Special Activities Division, backed up by a group of US special forces Green Berets, and a highly secretive special projects team from the CIA. Jugsy had been introduced to the commanders and sat at his console watching Sean's desert *mêlée* unfold in their ops room.

Sean ran across to Phil to get a better view of the point of attack on the group. 'Fuck,' Phil shouted as Sean arrived. 'Look. There's another five vehicles coming from the west. We're in deep shit now.'

Sean started laying down fire and shouted for more ammo to a Tuareg warrior who was relaying water and ammunition from the other vehicles, while Phil took full charge of the defensive counteractions.

'They took one out with a missile thank fuck, but where's the next one?' Phil shouted over the loud sound of rapid gunfire. 'What the fuck are they waiting for?'

'Watch out for that left-hand vehicle,' Sean shouted back, with his eye over the sights, and his rifle still firmly in his shoulder. 'I'll target the one on the right, but the left one is moving. Keep the fire rate up.'

Just as he finished shouting his orders, he heard the sound of a rocket-propelled grenade whistling through the air. 'Incoming,' he shouted, 'Get the fuck out.'

He sprinted as fast as he could away from the vehicle before throwing himself to the ground shielding his head and making himself as small a target as possible, before the shaped charge buried itself into the cab causing a huge explosion, spewing shrapnel everywhere.

'Fuck, fuck,' he shouted, looking up to see Maku and another Tuareg fall to the ground clasping their chests. They were both dead in seconds from the searing shards of copper fragmentation that had ripped through the cab. 'You OK mate?' Sean shouted to Phil who had run in the opposite direction.

'I'm OK, get some fire down for fuck sake.'

Just at that point, Sean watched something he had never seen before. But he had heard about it. A swarm of drones. High above him, sweeping fast and low towards the enemy vehicles. Jesus Christ, he thought, mesmerised at dozens of quadcopter unmanned aerial vehicles acting in perfect harmony as a murmuration of killer drones. Then he saw a second swarm swirling through a couple of low clouds and hammering through the air, coming directly out of the sun towards the ambushers.

He heard the fusillade of automatic gunfire being launched from below the first swarm of drones. Followed by the next missile strike, BOOM. The four terrorists had been vaporised. Smoke rose to the sky. Sean watched in relief as the terrorist vehicle burned, before he witnessed the next set of drones sweep in for the kill on the remaining vehicles. He noticed that below each drone was a metal frame. A four-posted frame that supported the weapons and housed the telemetry to enable artificial intelligence to track, trace, identify and then kill the enemy.

'Holy shit Sean,' came the shout from the other side of the desert berm. 'Are you seeing what I'm seeing mate? Swarms of drones with high-tech weapons. I thought that was all pie in the sky stuff.'

'Exploding pies,' Sean shouted back. 'It's bloody well real, and we're watching it right now. This is no dream. Got to be the CIA for sure.'

'The future is now. The future is here for fuck sake. Amazing,' Phil shouted back.

Both men relaxed a little to watch the ensuing battle of remotely operated swarms of killer drones take on, and take down a terrorist attack. The drones were swooping low, firing automatic bursts, then lifting high again in perfect formation, perfect synchronisation.

Through a system of flexibly connected plates, the quadcopters distributed the backward momentum of the four-post weapon frame in a way that kept the drone stationary in the air. A four kilogramme robot gimbal allowed six degrees of movement freedom, and the ability to rapidly retarget the weapon and camera onto the terrorists when they swooped into holding positions to fire the shots. Because they were driven by artificial intelligence, the robotic frame and weapon was totally agnostic to the payload. The plate system stabilised the drone and allowed the AI to get an accurate shot.

'Bet they're using this place as a test bed for live operations,' Sean shouted to Phil, watching him stand up for the first time since the attack had begun. 'They've been after this as a weapon for at least a decade, and now it's real, with us being the guinea pigs. Unbelievable tech.'

'I don't give a shit mate, it works. They can test away, they saved our bloody lives. What the fuck happens now?'

Sean took a few moments to think about that. And the new technology he had just witnessed for the very first time on live operations. He remembered that the Defence Secretary had recently said that 'swarm squadrons' will be deployed by the British armed forces in the coming years. He also knew that the US were well ahead of the game. They had been testing interconnected, co-operative drones that were capable of working together to overwhelm an adversary. Low-cost, intelligent and inspired by swarms of insects, these new machines would revolutionise future conflicts. From swarming enemy sensors with a deluge of targets, to spreading out over large areas for search-

and-rescue missions. They would have a range of uses on and off the battlefield.

Sean walked over to Phil who had trailed his weapon by his side. Then he heard a loud whoosh from the drones going around in a circle before flying back in to attack the last remnants of the terrorists. He stood side by side with Phil, two old and battered warriors watching the sun reach the distant horizon, a glow of orange in the sky, and a beaming smile on their face. Then came a gushing of red. Red piercing fire. A drone was hovering at the head of the swarm, directing a flamethrower onto the forward most vehicle. Rapid bursts of fire being projected with piercing force thirty metres ahead of it.

'Jesus Christ. What the actual fuck is that?' Phil asked, tapping Sean on the shoulder.

'That my friend, is most definitely the future. It's probably time for us old lags to hang up our boots I reckon.'

A short desert silence as both warriors tried to take in the immensity of what they were watching.

'Maybe you're right. But we need to finish this job first. Still a place for old-fashioned deception, boots on the ground, and some good old guts and glory.'

Sean glanced across at the bodies of the Tuareg warriors knowing the entire operation had now gone to rat shit. What now he wondered. He walked solemnly to kneel over the body of Maku. A proud and fierce warrior who had become his friend. Sean held Maku's head in his hands and began to close his eyes, noticing he had left the world with the tiniest of smiles on his face. Sean wondered about his children, his family and the deep passion he held for his Tuareg kinsmen. He had talked of one day seeing his dream come alive of a Tuareg state in the sands, a land they could call their own with the goal of gaining independence from corrupt Malian politicians. It would have been called '*Azawad*', Maku had said. Sean grimaced as a man's dream of a better life lay shattered, once again, in his hands.

Chapter 36

London

'Sorry to bother you at this late hour Sir, but something has come up.'

Jack studied the surprised face of Sir Justin Darbyshire who was sitting behind his desk, sleeves rolled up, and his polka dot tie loosened.

'I thought this would be urgent judging by your tone over the phone Jack. What's up?'

Jack felt his throat go dry for a moment as he heard Sir Justin asking him to take a seat. This would be a difficult conversation.

Jack had been sat punching out an operation order on his laptop when Laura had called him. He had been feeling dozy and tired from the day's meetings, but Laura's news jerked him into action. His adrenal glands were now reacting to the stressful news which had prepared him to act swiftly.

'It's gone tits up,' Laura had said in her gravelly voice. 'I'm changing the entire plan and within three hours I will have the approval of the President of the United States of America to move forward quickly.'

Jack was aghast, hardly containing his shock. He put Laura on speakerphone as he traipsed around his small office in Devereux Court. The running commentary was everything he hadn't expected. His meticulous planning had seemingly all gone to rot, his plotting for each step of the sting, now in tatters. His dismay only overtaken by some rapid thinking on how he could regain the initiative. But was it now out of his hands and into the Americans?

'The game plan and the mission is exactly the same,' Laura said fervently. 'The only difference is that I'm accelerating the plan on the ground. We're going for the jugular and we're going for bust.'

'What exactly do you mean?'

'I'm re-tasking your man on the ground, he's been compromised and I'm currently looking at dead bodies strewn all over the Sahara.'

Laura was sitting in the CIA operational HQ of Airbase 201 in the Agadez region of Niger monitoring the imagery feed from the CIA reaper circling above Sean on the ground. The $110 million dollar base was expected to be operational in 2019, but the rainy season and other environmental complexities had caused its delay. It was the largest ever American Air Force project outside of the USA and had been the subject of considerable debate in the Pentagon about abandoning it entirely. As part of a worldwide shift toward confrontation with Russia and China, the Pentagon had weighed up about a full drawdown in Africa. The debate was part of an effort to reshape the US toward its so-called great-power competition that had been outlined in the 2018 National Defence Strategy.

'We need to move quickly,' Laura said, continuing to provide her tactical and strategic narrative. 'The US Defence Secretary wanted Africa shut down, but he's lost that battle. I won it, and we've been quietly making overtures to the White House that it absolutely makes sense to project ourselves there as part of the power game with Russia and China. We've been planning this for a while Jack, but now the green light has been given. It's going to be a show of strength.'

'But what changed everything?'

'Two things. The President of Mali made contact with our ambassador asking for help, and the deaths of five US servicemen by Russian mercenaries in Niger. The President has had enough. He's countermanded everyone and told us to strike.'

'What about my team. What's the plan? I'll need to adjust things here in London and prepare the ground Laura. Don't leave me hanging now.'

'I won't. I know what you need for your sting, and I'll task your man to get it. In the meantime, the President is due to speak to your

Prime Minister in two hours time. I need some of your Special Forces Group on the ground alongside my teams.'

'Bloody hell Laura, what makes you think he'll make such a snap decision?'

'It's me remember Jack. I know everything. He's a good man, right? He wants to be seen working with the US and French as an emboldened Pan-Atlantic mission in Africa, right? Well here it is. On a dancing fucking plate with red roses and French berets on. It's all teed up my love.'

Jack couldn't help but smile. He could tell Laura was on a mission and it would be her way or no way. 'OK, I get it. America has woken up to the fact that the Chinese and Russians are buying up Africa, and the scramble for the continent just got real. I'll let Sir Justin know so he's primed. Look after my team for the next stages please.'

Jack adjusted his tie and leant forward to brief Sir Justin. He wasn't quite sure where to start and rustled up some saliva inside his cheeks to give him purchase on his stale mouth. 'Do you remember when Laura gave her speech to you about US involvement in Mali,' he began. 'Her words were that all avenues will need to lead to some kind of US intervention.'

'I do Jack. A fabulous woman with a turn of phrase like no other. I think she threw a few fucks in for good measure.'

'Indeed. Well, they've upped their game and plan to intervene imminently. By all accounts Russian mercenaries have taken over the Presidential Palace and they don't plan on stopping there.'

'Christ. Anything else I should know before I call the PM?'

'Well, Laura is asking for special forces support.'

'Cripes. To take down the mercenaries or what?'

'I can only assume that. She's got a full special activities team in place and is raring to go, but I've asked her to give me some assurances about my team on the ground and their mission too.'

'Bloody hell. She's not mucking about then. A gunfight in the desert with the Russians as if it's the Mojave Desert. What's the game plan Jack.? Why so quick?'

'Because the Russians have taken over. The Russian mercenaries have infiltrated the government and they'll be after the minerals, the gold and the economic benefits that come from that. The scramble for Africa is now a hotbed of skirmishes between China, France and Russia and it's about to blow up. So far, the Chinese have bought up all the land for slow time benefit, the Russians have done it on the cheap with force, and the US were caught napping. The French, well they're just fuming. The mercenaries ability to come in on the back of Russian military agreements has given the Kremlin extraordinary reach. They're now in more than twenty African countries and this is probably the most important one.'

'Well geopolitically it all makes sense. Russia's push is strategic, and not about Africa as such. The Russian President has made it pretty clear about winning his undeclared war against the West.'

'I agree Sir. I read a note the other day about these skilled soldiers of fortune who take their orders from an oligarch. Not from the Kremlin. And the note mentioned that two hundred mercenaries are involved in protecting Russian military intelligence officials at the Pico Basilé island spy base in Equatorial Guinea.'

'And then there's the opportunities for the US exploiting the mines. Only about six of the country's one hundred and thirty-three gold-rich reserves have been mapped out. Significant growth opportunities. It all makes sense but bloody hell they always need to rush don't they. Jesus.'

Jack watched Sir Justin tut a few times before rolling his sleeves down and tightening his tie ready to take his leave. 'I bloody well hope Laura knows what she's doing. Cold War 2.0 is about to get hot. Keep me updated Jack. I'll assure the Prime Minister we have this one.'

'Thank you, sir.'

'Oh, and get yourself home my boy. Have a safe journey. It's grim out there.'

Chapter 37

Mali

'We've found the weapons compound you're after,' was the first sentence Sean remembered from his inexplicable meeting with Laura Creswell in the middle of the Sahara desert. The next sentence had been etched into his mind, alongside her stunning facial features. 'Get in, find the evidence you're after, then lay the charges before blowing the place to kingdom come.'

That was pretty much the extent of his new orders. It came with a bark of '*kaboom*' at the end of the sentence and a lingering smile.

Deserts can be red hot by day, but freezing at night. Sean felt the chill inside his bones as he lay behind a sand berm waiting for the sun to go down. He would then covertly enter a large food processing compound just on the outskirts of a small desert commune called Bourem. The compound he was watching wasn't heavily guarded, but its discreet security belied the real story behind the poorly constructed mesh fencing that acted as its boundary. It was being used as a weapon store for illicit arms destined for sale on the Malian black market. Still disguised as a Tuareg, Sean watched a lone guard patrol the perimeter fence with an AK-12 rifle slung over his shoulder.

His mind shot back to his desert meeting with Laura. He still couldn't fathom out what the hell was going on, but she had assured him that if he got this job done, she'd have him on a plane and back in London within two days. That was all he wanted now. As well as a cup of tea and a good night's sleep.

Laura had arrived at the scene of the ambush on a US Air Force C-130J Super Hercules aircraft some two hours after a bunch of Green Berets had arrived to secure and cordon the entire area. She looked for all the world as if she was about to stroll along the promenade at Cannes as she walked gracefully down the ramp wearing white deck shoes and a green one-piece jumpsuit with a beige handbag in tow. Sean couldn't believe what he was seeing, but heard Phil behind him mutter the words, 'What the fuck.'

The Green Berets had hastily laid out two trestle tables near the base of the ramp and constructed a desert camouflage net to provide some shade from the heat. Sean slung the rifle over his shoulder and made his way to the tables closely followed by Phil and Yelena. Laura had waved enthusiastically at them, gesturing to come and greet her as if they were having a beach time picnic. A troop of Green beret soldiers, dressed in desert combats, fanned out into a circle around the aircraft while the air loadmaster brought a green Norwegian tea container down the ramp and into the makeshift gazebo.

'Hope you brought the crockery too Laura,' Sean quipped dusting his hand off before shaking hers. 'Some show you lot put on.'

'Lovely to see you again Sean. Different circumstances, same old shit. I know all too well how you Brits love to brew up in the middle of a battle to have some tea. So here we are. Tea now, tea and medals after we finish this little jaunt.'

Sean laughed at the notion. Phil shook Laura's hand and introduced Yelena to her. The four of them sat with tin mugs and a small plate of cookies for a social chat in the light desert breeze.

'I must say, you all look wonderful in your outfits you know. I'd like a nice picture on the ramp after our little meeting, and I'll show the President how cool the Brits are taking tea in the desert before the shit hits the fan.'

'For posterity and the love of our special relationship,' Phil chipped in, saying 'cheers' and toasting the Queen.

'Will this be another speech along the lines of a monster riding through a blue moon on Halley's fucking Comet,' Sean asked Laura in jest. She laughed loudly and stood up to kiss Sean on the cheek.

'You liked my speech didn't you? It's the same kinda speech as the last one my lovely man. Short and sweet.' Laura walked around the table before pausing. 'Enter the arms warehouse, lay some explosives, get out safely, then blow it to smithereens. Any evidence you collect while inside is a bonus for Jack.'

Sean watched her take a few sips of tea. She was wearing expensive gold earrings and had her hair neatly tied in a long ponytail. The woman was mesmerising. A legend of American CIA folklore and without a doubt, a future Chief. Laura was one lively lady, sharp and with a vernacular as inspiring as any leader he'd ever served under. He glanced across to Phil who was stuffing another two biscuits into his mouth, hardly taking his eyes off her. He was as struck by the effect this woman was having on him, as any legendary commander he had served under. Sean took a swig of his strong tea listening to her Californian accent.

'We're about to fuck the Russians over in the capital city and it will be a short sharp battle using Brit and American special forces to save the President, and free him from the hands of the Kremlin. Then we'll take up the fight with the jihadis on the ground in the coming months, the French will be grateful and bring us cheese, and we'll forge ahead together as a triumvirate keeping this place free of the Russian bear.'

'I'd call that a fightback at last,' Yelena suggested. 'The French have tried their hardest so far with only a handful of Brits and a small coalition. Are you saying you're now going to throw lots of people at this?'

'That's exactly right. And you're a French asset, right? Exactly why we need you on the ground with us over the next twenty-four hours or so. It looks good having the French play ball.'

'Those swarms of drones you threw around the desert suggest to me you're chucking a lot of money this way too,' Phil added.

'You liked that? Potent tech that we've tested here in Africa as well as in our own deserts away from prying eyes. We've developed them to operate in swarms, coordinating information among fleets of quadcopters, fixed-wing planes, ground assets, network enabled soldiers and boats. The teams have even developed tech to be able to identify humans and decide whether they represent a threat through facial recognition and AI.'

Sean was fascinated by this glimpse into the future of warfare but kept his counsel, reflecting on what had gone down. He was curious about what was coming his way next.

He listened to Laura and Yelena exchange their own views on the next generation world he was now entrapped in, wondering why all of a sudden the Americans were going to go big in Mali. And what about Jack's plans? How would they hold up? He knew he'd want to take Sir Rhys and his cabal down, but did he have enough? And how would they deal with Dozich who was always the slippery eel that got away?

'I want to make sure you play your role in this little venture,' Laura said to Yelena touching her hand briefly. Sean noticed how tactile she was as well as being hard as nails. 'It's a dangerous task with these two fine men, do you think you can do it?'

'Of course I can. Female skills are revered out here.'

'Yes, I heard that. Wonderful to hear. I want you to put that female stamp on this operation before we all go home. Jack tells me you've been a fine operator and he wants you to work with him in the future. What do you say?'

'Really? But I'm still officially a French agent?'

'Not anymore my friend. They're always on our periphery, but if you want to play with the big boys, it's the two-eyes community you need to belong to. The Americans and the Brits.'

Sean coughed politely, feeling a need to get on with the real reason Laura had flown two hundred miles for tea and biscuits in the desert.

'And our mission Laura?'

Laura smiled and paused for effect, knowing everyone would hold their silence. She was a shrewd operator. 'I want you to blow something up. At a specific time. When we assault the Presidential Palace, you'll simultaneously hit an arms and explosives compound. Get what you want from it before you blow it.'

Sean watched Phil demolish another biscuit and perk up. A demolition job. Right up his street. He looked like an excitable puppy but couldn't get any words out to ask more questions because his laughing gear, as he would call it, was stuffed with friable digestives.

Sean spied the part of the fence line he wanted to penetrate to make his entry into the compound. Laura had provided a set of aerial photos with close target analysis of the long building she'd been told was holding the weapons. He figured that they could easily get the job done within ten hours of entry. If there were no cock-ups.

Sean led the way to the insertion point. He used a pair of fence pliers to cut the mesh in a square that would be big enough for them to crawl through, and he ushered them into the compound quickly. Within a minute, he was replacing the mesh and fixing it back in place with black wire. He'd noticed how the guards were checking poor areas of fencing and hoped they wouldn't check this section too closely.

He led them to the central store warehouse where an astute imagery intelligence analyst had spotted an entry point on the northern face of the building, a high window that was always open. It was a tiny space to crawl through, but Phil stood on Sean's back telling him it was a goer. Sean would never get through it, so the plan was for Phil to enter and open the side door that was housed in a small annex. The Green Berets had provided all the kit they required for the insertion and the final act. They each carried a Colt 45 pistol harnessed on their waist, and a Heckler & Koch MP7 4.6mm chambered submachine gun slung over their backs. Phil had carried a small lightweight rucksack with enough detonating cord and C-4 explosives to create a detonation big enough to produce the explosive train needed to destroy the bulk of the weaponry inside.

Within minutes, Sean and Yelena had been ushered into the complex by Phil, who told them to be very careful where they trod and what they touched. He made no bones about the fact he was in charge now. The place was supposedly full of deadly weaponry, some of which had been tracked and traced from the deals Dozich had put in place. Only time would tell what they would find.

Chapter 38

Mali

The entire building reeked of machine oil. Sean walked carefully behind Phil where he cautiously made his way to a central workbench right in the middle of what looked like an arms factory. Then he saw them: dozens of explosively formed projectiles, EFPs. Improvised explosive devices: IEDs with shaped copper charges designed to penetrate armour and kill anyone inside their vehicles. Yellow wires were attached to their copper bases, each carefully laid out in boxes full of hay with small brown cards providing instructions on how to arm them.

'This ain't no weapons cache as Laura described it,' Phil shouted out to Sean. 'It's a fully-fledged Russian arms factory, probably run by the mercenaries using locally employed people under the threat of death if they squeal on the operation.'

'What do you mean?'

'Look at these here. High precision engineering of copper cases, probably lathed over there on those benches. They've been teaching them how to make high-grade IEDs by a master bombmaker I'd say.'

'But why? What's the game?'

'I can answer that,' Yelena chipped in. 'My father played a big role in bringing bomb making technology into Africa for the mercenaries. All to arm the jihadis and create chaos. He wanted to create the conditions for bloodshed and a new Caliphate where a country was ripe to be taken over by stealth. He's a bastard and he doesn't give a shit who gets killed.'

Sean and Phil looked at each other astonished at the extent of the weaponry in front of them. Merchants of death delivering carnage on a nation to take its government over by guile whilst arming hot-headed jihadis. Sean scanned the factory, trying hard to take in the immensity of what he could see around him. A vast open plan warehouse with crates stacked five high, precision machinery on messy workbenches, and munitions in varying states of assembly.

'Come on, we only have about seven hours to collect as much evidence as we can,' Sean said energetically as he crouched down to inspect a series of copper wiring and vices holding newly turned fuze pockets. 'This entire operation is right next to a tightly packed market to mask its purpose. No wonder they don't want high levels of security on the place, it would attract too many noses. A small part of Bourem has been turned into an industrial arms site.'

Sean followed Phil around the extremity of the workbenches. Improvised bombs lay around them in every stage of preparation and construction, along with assembly instructions written with marker pens on small easels. Each of the benches held a gold mine of intelligence on the Russian programme of arming ISGS, with Phil looking as if he was about to go into sensory overload.

'Jesus Christ Sean, come and have a look at this.'

Phil was like a kid in an old-fashioned sweet shop peering into each jar wondering which ones to inspect and take home.

'It's a fucking mortar mould. They're making their own bloody mortars. Holy shit this is big. Why don't we just preserve the lot and bring in the Americans to exploit all this intelligence?'

'Good bloody question. I don't know. You're gonna need to pick up and carry what you want, photograph the rest, and classify every munition you see. Catalogue it all. Then lay out the explosives. Ours is not to question why. We just do it. And I want to get home soon, so get a bloody move on.'

'Thanks a fucking bunch. You don't normally follow orders, what's changed?'

'I'm getting old and just want to get home. Main thing is to get the evidence Jack wants.'

'This will take hours and you pair better do what I tell you to.' Phil demanded.

'You crack on with that lot of IEDs,' Sean replied. 'I'm going to search for the weapons manifests and see what we can link. I know Jack. He only wants enough evidence to take the corrupt bastards down, so we can blow this place and stop it being used to manufacture stuff and kill people.'

'A full takedown then?'

'Yep.'

'Sweet. I like a good blow but be prepared - this place will go up with such a massive bang you'll see it from space. You're gonna need to evacuate everyone anywhere near here.'

'I know. I'm thinking about that. Now crack on Phil. We only have until just after daylight at a push.'

Just as Sean turned to begin his inspection of the conventional munitions, he heard the unmistakable sound of opera click into action. It was Phil and his opera. He was never without his small iPod which was now pumping out the tinny sounds of Rigoletto which flooded the oily air keeping Phil primed and focussed. Phil was a Welshman who had been brought up in a household that revered opera, rugby, and drinking. Sean recalled the story Phil had once told him about how his father used to serenade his mother through the dining room hatch, banging out Nessun Dorma in full baritone splendour whilst he cooked. Phil had spent many years as a youngster on the stages of small venues where his father was an amateur opera producer in his hometown of Penarth, South Glamorganshire. Often in nineteenth century operatic attire. He had been immersed by his father into the nuances of opera and rugby union from a young age where he played scrum-half throughout his military career, and always carried an iPod full of arias – but his real talent lay in taking bombs apart or blowing things up. Ideally with classical music playing in the background to provide inspirational energy to his handiwork.

Sean made his way to a series of wooden crates, stacked three high, on the opposite side of the warehouse from where Phil was inspecting the IEDs. Yelena passed him a large torch as he started to inspect the stencilled letters on the crates.

'How on earth are we going to look inside all these boxes?' she asked, curious as to what Sean was looking for.

'Well, I won't look through every single one, but I'm looking for particular consignments that have been diverted from the original buyer.'

'Like Nigeria or Ghana you mean?'

'Yup. Nearly all military munitions including rifles, rockets and big bombs are engraved and marked in some way. The codes will give me the factory where they were made, the type of explosive, serial numbers and filler, and quite often country codes too.'

'How on earth will we find the consignment you're after though. This will take ages.'

'Just by using my eyes, and a sense of what's right and wrong. Traffickers often leave tell-tale signs, change serial numbers, engravings might be brighter than the original stamps to avert their real lineage, and often I'm just looking for the absence of the normal, and presence of the abnormal.'

Sean knelt to look at a crate that was marked with white paint from a pre-cut stencil. The crate had been labelled 'Parts of a Tractor' that gave Sean immediate suspicion. 'Here you go, bet you a pound to a dollar this crate is not full of tractor parts. This kind of mislabelling of weapon crates is common practice among traffickers. Hold the torch and take pictures as we go.'

The lid was not sealed and had already been prized open by whoever wanted to check the contents were not tractor parts, but a stash of weapons. Removing the wooden cover, he got an immediate stench of machine oil and peered inside. Row after row of shoulder fired grenade launchers greeted him, all tightly packed with cardboard spacers, and plastic covers over the gaping muzzles. He lifted one of the weapons to inspect the serial number. It was a Bulgarian MSGL revolver-type 40 x 46SR grenade launcher in matt black. Yelena photographed the engravings and the pressed stamps on the side of the weapon, an identity card and a provenance that was hard to falsify. Sean would send the picture back to The Court where a team of small arms intelligence experts could decipher their markings as part of the project to track and trace their origins and who had signed their export.

Next, Sean moved to a set of crates that were standing alone sat between two industrial benches with a few bench grinders bolted to them. The slatted military green case was marked with black stencilled paint showing a gross weight of sixty-eight kilogrammes, alongside a batch number, year of production and factory code which he knew represented Romania. He opened the cover of the top case, removed the grease paper and spotted a single piece of A4 paper in a plastic folder.

Bingo! A delivery note. Vital intelligence.

He stood reading the note for a minute or so smiling at what he had found. Crucial data on the export contract dates, the order quantities, serial numbers, ports of transfer and country of origin.

'Looks like we've hit the jackpot. Here, look at this. Destination Nigeria. With end-user certificate numbers, weapons batch and model, and how nice, the inspector's signature at the port of entry. Fucking great.'

'What exactly are inside the crates then?' Yelena asked. She placed the papers on a bench to capture the contents on her camera.

'Six crates of AR-5MF assault rifles made in Bulgaria. Nice of them to leave the import and export details. The team won't take long to track and trace this consignment with the right access to export and transit databases.'

The whole area smelled acrid as Sean paced around the crates, occasionally placing crime scene cards with numbers on them which Yelena photographed next to the articles of interest. He checked the workbenches where an untidy work regime had resulted in remnants of circuit boards, stashes of 7.62mm bullets strewn around tables, lathes with aluminium shards at their base, and nosecones of self-manufactured mortars. It was a dystopian image of chaos.

'Be bloody careful around here and don't touch fuck all,' he said to Yelena as she followed him around the benches, pointing at artefacts to photograph. He leant for a moment on a work bench and started to sketch the entire warehouse, the beginnings of a detailed and accurate map. It was going to be a long haul and a long night.

'What exactly are these,' Yelena said pointing to the shiny nosecones.

'Made by ISIS. Looks like they shipped in their own engineers from Iraq in readiness to claim their next Caliphate here.'

'Engineers?'

'Yep, highly capable ones too. A terrorist organisation with their own arms manufacturers. They used to design their own munitions and mass-produce them using advanced manufacturing techniques. Wacky huh?'

'I had no idea.'

'Well the Iraqi oil fields provided the industrial base, so they had easy access to lathes, tool-and-die sets, injection-moulding machines and skilled workers who knew how to quickly produce intricate parts to spec. Their raw materials came from cannibalising engines and melting down scrap. Their engineers forged new fuzes, new rockets and launchers and small explosive cases to be dropped by drones, all designed and assembled by engineers trained in the West. They've migrated their *modus operandi* right here. And I'm guessing the Russians have been helping them.'

Sean carefully picked through a box of warheads and found another cache of weapons diverted from Nigeria with the same import code as before. This time it was a consignment of Serbian M80 Zolja rocket-propelled grenades with another delivery note. He lifted one and cradled it in both arms whilst Yelena photographed the engravings and stock numbers. Stock number 17-22-461. Jack had mentioned this consignment before, in fact he specifically referred to the stock number with some precision when Sean was laid up in hospital. It was if he'd memorised the entire code and wanted Sean to memorise it too. Jack used it as an example of how British ministers and officials had likely authorised the purchase of some 12,000 rocket-propelled grenades, known as the M80 Zolja from Serbia, with lot number 17-22-461. When the weapons were procured, the UK would have signed an end-use certificate, a document stating who the munitions would be used by, and not sold or diverted to anyone else. Jack's team had confirmed the sale via insiders in the Serbian government and he'd actually seen the end-user certificate and delivery verification document. And it wasn't Mali or their jihadi incumbents.

Somehow, and by nefarious means, small quantities had been diverted into Mali and Niger, or at least that was the intelligence Jack had revealed. But now, Sean had the evidence right in front of his face. There'd be quite some explaining to do about how it ended up here in a jihadi arms warehouse. Someone was violating the terms of their end-user certificate and, by extension, had failed to comply with the United Nations Arms Trade Treaty. Murky stuff probably involving corrupt officials and traffickers like Dozich. Sean remembered the story of how other nations were doing exactly the same. Qatar had bought multiple weapons that were later recovered from ISIS fighters in Iraq, and the case of a flight carrying six tonnes of munitions to Saudi Arabia where flight records show it failed to land, but was diverted into Jordan, proved a case where the arms made their way to fighters in Syria.

'This is pretty scary,' Yelena suggested handing Sean some water. 'Weapons factories, and Russia pushing arms into Mali to help form a jihadist Caliphate, while they take over the government. I hope Laura takes them down and quickly.'

'Well, I think she will. She's good. The worry for me is that this model can be replicated anywhere the jihadis go in the world. They have the tech, the engineers, money and machinery to make their own arms.'

'Probably using 3D metal printers in the future. Producing weapons at the push of a button.'

'That's the future, we saw it. Next generation terrorism using artificial intelligence, swarm drones and self-driving vehicle bombs. Bloody nightmare. Glad I'm gonna give all this up.'

'What do you mean give it all up?'

Sean ignored the question and wiped his brow. He headed for a small room he'd spotted and sat down on the floor next to a pile of steel sheeting. How the hell was he going to deal with this building? It was a hive of intelligence, but he'd been ordered to blow the place to smithereens. He wasn't sure about that.

'Do you think we can get the evidence that Jack needs?' Sean felt Yelena's hand being placed on his arm as she asked the question.

'Maybe. There's plenty to search through here. He's only got one aim, and now, we have a split mission. Get Jack the evidence to take down the corrupt officials and ministers helping the merchants of death do their dirty work. And the takedown of the Russian mercenaries intent on taking over this country. Laura is bold and ballsy. Let's hope she nails it.'

'What will you do after all this Sean? Well, I mean….I mean, what can we do?'

Sean turned to look her in the eyes. They told him everything he needed to know. She was in love with him. No mistake. And he was beginning to adore her. He thought in silence of all those drawers he wanted to stay shut, and nailed shut, in perpetuity. He thought of Maku. Of Jack. He hoped one-eyed Damon was keeping him safe from the chaos of Natalie who was still on the run. He really didn't know how to answer her question, so he left it. Like he always did. But he thought about an idea he'd had for a long time…maybe now was the time to call it a day and pursue that dream? Maybe with Yelena. He knew that was what she wanted. He thought the same in that moment. In that small space with the smell of engine oil, only masked by the lightest scent of her perfume.

'Listen, I have something to tell you,' he eventually said. He was still unsure whether it was the right thing to do, but he went with his gut anyway.

'Oh, what?'

Yelena looked nervous. He leant over to hold her hand.

'Sean, please - is it bad?' She looked for all the world as if she was about to be dumped.

'It might be, I don't know, but I can't hold it back any longer.'

'Sean, for fuck sake, please.'

Her tone was one of exasperation now, so he just let it blurt out. 'I know who your real father is.'

An awkward pause. A look of fear. Then a shuffle from Yelena to move away from him. Their hands pulled apart. He could tell she was scared.

'How, how the bloody hell do you know?'

'Jack told me. He has known for some time. Don't ask me how but he's verified it by DNA.'

Sean watched Yelena hold her head not knowing what would come next. Did she actually want to know? Or should he just keep his gob shut. He felt close to her though. Close enough to care. He held a hand out. She took it.

'Will it upset me? Do I know who it is?'

'You do.'

'Who?'

'Your father is Sir Rhys Eldridge.'

Chapter 39

Marlow, England

The Russian man pulled out a green beanie slipping it over his bald head ready for his surveillance shift in the hedgerow. He had dressed warmly for his three-hour stint, just a set of birdwatching binoculars over his shoulder, an aluminium water bottle and a pocket full of dried fruit. He walked along the hedge line glancing casually around him. The field was empty, but the sounds of pigs in a distant field could be heard above the gentle swell of the stream he walked through.

His job was a simple one. Send a text to a phone number he had memorised if he saw the man called Jack walking his dog along the lane. He had been ordered to await further instructions once he had spotted his prey, and not to venture from his position under any circumstances. Orders that had been provided to the other two Russian operators who rested from their shift in a pub bedroom some two miles away. The description of Jack was vague. Short black hair, five feet seven inches tall, a long nose, average build, with a large black mole at the bottom of his left cheek. He'd been told the man had a slight limp on his right leg, apparently caused from a bomb explosion in Beirut.

Three hundred metres away, a former Bulgarian Spetsnaz soldier sat in his surveillance van monitoring two screens for any movement from the covert cameras he'd deployed to watch for activity at the identified observation posts. In the three days he had been monitoring the OP's in the hedgerows, he had seen no one. Just the odd badger and lots of rabbits scuttling around in the undergrowth.

Little did he know that the Russians had chosen an observation post three hundred metres down the road to monitor people walking their dogs, and entering the pub. Two spy games, a red team and a blue team, three hundred metres apart, not knowing about each other, and a target that had just left his house to walk down to the pub. The black and tan Gordon setter boisterously led the way.

Jack lived in a small hamlet just to the west of Marlow. He had inherited the house from his late father, and despite living there for nearly fifteen years, he was never on first name terms with anyone in his avenue. He spoke occasionally to his closest neighbour, an insurance broker of an old family firm established in Lloyds of London, describing himself as a civil servant but never expanding on the detail. Jack was a discreet man, and a grey man in the village. His garden was always neat and tidy, and he bore no hallmarks of any wealth being very content with his ageing Range Rover despite most of the small avenue having large people carriers, and a second sportscar. He could never understand the need for such exuberance.

Jack was thankful for a Saturday afternoon at home after a mammoth couple of days adjusting his plans to suit Laura's in Mali. He'd had a thirty-five-minute call with Laura that morning where the satellite phone kept intermittently cutting out. He felt like he was talking into a tunnel, but in retrospect he hadn't done much talking at all. He was on receive for most of the call.

Jack walked along the leafy avenue and turned right onto the main road heading towards the Royal Oak. He fancied a pint. Maybe two, now that he felt a little more assured that Laura would make sure that he got what he wanted, and that Sean didn't end up as collateral damage from the merciless actions of a full-blown CIA operation.

'It could get noisy for a short time in the Presidential Palace,' she had said. Words that meant there would likely be a brutal shoot out with more than just the CIA on the ground. She never revealed the extent of the operation, and Jack didn't ask. Laura had always been the senior officer, even in their days together in Moscow. He hoped that the Prime Minister had seen it in his wisdom to support the Americans in what was now their full and unadulterated commitment to Mali, and a route at last, to taking on the jihadists with some might.

As he got closer to the pub, a number of thoughts shot across his mind. The closest crocodile to the canoe was Sir Rhys Eldridge. He wondered where he was now and wondered where and how he would finally break the news to him that the operation he was running was over. Closed down. Former intelligence officers and former government officials arrested and placed behind bars. He imagined the media fallout of his plot to take down the arms dealers, knowing that the time was right. Just a bit more evidence was needed to ensure his sting was pulled off.

Jack walked past a clutch of wildflowers and a series of lime and copper beech trees before approaching the small pond next to the pub. In times gone by, the drovers would have stopped here, watering their animals in the pond and spending a comfy night in the inn before crossing the Thames near Marlow and walking on to the London markets.

Jack tied Barny, his setter, to a post outside the main entrance, and walked in to order a pint of Rebellion beer.

Chapter 40

Mali

She internalised her hate, buried her rage deep inside her, despised the betrayal of the many men who had deceived her. She felt as if her heart had been ripped out of her body, dismembered, and replaced as if nothing had ever happened.

Her entire life had been a pretence. A sham. She felt as if she belonged to no one, had no true family, no one who had ever cared for her. In short, she felt entirely alone and abandoned. Even her mother had betrayed her, never told her, never felt that she should ever tell the truth of a fling with Sir Rhys decades ago that resulted in her own life being born. The sham of the years of childhood and the awkward moments when Sir Rhys had visited. She always felt something was amiss, but he had always been a kindly soul she thought.

In that moment, sat next to Sean in a weapons factory a long way from home, it suddenly hit her. Dozich never ever knew that she was not his daughter. Sir Rhys and her mother had probably kept the secret for decades, and in between, Yelena had been abused, manipulated, treated as a whore, a piece of shit worthy only of being used by Dozich for his criminal ends.

'Are you OK.' She heard the words but couldn't respond. Her mind was numb. No, it was spinning. She couldn't make head nor tail of it all. All she felt was deep sadness and depression, as if she was trapped in a chasm and being sucked deeper into its vortex. It was eating her. Her soul was dead. The thoughts of suicide splashed across her mind.

She looked around at all the weaponry. Maybe this was her only chance? A chance to find peace at last, and taking Sean down with her. She hadn't yet felt his love, his truth, his care for her. No one had ever truly cared for her. I've only ever been used and abused, she heard herself say. She glanced down to her waist where the Makarov pistol that Sean had handed to her, was sat.

A full two minutes later she tried to respond to the question Sean had posed. But no words came out. Then she tried again but couldn't look Sean in the face. She stumbled into an answer. 'I'm - I - No, not OK, no. I'm not OK.'

'Listen, I know it's a shock, but I felt you needed to know. I want to help you unravel your life. Try and make some sense and start again.'

The words came across as caring, but the sounds of Sean's words were in a vacuum being twisted by the evil part of her mind. The nemesis inside her. A voice of hatred against him. '*Kill them all, they all hate you, they all use you*.' Then came the good voice. '*He cares about you, use this as your launchpad for a new life. You're too young to give it all away*.' She felt sick in the stomach as the voices rumbled around in her head. '*Kill him, he's just like the others. Kill him. Take them all down in one go*.'

Yelena held her head in her hands and began to cry. She touched the revolver, almost in the hope it would save her. She tried to tamp down her anger, her pain. But it kept raging and rearing its head again. She didn't quite know what she would do next.

'Sean, quick. Get your arse over here.' Phil, shouted. He was finishing cataloguing and photographing a box of explosively formed projectiles and telemetry components laid beside them. But he'd spotted something happening on the other side of the wall.

Outside the warehouse, the very first glimpses of daylight were beginning to form as the sun gently crept over Africa's seventeenth parallel. Sean made his way toward the far side of the warehouse, noticing the sound of a few generators being sparked into action. He turned to where the sound was coming from. It was the market outside the northern perimeter. At this sleepy time of day people were starting to work, and the low hum of generators caused Sean to accelerate his escape plan.

'We need to get the hell out of here,' Sean shouted across the room where he spotted Phil was peering through a small blacked-out window. 'We've got thirty minutes maximum.'

'Look at this. Somethings going down.'

Sean peered through the small window. He could see a small convoy of trucks at the gatehouse being checked by the security guards. Paperwork was being exchanged through the truck window and signatures were being taken. A cursory search was made of the first vehicle before a black Range Rover pulled alongside with a man waving out of the window. An exchange of words with the guards saw the barrier open immediately and a guard saluting as he stood to attention.

'It looks like the guard's getting some sort of bollocking from the man in the passenger seat of the Range Rover.' Phil whispered.

'Someone pretty important then,' Sean replied.

'What do you reckon?'

'All four trucks are branded with UN markings. Looks like a big delivery.'

'Weapons?'

'Could be,' Sean said, continuing to watch the convoy enter. About half a dozen vehicles cut through the hazy, half illuminated sky, none of which were being searched as they swung around the sand-filled bollards at the gate, before accelerating through the checkpoint to a large parade square.

'It's certainly not the first time weapons have been smuggled around the hot spots of Africa under the guise of humanitarian aid,' Phil said, now looking through a gap in the wooden struts at the side of the window.

'Reminds me of the scam the Russians pulled off in Syria trying to get weapons to ISIS. A series of staged assaults by militants on the bases of Syrian government troops. Assad's army retreated without a fight, leaving the entire base unguarded, along with loads of weapons.'

'That was a way of delivering arms under the guise of them being war trophies. Bet they've done the same here.'

Sean shouted across the room asking Yelena to grab her stuff and make her way to the window. We need to get the fuck out of here and quickly he thought. But something had grabbed his eye and he wanted to wait. Then it came. Recognition.

'Jesus Christ, Phil. Do you see what I see?'

Sean felt Phil's eyes pierce the back of his neck, not knowing what the hell he was on about.

'Two men, yes. Do you not think it's time to scarper?'

'Not yet. Look. It's Dozich. He's walking right towards us. The twat is here. Right in front of us.'

'Bullet in him now, or later?'

'Just wait. Let's see what the fuck he's up to.'

'Delivering weapons Sean, that's what he's fucking well doing. Now are we going to leg it or what? I've got everything set up.'

Silence. Sean kept watching. Thinking. Then he stepped away and turned towards Phil.

'That annex just over there. It's an extension of this warehouse and they're making their way into it. What's inside?'

The door is locked, but I'm guessing it's the office space at the front of the warehouse.'

'Can you get some eyes on inside?'

'Not sure. I've got a hand drill.'

'Do it quick, get me eyes on. If they come through the door, we deal with them.'

'Rightio. Standby.'

'Yelena, get down here. Stay down, and stay with our kit until we've dealt with this.'

'Dealt with what?'

'Visitors. Bad ones. Stay quiet and stay hidden.'

Chapter 41

Marlow

Natalie Merritt was in no mood for fucking about. The excitement she felt when she read the text that stated Jack was in the pub was as good as any drug she had ever taken, and equatable to the sensation of knowing she was about to have sex. The chemicals in her brain surged with pleasure as she played out in her mind how she would torture this man before finally killing him slowly. She thrived on the *chase* and the *crush* as she called it. Revelling in the power of taking a man's life.

Natalie pulled on a set of navy jeans and a black bra, hooking it up skilfully as she made her way to the bathroom mirror. She pulled on a brunette wig and began to apply makeup that would see her age increase by at least ten years. The skills of disguise had never left her.

She tutted as she glanced across to the blonde woman lying in the bed who was snoring intermittently. Natalie had seen fit to have a long night out on the town and picked up a particularly drunk lady in the early hours of the morning at a local club. The early morning session of sex never materialised, and she'd have to wait a little longer to get her next fix. She touched up her lipstick, picked up her suitcase, and opened the door.

Natalie sat in the rear of the chauffeur driven car, wearing a cashmere sweater and low-heeled boots, placing a set of expensive sunglasses over her eyes to shield them from the bright autumn sunshine. She mentally played out her next moves in her native Russian language, at times reminiscing her childhood in Rostov-on-Don before she became part of the Russian illegals programme. Is part of that girl still with her? Or had every strain of emotion and empathy been drained out of her during the decade or so of being ingratiated as an SVR agent, with nothing left but a mind set on revenge?

Natalie's father was a relatively unknown KGB General and he sent Natalie at the age of nine to study in the Czech Republic where she was fostered to a family with Canadian and Russian roots who were embarking on their own *illegal* careers. The family emigrated to Canada under the Russian illegals programme in 1991 where they built a backstory as a typical North American family and awaited instructions from superiors. She was provided with the name of a deceased Canadian child and the beginnings of her legend took hold.

As they drove to the quiet Marlow pub where her target was ensconced, she wondered why her mind kept drifting back to the glamorous life she once had before the bastard she was about to kill had ruined her entire life. She wanted that life back, and one day she would set up a new life in America and start again as a freelancer. A freelance agent to one day prove to Moscow she was worthy.

A buzz on her phone brought her back to the here and now.

'*He's in the tent. Just him and the dog.*'

Her senses were electric as she punched out a reply to her thugs on the ground, who remained ready to serve her every order.

As Natalie walked across the lawns of the pub towards the colourful teepee, she saw a well-muscled dog sipping water from a plastic expandable pot. She looked professionally anonymous, carrying two drinks towards a lone man inside the teepee who she could now see was sat on one of the small stools reading a book with a pint of beer in front of him.

'Jack,' she exclaimed. 'It's been so long. I saw you earlier and thought I'd buy you a drink. How are you?'

She watched Jack struggle to comprehend what was going on and who she was. He was indeed a handsome man she thought. Small, but proportionate, dressed smartly in a black polo neck jumper and exuding a gentle smell of decent aftershave. She threw a beaming smile and placed the two glasses on the table.

'I'm sorry, I don't think I know you?' Jack responded in bemusement. She could see the beginnings of a face that knew she was a threat. He was after all a seasoned British spy, perhaps a bit slow on his feet in his elder years, but none the less, an astute man.

'When you look behind you Jack, your current thoughts will be fully verified. He's holding a Romanian Tokarov pistol, cheap I know, but I know you won't mind.'

As Jack turned to check for the threat, Natalie lunged forward to drive a hypodermic syringe deep into his thigh. She pushed the plunger into the syringe's barrel and injected a dose of dihydroetorphine: a thousand times more potent than morphine. The onset of the anaesthetic effects of the drug were rapid, providing Natalie with a couple of minutes to explain to Jack what she would subject him to in the coming hours. She studied Jack's face as she talked, watching his eyes dart around and a look of deep fear cemented in his mind.

Three or four patrons of the pub who were sitting on the adjacent lawn, witnessed the escapade of a dark blue Mercedes sprinter reversing at speed towards the teepee, before they saw two polo shirted men bundle the limp body of a man into the rear of the van. They watched a slender lady walk around the van, smile at each of them, before jumping into the passenger seat and fitting her seat belt.

At 2.30pm that afternoon, Chief Inspector Alan Fox of Thames Valley Police was viewing the pubs CCTV coverage in the small office behind the bar, curious about one thing. Why had the woman killed the dog? Was there really any need? He nodded at the landlord who asked if he took sugar in his coffee and leant forward to view the face of the brunette who had walked into the bar earlier that afternoon and ordered two vodkas with lemonade.

He'd heard the bar staff passing rumours amongst themselves that the local man who had been kidnapped was the son of a wealthy banker and that there was some sort of ransom to be paid. He wasn't sure about that, rumours were generally always rumours.

He walked out to view the garden teepee again, the scene of a crime that was now fully cordoned and manned by a few police officers, with a lone photographer working alongside the suited forensics officers inside the tent.

'Chief Inspector,' came the call from behind him. He turned to see three men, all in suits. The stockier one in a light blue three piece thrust his hand out and held a piece of paper in his other.

'Alan, my name is Piers from SO15.'

'OK. And these chaps are?'

'Ian, and Gary. They're from Box. MI5. I have an official order here that I will now be taking over this investigation, and we'll require your teams here to provide all evidence and photography to us.'

Chapter 42

Mali

Sean peered through the spy hole Phil had drilled into the wooden door enabling him to look into the room that Goran Dozich was just walking into. The room was partially lit with two flickering strip lights that cast shadows across the central table onto the green wooden panelled walls. A second man followed Dozich into the room. A jihadist that Sean recognised. It was the ISGS leader Andooha al-Saqahrawi.

The low-ceilinged room had a stained blue rug that sat beneath the six legs of an old teak table, a couple of rusted filing cabinets close by, and a dreary looking leather sofa at the far end of the room next to the door that Dozich had now entered.

Sean tried to figure out the consequences of what he was about to do. Not quite knowing what might happen, but knowing it was the right thing to do. He had to kill Dozich. He'd wished he'd done it long ago, now that he knew the extent to which he had brutalised Yelena. He felt an instinctive desire to protect her, a yearning to care for her, and a wish to save her from the pain she had suffered at the hands of a man she once thought was her father. He never saw himself as a knight in shining armour, never really felt it that way. But subconsciously, that was exactly what he was thinking. He cared. Looking through the spy hole at Dozich, he began to feel an intense rage rise deep inside his soul. Only the tap on his shoulder stopped him bursting straight into the room.

'Slowly Sean, let's see what happens before we take him down.'

Sean paused and looked Phil in the eye. He didn't need to say it, he could see Phil understood him straight away. But he said it anyway. 'We kill them both, get this done, and we get the fuck out of here.'

'Give me a few minutes to rig the final explosive charges,' Phil said. 'I just need to plug them all in, then we're good to go. I'm using a slow burn fuse to get this lot blown. Maybe tie the bastards up inside the warehouse, or what...'

The thought from Phil was a worthy one. Sean pondered his options as he spied on Dozich, who was sat at the table with the jihadi sat opposite him. He watched a third man enter the room carrying a silver coffee jug and some small glasses. The man who entered the room was slim and tanned, wore a pistol in a thigh holster and sported a thick salt and pepper beard. He left a packet of cigarettes on the table, smiled at Dozich, and walked to the corner of the room where he opened the glass door of a full-length glass cabinet that hosted a small rack of IT servers. The man pressed a few buttons, then left the room.

Sean watched Dozich open a small laptop and boot it up. He could hear Phil in the background rustling a bunch of wires, getting them primed and ready for their escape. Then he saw the jihadi hand an old-fashioned compact disc to Dozich, who in turn punched a button on the side of the laptop before inserting it. It looked like a transaction was in play, and Sean wondered what type of data was being exchanged.

Seconds passed. Sean still wasn't sure how he'd play this one. The laptop and disc would provide key evidence for Jack, and the servers would store a wealth of intelligence useful for taking down considerable numbers in the illegal arms trade. He smelled the sweat of Phil return to the space behind him, but didn't take his eye from the peep hole in the doorframe.

'Good to go, I can blow this place in less than fifteen seconds,' Phil whispered over Sean's shoulder. 'The place will go up in small bursts, ninety seconds apart, all set as a chain reaction with the charges detonating in a staggered manner.'

'Good. You ready? Weapon cocked?'

'Yep.'

'OK, let's do this.' Sean stepped back, leant over to check that Yelena was still hidden, then lunged forward to kick the door in. He lifted his Makarov pistol to aim the barrel right at Dozich's head, noticing Phil had dropped to one knee, his weapon trained on the jihadi.

'Hands on the table now,' Sean shouted at the top of his voice, the shock of entry was written across Dozich's face who froze in fear. Sean looked straight into his eyes. 'One fucking move and I kill you. Tilt your head up and keep your hands on that fucking table. Don't move.'

Both men were now staring at the wooden ceiling with their hands on the table, so Sean moved forward to pull the laptop from between the trembling hands of Dozich. He tapped the button holding the disc, heard the short ping and watched the casing flip out. Sean lifted the compact disc and placed it in his jacket pocket, all the time keeping a sharp eye out for any movement from Dozich.

'I can pay you,' Dozich said assertively, now slowly lowering his head to glance at Sean. 'I have men outside that can take you straight to my gold mine. I have thousands of dollars there and you can have what you want. Gold, dollars, vehicles, aircraft home.'

'Nice try,' Sean uttered, making a point of tensing his finger on the trigger. 'You look like a dead man to me, but you can tell me plenty before I decide, and who knows, I might even feel the urge to spare you.'

Silence in the stale air. The sense of nervous tension focussed Sean's mind. He watched Dozich close his eyes for a moment, hearing the dull sounds of his fingertips tap on the table.

'What do you want to know? I can give you millions by the way. I can transfer it all into an account right here and now, just as my friend was about to do.' Dozich paused. 'This is a lucrative business you know, why not be a part of it. There's plenty for everyone here, and you know it makes sense.'

'Oh, I know there is,' Sean said scraping a chair into place at the head of the table, before sitting to face Dozich. 'Now, tell me about your friendship with Sir Rhys Eldridge.'

Dozich laughed out loud. Then a pause. And then a nervous laugh again. 'So that's what this is all about? You're MI6 or something and want to take him down. I'll gladly help with that, the bastard was shagging my wife decades ago. And he thought I never knew. I just used him for what I needed. He's an asshole but a very useful one.'

Sean frowned. He'd wondered about this family secret when Yelena was telling him her backstory. Then he felt himself grating his jaw, glaring angrily at Dozich. He stood and walked across the room to the window to try and calm his thoughts. The daylight was getting stronger. The security lights in the compound were beginning to switch off, and two guards were merrily chatting and smoking cigarettes next to Dozich's vehicle.

Sean returned to his seat and leant across the table, hardening his gaze. 'Who's the father of Yelena then?'

'You really want to know?'

'Yes.'

'It's Eldridge of course. It could only ever be him. It was obvious.'

'A little game you played with her mind then. Bringing her up as your child, abusing her for decades. You utter bastard. I should slot you right here and now.'

'She got everything she ever needed from me…'

Sean interjected angrily. 'Including your abuse. You're evil. Your hatred for Eldridge fed your evil, narcissistic soul by abusing her. You fucking sick bastard.'

'Listen. You're an intelligent man. Forget all that, she doesn't care for you anyway, and you used her too. Let me give you this opportunity, take the deal, take the money and live happily ever after. Take her too if you want.'

Sean stood, clenched his fists, and turned his back on Dozich for a second time. 'Who else is helping you in this operation in Britain. Names. Who else is working with Eldridge.'

'Come on, what is this? You don't want all this grief dealing with me. It's a waste of all our time. Let me live, you get to become a rich man, I give the names once it's all done, and you're on your way. None of this is personal you know. It's about money and wealth.' A pause, and a piercing eye contact from Dozich as he leant forward to make a point. 'You know - you know that you'll never get to Eldridge, he's well protected by your government and those above him are probably on the take too. Surely you know that right? Even if I give you some other names, they'll eventually end up slotting you too. Once they know you know a bit too much, they'll take you down. You're just a pawn in this game of interconnected groups, just like me. The Kings and Queens of these games are in power across the globe, so it's better for the likes of you and I to keep our guard, keep it non personal, and keep taking the money. What do you say?'

Sean leant back and began to think. He glanced momentarily at Dozich who beamed the challenge through his eyes. Dozich spoke again. The words dulled. His voice fluttered away into the musty air of the cabin. Sean didn't mind being shunted around the world by Jack to solve problems, nor did he mind being the fall guy to trap evil merchants of death, but he drew the line at being kept in the dark about saving the careers of politicians who might be tinkering with arms deals, making their fortunes, and shoring up the defence of the elite who might be embroiled in this murky world. What exactly was Jack up to here? What was he missing? Something wasn't quite right.

Sean's eyes narrowed as he thought about the offer. Time was getting on and he couldn't fuck around much longer. He visualised the bullet penetrating Dozich's face: right between his eyes. He visualised this piece of shit being gone from the world. It was the right thing to do. He began to feel Yelena's pain, and at that moment, he realised how much he loved her. His heart began to thump rapidly, and the hot thrill of adrenaline shot through his veins.

Just as he raised his pistol, he heard the door behind him clank open. A threat? Footsteps, yes.

Then a voice.

'Drop the gun, asshole. Drop it now.'

Sean could just make out the stance of Phil in his peripheral vision a few metres away. He nudged his head to see Phil lower his pistol, move into a crouch position, and place his weapon on the floor.

'Don't turn around. Move slowly, and place that tool on the ground. Now!'

Sean's mind rapidly burnt an image into his brain of a man stood behind him, holding a weapon aimed at his back, and easily able to kill him - swiftly if he made any sharp movements. There was no way out. He had no choice. He placed the weapon on the ground cursing his lack of caution. As he rose, he noticed the triumphant smile of Dozich glaze across his face.

'Hands on your head, stand up, and turn and face me.'

Sean slowly did as he was told. His mind flashed through the options of how he could evade this threat to his life. He turned. Just as he thought. It was the tall man with the beard who had brought the coffee into the room earlier and had somehow entered through the warehouse catching Sean completely unawares. *Fuck* was all he could think. *Fucking hell.* Maybe that quack was right at the psychiatry session. He wasn't up to this kind of game anymore.

'It seems you might not be MI6 after all,' Dozich said cheerfully as he stood up to collect the weapons. 'Pretty bloody slack drills all round, and now you're pretty fucked eh?'

'Fuck off,' was all Sean could muster, a desperate feeling of dread inside him. Maybe he was too battered for this world of war now. Past his sell by date, and way past the time he should have retired gracefully to paint pictures in the wilderness.

Sean shifted his eyes between Dozich and the bearded man. Then he glanced at Phil who shifted his eyes as a signal not to make the move he could see Sean was thinking of. Sean reckoned with a bit of speed and power he could take down the bearded man, whilst Phil could get to Dozich, turning the tables through sheer brute force, speed and skill. He knew Phil would react quickly if he made the first move, and the half-second of his dynamic thought meant he either went for it now, or he'd never get another chance. He'd be happy to go down fighting, he knew the risk of being killed, and there was little left now in his life anyway, except perhaps Yelena. And his son. God, his son. What the fuck was he thinking putting himself in all this danger time after time when he had a young boy who needed him alive. *Get a grip*, he told himself, get out of this game, stay alive and get out. Those thoughts all happened in the seconds he had to react. He did nothing. He kept his hands on his head.

A noise. A weapon being cocked. The slider being pulled back sharply, then released to chamber a round in the barrel.

'Put your fucking weapon down, now.' Yelena shouted harshly at the bearded man.

Sean turned to see Yelena stood in the shadowed gap of the doorframe. He saw the glint of the sun on the barrel of the weapon she was holding, and he witnessed the sheer rage in her eyes.

'Put it down and don't fucking move. Nobody moves. You all stand still because I'm in the mood to shoot the fucking lot of you, and probably will.'

Yelena's left fist was clenched with her nails gnawing into her hand, and her face tight with anger. Sean's eyes wandered to see the bearded man place his weapon on the floor and Dozich place his hands in the air, palms out, as if fending off a series of blows. Four men standing around a table, a jihadi sat watching the episode of mayhem unfurl in front of his eyes, and a woman intent on revenge, harbouring a rage of intense proportions, with a pistol swinging from one man to the other. Who first, Sean wondered, now fearing for his own life again. Yelena did not look at all stable.

'Darling,' Dozich shouted starting to move towards her. 'It's me, your father. Don't worry, everything will be fine.'

Yelena seemed to be fully disassociated. Disassociated from what and who stood in front of her. She seemed in a daze gripped by an alien mind.

'Shut the fuck up. You're not my father. You're my rapist, torturer and the devil. Stop right there before I blow your brains out.'

Sean took a step forward towards Yelena who was caught in the sunlight spilling into the room. 'Good work Yelena. Let's get out of here. We'll tie them up in the warehouse, it's all set to blow.'

'Shut up. Stand fucking still. Don't you dare think you can get out of this, you fucked with my mind too you bastard. I loved you, and you used me too. Just like that bastard.' Yelena swung the barrel at Dozich, then back at Sean's chest.

Sean was stunned. Yelena was raging inside now, swinging the muzzle between him and Dozich, back and forth, until it came to rest again on Sean.

Sean stiffened. His jaw grated. He couldn't believe she was pointing a loaded gun at him. She's going to do it, he thought, she's going to kill me, and every last one of us in this room.

'He played you Yelena, he doesn't love you,' Dozich said. 'Let me give you a million dollars, set yourself up for the rest of your life. We can do it right now, on this laptop, and you go free. Just kill him now. He betrayed you.'

'You know that's not true,' Sean yelled. 'Come on, give me the weapon.'

The weapon didn't move. Then she lifted it a notch. It was aimed right at Sean's head now. A smile began to form on Yelena's face, then it happened. She started to pull the trigger, tensing it, grimacing now, shaking the weapon ready to release the bullet. Sean closed his eyes. 'You know someone loves you,' he said calmly. 'And you know that someone is me.'

He opened his eyes again. He watched a tear rolling slowly from Yelena's right eye. He saw her take a deep breath before moving the weapon back to Dozich, placing a second hand on the grip, then tensing her shoulders.

A grim realisation of death came across Dozich's face. He was white as a sheet. Looking down the barrel of a weapon that was about to take his life.

Yelena pulled the trigger and the booming sound of the discharge raged through the room, the flash from the muzzle momentarily catching Sean by surprise. Dozich howled in agony as he clutched his chest, the bullet having ripped through his right lung, before he collapsed into a bundle on the ground. His body began to jerk wildly and the rasping sound of his last gasps of air brought his life to an end in seconds.

A second shot. Yelena fired again at the bearded man. The round smashed into his chest causing him to bellow loudly before he fell backwards onto the table, ricocheting his body onto the rug that was now covered in deep red blood.

Phil sprang into action grabbing his weapon from the table and trained it on the jihadi who still hadn't moved. Sean ran forward to grab Yelena, who was now a quivering wreck having dropped the weapon with her weakened legs causing her to collapse into his arms. It was over. She had killed her lifelong tormentor and destroyed the evil that had subsumed her life for too long.

'Let's not fuck around Sean, get bloody moving,' Phil shouted.

Just as Sean was about to reply, a volley of bullets flew through the window, one round whizzing past Sean's neck into the wooden doorframe behind him. Out of the corner of his eye, Sean saw the jihadi lurch forward and reach behind him for a pistol lodged in the back of his jeans under his traditional agbada shirt. Everything was happening now in slow motion, but Sean turned to see Phil spring into action. In a single motion, Phil ducked, watched the jihadi grab the pistol, and rolled onto his back firing a double tap of rounds into his neck.

'Move. Move now into the warehouse,' Sean shouted as he heard the commotion of security guards shouting at each other outside, seemingly in some disarray.

The three of them ran into the warehouse with Phil shouting and steering them towards the far end of the complex where he had prepared their escape through an air vent that linked the building to a separate power room that was close to the perimeter fence. Sean grabbed Yelena's hand, forcing her to run quicker, sweating now with the realisation that this could all go pear-shaped pretty quickly and they might never escape if the guards surrounded the warehouse. Only Phil's handiwork could possibly save them now, and he hoped that it wouldn't be too long before the first of the detonations took place.

'Keep going, pull the vent open, and start crawling along it,' Phil shouted. 'I'll prime the initiator and get this place to go very loud.'

Chapter 43

Mali

Phil 'the nose' had established a complex configuration of slow burn detonation fuse that had been rolled out to six separate areas of the warehouse ready to blow the munitions in a staggered manner. The black detonating fuse would burn its thin explosive powder strands inside its quarter inch core at thirty seconds per foot, all neatly wrapped in reinforced and waterproof plastic coating. Each detonating fuse led to the C-4 plastic explosives that Phil had placed next to munition crates that would sympathetically detonate next to each other, after the main charge had been detonated. All manner of rockets, grenades, and explosively formed projectiles would create the explosive train that Phil wanted to render them all utterly useless for future use. Yes, the carnage of the explosions that would ensue would create huge panic, chaos and devastation, but he'd planned it so that he could mitigate as many deaths as possible to the locals who were now starting to come into work around the site, and into the adjacent markets.

The detonating fuse was placed in the natural corridors between the five-metre high industrial shelving, and led to tight connections of the non-electric, pre-crimped detonators that would act as the priming initiator into the five-kilogramme plastic explosive moulds. From a central point in the warehouse, Phil could fire a flash initiator into the detonating cord and set an explosive train at staggered times around the entire complex. It wasn't without high-risk, especially as they had to escape at the same time, and the risk of detonating cord catching fire from separate explosions could wreak havoc if they all blew at once.

Phil looked down at his flash initiator where he would simultaneously push two black buttons with his thumb and forefinger. He briefly pulled his hand through his short hair and let out a big sigh as he tried to regulate his breathing. His plan was that the first explosion would create the chaos needed to allow them to escape from the guards who would then be plummeted into panic, stopping them from entering the building. Then the next explosion would take place, then the next, and then the next.

Each explosion would force anyone in the surrounding area to escape the conflagration and run for their lives whilst most of the fragmentation slugs of the munitions would be lodged into the mud walls of the warehouse.

He'd thought it through well, but he couldn't be sure it would all go off as he wanted. The absolute key to their own survival was to be clear of the inside of the warehouse before the fragments started flying in all directions, throwing searing blades of hot metal across the entire arms factory, killing anything stone dead in its way.

Phil started to crimp the final length of black fuse into the flash initiator which he placed between his knees. As he did so, he sang the first verse of Calon Lân, a favourite Welsh ballad that always reminded him to be pure, genuine, and love the simple things in life. He hoped and prayed that innocent bystanders would not be killed by what he was about to unleash.

'*Calon lân ywn lawyn daiowny*,' he sang loudly, pushing the thick fuse into place. He looked up briefly to check his escape route to the vent, a throwback to his training on slow burn fuses, where it had been drilled deeply into him to always check twice that the escape route was clear before pulling the trigger.

'Fuck.'

He couldn't believe what he was seeing. 'Jesus Christ,' he murmured to himself.

Yelena was clambering back out of the vent with Sean grappling to stop her, trying hard to get her to leave. She looked like she was having none of it. Crying and now screaming, in a total meltdown.

'Leave me, leave me here to die. I don't want anymore,' Yelena shouted in panic.

Phil stood and shouted at them both. 'Get the fuck out. There's no time left now, just get going, fix it later.'

Phil was gripped and fuming. Two buttons left to press, eighty seconds to the first explosion, and now he had a domestic scene happening right in front of him. He watched Sean grapple with her, trying to console her, trying his best to show her life could go on. It was awful to watch. A brave woman emotionally devastated, and a man of honour trying to avert her crying, showing her the way to salvation. A small tunnel and a short run through the perimeter was all that was needed to escape this madness, back to a safe place, and a world that could repair her. But no, it all had to happen just as he was about to plunge the environment into utter devastation, not knowing right now whether any of them would survive.

'Sean, just get her out. Now.' Phil pleaded. 'I'm firing this gun whatever happens, and I'm pressing the trigger in five seconds.' He watched Sean nod from beyond Yelena's shoulder, and started counting down from five. Yelena finally began to lift herself back into the air vent. Just as he counted down to three, he heard the first distant report of a bullet being fired.

Whoosh. Clink.

'Shit,' he said, taking cover on his knees as a bullet ricocheted off the central iron stanchion between him and the shooter, who was some fifty metres away at the other end of the warehouse. 'It's all gone tits up now,' he said shaking his head.

He grabbed the green flash box into the palm of both his hands, said a little prayer in Welsh, and mouthed his final words before making good his escape. 'Three, two, one, firing now.'

He pressed the two black buttons simultaneously as hard as he could, praying that the flash initiator would cause the fuse to start burning the powder inside its protected casing towards the first detonator some twenty feet away.

He watched the detonation cord burn, knowing he had exactly eighty seconds to exit the danger zone and shield himself from the first sets of explosive blast and fragmentation that would surely cause the conflagration he hoped for. He was now fully aware that the angry men entering the warehouse would soon be stood on top of the explosives that would send them to their deaths.

'Come on Phil,' Sean shouted, waving an arm fiercely from inside the vent. 'Give me your hand.'

Phil grabbed Sean's hand, at the same time, driving his right foot onto a protruding shelf to lever his way swiftly into the air vent. Phil started to crawl a metre or so behind Sean, noticing that Yelena was a good ten metres ahead of them making quite a racket as she clambered through the shiny steel vent to what looked like a fluorescent light ahead of them in the distance. He leopard crawled fiercely on all fours, swatted a dead mouse out of the way, and made fast progress into the void, sweating profusely now. He was counting the seconds from detonation in his mind when he got to ninety-seven, wondering if he'd fucked it all up. He knew there was a margin of error on the fuse burn rate, but hoped and prayed it hadn't been a batch of old stuff that would fail a couple of feet down the fuse. Just as he got to one hundred and five, he heard the thunderous explosion behind him.

Phil pictured the armed guards who were probably blown savagely from their feet by the blast wave, and writhing in agony from the burning metal that would have entered their bodies at a velocity of hundreds of miles per hour.

Grimacing, Phil tucked his body tight, waiting for the blast wave to follow him down the vent. He hoped he wasn't about to get a stray piece of shrapnel up the arse and gripped himself hard, tensing every muscle in his body awaiting whatever would come at him. In the end, it was just a meek blast of air, but the smell of cordite and chemicals made him gag. He made his way to the end of the vent and climbed out into the noisy surroundings of a power room, noticing its high voltage buzz bars and transformers.

Sean gave him a high five handshake and they said nothing for a good few seconds. It was the grim thought of what was about to come that spurred them back into action.

Chapter 44

Mali

P hil 'the nose' was pumped. 'I reckon, another minute and the second blast will crack off,' he said, peering over Sean's shoulder to see if Yelena was OK. 'Let's check the route to the fence, and we make a run for it just after the second blast.'

'How long to the third?' Sean asked.

'Another thirty seconds after that.'

'And the fourth?'

'Same.'

'Jesus Phil, how many blasts in total.'

'Six, but you might get one or two extra thrown in for good measure as the other munitions start sympathetically detonating.'

'Sympathetically?'

'A good old-fashioned bomb doctor term for explosives sat next to other explosives that go bang, because of its proximity.'

'Fuck. This is going to be some firework display.'

'Yep. Enough to create lots of chaos for us to get the fuck out of here and get back home sharpish.'

Phil watched Sean hold Yelena by the shoulders, steadying her for the next phase. 'You OK now?' he asked.

'I think so. I'm sorry about that, but it was quite traumatic killing him in that way, and I just lost my mind for a moment.'

'Twenty seconds,' Phil shouted, hoping Sean would get a move on.

'It's always traumatic,' Sean whispered into her ear, giving her a kiss on the cheek. 'But you're safe with us. A road to the future now.'

'Ten seconds. Get to the door,' Phil said peering out at the sandy void through the louvred slats. 'It's clear. Follow me. And be ready to fucking shoot anyone who tries to stop us.'

'Roger that,' came the reply. 'Poised. You move first. I'll steer you.'

With that, Phil tutted, then rolled his eyes, knowing Sean was taking the piss. Sean never did like taking orders from anyone, never mind being told to follow them. Phil pulled the small brass latch on the door lock to release it from its housing and opened the hefty door a couple of inches. Nothing. No sign of anyone. A thirty-metre dash to the fence line to the location they had entered, where they had patched a three foot square panel of fencing with twisted cable wire to hold it in place.

He reckoned it would take them about fifty seconds to unravel the wire coils, pop out the panel, then crawl out through the hole. Perfect timing, he thought. The second explosion would avert any attention from the guards on the perimeter, and all their eyes would be on the pummelling of the mud walls, and the flashes of fire crashing into the early morning sky.

'How long?' Sean asked, an intensity now in his gravelly voice.

'It's gone over the detonation time. The fuse isn't that accurate on burn rate.'

'Oh great. So, we could be standing here for a while then…'

Boom!

The second explosion ripped through the warehouse, at a magnitude of sound that was double the first one.

'Go, go, go,' Sean barked.

Phil ran to the fence checking to his left and right as he crossed the gravel trackway. Just as he got to the fence line, he looked behind him. Reams of smoke were bellowing from the top of the warehouse, with bursts of flames piercing through the roof into the light blue skyline.

He focused on the fence cables and turned the first twisted wire with his thumb and finger, cursing as a sharp sliver of metal cut his forefinger. He unravelled the second, then the third, before punching the panel through ninety degrees allowing him to shuffle his head and shoulders through the gap. He thrust his torso forward, followed by his legs, and scampered through the small hole before ending with a forward roll into the sand, alert to anything that might confront him.

On one knee now, he scanned the environment, looking for any threats around him, and urged Sean and Yelena to move much quicker than they had been going so far. Only a few more minutes he thought, hoping that the escape vehicle would be in place. A hidden vehicle prepared and manned by the CIA to get them speedily to a Black Hawk helicopter at a desert rendezvous some five kilometres away. Granted, they were an hour or so late, but the plan had accounted for that. The adrenaline shot through his neuro receptors, all of them now revelling in the danger of yet another escapade with his best mate.

'Come on you pair, stop fucking around,' he urged making his way up the gravelled sand berm to where the escape vehicle would be covered from view in the wide culvert below.

A wry smile came across his rugged face as he heard another blast of munitions shoot across the basin expanse, quickly followed by a series of smaller explosions that he recognised as grenades going off inside the warehouse. Happy with his handiwork, he placed one knee on the ground, and watched Sean and Yelena make their way up the hill, breathing hard. He looked back at the warehouse, now some half a kilometre away. His explosive train had worked a treat.

It's an old adage on high-risk operations. And this was no exception. 'It's never over until it's over.' And this one wasn't. Phil watched the third explosion rip through the roof of the warehouse, and a vast plume of smoke exit the void of the destroyed corrugated steel roof. Flames were pouring through the building, and the odd orange burst zipped in and out of the windows that had been obliterated by the series of explosive blasts. He watched the tiny silhouettes of men scurrying around the compound, most trying to escape, some looking for cover, and some starting to drive their vehicles through the now abandoned gatehouse barriers.

Then it came. The small sounds of gunfire. Insignificant at first, he thought. Tiny aberrations set against the sound of high explosives going off all around the skyline. Then he felt the sand being splattered all around him.

'Shit,' he shouted loudly scrambling to get over the berm.

'Keep your heads down, move quickly,' he shouted again to Sean and Yelena, now about ten metres behind him.

He dived over the berm, and in a singular motion swivelled his body in a star shaped manner, to turn back and face the incoming fire, pushing hard with his feet to get to the prone position he needed, hidden just behind the crest of the berm.

'Come on, come on,' he shouted again, seeing Sean struggle to the top of the berm, bullets now landing all around his feet.

He saw the face of Yelena slightly behind Sean. She was now covered in sweat, grunting hard to make her final lurches to freedom, sweeping her hair out of her face, pushing hard on her legs to get the grip she needed to propel her up the slope. Phil could see she couldn't get the purchase she needed in the tumbling sand. Her legs kept going in a cycling motion at full tilt, but the momentum didn't throw her forward at the rate she needed.

'Arghhhh,' was all he heard as the bullet smashed into her back between her shoulder blades. The last thing he witnessed, before Yelena fell face first into the sand, was her bulging eyes looking him straight in the eye, paralysed with fear.

What happened next, was all in frantic slow motion. The dull sounds of gunfire tailing off into a vacuum of mysterious echoes. It was like a freeze frame to him. It was etched into his skull. The sounds of Sean shouting 'Noooooo, No, No…' followed by the sight of him grabbing her jacket lapels to pull her over the berm.

He watched Sean turn her body in the sand, check her pulse, place his ear to her mouth to check to see if she was breathing. Frame by frame, all in slow motion, Phil couldn't believe it. He watched Sean turn towards him. It was a grim scene. A scene of trauma never to be locked away.

The flames seared away in the background, and the thud of the fourth explosion caught Phil's ear in the slow motion vacuum he'd been pulled into.

She was dead. Yelena was gone.

Chapter 45

London

S ean sat at the far end of the bar, facing the pub entrance with a clear view through the large expansive windows to the Smithfield Rotunda gardens. The Butchers Hook and Cleaver was a favoured haunt of his, now providing him with the stimulus he needed to think through carefully what to do next. Formerly a branch of The Midland Bank and a wholesale meat supply shop, the Butchers Hook and Cleaver was an historic City pub right next door to Smithfield, the oldest meat market in London.

Sean was in pain, and it hurt badly. A new type of pain to lay on a shelf alongside all of his others. His age-old mantra of hogging the pain had long been subdued, fiercely punctured by the loss of the woman he loved. The image of Dozich being obliterated by Yelena gave him some solace. She may have been badly pained, but she was a good woman inside. A kind and loving woman. If only he'd run behind her, shielded her, he thought with a pang of deep sadness.

Sean glanced out of the windows to the circular gardens where in days gone by jousters, tournaments and grim public executions had once taken place. Heretics, rebels and criminals were slain, beheaded or boiled and hundreds were burnt at the stake during Queen Mary's reign in the 1550s. Sean's gaze turned into a lingering stare. He felt numb, sedated even. Despite his hurt, he had one more act to fulfil. An execution, possibly two, and he needed to plot the sequencing with one-eyed Damon in detail.

He placed his phone on the bar and pushed an empty plate to one side before picking up a mug of builder's tea. He wasn't quite ready for beer. He thought back to the last thirty-six hours, the reality hardly registering with him. Was it all a dream? What had happened to Laura's planned attack? Maybe he'd find out one day.

The American soldier had crouched at the base of a white column adjacent to the Mali Presidential Palace. He had awaited the signal for the assault to begin which would come from a codeword into his earpiece, at which point he would raise the pistol grip of the recoilless AT4 gun, release the safety, and fire the eighty-four millimetre rocket at the Black Toyota Landcruiser parked in front of the palace entrance where two Russian mercenaries were awaiting their VIP passenger, and another had stood holding the rear door open.

At this distance, the Texan, a veteran of ten years in the CIA Special Activities Division, was confident that he could take down all three men with the enhanced lethality of the copper projectile that would force a thin copper charge liner into a jet-like penetrator on detonation.

'OPTICAL, OPTICAL, go now,' came the shout across the radio. The Texan released the safety, drew his eye closer to the sighting mechanism, steadied his aim, and simultaneously placed his finger on the trigger. He took up the pressure, watched a man in a grey suit with an eyepatch walk towards the Toyota, then squeezed.

For anyone looking through the large French colonial gates at the far end of the driveway, what they would have seen next would have astonished them. Almost to the exact second of synchronisation, three explosive events happened that indicated that the Presidential Palace was under sustained attack.

As the copper penetrator slashed through the armour-plated vehicle, whipping its molten metal around the cab, two Black Hawk helicopters emerged over the roof of the palace, and streams of assaulters in black fatigues fast roped onto the terrace of the Palace. At the same time as the vehicle occupants were sheared by the fragmentation, a distant sniper waited until the grey suited eyepatch was thrown to the floor from the blast. Half a second later a single .300 Winchester Magnum low drag bullet had penetrated his skull.

Behind him, a whirlwind of activity had been taking place. Sixteen SAS soldiers had stormed the Palace, killing four Russian mercenaries within three minutes of hitting the terrace, and in front of them a dozen armoured vehicles had crashed through the Palace gates and were putting down effective fire on the two lower floor offices where the mercenaries had been headquartered.

A hail of AT4 rounds had been fired into the middle floor offices, causing thunderous explosions. A number of mercenaries had taken cover behind a truck from the hail of 7.62mm bullets that had been pummelled into them from SAD agents who had now overpowered the bulk of the enemy through shock and awe, and the full force of surprise. A lone mercenary in desert fatigues with only a pistol to hand, bolted for the perimeter, but at the point he heard the sickening whir of a thirty-millimetre chain gun from an Apache gunship, he knew he was a dead man. The bullets ripped his torso apart, cutting him down in his tracks.

Within fifteen minutes of the attack, the President had been whisked away safely by the gloved hands of four American SAD operators who had lifted him into a Black Hawk helicopter hovering above the roof of the palace. All that was left were two Russian mercenaries, kneeling on the dirt in front of the palace steps, hands clasped behind the back, with two Armalite rifles pointed at their heads.

In London, the Prime Minister and COBRA officials watched live imagery of the SAS storming the Palace, followed by the aerial imagery of the entire attack from an American RQ-4 Global Hawk unmanned aerial vehicle. Officials in COBRA were scrambling to check that Washington had initiated the follow-on attacks to be mounted by the French on Jihadi strongholds, backed up by American special operations teams. At the point where the mission had been achieved, Sir Justin Darbyshire left the room to make a secure phone call to Laura in Niger.

'Is he safe?' Sir Justin had asked nervously.

'He is,' came the reply. 'We fucked up though. I should have had more teams on the ground to help him. Yelena was killed during the extraction.'

'Shit. That's bad. Can you get him back quickly? I have a bit of a problem going on back here. We've lost Jack.'

When One-Eyed Damon walked into the Butchers Hook and Cleaver, he tapped his white cane on the first set of table and chairs not knowing to go left or right around them. One-eyed Damon preferred pubs he knew, and ideally ones on his patch, it just made things easier. Sean noticed he was confused and shouted out to him.

'Ten o'clock mate. At the bar.'

One-eyed Damon growled a bit, then made his way clockwise around the opposite side of the table he had begun to circumvent the other way. 'Roger. Two pints please.'

Sean nodded to the barman and ordered three pints of Fuller's ESB cask ale. One-eyed Damon sat on a stool and tapped the bar. He launched straight into his apology.

'Look, we fucked up mightily. Thought we had it nailed, but we chose the wrong OPs mate. I'm really, really sorry - this hurts me.' Sean noticed him slurp half a pint of the ale in one go.

'We did manage to get a regain though, when it all went noisy.'

'What do you mean noisy? What the hell happened?'

'Well, you were spot on with your thoughts about Natalie's thugs lifting him at his local. Trouble was, when Jack arrived at the pub, we should have got closer. The Bulgarians missed the woman entering. They reckon she was disguised. I reckon they were just shit fucking lazy.'

'And?'

'It went noisy when a Mercedes hard reversed to a big tent in the garden. One of those pointed native American things.'

'A teepee.'

'That's the one. Jack was chucked in and they belted out of the car park.' One-eyed wiped his brow and drunk the final half a pint of ale. 'The dipshits did manage to follow them though. Right into the centre of London.'

Sean tutted. 'He could well be dead now you know. Tortured and murdered.'

'What makes you think that? She must be after something in return right? Extortion?'

'Doubtful. She a sociopathic killer. I'll tell you later.'

'OK.'

'Now, I'm guessing you've got eyes on the location, right?'

'Yes. But it's a tricky place to watch.'

Sean took a moment to take a drink. He had spoken to Sir Justin Darbyshire that morning, and he'd delayed his request to meet him. He needed to figure out what to do and he'd decided not to let Sir Justin know that Jack had been under his surveillance. It was nagging him now though. Should he tell him? The security service would be going wild trying to track Jack down, one of their top agents, their top executives, now kidnapped. A massive security blow to MI5 and a huge risk to them and The Court operations. Bloody hell, Natalie could blow the whole thing up. Years of covert planning to get to the stage where it was with the CIA. Sean knew he ought to cough up the information to Sir Justin, but he wanted to know more before he did.

What about Laura? She had a lot invested in The Court. It suddenly dawned on him that a lone Russian sociopath could do untold damage to the British and American Intelligence services. Maybe that was her plan all along, he thought? What exactly did he reveal to her under interrogation? He couldn't remember.

For an hour, as customers came and went, Sean discussed the options with one-eyed Damon to rescue Jack, if indeed he was still alive. They discussed weaponry and avenues of approach to the site where he was detained. Sean shivered at the very thought of him going through the same torture ritual that Natalie had used on him. He wasn't completely sure he hadn't given anything more away which would cause problems to The Court.

It didn't help that one-eyed Damon now disagreed with his plan. Yes, he knew he should call Sir Justin. And yes, he knew this was a risky thing to do. But he wanted revenge and revenge is a potent driver of action. He wanted to kill Natalie himself, and not allow some anonymous trooper to take her down during an armed assault. The rescue of an MI5 Director would have all manner of special forces officers crawling all over it, police cordons in place, residents evacuated. Was that the best way forward?

Then he thought of Swartz. Just when he needed his former SAS friend, he was no longer there. Dead. The victim of a mole or insider on the operation who had leaked the details of the operation he was on. Sean immediately suspected Sir Rhys was at the heart of all this, and made a vow to deal with him after Natalie. He was incensed now, raging deep inside.

Later, at Millbank, Sean looked west across the river to spy the location where Jack was being held hostage. It gave him quite a surprise.

'A bloody penthouse suite?' He asked.

One-eyed Damon stammered his answer. 'Yes, looks like it is - it is.'

'Have the guys been up there?'

'No. Tough security to crack but we can have a look at different ways to get in. Or…'

'Or what…?'

'Look at those windows. We saw her on the eleventh floor apartment. You could use a half inch armour piercing round from a sniper rifle to kill Natalie in one go.'

Sean took a moment to think through what was effectively, a very valid option. Then he made a phone call. Luckily, Sir Justin Darbyshire was available and asked if he could help with anything. Sean said yes, he could.

Chapter 46

London

J ack sat at a Carvelle pedestal dining table wondering whether to eat the crab rosti with cress and chives. Or should he simply forgo the starter and push straight onto the sirloin of beef & braised oxtail, with mushroom puree and wilted spinach?

He looked across the marble table towards the London skyline. The eleventh floor Penthouse, where he was dining alone, provided superb views across the Lambeth Palace gardens and down the River Thames to the Palace of Westminster and the City of London.

His eyes focused for a moment on the terrace pavilion of the House of Commons, a short social space, snuggled neatly within the Palace's 260 metre gothic façade along the northern bank of the River Thames. His mind wandered back to when it all began.

Jack's entrée into the Houses of Parliament, the corridors of Westminster and the machinations of British politics, all began in the early nineties when he had been asked by an old school friend to speak at a select committee dinner who were considering the questions of what to do about the Bosnia situation, which was rumbling badly in the Balkans. He and his friend had both attended Haberdashers' Aske's Boys' School near Borehamwood but had departed sixth form into completely different careers. It had been some twelve years since they had last met when Jack decided it was time to discover what the mystical, ceremonious halls of Westminster fame looked like in the stony flesh.

It was a curious dinner, only eight members of the select committee, and Jack as their guest in one of the tiniest dining rooms he had ever had the pleasure to eat in. The oak panelled walls, historic paintings of the Palace, and the musty smells of the room made him recognise that his choice of career in the Secret Intelligence Service was exactly the right move.

Jack had never been comfortable around the political class, and being right in the centre of it, with all eyes focussed on him as a guest speaker, he began to feel deeply uncomfortable with it all. It was only later that evening, when he was drinking a gin and tonic on the pavilion terrace with a few of the committee members, that he began to despise, not the place, but some of the people within it.

Jack brought his eyes back to the issue in question. To eat the crab rosti or not. His choice was interrupted when the door opened behind him and he heard the distinctive clatter of high heels walking across the solid wood floor.

'I hope you're enjoying the view of your office right in front of you,' Natalie said chirpily. 'A wonderful sight to see. Thames House in all its glory, and look, the sweeping views down to Westminster. Pure nostalgia. That's what you all love in MI5 isn't it?'

Jack didn't turn to speak or even look at her, but he did smell her distinctive Caron Poivre perfume as she breezed past him to stand beside the full-length glazing before she turned on her heels.

'So, can we get down to business Jack? I trust you've been happy with the arrangements so far?'

'Delightful. Though the food is a bit too exotic for my vanilla palate.'

Jack pushed the rosti away and forced a smile. The light behind Natalie provided only a silhouette of her shape, but he did make out that she was wearing a navy sleeveless dress. The prismed light that streamed through the glazing glinted across the chunky silver chain that she wore. Natalie picked up a banana from the grey carbonised bowl on the table and started to peel it.

'I enjoyed my time in there,' she said beguilingly. She pointed to the Houses of Westminster. 'I fucked a lot of men in there, and the occasional woman you know.'

Jack sensed from the silence, that she wanted some sort of reaction from him. He breathed deeply and sighed. 'What's this all about Natalie? It's been a nice game so far, but can we get on with it please?'

'Oh, you want me to fuck you now, or later?'

'You've already done that. At least to my career. The damage is pretty deep I'm sure.'

Natalie peeled the last bit of the banana and shrugged. She glided across the room to sit next to Jack and started to lick the banana erotically, occasionally pouting her perfectly symmetrical lips. Only a touch of Botox Jack thought, but a hefty sliver of red lipstick. He knew exactly what she was doing, and sensed this would be a long afternoon of power plays from Natalie. But what the hell did she actually want?

'Did Sean ever tell you much about me Jack?'

'What do you mean?'

'When he fucked me. Did he tell you how wonderful it was, how crazy it was?'

A pause in which Jack wasn't sure whether to answer, or how he could answer. 'Umm, well - he most certainly told me about the crazy bit - which is why we took you down with an armed assault. We weren't going to take any chances with you.'

Natalie purred. 'Well, your reward was taking down a lot, but not all of my Russian agents in Britain. I got jail, embarrassment and the loss of my career. But I got my revenge too, and that's all that matters now.'

'Revenge?'

'Killing Sean was as sweet as taking the honey nectar from a hungry bear's paw. I thought I'd let you know he suffered immensely.'

Jack felt the bait and decided to play dumb. He looked over his shoulder and glanced around the Goddard Littlefair interior that accentuated the classical size of the room with its floor-to-ceiling windows. It reflected the size of the shit he was in. The Russian guard behind him smiled. His weapon was already cocked in case Jack gave him any trouble.

'Why the five-star welcome?' Jack asked reaching for a napkin. 'Or does the torture and brutality come later?'

Natalie leant back to finish the banana. It was hard for Jack not to notice her low-cut dress, and ample cleavage. 'Well, we want to give you a chance first Jack. Maybe a bit of fun too. You get my drift. All of this can be done in a very nice amicable way you know.'

'We?'

'Ah, yes. I forgot to say.' Natalie looked at her watch. 'My father will be here shortly. He can join you for your main course.'

'*Bollocks*,' Jack thought. He knew something wasn't quite right, and now he was about to meet a Russian nemesis from his time in Moscow in 2006. Andrey Katchalyna was a former KGB General, but when Jack knew him, he had become the Deputy Director of the FSB responsible for Russian counterespionage. Jack had had the unfortunate experience of an interview with him after a particularly sensitive cock-up by MI6 on the streets of Moscow. Jack fleetingly thought of those moments, which made him wince. The very name Katchalyna had been etched deep into his memory. He must be in his late seventies by now Jack thought.

It wasn't long before Jack was able to confirm his own thoughts. There was no knock at the door, no sudden entry by Katchalyna, but Jack sensed something was going down when four suited men entered the room and started inspecting the walls with non-linear junction detectors. They looked like metal detectors but smaller. Black, sleek, and high-tech, emitting a continuous beeping sound as they sought to find hidden electronic bugs behind the plasterboard, behind pictures and within the expensive furniture.

Twenty minutes later, the team leader gave the nod to Natalie, and she punched a text to her father.

Chapter 47

London

Jack was a little surprised at how well Katchalyna had aged. Fine living from his wealth, all made from a lifetime of crooked deals in Moscow and across the globe, he thought.

'You look well Jack, much better than the last time we met,' the elderly man said. 'When was that. Fourteen years ago, maybe?'

'Fifteen,' Jack said tersely. Not at all pleased to see the man who had ordered his brutal interrogation in a bare cell somewhere on the outskirts of Moscow all those years ago. It was a memory so bad, that he could hardly look Katchalyna in the eye. He was faced by a known KGB murderer, but his destiny was likely to be far worse than the last time they had met.

Jack forced himself to look across the table at Katchalyna. It was as painful as any victim looking at their abuser, at their persecutor. He now felt immensely vulnerable, despite Katchalyna explaining that he had a proposition to make to him. Katchalyna wore a tailor-made grey suit, white shirt and yellow tie, but he looked slightly fragile now. His hands were clasped as he spoke. A slight shake. Jack's eyes were drawn to his distinctive white hair, immaculately parted on the left, with a dash of Brylcreem keeping the coiffure neatly in place. His thinning features suggested that the man was now approaching his eightieth year, or a touch inside it. He still looked agile though and spoke perfect English with a slight Slavic accent.

'Natalie, if you please.' Katchalyna pointed to the brown envelope placed on the table in front of him. Natalie picked up the envelope, walked daintily to Jack as if she was on a catwalk, opened the envelope and placed a ten-inch photograph in front of him.

'As you can see Jack, your agent is doing well. Well, he's alive, and doing as well as can be expected I suppose.'

Jack took one look at the photograph and gagged. The man was sat in a solitary confinement cell, naked except his underpants, posing for a photograph with a uniformed Russian guard holding his head by his long brown hair. It was distressing to look at. His eyes were blackened, and his lips were swollen. The man was Andre Sukonov.

Now in his sixties, Sukonov had been recruited by Jack in Moscow to provide information on Russian arms sales to Middle Eastern countries in return for cash incentives. He was one of Jack's first agents that he had personally recruited.

'You British always had an interest in our arms trade, and now it seems you've taken that interest a few steps further and made it very personal Jack. So much further, that you have caused me considerable aggravation with my commercial interests supporting the Kremlin.'

Jack took a moment to compose himself. He could see where this might be going. After Sukonov was arrested by the Russian FSB, a television commentator suggested that MI6 had managed to recruit Sukonov by gathering compromising information on him. He was said to have received $12,000 from Jack on two occasions: payment for providing secret intelligence before he was finally arrested for high treason.

'What do you want from me Andrey?' Jack asked, still angry at the condition of his former agent.

'Well, I propose we start with a civil chat on how you have decimated my mercenary business, perhaps something to eat and drink, then we can get onto my proposition. One that you will choose between being killed or providing me with what I want. How does that sound?'

Jack made a face and sighed. 'I can see you've enjoyed being Chairman of Keystone Security Corps Andrey. I've investigated all of your businesses over the years, and it's given me quite a kick too. Keystone Corps gave me a particularly good insight into your arms deals and how you set up the front companies. Technically registered in the breezy happy go lucky Honduras, it's fifty-one percent owned by an entity called Pryston Holdings Limited, which itself is registered in the British Virgin Islands. A favourite offshore destiny for Russian enterprises trying to conceal their ownership structures. Luckily for me, it's a British overseas territory, and I could easily get to the right people to probe your financial deals across the globe.'

'You have been doing your homework Jack.'

'I have. It seems you had quite a good run in your retirement, contracted illicitly by the Kremlin as a private security company to supply arms to all parts of the globe. I have to say, it was quite nice to see your operation shut down in Africa, but I know you have other global deals too. It seems you've established another two companies in the same manner, and you might just find you're on the wrong side of a few law enforcement inquiries that are, well … imminent.'

Katchalyna waved a dismissive arm. 'I was your target all along wasn't I?'

'You could call it a hobby of mine.'

'I see. So, you've been planning your revenge for over fifteen years. Your own sweet payback against a man who ordered your torture and interrogation. It must have been eating away inside you for all those years. The jealousy, the hate, the bitterness.'

Jack held his gaze on Katchalyna's face. He began to feel exactly the emotions the ex KGB hardman had described. The hatred had seeped into his stare. He watched Katchalyna's expression harden.

'You see Jack, I was a fool. I underestimated you all those years ago. I thought you were just a typical officer in the British Embassy. An MI6 lacky. But I've recently seen what you've been up to and looked deeply into your activities over the last five years. It shocked me. Granted, I had no idea you'd take fifteen years to plug away at retribution, but now I've seen how you take down your own brethren too. Ministers who you hate, disloyal ambassadors that you hunted down, even rogue intelligence officers that you investigated with vigour. You trapped them all. And for that I salute you. You'd have had a fine career in the Russian intelligence services.'

'Well thank you. Recognition at last,' Jack replied sardonically. He wasn't going to go down without a good fight and a bit of British sarcasm to boot. 'Maybe I underestimated you too. My mistake was thinking that you wouldn't be able to get to your daughter, and that she'd spend the rest of her life behind British bars. Call it a Tiger Kidnap if you like. I knew it would be a spear in your back. I was the one who made sure she'd never get released under any deal, under any spy swap, under any circumstances. You see, my now deceased boss, knew all along that my focus was on you, and that one day we'd both make you pay for taking down sixteen of our best agents in Russia during our time in Moscow as enemies. We've been watching your Chairmanship of the largest mercenary gang that's affiliated to the Kremlin. I hope they now see you as unreliable, as a burden on them. Washed away, zero political favour left, and a has-been.'

'Oh, they do, which is why I'm here now. To get my own vengeance, and to make you pay for your total disrespect for the unwritten rules we have. You made it too fucking personal.'

'And you were the fucking arsehole who had me beaten to within an inch of my life.'

Jack knew that Katchalyna was deranged with power, and this was his last toss of the dice. The Court surely knew he had been kidnapped, and he hoped it was just a matter of time for them to find him. But how much time?

'The one thing I still can't work out Jack, is how you knew about Natalie? And how you trapped her?'

'That's easy. She was your star, the woman who seduced everyone in Westminster, the woman who ran your illegals in this country, and the one who we knew about many years ago. In fact, it was in that office right over there, that I first read the report of Natalie. From a source who knew all her contacts, and all her hidden links back to Moscow.' Jack pointed to his office on the fourth floor of Thames House wondering if he'd ever get to see the inside of it again.

'Mmmm,' was the only response from Katchalyna. Jack heard Natalie stamp her foot behind him.

'Why don't you tell me about your business now that we're having a cosy chat. Hopefully it's all imploded.'

Katchalyna's eye narrowed. Jack could see he was pained, he had damaged him. He had wrecked his business and his credibility.

It wasn't obvious by his responses, but Katchalyna was mightily pissed off with Jack.

'I admire you Jack, you did well up until this point, but now I hold all the cards. Your fifteen years of plotting might just come to an end today.' Katchalyna stood to deliver his lecture. 'Keystone Corps is simply the latest expression of an evolving policy. I'll build it again. My president wants companies like mine to act as a way of implementing his national interests without the direct involvement of the state. He calls it elastic power. We operate as a structure, financed through private contracts, but essentially, we are a deniable instrument of the state.'

'You mean you were. You're out of favour now. All your chips are gone.'

'You're a smart man Jack. You know how Moscow works. The true currency of Russia is not the rouble, it's political favour as you know. Without it, millionaires like me become tomorrow's villains. With it, people like me can become rich on preferential contracts and that's why my country is full of political entrepreneurs who generate initiatives which we believe will please the Kremlin. I'm a Kremlin agent of influence, both out of conviction, and because of the political advantage I gain. I never left the intelligence services, I just put a suit on to run a different arm.'

Jack knew what Katchalyna was doing. Trying to justify his way of life and manipulate his thoughts for whatever it was he was going to demand - in return for Jack's life. He and his private military company would have had frequent contact with the Russian security organs, and he could still rely on the state apparatus to support him where it was favourable to them.

'It seems to me that your political favour has been broken, and you are now the villain.' Jack sniped. 'There may never be a way back for you. You might as well throw it all in and work for me. We can provide you with the protection you need, and you can see your retirement years played out coaching our agents in the doctrine and training of the FSB. What do you say?'

'You're as corrupt as I am Jack. It's just you think in your British mind that being morally corrupt is ok.'

The comment hurt Jack. His entire life had been dedicated to rooting out the corrupt. He bit his lip and grasped for his tie which was missing. He was wearing a fresh light blue shirt that Natalie had provided following his capture. He felt underdressed.

Katchalyna prodded again. 'I know you were responsible for the murder of my quartermaster, and that has really annoyed me. It cost me a lot of money.'

'Quartermaster?'

'Goran Dozich.'

'How?'

'He was killed in an explosion that took out millions of pounds worth of my weaponry in Mali. He was my quartermaster. Keystone's quartermaster.'

'Very strange. My intelligence shows that he was also working for others.'

'Who?'

'You don't know?'

'No, I fucking well don't.'

'He was making a bit on the side with a Russian oligarch I recruited to trap you both.'

Katchalyna scowled. 'You've made me an offer Jack, now I shall make mine.'

Jack thought momentarily of his plot. He'd managed to bring down Keystone Corps in West Africa, but now he wanted the scalps of twenty-one-club. Maybe he'd never live to see that day, knowing he would never agree to any deal put to him. 'Go on,' he said.

'Do you remember when my team watched you receive a package from Sukonov? You were sat on a bench in Ismailovsky park. Do you remember Sukonov's face? It was the last time you saw him in the flesh. We filmed you both and ran it across all the Russian news channels. If you remember, we had a small chat in a cell, and a few days later you became *persona non grata*. Your life was saved by a sheer stroke of luck and a payment.'

Jack nodded. A sense of shame hit him from hearing those words. A spy's worst fear. Getting caught and being publicly embarrassed during the act of being kicked out of a country.

'Well, you can see him again, and I'll arrange the swap,' Katchalyna continued.

'Swap? There are deep protocols for that, and you know it.'

'Yes, well I need to curry some favour again with the Kremlin. So, the deal is simple. You give me your top Russian agent that you have been personally running, I'll give you Sukonov. Or else he dies, and you die. I like to keep things simple Jack. Two lives for one. A pretty fair deal I'd say.'

Jack sighed. 'So, let me get this straight. You tell the Kremlin you've flushed out a Russian traitor, exchange him for a former traitor, you gain some political favour and they invest in you to start your corrupt businesses again. I don't gain anything.'

'You gain your life.'

'No one in my service will ever agree to any swap under these circumstances,' Jack replied, his face expressionless.

'You'll find a way Jack. You're smart. The whisper in Moscow is that you personally recruited an agent that no one else in MI5 knows about. I suspect that's true. And I want him.'

Shit, Jack thought. He has an inkling about Sergei. Is he bluffing? Is he trying to tease it out of him? The room's silence began to swirl dizzyingly around him. He stayed quiet.

'You see Jack, people talk and good friends talk. The spotlight is on the man you're running. You either give him up now, or I speak to the GRU and they'll hunt him down. Your Russian spy is a dead man walking. Give him up now and save two lives.'

'So, Moscow rules are out of the window then? I assumed so, especially when you brazenly busted Natalie out of jail with all guns blazing.'

'Those gentlemen's agreements were lost long ago Jack. You know that. Our objectives have changed, and we have no time now for such frivolity.'

'Well it's frivolous to suggest I am running such an agent. You know we don't run agents without any oversight. He doesn't exist, except in your imagination.'

'Not true Jack. He exists. You've been a bit slack in your tradecraft.' Katchalyna nodded to Natalie again.

A map with interconnecting lines was placed in front of Jack.

'Running an agent needs tight security and it seems you were both running burner phones whenever you did need to speak.'

'I'm not sure what you mean?'

'We have some really good analysts in Moscow who discovered that Sergei had been making a lot of calls from burner phones, but he made one big mistake. He didn't destroy one of them, and he used it at least four times from the same location using the same cell phone masts to connect with. He set a pattern that had us all intrigued.'

Jack's instinct was that Sergei had been rumbled, but he also knew Katchalyna was checking for his reaction. 'I've never heard of this man you call Sergei, and actually, so what? The man could be contacting anyone. Nothing to do with me.'

'But we found a connection between the both of you.'

'Go on.'

'He made one phone call to a cellphone in the Connaught hotel in Mayfair, at exactly the same time that you had entered for lunch with your CIA chum. Or is she your lover Jack?'

'Shit.' Jack's stomach sank.

Chapter 48

London

Sean looked at his watch. The timing had to be immaculate. He'd researched the layout of the Penthouse suite that Jack was holed up in, noting the precise layout of the two-storey residence that stretched exotically over the tenth and eleventh floors.

The gargantuan development was a mass of glazing and curvatures that gave it a feel of a boutique hotel. Think sophisticated furnishings, luxurious materials, crystal chandeliers and glitzy surfaces. Natalie must have pulled in a big favour from somewhere he thought. Who else might be helping her? Surely the Russian SVR had now disavowed her? Sean wasn't quite sure whether she was acting as a lone wolf, or had the backup of the Russian state. All he knew, was that he needed to get Jack out of there quickly.

Sean studied the floor plans again as he waited for the appointed time to arrive when he would assault the complex with a deception plan that could easily backfire. He noticed the Penthouse had an expansive dining room and separate lounge on the upper floor, with a kitchen, office, open plan pantry and two bedrooms on the lower floor. The building plans included the room data sheets which provided the full detail of how the architect had designed the opulent residence. Reflective flooring, two crystal chandeliers, a rare stone finish in the bathroom and a full range Poggenpohl kitchen. No less than the well-heeled residents would expect in such a prestigious development.

Sean's plan was a simple one. Perhaps too simple. Gain entry surreptitiously and alone, make his way to the dining room where Jack had been spotted by one-eyed Damon's surveillance team, then mount a surgical strike to kill Natalie and any minders in her presence. Speed and coordination would be of the essence.

He checked his watch again. Thirty minutes to the designated time that the plan would spark into action. A three-pronged supporting attack. He began to feel nervous about the one part of the plan he had no control over. One-eyed Damon's former Spetsnaz mates, and a Bulgarian sniper who had convinced Sean he had been the best shot in his regiment. One-eyed Damon used his Bulgarian friends for all manner of off-the-books work.

Sean had only met the sniper once before, deep in the bowels of a Soho club owned by a high-grade Bulgarian syndicate that was fronted as a legitimate business by one-eyed Damon's former Sergeant Major. They were close friends who'd operated together in the Balkans, and one-eyed Damon's go-to team for weapons, explosives and strong-armed men when dirty business needed to be done.

Naz was a small beast of a man. Built like a beer barrel with a thin face and two gold front teeth. 'How can I help this time?' Naz had asked Sean when they met in the Birdhouse café in Clapham. Sean had been convinced by one-eyed Damon that Naz could pull the shot off and had the perfect sniper rifle in his vast armouries that were scattered across the south of England in multiple caches. Sean never asked who his other clients were. Naz had indicated that all he needed was the target, and the type of glazing. He could then research the best rounds to be used to penetrate the glass.

'It's five millimetres with an air gap of ten millimetres,' Sean had quietly confirmed in a corner of the café. 'Can it be done?'

'Depends,' Naz said stroking his deep black beard. 'Laminated or tempered?'

'Seems to be heat strengthened. Here, have a look at the spec.'

Naz studied the specification, nodding enthusiastically as he read each line using his forefinger to steer him. 'I need a location to give me a ninety-degree shot. Have you looked at that?'

One-eyed Damon chipped in. 'Sean's pulled a government favour in. A building opposite the river, a three hundred and fifty metre shot. Same level, same height, perfect angle into the sheet of glass.'

Sean passed Naz an ordnance survey map showing the two buildings with the River Thames in the middle. He pointed to the location using a pencil, without drawing on the map, and used a piece of paper on its length to measure the precise distance.

'Mmmm. OK. It looks doable,' Naz murmured, still stroking his beard. 'It will need a heck of a lot of velocity though. The good thing is that the tempered glass will crumble like dust on impact. This type of glazing crumbles into particles instead of large jagged sheets.'

'Have you got the kit for this Naz?'

Sean knew he had to ask the question. But wished he hadn't. The lingering stare that came back across the table at him was one of pure disdain, as if he'd asked a tank commander if he had any big shells.

'I have exactly the right *kit* as you describe it, if you can match the price. 'I'm a thirty-two-year veteran of a Spetsnaz unit and sniping was my career. Sniping is a complicated skill that requires an extensive amount of practice, dedication to the craft and a fair bit of geometry too, so forgive me while I think through the mathematics. Pass me a piece of paper and I'll teach you.'

Sean handed him a notebook and refrained from saying anything more on the subject of weapons and firepower, lest he got bogged in too far with more lessons. He watched Naz draw a few lines of what looked like trigonometry, a few decimal figures, and a stickman as target.

'Velocity,' Naz explained. 'The crux to this is the right bullet, and the right levels of velocity to maintain trajectory. The more velocity the better. This is where the 7.62mm calibre doesn't play well, but Magnums, point 338s, and half inch calibres are my choice. Then there's the angle of firing. The further you are off a ninety-degree hit, the angle of deflection grows in larger increments, a bit like playing snooker. A little bit of angle makes a big difference in direction. As I mentioned before, there are lots of specialty rounds out there for penetrating different kinds of materials, such as glass. But to make my shot perfect I need accurate data for each type of round. My point is, I've done all this before on special ops shooting into aircrafts and government buildings, as well as armour-plated vehicles on the move. Shooting through glass was a common task for me.'

Sean made a radio check to all the callsigns as he waited for Jugsy to launch his specially adapted quadcopter from a disused brewery courtyard a couple of kilometres away. He checked he had a visual from the quadcopter camera on his phone screen, and tapped one-eyed Damon on the shoulder in readiness to bolt up the stairs. He asked every man on the team for their status, and gave some thought to his entry plan before clipping a magazine into his Sig Sauer XFIVE. Sean fitted the titanium suppressor and momentarily admired the legion grey tungsten grip. He hoped the chambered bullet would be the one that neutered the festering itch.

'It's in the air, seven minutes to target,' came the call into Sean's earpiece. He checked the phone screen, and sure enough, Jugsy's drone was airborne providing perfect telemetry to beam live imagery of the south London skyline right into the secure application that would give him eyes on the target. Sean's heart began to pound, his mind hungry for the kill he so badly wanted for himself. Within half a second, he was moving quickly up the two flights of stairs to the target penthouse with one-eyed Damon right behind him.

Taking out the fibre optic endoscope, Sean knelt, and slid the flexible two-millimetre cable underneath the door while one-eyed Damon stood guard with his white stick at the ready. He'd use the aid as a blag if anyone came along wondering what the hell was going on.

Sean leant forward and placed an eye to the probe. A brightly lit room showed a staircase to the upper level, and an empty hallway. The hallway looked quite wide with beech wood flooring and gloss white woodwork leading straight to the two bedrooms. Silence. All quiet. So far so good, but now came the point in the operation he wasn't completely happy about. Hacking into the lock.

Billy the Phish had manufactured a mobile hack card that he'd soldered onto a handle for Sean to use with some ease. He'd explained to Sean that it would take less than five seconds, but Sean was not so sure.

Billy the Phish had bastardised a three-hundred-pound RFID reading and writing tool, linked it to an expired hotel key card that had been pulled from the trash of the nearby Hilton, and set a series of cryptographic tricks to electronically deceive the lock.

Sean placed the card on the chrome door reader, breathed deeply, and prayed for access. The device had begun to cycle through all the possible codes on the lock, had identified the correct one in about eighteen tries, and then wrote that master code to the card giving Sean free reign to roam any room in the building. The whole process took just under ninety seconds. Billy Phish had said the hack would normally work on 140,000 hotels in more than 160 countries, and he gave Sean the probability of a ninety-six percent chance of cracking the door he was about to enter.

Silently, Sean pushed the handle down and entered the residence, before turning to his left. He was immediately greeted by a vast painting of a cartoon in the small alcove that led to the upper storey. *The Drowning Girl* was a copy of its original painted in the new Pop Art style by Roy Lichtenstein. Sean studied the large commercial painting for a second. A masterpiece of melodrama he thought. Perfect symmetry to the mission in hand. To kill Natalie. He moved swiftly past the painting noting the clichéd narrative in a bubble coming from the drowning girl's mouth. *'I don't care, I'd rather sink than call Brad for help.'* He couldn't help but think of Yelena.

Sweating now, Sean moved slowly to approach the corner that gave entry into the vast dining room. He glanced around the large corridors. Sahara Noir marble floors pervaded every corner with other luxurious details that lined the routes to the dining room and an even bigger lounge. He edged silently with his back to the wall, pistol and suppressor now held high, until he arrived at the corner where he'd launch his attack. Voices. Was it Jack's? Yes. Quiet and slightly muffled. Then another voice he didn't recognise. Sean checked his phone screen. The quadcopter was high above the development, laid off at an angle, but providing a perfect view into the dining room.

'Jugsy, can you hear me?' Sean whispered.

'Roger. Poised, ready to go.'

'Standby. On my call. Out to you. Naz, are you good?'

A short pause. 'Roger. Good to go. Sights raised.'

Sean didn't know it, but Naz had gone through a cycle of meditation and mental preparation before he'd arrived at this point. The moment he awaited the order to kill. He'd tucked the butt of his rifle into the crook of his shoulder, pressed his cheek against the stock, and adjusted it to get a good weld that would ensure his shot was stable. He checked his range finding, confirmed the wind speed, which was thankfully low, and eyed the target some 350 metres away. He used the silhouette of his target in his scope to compensate for bullet drop, clicking the scope dial to adjust for the distance.

'Target's seen, two men, one woman,' Jugsy reported. Sean looked at the imagery on his screen. It looked perfect. He wasn't sure how many minders were in the room, but so far, only one had been seen. But were there others elsewhere? Too late. He was totally committed, revelling in the risk, and knew the moment had come.

'Go, go go,' Sean whispered into his microphone.

Bizarre happenings catch people unaware. Too surprised with shock to act quickly. This was one such moment for the gathering inside the dining room.

From out of nowhere, a black drone appeared in front of the eleventh floor glazing, catching Natalie totally by surprise with her mouth now open. Jack caught sight of her surprise, which immediately turned to sheer horror when she shouted out to Katchalyna. 'What the fuck is going on?'

Jack was dumfounded. A drone hovering at the window some three feet away from the building, a hundred and ten metres above the ground. The surprise achieved the effect. He watched Katchalyna move three paces forward to look the drone in the eye. Jack could make out four rotors, a camera lens within a three-legged cage and what appeared to be a short barrel underneath, all held in balance by a circular frame. Then everything seemed to happen in slow motion.

First, the outside window shattered like dust from what appeared to be a blasting cap shot from the drone. A softening blow from another weapon close to the intended target, spidering the surface, allowing for a cleaner penetration for the next bullet.

Naz had chosen a point 408 Chey-Tac copper nickel round to deliver a blistering bore of 3,450 feet per second through the second window. He took a deep breath, exhaled evenly with pursed lips to dry lung in preparation for the shot. Just two pounds of pressure on the trigger, being careful not to jerk, he watched the first glass pane shatter. Then within a half-second, he fired the shot across the River Thames. A little pop, and no smoke.

Jack heard the meaty thwack first as the bullet penetrated the window before passing straight into Katchalyna's chest. He appeared to try and regain balance. First on his right leg, then his left, before he spun round, rocked on his feet, and slumped to the floor. Jack sensed movement in the corner of the room before he heard the first muffled pop from a weapon, then a second in short order. A double tap. The minder who was once stood in the corner of the room overseeing the conversation, was now gasping for breath with Sean Richardson stood behind him, aiming a pistol with a suppressor fitted, right at Natalie. The next thing he heard was a deathly silence except for the sucking of the minder's chest. Then a second double tap.

A tidal wave of anger rushed through Sean's veins as he watched his shots miss Natalie by half an inch as she ducked, before darting into the lounge. His millisecond of hesitation had cost him. It was as if her survival was being written by the merciful spirit of a theatre producer.

He heard Natalie's high heels clatter across the lounge floor followed by a double thud of something being thrown against a wall. Sean charged through the lounge, jumped the white leather sofa that was between him and a small spiral staircase leading to the lower storey, spotted the red high heels that had been ejected, and swung around a stone pillar before landing at the top of the gunship grey stairs. He stopped, pushed his head forward to check the route, then pulled it back. Two shots blasted through the railings creating an air vacuum that ran through his hair before it crashed into the ceiling. Natalie or a guard? He didn't know.

Sean reached around the staircase pole and fired two shots into the chasm below trying to see who was at the bottom. He heard the ricochet of both bullets fly off the steel flooring at the base, then pulled his head back again. Nothing. No one returned fire. He ran for the corner of the staircase to get a better view below. Bracing both arms, bending his knees, and with the pistol aimed below, he scoured the route. Safe.

He held the pistol at chest height as he descended the staircase, listening intently for any movement below him - then all in one sequenced movement, he jumped to the floor, rolled across the corridor, and landed in the prone position before firing four shots towards the glimpse of navy cotton that had darted into the kitchen.

This would now be tricky. Sean couldn't recall any exit from the kitchen, but he couldn't be fully sure. He had no choice but to enter with all the risk that entailed. She could be standing just inside the entrance and he'd have no chance.

Sean dropped the mag and pushed home a new one. He was concerned about a failure to eject a case on the last shot which was unusual for his favourite weapon. He didn't think it was a dirty extractor and went for a new magazine just to be sure. He took a deep breath, edged along the wall, and reached around the corner pumping two shots as a sharpener to anyone inside. Nothing. No return of fire again. To give himself a chance, he lunged for the far wall, crouched into position and looked fully inside the kitchen entrance. All quiet. Nothing there. Getting annoyed now, he burst into the kitchen and rolled across the graphite noire floor landing by a central stanchion. Again nothing. He scoured the enormous expanse of the kitchen before carefully rising to his feet. Then he saw it. *Bollocks*.

A small door that was ajar and led into the second corridor that traversed all its rooms in the centre of the residence. Where was she going?

'Are you still chasing me Sean? Drop it now. Don't fucking move.'

Idiot. In that vital moment, there was no time for any thought. No choice. Just muscle memory and a shot to nothing. In the blink of an eye, Sean dropped to the floor, twisting onto his back and took the shot as gravity pulled him to the ground. The pop of the suppressor fired off, and Sean could see the distant Natalie fire a round too. The bullet zinged off the tiles just to his right as he rolled onto his stomach. He wasn't sure if his shot had landed but he'd managed to dodge the first round and waited for the second. Nothing. Then he heard gurgling. And a hand smacking the granite tiles.

He jumped up, looked over the sights of the pistol, and saw Natalie rocking on her back hitting the floor again with her hand. Her eyes were open, blood gushing from her throat. She watched him approach and seemed to throw him a smile.

Sean raised the weapon barrel, held his breath, and fired a double tap through her skull. Blood and brain matter spewed onto the floor.

A long silence. A long thought.

'Time to go,' Jack shouted from behind. 'Give me your phone and I'll get this place sealed off.

Sean turned. Jack was smiling as if to say well done, but he didn't actually say anything.

'This would be the perfect moment to offer me a full-time job you know,' Sean uttered. 'An office-bound one.'

'Very sharp Sean. You may well have earned that.'

Sean pulled a hand through his hair. 'As long as you're plotting, I'm never safe. It's time, and you know it.'

'Thankfully we're both alive to fight and plot for another day,' Jack said nodding towards Natalie's corpse. 'Katchalyna bred an evil psychopath there.'

'You're right. But I still don't get one thing.'

'What?'

'I don't understand how I get tortured and you get a five-star dining experience with all the trimmings.'

'Rank, my dear boy. Just rank I'd say.' They laughed.

Chapter 49

London

Sean's thoughts drifted between Swartz and Yelena as he walked through the Knightsbridge mews stopping occasionally to glance in the shop windows. It was always a long while after a mission that the reality of losing good people struck him. Always after the fitful nights of mind-numbing rumination, and always another set of scars to add to the collection stuffed away in his virtual drawers.

Reluctant to spend any more time than necessary talking about this episode of his life, he had agreed to meet Jack one last time before flying back to his retreat in the south of France.

'This way, Mr Richardson,' the breezy club secretary said. The Chairman is dining with you today, I think there are five of you, is that right?'

'Chairman?' Sean asked inquisitively. 'Who is that?'

'Sir Justin Darbyshire, the Cabinet Secretary.'

It's another bloody trap. Five people? What the hell was Jack up to now?

He followed the club secretary up the stairs, stopping for a moment to look at a photograph of a friend he knew. The club's staircase was decorated on every spare inch of space with portraits of numerous legends, male and female, ranging from the second world war to the recent episodes in Afghanistan and Iraq - including many heroes from overseas nations. Those members killed in action had their photograph framed in black. Sean wondered if Swartz would ever have his picture sized, framed and hung alongside many of his compatriots. Probably not, he thought. There are no medals for us. No accolades. We're the hidden mercenaries of the crown, in a way, no different from the Russian mercenaries he'd been tasked to take down.

'Here we go Mr Richardson, I hope you enjoy your lunch.'

Sean entered the small dining room and was greeted by three men and a woman. The first person he recognised was Jack who sat in the far corner already fiddling with his tie. The woman sat next to him was Laura Creswell whose amenable wide smile was accentuated by her deep red lipstick. This could be interesting he thought.

Sir Justin Darbyshire rose to greet Sean. 'Great to see you again Sean, and I hope you're well rested. Now, I think there's only one person you don't know.'

Sir Justin swept an arm towards a man who turned to face Sean as he rose from his chair. He was wearing a white open necked shirt, and a light grey jacket with black slacks.

'This is Sir Rhys Eldridge. He's been wanting to meet you for a while now.'

Sean was instantaneously gobsmacked. The target of the sting operation. He looked across the table toward Jack unsure if he should take the hand that was now outstretched in front of him. Jack nodded a gesture of assurance as he did so.

'What on earth is going on?' Sean asked Sir Justin. 'I really don't understand.'

Sir Justin paused, and glanced over to Laura who was now also nodding. 'I understand. Let me explain what's been happening over lunch, but the first thing you need to know is that Sir Rhys is one of us. He is a British spy. Recruited by Jack some many years ago to get deep inside Westminster and beyond. He's been one of our finest and most secret assets, a little like yourself Sean. Who knows, maybe you'll both grace the staircase of fame one day...'

'When I'm dead,' Sir Rhys interrupted, still shaking Sean's hand vigorously. 'Very well done on this job, I've heard all about you Sean. And please accept my most sincere condolences about Yelena and Swartz. I hope you'll allow me the time to explain some of the intricacies which caught us all by surprise.'

Sean could hardly move. His legs felt like cement and his mouth was dry as a bone. He couldn't register what he was hearing. This was supposed to be the man responsible for Swartz's death and was supposed to be Yelena's father. *What the actual fuck*, he thought.

Sean sat down and tried to relax a little but wanted to know more. He gave a warm smile to Laura, noticing that he was grating his jaw again.

'I expect you want to know what this is all about,' Sir Justin said reaching for his napkin. 'The first thing I'll say is you're amongst good friends, good servants of the crown, despite what your perceptions might be telling you right now.'

Sean nodded, his jaw still grating. He breathed deeply and took a hefty drink of water before speaking. 'So, I guess this is where you reveal everything?'

'In a manner of speaking, yes.'

'Presumably, you already know that all I'm interested in is who was ultimately responsible for Swartz's death?'

'Ah, well, yes of course,' Sir Justin said, directing an arm at Jack to take over the proceedings.

Jack touched his tie and cleared his throat. Sean had rarely seen him so nervous in any of his debriefs. This mission was far messier than he'd probably thought at the outset.

'I think I should start with the obvious if I may,' Jack began. 'Sir Rhys and I are very good friends, in fact we went to school together...'

'Posh one, I bet,' Sean interrupted, elbows now leaning on the table with hand clenched and knuckles touching his lips. He was already engrossed and chipper with it.

'Haberdashers.'

'Right, OK. Very nice for you both.'

'We grew up together then went our different ways. One into the oil industry then politics, one of us into spying for the nation.' Jack paused. 'I'll be honest with you, I never had much time for politicians in this country, some are good yes, but eventually many of them lose their way and get vacuumed into a world they never knew existed. There are of course some fine ones, but I learnt one day long ago, that many are simply too naïve to lead the nation. Sir Rhys was different.'

'Quite,' Sir Justin chipped in. 'Remember it's house rules here. We're safe to talk honestly inside these marvellous four walls.'

Sean smiled, intrigued about what else might be disclosed within the private club. 'This is why you seem to spend all your time plotting to take down the bad apples within the system, I presume?'

'You could say that. Yes. No one else was doing it in the intelligence services, unless they formally came across our radar for investigation, but much was being missed, and that was very dangerous to the nation. So, I decided to recruit and run Sir Rhys nearly twenty years ago to act as my first insider in the Palace of Westminster.'

'You have more?'

'Yes. As do the Russians across the globe of course. Not just as politicians, but as agents of influence operating everywhere from lobbyists, to academics, scientists and of course administrators. That's exactly how Natalie infiltrated so deep inside the Westminster walls using every skill she could from her Russian illegals training and playbooks. Silent undercover agents who are only activated when absolutely necessary. Which is exactly why we need our very best agents to counter that, and I'm pleased to say that Sir Rhys was our very own illegals if you like. A man who sat and watched for many years, who infiltrated secret cabals, fed back intelligence to me, and then rose to such a high position as an MP and in the twenty-one-club, that we could start the operation to take down the most senior men who were acting against the nation.'

'A silent sleeper agent deep in Westminster to lure out traitors. Genius.'

'But fraught with danger, and on occasion, mistakes. Such as this mission. Yes, we had some great success over the years as we smoked out, amongst others, the likes of Dominic Atwood. You remember him don't you.'

Sean looked over towards Laura who had been remarkably quiet so far. She was now touching up her lipstick. 'I do, evil bastard. That was some sting you laid on him, sticking me right in the eye of the storm with Natalie.'

'Indeed, and I'm sorry you've had to bear the brunt of all this over the years. And I'm truly sorry about Swartz and Yelena. Absolute tragedy for you and us all. But we all feel we owe you much more than just our apologies. We are very proud of what you have achieved, on behalf of us all.'

For some reason, Sean felt he and his team were nothing but disposable collateral. Deniable assets to achieve a government effect. But Jack was intimating now that he might be offered more. He was curious as to why Jack was telling him highly secret information that he really didn't have to disclose. Then it dawned on him. Jack had previously ensured that he had been rescued from the Afghan jail, and had told him it was because he wanted to keep an eye on him - perhaps because Jack had somehow understood the trauma that he had endured when he was left to rot in an overseas jail. Maybe he had too?

'Tell me Jack, have you ever been jailed and tortured?'

Jack paused. He reached for his tie but pulled back. 'Yes.'

'I thought so. It's all beginning to make sense now, when I look back on each of your plots and your detailed operations. You saved me from myself because you pretty much went the same way, right? Into a deep dark hole.'

'I think you're right Sean. It was Katchalyna,' Laura barked matter of factly. 'The bastard nearly killed him, but hey guys, we're going off point here. Let's get back on track, I need to eat you know. Offer him the job for fuck sake Jack.'

The atmosphere eased with Laura's no-nonsense American vernacular. Sir Justin and Sir Rhys laughed out loud.

'Well come on guys, you Brits don't half like to string things out a bit. This is like watching Ice Cold in Alex for fuck sake. Let's talk new missions and new jobs.'

'Job?' Sean asked, looking to get to the crux.

'All in good time, Sean. Let's eat a little first,' Sir Justin said, leaning over to call a waiter through from the bar, throwing Laura a wink.

Sean needed a break but couldn't help himself. He adjusted his chair to have a chat with Sir Rhys while the others started checking the menus as the smartly dressed waitress hovered discreetly.

'Forgive me for asking this, but I need to know Sir Rhys. Are you Yelena's father?'

Sir Rhys looked drained but answered calmly. 'Yes, by all accounts I am her father. I'm carrying as much weight on my shoulders as I'm sure you are, and I must say, if I'd have known much earlier, I'd have done things very differently. I'm quite devastated.'

'You mean you didn't know?'

'No, I didn't. Until Jack told me shortly after he briefed you. By that time, it was too late to even think about intervening. He's a smart man you know Sean. Jack spent every hour of every day digging into people. Researching, collecting intelligence, squeezing it all into a receptacle of bait where he'd use it to hook the big fish. He was like that at school too. Always researching.' Sir Rhys took a moment to steady himself. He seemed out of breath. 'I confided in Jack about a very short affair I had with Yelena's mother while Dozich was away on business. I was a young man then, far too sure of myself, but for the affair I remain ashamed. You see, I didn't know Yelena was my child. Until Jack started asking me questions at the same time as developing this plot. Then he asked me to collect DNA samples from Dozich's house, and it dawned on me what he might be looking for. I took toothbrushes, loose hairs, even cigarette butts, and then Jack took my own hair and had it analysed without me knowing. His hunch paid off. If only we could have dealt with this in another way Sean. If only.'

Sean noticed Sir Rhys was now quite emotional as he paused to wipe his forehead with a white handkerchief. Sir Rhys continued to tell the story of how he had first met Dozich in the oil industry, was asked by Jack to maintain his connection with him when Sir Rhys became an MP, and how he had provided secret intelligence on the covert activities of Dozich for many years which led to the disruption of a considerable number of his Russian proxy operations. It must have been a massive job to protect Sir Rhys as the source of intelligence during that period of time. He was at very high-risk and could easily have been outed.

'How does it feel to have been immersed with such mobsters over the years,' Sean asked. 'That's not a job that most people could manage for long, and you were immersed in it for decades.'

'It's taken its toll on me in many ways. I feel that you understand Sean. Your role, from what I've heard has been far more dangerous than my own. But the emotions are probably the same. The never-ending anxiety, the voices in your head telling you to get out and stop what you're doing, the fear of being caught and killed. It never really goes away being a covert agent for so many years, and my health has now suffered because of the incessant stress. That's why Jack agreed that once I became elected into Le Cercle I'd work my way into becoming the figurehead and Czar of the breakaway unit, and then he'd act to take everyone down.'

'You mean the twenty-one-club?'

'Yes. Once I was asked to chair that group, I had insider intelligence that was dynamite. Then Jack began to unravel all of the connections inside the group that we really didn't know much about at all. Especially, the clandestine linkages of former intelligence officers who were a deeply hidden part of the group, as well as their links to the European political elite. Their operations were far and wide, deep corruption inside nation state apparatus creating legal mechanisms for exporting weapons, and a surprise we didn't really know about - extortion from large corporates using the intelligence they had collected. They were their own private intelligence agency designed to create wealth.'

Sean felt himself beginning to form a rapport with Sir Rhys. He could see that he too was grappling with the ethics of his work. The duplicity, the deceit, the incessant questioning in your mind of whether this was the right thing to do. The cloaked knife of treachery that could take your life as an agent at any moment.

He took a minute to place his lunch order with the slim waitress then reached for his phone. He tapped a few buttons before a photograph appeared on the screen of Swartz in black kit during the London bombings of 2005.

'This is Swartz,' Sean said, passing the phone to Sir Rhys who reached inside his jacket for his glasses. 'We were the closest of friends. Went through lots together, and he always joked that he'd never reach his military pension age being connected to me and the danger it brought. He was wrong though. He got his pension, we had a great party and did a few more jobs together. Then he was murdered by the twenty-one-club. Who gave the order to kill him?'

'A good man I'm sure. You know Sean, we have lots of admiration for how you handled this operation, and I'm truly sorry you lost your best friend. But I swear that none of us knew about the plan to kill the men on the terrace. Dozich and his henchmen committed the act, but the order came from another Brit in the twenty-one-club. A man called Hoover. Vincent Hoover. The minister for state at the foreign office. The man Jack sought to trap all along. The man I'd been tasked to watch like a hawk in Parliament and the Foreign Office. He's the de facto leader of the twenty-one-club. I was simply a figurehead as the Chair.'

Sean sat back aghast. The order to kill many men given by a minister of state, and Swartz was the collateral damage. He had no choice but to believe Sir Rhys, studying his face carefully as he answered that question in detail. He felt assured that Dozich was now dead.

'Now then everyone, I propose a small toast.' Sir Justin bellowed to everyone sat at the table. He stood, nodded gently to each person, and made the toast. 'To the third avenue,' he said gleefully.

'The third avenue.' Everyone responded, except Sean.

'Sounds like the title of a good spy book,' Sean said cheekily, now a bit more chipper.

'Or a good painting,' Sir Justin replied, smiling broadly. 'We've all heard of your talents with a paint brush Sean. Perhaps you can turn us all into one. Plotting away in here maybe?'

Sean smiled, conscious that all eyes were on him. He suspected that some sort of offer would be made to him. But you never could tell with this lot.

'Now, let's turn to the business of the day everyone,' Sir Justin said, clearing his throat a little before continuing. 'Laura here heads up the third option with her Special Activities Division, Jack heads up The Court as the third way, and together we form the third avenue. I'd be delighted if you'd join the team on a full-time basis Sean, working for Laura initially.'

Jesus Christ.

An air of taut silence drew across the room. Sean never liked being centre stage, everyone watching for his reaction, a sense of anticipation and eagerness in each of their eyes. Maybe this might be a new way out, or perhaps it might suck him even deeper into his own strife. Maybe he needed to sever the links completely. The swirl of emotion was too fast for him. He didn't know what to say. God, how he had hated how Jack had always kept him in the dark like a mushroom being fed shit. Maybe the offer of a full-time role in The Court would open up the gates to having better control? Then he remembered the words of Swartz. *'They're all treacherous bastards you know.'* Maybe he was right.

'What exactly does this involve? The offer is interesting to say the least.'

'Plenty of stuff that you like,' Laura answered. 'With more chance to develop the operations, leading on the UK side, working with my officers on Top Secret international intelligence operations. You know, like you used to do.'

'Not quite in this sense though. It sounds as if I'm crossing the line again. Back in, so to speak.'

'That's exactly right. The line is right here in front of you. You know it makes sense.' Laura drew the imaginary line with her neatly manicured forefinger. 'No rush. But we have a few things that need tackling right away. Things are about to get very heavy with the Chinese now.'

The appeal of working with Laura was plain as day. One of the finest motivators he had ever worked with. Attractive and engaging, she had a way of getting senior staff to come around to her way of thinking. Sean had imagined she was at the very heart of this offer and had probably convinced Sir Justin of its merits. She exuded trust, using compelling arguments.

'Anything specific?' Sean asked taking a sip of the club branded red wine.

'Ah, well that would be telling. Look, if this is something you fancy, you and I can have a quiet chat tomorrow over coffee. If it's not, I wish you luck with your dreams. Art shop wasn't it?'

Sean pondered his often-thought dream of disappearing overseas to open an art shop and linger away taking it easy for the rest of his life. Then his gut feeling kicked in, as it always did. He was never one for pontificating too long.

'I'm in.'

Chapter 50

London

Lunch had been both insightful and delicious as Jack led everyone to the bar for a celebratory drink. Jack and Sean sat at the bar whilst the others took a seat on the velvet upholstered bench seats underneath a painting of Princess Anne, the patron of the club.

'You've done it again Jack,' Sean said clinking his beer glass with his handler's. 'Taken more of the bastards down.'

'Thanks. But at great cost this time. To both of us, and our teams. It's time to be a bit less risky.'

'You know that's not true, that's why we exist. Chin up, we move on and make a difference. That's what we do.'

'Maybe you're right. We've built something special with Laura and Sir Justin, and I can see the true merits of D's vision now. He was a man before his time, shaping this niche world we exist in, working as a covert two-eyes outfit.'

'What about Hoover, this minister who was your target all along. What's happened to him?'

'Taken down quietly. We conducted a covert search of his home in Sussex, downloaded data from his secure desktop, and discovered multiple files showing payments into a numbered account in Luxembourg. In excess of seven million paid by Dozich via an intermediary company in London. Conclusive evidence of collaboration in illegal weapons deals.'

'And next?'

We threaten with exposing him, shame him, prosecute him, then wring him dry of intelligence on the other politicians and former intelligence officers he has in the twenty-one-club. Then we take them down one by one.'

'And Sergei?'

'Compromised. But now safc.'

'Compromised by who?'

'Major General Katchalyna, former Deputy Director of the FSB, killer in the KGB, and Natalie's father. Sergei got a bit slack and the whispers rolling around Moscow eventually led to Katchalyna digging deep on him. He became the prime suspect for passing information to us that was related to Katchalyna's mercenary operations. All true of course, but he was outed.'

'And you know he wasn't the mole, right? He was clean all along.' Sean studied Jack's face carefully to gauge his reaction.

'I do. Samantha did a brilliant job on investigating who it might have been. But how do you know that Sergei wasn't the mole?'

'Samantha told me.'

'Ah, OK. I thought you might pay her a visit. She's a good woman you know.'

Sean smiled coyly. 'I know that. We're close, and who knows what's down the line eh?'

'Did she tell you who leaked the information?'

'Yes. A bloke called Galloway.'

'Indeed. But that's the loose end that worries me. He's still a threat and we can't find him. He's gone dark.'

'You won't find him either,' Sean said knowingly.

'What do you mean?'

'Let's just say that I have him nicely tucked up with one of my friends explaining the error of his way's. The slate is clean, and you can have arrested whenever you want. Or…'

Jack's first reaction looked as if it would be to berate Sean for going off-piste again. But he didn't, he simply grinned, and ordered another beer.

Something still didn't make sense to Sean. It was a niggle. Jack rarely disclosed the whole story about what had been kept in the background and hidden from view on his operations, and Sean had been the bait for far too long. He instinctively knew there was more to this story.

'Two whiskies please,' Sean asked the barman, before challenging Jack. 'You're not leaving here until you tell me exactly what it is that you're not telling me. On previous jobs, I've let it go. This time I won't. I've got all evening, and I'm in the mood for drink.'

Sean watched Jack's eyes drop. Then unbelievably he took his tie off. His security. Nothing left to fiddle with. What on earth is he doing Sean wondered.

'I might just be in for a few more too,' Jack replied. 'But I warn you, you might not like what I tell you.'

'Try me.'

'Well, like you I was tortured and beaten up for a number of days, but this time it was Katchalyna and his FSB men who did the damage. Katchalyna has been my target for many years, fifteen to be precise. But we had to stage things a little bit awkwardly to get at him - and his daughter Natalie, was the first to be put in place.'

'Jesus. I have a funny feeling I've been the front man getting smashed time and again to let you get your own revenge on an ancient nemesis.'

'Possibly. A means to an end. Moscow was harsh for me back in the day, and I was in your position being the point man on many occasions. The bait and the lure. For someone much higher up than me, and a handler that put me in the line of fire time and time again too. I was operating on that occasion off the books of the British, and working for someone else when I was captured and tortured. As a deniable asset to another nation. Katchalyna had been the target of my own handler and I'd been collecting intelligence from one of his closest allies whom I'd recruited.'

'How'd it go wrong then?'

'I made a mistake. Just one. But enough to see my agent nearly killed, and me interned by his cronies. So you see, I know all too well how you feel and we have much in common Sean. Only this time, the tables have been turned. You see, my handler back in those days was Laura. I was working for the CIA on a case that MI6 couldn't touch. But we were lovers at the time, and she needed a favour…'

Sean was dumbfounded. He'd always wondered about the link with Jack and Laura. Lovers in Moscow, a handler and an agent, and now Sean was the junior agent of them all. Played as a pawn, or coached and mentored by them both for bigger things? He wasn't quite sure.

Sean glanced across to Laura who raised her glass of wine and smiled.

'Who rescued you then Jack?'

'The wonderful woman in the corner,' Jack said, stuffing his tie into his jacket pocket as if he'd finally neutered his own pain. 'She's a better shot than the sniper who took Katchalyna down. But equally deadly.'

***

Acknowledgements

I thoroughly enjoyed writing this novel, especially when I was joined at times by my five-year-old daughter who sat on my knee, while I typed one-handed. As the months went by, she pulled up her own small kiddies' desk, sat beside me, mimicked me, and wrote her own novel. It was wonderful to experience, and little Holly Jenkins helped me through the tough weeks writing this story, as did my son Matthew. They are my inspiration.

I have many people to thank but only one who encourages me like no-one else. My wife Rebecca has been a rock and a wonderful wife as well as a thoroughly competent advisor to me as I write the stories. Her selfless support and enduring inspiration has been magnificent. My heartfelt thanks.

I'm indebted to a number of good friends and first among them is Kaaran, a Kiwi rugby friend of mine who provides great advice. Thanks also to some superb friends who acted as the catalyst for the Failsafe Thrillers: Phil Sullivan, Chris Hawthorne, John Sykes, Martin Grime, Warren Melia, Jim Blackburn, Bob Shaw and John Almonds, my long-time mentor. Thank you once again to my beta readers who continue to give great feedback: Bryan Miller, Nick Milne, Liane Hard, Trevor Foster, Natalie and Mark Kane, Tony Hodson, Drew Johnson, Andy Nicholl, and Peter Wilson.

Finally, to you all. My wonderful supporters and readers who continue to inspire me with the superb feedback I have received, the letters, and the encouragement. The fourth novel is now well and truly set in my mind because of you all. Thank you for your generosity and support.

Michael Jenkins MBE
London
June 2020

Did you enjoy this book? If so, I'd be delighted if you would take the time to submit a review on Amazon and Goodreads, which really helps make a difference to authors. Honest reviews are our lifeblood and are so helpful for readers and authors alike. I'm very grateful to every one of my readers and supporters, who inspire me to write more.

Other novels by Michael Jenkins:

The Failsafe Query
The Kompromat Kill

You can follow me or join my readers club at:
www.michaeljenkins.org and facebook.com/thefailsafethrillers

Featured author on www.londoncrime.co.uk

Coming soon in 2021

THE THIRD AVENUE

On the brink of a world crisis, the fate of one of America's most powerful female spy's rests on a knife edge.

A pulsating spy novel with a perilous mission against a new and terrifying enemy.

Printed in Great Britain
by Amazon

45037889R00208